Three women meet at a crossroads in their lives, each searching for new ways to grow—and find in each other the courage to take chances and embrace the future.

With the undying support of her friends, Hayley and her new daughter have laid down roots in a new town. But when one of those friendships blossoms into something more, Hayley must choose between two different kinds of love…

Third in a new trilogy from the
#1 *New York Times* bestselling author.

Dear Reader:

Toward the end of summer, with its hot, sticky days, I like to bring some of my garden inside. Daisies and dianthus, spears of gay feather, flat cups of yarrow, long elegant lilies. I always hesitate—it seems a shame to snip them. But on a long, rainy day, or one where the heat blasts me back indoors, it's a lovely thing to have flowers I've helped grow keeping me company around the house.

If I am outside, and the weeding and deadheading is done for the day, I can sit in the shade, on a bench or glider or garden wall, and just enjoy. Or I can take my granddaughter for a walk, show her the flowers, tell her their names as my mother and father did for me. I like to think I'm helping instill this love of growing things in her—and will do the same for my grandson soon, as my parents instilled it in me, and as I passed that love to my boys. My family is another passion for me, another garden full of color and bloom and unlimited potential.

Every year, from spring planting through summer bloom, through fall when my zinnias and mums give me flowers and the trees begin to flame, I'm given the gift of seasons. Through the long, cold winter while my gardens sleep, I think of what they'll give me when they wake in spring, and what I'll give them. When the first crocus pops its brave head out of the frosty ground, I know soon I'll be digging up rocks, chasing deer, pulling weeds, wandering through my gardening center to see what I can't resist this year. And watching life renew, watching hope flower, even while I plant.

In the garden is joy and beauty, work and reward. I hope you make your own.

NORA ROBERTS

Three women learn that the heart of their historic home holds a mystery of years gone by, as number-one bestselling author Nora Roberts brings her In the Garden trilogy to a captivating conclusion . . .

A Harper has always lived at Harper House, the centuries-old mansion just outside of Memphis. And for as long as anyone alive remembers, the ghostly Harper Bride has walked the halls, singing lullabies at night . . .

Hayley Phillips came to Memphis hoping for a new start, for herself and her unborn child. She wasn't looking for a hand-out from her distant cousin Roz, just a job at her thriving In the Garden nursery. What she found was a home surrounded by beauty and the best friends she's ever had—including Roz's son Harper. To Hayley's delight, her new daughter Lily has really taken to him. To Hayley's chagrin, she has begun to dream about Harper—as much more than a friend . . .

If Hayley gives in to her desire, she's afraid the foundation she's built with Harper will come tumbling down. Especially since she's begun to suspect that her feelings are no longer completely her own. Flashes of the past and erratic behavior make Hayley believe that the Harper Bride has found a way inside of her mind and body. It's time to put the Bride to rest once and for all, so Hayley can know her own heart again—and whether she's willing to risk it . . .

"[Roberts's] considerable talents at creating richly compelling characters and witty, spellbinding stories come into full bloom."
—*Booklist* on *Blue Dahlia*

DON'T MISS THE FIRST TWO BOOKS IN THE TRILOGY

BLUE DAHLIA
BLACK ROSE

Turn the page for a complete list of titles by Nora Roberts and J. D. Robb from The Berkley Publishing Group . . .

Nora Roberts & J. D. Robb

REMEMBER WHEN

Nora Roberts

HOT ICE	TRUE BETRAYALS
SACRED SINS	MONTANA SKY
BRAZEN VIRTUE	SANCTUARY
SWEET REVENGE	HOMEPORT
PUBLIC SECRETS	THE REEF
GENUINE LIES	RIVER'S END
CARNAL INNOCENCE	CAROLINA MOON
DIVINE EVIL	THE VILLA
HONEST ILLUSIONS	MIDNIGHT BAYOU
PRIVATE SCANDALS	THREE FATES
HIDDEN RICHES	BIRTHRIGHT
NORTHERN LIGHTS	

Series

In the Garden Trilogy

BLUE DAHLIA
BLACK ROSE
RED LILY

Key Trilogy	*Three Sisters Island Trilogy*
KEY OF LIGHT	DANCE UPON THE AIR
KEY OF KNOWLEDGE	HEAVEN AND EARTH
KEY OF VALOR	FACE THE FIRE

Gallaghers of Ardmore Trilogy	*Born In Trilogy*
JEWELS OF THE SUN	BORN IN FIRE
TEARS OF THE MOON	BORN IN ICE
HEART OF THE SEA	BORN IN SHAME

Chesapeake Bay Saga	*Dream Trilogy*
SEA SWEPT	DARING TO DREAM
RISING TIDES	HOLDING THE DREAM
INNER HARBOR	FINDING THE DREAM
CHESAPEAKE BLUE	

Anthologies

FROM THE HEART
A LITTLE MAGIC
A LITTLE FATE

MOON SHADOWS
(with Jill Gregory, Ruth Ryan Langan, and Marianne Willman)

The Once Upon Series
(with Jill Gregory, Ruth Ryan Langan, and Marianne Willman)

ONCE UPON A CASTLE	ONCE UPON A ROSE
ONCE UPON A STAR	ONCE UPON A KISS
ONCE UPON A DREAM	ONCE UPON A MIDNIGHT

J. D. Robb
(in order of publication)

NAKED IN DEATH	JUDGMENT IN DEATH
GLORY IN DEATH	BETRAYAL IN DEATH
IMMORTAL IN DEATH	SEDUCTION IN DEATH
RAPTURE IN DEATH	REUNION IN DEATH
CEREMONY IN DEATH	PURITY IN DEATH
VENGEANCE IN DEATH	PORTRAIT IN DEATH
HOLIDAY IN DEATH	IMITATION IN DEATH
CONSPIRACY IN DEATH	DIVIDED IN DEATH
LOYALTY IN DEATH	VISIONS IN DEATH
WITNESS IN DEATH	SURVIVOR IN DEATH

Anthologies

SILENT NIGHT
(with Susan Plunkett, Dee Holmes, and Claire Cross)

OUT OF THIS WORLD
(with Laurell K. Hamilton, Susan Krinard, and Maggie Shayne)

Also available . . .

THE OFFICIAL NORA ROBERTS COMPANION
(edited by Denise Little and Laura Hayden)

NORA ROBERTS

RED LILY

JOVE BOOKS, NEW YORK

THE BERKLEY PUBLISHING GROUP
Published by the Penguin Group
Penguin Group (USA) Inc.
375 Hudson Street, New York, New York 10014, USA
Penguin Group (Canada), 90 Eglinton Avenue East, Suite 700, Toronto, Ontario M4P 2Y3, Canada
(a division of Pearson Penguin Canada Inc.)
Penguin Books Ltd., 80 Strand, London WC2R 0RL, England
Penguin Group Ireland, 25 St. Stephen's Green, Dublin 2, Ireland (a division of Penguin Books Ltd.)
Penguin Group (Australia), 250 Camberwell Road, Camberwell, Victoria 3124, Australia
(a division of Pearson Australia Group Pty. Ltd.)
Penguin Books India Pvt. Ltd., 11 Community Centre, Panchsheel Park, New Delhi—110 017, India
Penguin Group (NZ), Cnr. Airborne and Rosedale Roads, Albany, Auckland 1310, New Zealand
(a division of Pearson New Zealand Ltd.)
Penguin Books (South Africa) (Pty.) Ltd., 24 Sturdee Avenue, Rosebank, Johannesburg 2196,
South Africa

Penguin Books Ltd., Registered Offices: 80 Strand, London WC2R 0RL, England

This is a work of fiction. Names, characters, places, and incidents either are the product of the author's
imagination or are used fictitiously, and any resemblance to actual persons, living or dead, business
establishments, events, or locales is entirely coincidental. The publisher does not have any control over
and does not assume any responsibility for author or third-party websites or their content.

RED LILY

A Jove Book / published by arrangement with the author.

PRINTING HISTORY
Jove mass-market edition / December 2005

Copyright © 2005 by Nora Roberts.
Excerpt from *Blue Smoke* © 2005 by Nora Roberts.
Cover design by Steven Ferlauto.

ISBN: 0-515-13940-8

JOVE®
Jove Books are published by The Berkley Publishing Group,
a division of Penguin Group (USA) Inc.,
375 Hudson Street, New York, New York 10014.
JOVE is a registered trademark of Penguin Group (USA) Inc.
The "J" design is a trademark belonging to Penguin Group (USA) Inc.

PRINTED IN THE UNITED STATES OF AMERICA

10   9   8   7   6   5   4   3   2   1

To Kayla, child of my child,
and all those lights who've yet to shine
when this was written.

Grafting and budding involve joining two separate plants so that they function as one, creating a strong, healthy plant that has only the best characteristics as its two parents.

AMERICAN HORTICULTURE SOCIETY
PLANT PROPAGATION

Youth fades; love droops, the leaves of friendship fall; a mother's secret hope outlives them all.

OLIVER WENDELL HOLMES

PROLOGUE

SHE WAS DESPERATE, DESTITUTE, AND DEMENTED.

Once she'd been a beautiful woman, a clever woman with one towering ambition. Luxury. She'd achieved it, using her body to seduce and her mind to calculate. She became the mistress of one of the wealthiest and most powerful men in Tennessee.

Her house had been a showplace, decorated at her whim—and with Reginald's money. There'd been servants to do her bidding, a wardrobe to rival the most sought-after courtesan in Paris. Jewelry, amusing friends, a carriage of her own.

She'd given gay parties. She'd been envied and desired.

She, the daughter of a biddable housemaid, had all her avaricious heart had desired.

She'd had a son.

It had changed her, that life she hadn't wanted to carry

inside her. It had become the center of her world, the single thing she loved more than herself. She planned for her son, dreamed of him. Sang to him while he lay sleeping in her womb.

She delivered him into the world with pain, such pain, but with joy, too. The joy of knowing when the pain was done, she would hold her precious son in her arms.

They told her she delivered a girl child. They told her the baby was stillborn.

They lied.

She'd known it even then, even when she was wild with grief, even when she sank into the pit of despair. Even when she went mad, she knew it for a lie. Her son lived.

They'd stolen her baby from her. Held him for ransom. How could it be otherwise when she could *feel* his heart beat as truly as she felt her own?

But it hadn't been the midwife and doctor who'd taken her child. Reginald had taken what was hers, using his money to buy the silence of those who served him.

How she remembered the way he'd stood in her parlor, coming to her only after her months of grief and worry. Done with her, she thought as she buttoned the gray dress with trembling fingers. Finished now that he had what he had wanted. A son, an heir. The one thing his cold-blooded wife hadn't been able to provide.

He'd used her, then taken her single treasure, as if he had the *right*. Offering her money and a voyage to England in exchange.

He would pay, he would pay, he would pay, her mind repeated as she groomed herself. But not with money. Oh no. Not with money.

She was all but penniless now, but she would find a way. Of course she would find a way, once she had her darling James back in her arms.

The servants—rats and sinking ships—had stolen some of her jewelry. She *knew* it. She'd had to sell most of the rest, and had been cheated in the price. But what could she expect from the thin-lipped scarecrow of a jeweler? He was a man, after all.

Liars and cheats and thieves. Every one of them.

They would *all* pay before she was finished.

She couldn't find the rubies—the ruby and diamond bracelet, heart-shaped stones, blood and ice, that Reginald had given her as a token when he'd learned she was pregnant.

It was a trinket, really. Too delicate, too *small* for her tastes. But she *wanted* it, and tore through the messy maze of her bedroom and dressing area in search.

Wept like a child when she found a sapphire brooch instead. As the tears dried, as her fingers closed around the pin, she forgot the bracelet and her desperate desire for it. Forgot that she'd been searching for it. Now she smiled at the sparkle of rich blue stones. It would be enough to provide a start for her and James. She would take him away, to the country perhaps. Until she felt well again, strong again.

It was all very simple, really, she decided with a ghastly smile as she studied herself in the glass. The gray dress was quiet, dignified—the proper tone for a mother. If it hung on her, drooping at the bodice, it couldn't be helped. She had no servants now, no dressmakers to fuss with alterations. She would get her figure back once she and James found their pretty country cottage.

She'd dressed her blond hair in top curls and, with considerable regret, eschewed rouge. A quiet look was better, she concluded. A quiet look was soothing to a child.

She would simply go get him now. Go to Harper House and take back what was hers.

The drive out of the city to the grand Harper mansion was long, cold, and costly. She no longer had a carriage of her own, and soon, very soon, Reginald's agents would come back to the house and remove her as they'd threatened already.

But it was worth the price of a private carriage. How else could she bring her James back to Memphis, where she would carry him up the stairs to his nursery, lay him tenderly in his crib, and sing him to sleep?

"Lavender's blue, dilly dilly," she sang softly, twisting her thin fingers together as she stared out at the winter trees that lined the road.

She'd brought the blanket she'd ordered him from Paris, and the sweet little blue cap and booties. In her mind he was a newborn still. In her shattered mind the six months since his birth didn't exist.

The carriage rolled down the long drive, and Harper House, in all its glory, stood commanding the view.

The yellow stone, the white trim were warm and graceful against the harsh gray sky. Its three stories were proud and strong, accented by trees and shrubs, a rolling lawn.

She'd heard that peacocks had once wandered the estate, flashing their jeweled tails. But Reginald hadn't cared for their screaming calls, and had done away with them when he'd become master.

He ruled like a king. And she'd given him his prince. One day, one day, her son would usurp the father. She would rule Harper House with James. Her sweet, sweet James.

Though the windows of the great house were blank and glazed by the sun—secret eyes staring out at her—she imagined living there with her James. Saw herself tending him there, taking him for walks in the gardens, hearing his laughter ring in the halls.

One day, of course, that's how it would be. The house

was his, so in turn, the house was hers. They would live there, happily, only the two of them. As it was meant to be.

She climbed out of the carriage, a pale, thin woman in an ill-fitting gray dress, and walked slowly toward the front entrance.

Her heart thudded at the base of her throat. James was waiting for her.

She knocked, and because her hands refused to be still, folded them tightly at her waist.

The man who answered wore dignified black, and though his gaze swept over her, his face revealed nothing.

"Madam, may I assist you?"

"I've come for James."

His left eyebrow lifted, the barest fraction. "I'm sorry, Madam, there is no James in residence. If you're inquiring about a servant, the entrance is in the rear."

"James is not a servant." How *dare* he? "He is my son. He is your master. I've come for him." She stepped defiantly through the doorway. "Fetch him immediately."

"I believe you have the wrong house, Madam. Perhaps—"

"You won't keep him from me. James! James! Mama is here." She dashed toward the steps, scratched and bit when the butler took her arm.

"Danby, what is the problem here?" A woman, again in servant black, bustled down the wide hall.

"This . . . woman. She's overwrought."

"To say the least. Miss? Please, Miss, I'm Havers, the housekeeper. You must calm yourself, and tell me what is the matter."

"I've come for James." Her hands trembled as she lifted them to smooth her curls. "You must bring him to me this instant. It's time for his nap."

Havers had a kind face, and added a gentle smile. "I see. Perhaps you could sit for a moment and compose yourself."

"Then you'll bring James? You'll give me my son."

"In the parlor? There's a nice fire. It's cold today, isn't it?" The look she gave Danby had him releasing his hold. "Here now, let me show you in."

"It's a trick. Another trick." Amelia bolted for the stairs, screaming for James as she ran. She made it to the second floor before she collapsed on weak legs.

A door opened, and the mistress of Harper House stepped out. She knew it was Reginald's wife. Beatrice. She'd seen her at the theater once, and in the shops.

She was beautiful, sternly so, with eyes like chips of blue ice, a slender blade of a nose, and plump lips that were curled now in disgust. She wore a morning dress of deep rose silk, with a high collar and tightly cinched waist.

"Who is this creature?"

"I'm sorry, ma'am." Havers, swifter of foot than the butler, reached the door of the sitting room first. "She didn't give her name." Instinctively, she knelt to drape an arm around Amelia's shoulders. "She seems to be in some distress and chilled right through."

"James." Amelia reached up, and Beatrice deliberately swept her skirts aside. "I've come for James. My son."

There was a flicker over Beatrice's face before her lips clamped into a tight line. "Bring her in here." She turned, strode back into the sitting room. "And wait."

"Miss." Havers spoke quietly as she helped the trembling woman to her feet. "Don't be afraid now, no one's going to hurt you."

"Please get my baby." Her eyes pleaded as she gripped Havers's hand. "Please bring him to me."

"There now, go on in, talk to Mrs. Harper. Ma'am, shall I serve tea?"

"Certainly not," Beatrice snapped. "Shut the door."

She walked to a pretty granite hearth and turned so the

fire smoldered behind her, and her eyes stayed cold when the door shut quietly.

"You are—were," she corrected with a curl of her lips, "one of my husband's whores."

"I'm Amelia Connor. I've come—"

"I didn't ask your name. It holds no interest for me, nor do you. I had assumed that women of your ilk, those who consider themselves mistresses rather than common trollops, had enough wit and style not to step their foot into the home of what they like to call their protector."

"Reginald. Is Reginald here?" She looked around, dazedly taking in the beautiful room with its painted lamps and velvet cushions. She couldn't quite remember how she came to be here. All the frenzy and fury had drained out of her, leaving her cold and confused.

"He is not at home, and you should consider yourself fortunate. I'm fully aware of your . . . relationship, and fully aware he terminated that relationship, and that you were handsomely recompensed."

"Reginald?" She saw him, in her fractured mind, standing in front of a hearth—not this one, no not this one. Her hearth, her parlor.

Did you think I'd allow someone like you to raise my son?

Son. Her son. James. "James. My son. I've come for James. I have his blanket in the carriage. I'll take him home now."

"If you think I'll give you money to ensure your silence on this unseemly matter, you're very mistaken."

"I . . . I came for James." A smile trembled on her lips as she stepped forward, arms outstretched. "He needs his mama."

"The bastard you bore, and that was forced on me is called Reginald, after his father."

"No, I named him James. They said he was dead, but I

hear him crying." Concern covered her face as she looked around the room. "Do you hear him crying? I need to find him, sing him to sleep."

"You belong in an asylum. I could almost pity you." Beatrice stood, the fire snapping at her back. "You have no more choice in this matter than I. But I, at least, am innocent. I am his *wife*. I have borne his children, children born within the bounds of marriage. I have suffered the loss of children, and my behavior has been above reproach. I have turned a blind eye, a deaf ear on the affairs of my husband, and given him not one cause for complaint. But I gave him no son, and that, *that* is my mortal sin."

Color rushed into her cheeks now, all fury. "Do you think I want your brat foisted on me? The bastard son of a whore who will call me mother? Who will inherit this?" She threw her hands out. "All of this. I wish he had died in your womb, and you with him."

"Give him to me, give him back to me. I have his blanket." She looked down at her empty hands. "I have his blanket. I'll take him away."

"It's done. We're prisoners in the same trap, but at least you deserve the punishment. I've done nothing."

"You can't keep him; you don't want him. You can't have him." She rushed forward, eyes wild, lips peeled. And the blow cracked across her cheek, knocking her back and to the floor.

"You will leave this house." Beatrice spoke quietly, calmly, as though giving a servant some minor duty. "You will never speak of this, or I will see to it that you're put in the madhouse. My reputation will not be smeared by your ravings, I promise you. You will never come back here, never set foot in Harper House or on Harper property. You will never see the child—that will be your punishment, though it can never be enough in my mind."

"James. I will live here with James."

"You are mad," Beatrice said with the faintest hint of amusement. "Go back to your whoring. I'm sure you'll find a man who'll be happy to plant another bastard in your belly."

She strode to the door, flung it open. "Havers!" She waited, ignoring the wailing sobs behind her. "Have Danby remove this thing from the house."

BUT SHE DID COME BACK. THEY CARRIED HER OUT, ordered the driver to take her away. But she came back, in the cold night. Her mind was broken to pieces, but she managed the trip this last time, driving in a stolen wagon, her hair drenched from the rain, her white nightdress clinging to her.

She wanted to kill them. Kill them all. Slash them to ribbons, hack them to pieces. She could carry her James away then, in her bloody hands.

But they would never let her. She would never take her baby into her arms. Never see his sweet face.

Unless, unless.

She left the wagon while shadows and moonlight slid over Harper House, while the black windows gleamed and all inside slept.

The rain had stopped; the sky had cleared. Mists twined over the ground, gray snakes that parted for her bare, frozen feet. The hem of her gown trailed over the wet and mud as she wandered. Humming, singing.

They would pay. They would pay dearly.

She had been to the voodoo woman, and knew what had to be done. Knew what would be done to secure all she wanted, forever. For always.

She walked through the gardens, brittle with winter, and to the carriage house to find what she needed.

She was singing as she carried it with her, as she walked in the damp air toward the grand house with its yellow stones alit with moonlight.

"Lavender's blue," she sang. "Lavender's green."

ONE

᠀

Harper House
July 2005

TIRED DOWN THROUGH THE MARROW, HAYLEY YAWNED until her jaw cracked. Lily's head was heavy on her shoulder, but every time she stopped rocking, the baby would squirm and whimper, and those little fingers would clutch at the cotton tank Hayley was sleeping in.

Trying to sleep in, Hayley corrected and murmured hushing noises as she sent the rocker creaking again.

She knew it was somewhere in the vicinity of four in the morning, and she'd already been up twice before to rock and soothe her fretful daughter.

She'd tried at about the two A.M. mark to snuggle the baby into bed with her so they'd both get some sleep. But Lily would have nothing but the rocker.

So Hayley rocked and dozed, rocked and yawned, and wondered if she'd ever get eight straight again in this lifetime.

She didn't know how people did it. Especially single mothers. How did they cope? How did they stand up under all the demands on heart, mind, body—wallet?

How would she have managed it all if she'd been completely on her own with Lily? What kind of life would they have had if she had no one to help with the worry, the sheer drudgery, the fun and the foolishness? It was terrifying to think of it.

She'd been so ridiculously optimistic and confident, and *stupid,* she thought now.

Sailing along, she remembered, nearly six months pregnant, quitting her job, selling most of her things and packing up that rattletrap car to head out.

God, if she'd known then what she knew now, she'd never have done it.

So maybe it was good she hadn't known. Because she wasn't alone. Closing her eyes, she rested her cheek on Lily's soft, dark hair. She had friends—no, family—people who cared about her and Lily and were willing to help.

They didn't just have a roof over their heads, but the gorgeous roof of Harper House. She had Roz, distant cousin and then only through marriage, who'd offered her a home, a job, a chance. She had Stella, her best friend in the world to talk to, bitch to, learn from.

Both Roz and Stella had been single parents—and they'd coped, she reminded herself. They'd better than coped, and Stella had had two young boys to raise alone. Roz *three*.

And here she was wondering how she'd ever manage one, even with all the help only an offer away.

There was David, running the house, cooking the meals. And just being wonderfully David. What if she had to cook every night after work? What if she had to do all the shopping, the cleaning, the hauling, the *everything* in addition to holding up her end at her job and caring for a fourteen-month-old baby?

Thank God she didn't have to find out.

There was Logan, Stella's gorgeous new husband, who was willing to tinker around with her car when it acted up. And Stella's little guys, Gavin and Luke, who not only liked to play with Lily but were giving Hayley a hint of the sort of things she had coming in the next few years.

There was Mitch, so smart and sweet, who liked to scoop Lily up and cart her around on his shoulders while she laughed. He'd be officially here all the time now, she thought, once he and Roz got back from their honeymoon.

It had been so nice, so much fun, to watch both Stella and Roz fall in love. She'd felt a part of it all—the excitement, the changes, the expansion of her new family circle.

Of course, Roz's marriage meant Hayley'd have to stop dragging her feet on finding a place of her own. Newlyweds were entitled to privacy.

She wished there was a place close by. Even on the estate. Like the carriage house. Harper's house. She sighed a little as she rubbed a hand over Lily's back.

Harper Ashby. Rosalind Harper Ashby's firstborn, and one delicious piece of eye candy. Of course she didn't think about him that way. Much. He was a friend, a co-worker, and her baby girl's first crush. From all appearances, that love affair was mutual.

She yawned again, lulled like the baby by the rhythm of the rocking and the early-morning quiet.

Harper was, well, just flat-out amazing with Lily. Patient and funny, easy and loving. Secretly she thought of him as Lily's surrogate father—without the benefits of smoochies with Lily's mother.

Sometimes she played pretend—and what was the harm in that?—and the surrogate part of father didn't apply. The smoochies did. After all, what red-blooded American girl—currently very sex-deprived girl—wouldn't fantasize now and again about the tall, dark, and ridiculously handsome type, especially when he came with a killer grin, heart-melting brown eyes, and a pinchable butt?

Not that she'd ever pinched it. But in theory.

Plus he was completely smart. He knew everything there was to know about plants and flowers. She loved to watch him working in the grafting house at In the Garden. The way his hands held a knife or tied raffia.

He was teaching her, and she appreciated it. Appreciated it too much to indulge herself and take a nice hungry bite out of him.

But imagining doing it didn't hurt a thing.

She eased the rocker to a stop, held her breath and waited. Lily's back continued to rise and fall steadily under her hand.

Thank God.

She got up slowly, moving toward the crib with the stealth and purpose of a woman making a prison break. With her arms aching, her head fuzzy with fatigue, she leaned over the crib and gently, inch by inch laid Lily on the mattress.

Even as she draped the blanket over her, Lily began to stir. Her head popped up, and she began wailing.

"Oh, Lily, please, come on, baby." Hayley patted, rubbed, swaying on her feet. "Ssh now, come on. Give your mama a little break."

The patting seemed to work—as long as she kept her hand on Lily's back, the little head stayed down. So Hayley sank to the floor, stuck her arm through the crib slats. And patted. And patted.

And drifted off to sleep.

* * *

IT WAS THE SINGING THAT WOKE HER. HER ARM WAS asleep, and stayed that way when her eyes opened. The room was cold; the section of the floor where she sat beside the crib a square of ice. Her arm prickled from shoulder to fingertip as she shifted to keep a protective hand on Lily's back.

The figure in the gray dress sat in the rocker, softly singing the old-fashioned lullaby. Her eyes met Hayley's, but she continued to sing, continued to rock.

The jolt of shock cleared the fuzziness from Hayley's head, and had her heart taking one hard leap into her throat.

Just what did you say to a ghost you hadn't seen for several weeks? she wondered. Hey, how are you? Welcome home? Just what was the proper response, especially when the ghost in question was totally whacked?

Hayley's skin was slicked with cold when she pushed slowly to her feet so she could stand between the rocker and the crib. Just in case. Because it felt as if a few thousand needles were lodged in her arm, she cradled it against her body, rubbing it briskly.

Note all the details, she reminded herself. Mitch would want all the details.

She looked pretty calm for a psychotic ghost, Hayley decided. Calm and sad, the way she had the first time Hayley had seen her. But she'd also seen her with crazed, bulging eyes.

"Um. She had to get some shots today. Inoculations. She's always fussy the night after she gets them. But I think she's settled down now. In time to get up again in a couple of hours, so she'll probably be cranky for the babysitter until she gets her nap. But . . . but she should sleep now, so you could go."

The figure faded away seconds before the singing.

* * *

DAVID FIXED HER BLUEBERRY PANCAKES FOR BREAK-fast. She'd told him not to cook for her or Lily while Roz and Mitch were gone, but he always did. Since he looked so cute fussing in the kitchen, she didn't try very hard to discourage him.

Besides, the pancakes were awesome.

"You've been looking a little peaky." David gave her cheek a pinch; then repeated the gesture on Lily to make her giggle.

"Haven't been sleeping much lately. Had a visitor last night."

She shook her head when his eyebrows rose, and his mouth curved into a leer. "Not a man—too sad for my bad luck. Amelia."

Amusement faded immediately, replaced by concern as he slid into the breakfast nook across from her. "Was there trouble? Are you all right?"

"She was just sitting in the rocker, singing. And when I told her Lily was fine, that she could go, she did. It was completely benign."

"Maybe she's settled down again. We can hope. Have you been worried about that?" He took a careful study of her face, noted the smudges under the soft blue eyes, the pallor beneath the carefully applied blush on her cheeks. "Is that why you haven't been sleeping?"

"Some, I guess. Things were pretty wild around here for a few months. Our gooses were constantly getting bumped. Now this lull. It's almost creepier."

"You've got Daddy David right down here." He reached over to pat her hand, his long, concert pianist's fingers giving it a little extra rub. "And Roz and Mitch will be back today. The house won't feel so big and empty."

She let out a long breath, relieved. "You felt that way, too. I didn't want to say, didn't want you to feel like you weren't enough company or something. 'Cause you are."

"You, too, my treasure. But we've gotten spoiled, haven't we? Had a houseful for a year around here." He glanced toward the empty seats at the table. "I miss those kids."

"Aw, you softie. We still see them, everybody, all the time, but it's weird, having everything so quiet."

As if she understood, Lily launched her sip-cup so that it slapped the center island and thudded on the floor.

"Atta girl," David told her.

"And you know what else?" Hayley rose to retrieve the cup. She was tall and lanky, and much to her disappointment, her breasts had reverted to their pre-pregnancy size. She thought of them as an A-minus cup. "I think I'm getting in some sort of mood. I don't mean rut, exactly, because I love working at the nursery, and I was just thinking last night—when Lily woke up for the millionth time—how lucky I am to be here, to be able to have all these people in our lives."

She spread her arms, let them fall. "But, I don't know, David, I feel sort of . . . blah."

"Need shopping therapy."

She grinned and got a washcloth to wipe Lily's syrupy face. "It is the number-one cure for almost everything. But I think I want a change. Something bigger than new shoes."

Deliberately, he widened his eyes, let his jaw go slack. "There's something bigger?"

"I think I'm going to cut my hair. Do you think I should cut my hair?"

"Hmm." He cocked his head, studied her with his handsome blue eyes. "It's gorgeous hair, that glossy mahogany. But I absolutely loved it the way you wore it when you first moved here."

"Really?"

"All those different lengths. Tousled, casual, kicky. Sexy."

"Well . . ." She ran her hand down it. She'd grown it out, nearly to her shoulders. An easy length to pull back for work or motherhood. And maybe that was just the problem. She'd started taking the easy way because she'd stopped finding the time or making the effort to worry about how she looked.

She wiped Lily off, freed her from the high chair so she could wander around the kitchen. "Maybe I will then. Maybe."

"And toss in the new shoes, sweetie. They never fail."

IN HIGH SUMMER BUSINESS SLOWED AT THE GARDEN center. It never trickled down too far at In the Garden, but in July, the heady late winter through spring rush was long over. Wet heat smothered west Tennessee, and only the most avid of gardeners would suffer through it to pump new life into their beds.

Taking advantage of it, and her mood, Hayley wheedled a salon appointment, and an extra hour off from Stella.

When she drove back into work after her extended lunch break, it was with a new do, *two* new pair of shoes, and a much happier attitude.

Trust David, she decided.

She loved In the Garden. Most days, she didn't feel as if she was going to work at all. There couldn't be a better quality in a job than that, in her opinion.

She enjoyed just looking at the pretty white building that looked more like someone's well-tended home than a business, with the seasonal beds spreading out from its porch, and the pots full of colorful blooms by its door.

She liked the industry across the wide gravel lot—the

stacks of peat and mulch, the pavers and landscape timbers. The greenhouses that were full of plants and promises, the storage buildings.

When it was busy with customers, winding along the paths, pulling wagons or flatbeds full of plants and pots—everyone full of news or plans—it was more like a small village than a retail space.

And she was a part of it all.

She stepped in, and did a turn for Ruby, the white-haired clerk who manned the counter.

"Don't you look sassy," Ruby commented.

"I feel sassy." She ran her fingers through her short shaggy hair, then let it fall again. "I haven't done anything new with my hair in a *year.* More. I almost forgot what it was like to sit in a beauty parlor and have somebody do me."

"Things do slide with a new baby. How's our best girl doing?"

"Fussy last night after her shots. But she bounced back this morning. My butt was dragging. Pumped now though." To prove it, she flexed her arms to show little bumps of biceps.

"Good thing. Stella wants everything watered, and I do mean everything. And we're waiting on a big delivery of new planters. They'll need to be stickered and shelved once they come in."

"I'm your girl."

She started outside in the thick, drowsy heat, soaking the bedding plants, the annuals and perennials who'd yet to find a home. They made her think of those awkward kids in school who never got picked for the team. As a result, she had a soft spot for them and wished she had a place where she could dig them into the soil, let them bloom, let them find their potential.

One day she would have a place. She'd plant gardens,

take what she'd learned here and put it to use. Make something beautiful, something special. There would have to be lilies, naturally. Red lilies, like the ones Harper brought to her when she was in labor with Lily. A big, splashy pool of red lilies, bold and fragrant that would come back year after year and remind her how lucky she was.

Sweat trickled down the back of her neck, and water dampened her canvas skids. The gentle spray annoyed the gang of bees covering the sedum. So, come back when I'm finished, she thought as they flew off with an annoyed buzz. We're all after the same thing here.

She moved slowly, half dreaming, down the tables holding the picked-over stock.

And if one day she had a garden, and there was Lily playing on the grass. With a puppy, she decided. There should be a puppy, all fat and soft and frisky. If she was able to have all that, couldn't she add a man? Someone who loved her and Lily, someone funny and smart who made her heart beat just a little faster when he looked at her?

He could be handsome. What was the point of a fantasy if the guy wasn't great-looking? Tall, he would be tall, with good shoulders and long legs. Brown eyes, deep delicious brown, and lots of thick dark hair she could get her hands into. Good cheekbones, the kind you just wanted to nibble your way along until you got to that strong, sexy mouth. And then—

"Jesus, Hayley, you're drowning that coreopsis."

She jerked, whipping the sprayer, then on a little yip of distress whipped it back again. But not before the water hit Harper dead-on.

Gut shot, she thought, torn between embarrassment and inappropriate giggles. He looked down at his soaked shirt, his jeans with a kind of grim resignation.

"Got a license for that thing?"

"I'm sorry! I'm so sorry. But you shouldn't sneak up behind me that way."

"I didn't sneak anywhere. I walked."

His voice was aggravated, but so Memphian, she thought, where she knew hers hit twang when she was excited or upset. "Well, walk louder next time. I really am sorry though. I guess my mind was wandering."

"This kind of heat, it's easy for the mind to wander, then lie down to take a nap." He pulled the wet shirt away from his belly. His eyes crinkled at the corners when he narrowed them. "What did you do to your hair?"

"What?" Instinctively she reached up, pulled her fingers through it. "I had it cut. Don't you like it?"

"Yeah, sure. It's fine."

Her finger itched on the trigger of the sprayer. "Please, stop. That kind of flattery'll just go to my head."

He smiled at her. He had such a great smile—sort of slow, so that it shifted the angles of his face and lit up in those deep, dark brown eyes—she nearly forgave him.

"I'm heading home, for a bit anyway. Mama's back."

"They're back? How are they? Did they have a good time? And you don't know yet because you haven't been home. Tell them I can't wait to see them, and that everything's fine over here, and Roz shouldn't worry and come over and start in working when she's barely walked in the door. And—"

He cocked his hip, hooked a thumb in the front pocket of his ancient jeans. "Should I be writing any of this down?"

"Oh, go on then." But she laughed as she waved him away. "I'll tell them myself."

"See you later."

He walked off, the man of her daydreams, dripping a little.

She really had to get her mind off Harper, she warned herself. Get it off and keep it off. He wasn't for her, and she knew it. She walked over to give the potted shrubs and climbers a good soak.

She wasn't even sure she wanted anybody to be for her—right now, anyway. Lily was number one priority, and after Lily came her job. She wanted her baby happy, healthy, and secure. And she wanted to learn more, do more at the nursery. The more she learned, the less it would be a job, and the more it would be a career.

Pulling her weight was fine, but she wanted to do more.

After Lily, her work, and the family she'd made here, came the fascinating and spooky task of identifying Amelia, the Harper Bride—and laying her to rest.

Most of that fell to Mitch. He was the genealogist, and along with Stella the most organized mind of the bunch. And wasn't it cool that he and Roz had found each other, fallen in love, after Roz had hired him to research the family tree to try to find where Amelia fit in? Not that Amelia had cared for the falling-in-love part. Boy, she'd been a stone bitch about it.

She might get mean again, too, Hayley thought. Now that they were married and Mitch was living at Harper House. She'd been quiet for a while, but it didn't mean she'd stay quiet.

If and when the whirlwind resumed, Hayley intended to be ready for it.

two

HAYLEY WALKED INTO HARPER HOUSE—AH, THE
blessed *cool*—with Lily on her hip. She set Lily on her
feet, then dumped her purse and the diaper bag on the bottom step so they'd be handy for her to carry up. Up's where
she wanted to go. She wanted to shower for, oh, two or
three days ought to do it, then drink an ice cold beer,
straight down.

But before she did anything, she wanted Roz.

Even as she thought it, Roz came out of the parlor. She
and Lily gave mutual cries of delight. Lily changed direction, and as she headed toward Roz, Roz closed the distance and scooped her up.

"There's my sweet potato." She gave Lily a fierce hug,
nuzzled her neck, then with a grin for Hayley, looked back
at the baby and listened with amazement to the excited and
incomprehensible babbling. "Why, I can't believe all that

happened in just one week! Don't know what I'd do if you weren't here to catch me up on all the local gossip." She grinned at Hayley again. "And how's your mama?"

"I'm fine. I'm great." Hayley dashed over to lock them both in a hug. "Welcome home. We missed you."

"Good. I like being missed. And look at this." She flipped her fingers over Hayley's hair.

"I just did it. Just today. Woke up with a bug up my butt. Oh, you look so beautiful."

"Listen to you."

But it was true, always true. And now a weeklong honeymoon in the Caribbean had added a dewy glow to innate beauty. Sun had turned the creamy skin pale gold so that Roz's long, dark eyes seemed even deeper. The short, straight hair capped a face with the sort of classic, timeless beauty Hayley knew she could only envy.

"I like that cut," Roz commented. "It looks so young and easy."

"Gave my morale a boost. Lily and I had a rough night. She got her shots yesterday."

"Mmm." Roz gave Lily an extra hug. "No fun there. Let's see if we can make up for it. Come on in here, baby girl," Roz said, snuggling Lily again as she went back in the parlor. "See what we got you."

The first thing Hayley saw was a life-sized doll with a mop of red hair and a sweet and foolish smile.

"Oh, she's so cute! And almost as big as Lily."

"That was the idea. Mitch spotted her before I did, and nothing would do but we bring her home to Lily. What do you think, sweetie?"

Lily poked the doll in the eye a couple of times, pulled its hair, then was happy to sit on the floor and get acquainted.

"It's the kind of doll she'll name in a year or so, then keep in her room till college. Thank you, Roz."

"We're not done. There was this little shop, and they had the most adorable dresses." She began to pull them out of the bag while Hayley goggled. Soft smocked cotton, ruched lace, embroidered denim. "And look at these rompers. Who could resist?"

"They're wonderful. They're beautiful. You'll spoil her."

"Well, of course."

"I don't know what to . . . She doesn't have any grand— anybody to spoil her like this."

Roz arched a brow, folded a romper. "You can say the G word, Hayley. I won't faint in horror. I like to think of myself as her honorary grandmother."

"I'm so lucky. We're so lucky."

"Then why are you tearing up?"

"I don't know. All this stuff's been going on in my head lately." She sniffled, heeled a hand under her eyes to rub away the dampness. "Where I am, how I got here, how it might've been for us if I'd been on my own with Lily the way I thought I'd be."

"Might've beens don't get you very far."

"I know. I'm just so glad I came to you. I was thinking last night that I should start looking for a place."

"A place to what?"

"Live."

"Something wrong with this place?"

"It's the most beautiful house I've ever seen." And here she was, Hayley Phillips from Little Rock, living in it, living in a house that had a parlor furnished with beautiful antiques and deep rich cushions, with generous windows that opened up to acres of more beauty.

"I was thinking I should look for a place, but I don't want to. At least, well, not right now." She looked down, watched Lily struggle to carry the doll around the room. "But I want you to tell me, and I know we're good enough friends that you will, when you want me to start looking."

"All right. That settled then?"

"Sure."

"Don't you want to see what we brought you?"

"I got something, too?" Hayley's lake blue eyes went bright with anticipation. "I *love* presents. I'm not ashamed to say it."

"I hope you like this one." She took a box out of the bag, offered it.

Wasting no time, Hayley took off the top. "Oh, oh! They're gorgeous."

"I thought the red coral would suit you best."

"I *love* them!" She took the earrings out of the box and holding them to her ears rushed to one of the antique mirrors on the wall to study how they looked. The trios of delicate and exotic red balls swayed from a glittery triangle of silver. "They're wonderful. God, I have something from Aruba. I can't believe it."

She dashed back to give a chuckling Roz a hug. "They're just beautiful. Thank you, thank you. I can hardly wait to wear them."

"You can give them a test drive tonight if you want. Stella, Logan, and the boys will be over. David tells me we're having a welcome-home dinner."

"Oh, but you'll be tired."

"Tired? What am I, eighty? I just got back from vacation."

"Honeymoon," Hayley corrected with a smirk. "Bet you didn't get a lot of rest either."

"We slept in every morning, you smart-ass."

"In that case, we'll party. Lily and I'll go upstairs and get ourselves all clean and pretty."

"I'll give you a hand up with all these things."

"Thanks. Roz?" Everything inside her had settled down to a glow. "I'm really glad you're home."

* * *

IT WAS SO MUCH FUN TO PUT ON HER NEW EARRINGS, to dress Lily in one of her pretty new outfits, to fuss a little over both herself and her daughter. She shook her head just for the pleasure of feeling the way her hair fell and her earrings swung.

There now, she thought, not feeling dull and blah anymore. Since she was feeling celebratory, she capped it off with new shoes. The thin-heeled strappy black sandals were impractical and unnecessary. Which made them perfect.

"And they were on sale," she told Lily. "Gotta say, they've got to be more fun than Prozac or whatever."

It felt great to wear a dress—a short dress—and sexy shoes. A new haircut. Red lipstick.

She gave a turn for the mirror and struck a pose. Maybe she had a skinny build, but there was nothing much she could do about that. Still, she wore clothes pretty well, if she did say so. Kind of like a clothes hanger. Add new hair, new earrings, new shoes, and you had something.

"Ladies and gentlemen, I do believe I'm back."

DOWNSTAIRS, HARPER WAS SPRAWLED IN A CHAIR, sipping a beer and watching the way Mitch touched his mother—her hair, her arm—while they related some of the highlights of their trip for Logan and Stella and the boys.

He'd heard some of it already when he'd buzzed home for an hour that afternoon. He wasn't really listening. He was just watching, and thinking it was good, it was time his mother had someone so obviously besotted with her.

He was happy for her—and relieved. No matter how

well his mother could take care of herself, and God knew she could do just that, it was a comfort to know she had a smart, able man at her side.

After what had happened last spring, if Mitch hadn't moved in, he'd have done so himself. And that might've been a little sticky with Hayley living there.

It was more . . . comfortable, he decided, for everybody, if he continued to live in the carriage house. It might not have been much distance geographically, but psychologically it did the job.

"I told him he was crazy," Roz continued, gesturing with her wine in one hand, patting the other on Mitch's thigh. "Windsurfing? Why in God's name would we want to teeter around on a little hunk of wood with a sail attached? But he just had to try it."

"I tried it once." Stella sat, her curling mass of red hair spilling over her shoulders. "Spring break in college. It was fun once I got the hang of it."

"So I hear." Mitch's mutter had Roz grinning.

"He'd get up on the thing, and in two seconds, splash. Get up, and wait, I think he's got it. Splash."

"I had a defective board," Mitch claimed, and poked Roz in the ribs.

"Of course you did." Roz rolled her eyes. "One thing you can say about our Mitchell is he's game. I don't know how many times he hauled himself out of the drink and back on that board."

"Six hundred and fifty-two."

"How about you?" Logan, big and built and rugged beside Stella, gestured toward Roz with his beer.

"Oh, well, I don't like to brag," Roz said and examined her fingernails.

"Yes, she does." Mitch gulped down club soda, stretched out his long, long legs. "Oh, yes, she does."

"But I enjoyed the experience quite a lot."

"She just . . ." Mitch sailed his hand through the air to illustrate. "Sailed off as if she'd been born on one of the damn things."

"We Harpers do tend to have excellent athletic abilities and superior balance."

"But she doesn't like to brag," Mitch pointed out, then glanced over at the click of heels on hardwood.

Harper did the same, and felt his reputed superior balance falter.

She looked frigging amazing. The skinny little red dress, the mile-high shoes combined to make her legs look endless. The sort of legs a man could imagine cruising over for miles and miles. Her hair was so damn sexy that way, and her mouth was all hot and red.

She had a baby on her hip, he reminded himself. He shouldn't be thinking about what he'd like to do to that mouth, that body when she was carrying Lily. It had to be wrong.

Across the room, Logan let out a long, low whistle that had Hayley's face lighting up.

"Hello, beautiful. You look good enough to eat. You look good, too, Hayley."

At that, she gave one of those husky rolls of laughter, and hip-swayed over to drop Lily in Logan's lap. "Just for that."

"How about some wine?" Roz offered.

"To tell you the truth, I've been wanting a cold beer."

"I'll get it." Harper all but sprang out of his chair, and was heading out of the parlor before she could respond. He hoped the trip to the kitchen and back would bring his blood pressure back to normal.

She was a cousin, sort of, he reminded himself. And an employee. His mother's houseguest. A mother. Any one of those reasons meant hands-off. Tally them up, and it put Hayley way off-limits. Added to that, she didn't think of him that way, not even close.

A guy made a move on a woman under those circumstances, he was just asking to screw up a nice, pleasant friendship.

He got out a beer, got out a pilsner. As he was pouring, he heard the squeal, and the rapid clip of heels on wood. He glanced over and spotted Lily running, with Hayley scrambling behind her.

"She want a beer, too?"

With a laugh, Hayley started to scoop Lily up, only to have her baby girl go red in the face and arch away. "You. Like always."

"That's my girl." He hoisted her up, gave her a toss. The mutinous little face went sugar sweet and bright with smiles. Pretending to pout, Hayley finished pouring her beer.

"Shows where I am in her pecking order."

"You got the beer, I got the kid."

Lily wrapped an arm around Harper's neck, dipped her head to rest it on his cheek. Hayley nodded, lifted her glass. "Looks like."

IT WAS WONDERFUL TO HAVE EVERYONE AROUND THE table again, the whole Harper House family, as Hayley thought of them, sitting together, diving into David's honey-glazed ham.

She'd missed having a big family. Growing up, it had been just Hayley and her father. Not that she'd felt deprived, she thought, not in any way. She and her father had been a team, a unit, and he was—had been—the kindest, funniest, warmest man she'd ever known.

But she'd missed having meals like this, a full table, lots

of voices—even the arguments and drama that went hand-in-hand in her mind with big families.

Lily would grow up with that, because Roz had welcomed them. So Lily would have a lifetime of meals like this one, full of aunts and uncles and cousins. Grandparents, she thought, stealing a glance toward Roz and Mitch. And when Roz's other sons, or Mitch's son, came to visit, it would just add to the rich family stew.

One day, Roz's sons, and Mitch's Josh, would get married. Probably have a herd of kids between them.

She shifted her gaze toward Harper and ordered herself to ignore the little ache that came from thinking of him married, making babies with some woman whose face she couldn't see.

Of course, she'd be beautiful, that was a given. Probably blonde and built and blue-blooded. The bitch.

Whoever she turned out to be, whatever she looked like or *was* like, Hayley determined she'd make friends. Even if it killed her.

"Something wrong with the potatoes?" David murmured beside her.

"Hmm. No. They're awesome."

"Just wondered why you looked like you were forcing down some bad-tasting medicine, sugar."

"Oh, just thought about something I'm going to have to do, and won't like. Life's full of them. But that doesn't include eating these potatoes. In fact, I was wondering if you could show me how to cook some things. I can cook pretty good. Daddy and I split that chore, and we were both okay with the basics—I could even get a little fancy now and then. But Lily's growing up on your cooking, so I ought to be able to fix it for her myself when need be."

"Hmm, a kitchen apprentice. One I can mold into my own likeness. Love to."

When Lily began to drop the bits of food still on her tray delicately to the floor, Hayley popped up. "Guess who's done."

"Gavin, why don't you and Luke take Lily outside and play awhile?"

"Oh." Hayley shook her head at Stella's suggestion. "I don't want them to have to mind her."

"We can do it," Gavin piped up. "She likes to chase the ball and the Frisbee."

"Well . . ." At nearly ten, Gavin was tall for his age. And at just-turned-eight, Luke was right behind him. They could—and had—handled Lily at play on the backyard grass. "I don't mind if you don't, and she'd love it. But when you're tired of her, you just bring her back."

"And as a reward, ice cream sundaes later."

David's announcement got a couple of cheers.

When playtime was over, the sundaes devoured, Hayley carried Lily up to get her ready for bed, and Stella brought the boys up to the sitting room they'd once shared to watch television.

"Roz and Mitch want an Amelia talk," Stella told her. "I didn't know if you'd gotten the word."

"No, but that's fine. I'll be down as soon as she is."

"Need any help?"

"Not this time, but thanks. Her eyes are already drooping."

It was nice, she thought, to hear the muted crash and boom of some sort of space war on the sitting room television and the bright chatter of the boys' commentary on the action. She'd missed those noises since Stella had gotten married.

She settled Lily in for the night—hopefully—checked the monitor and the night-light. Then left the door ajar as she returned downstairs.

She found the adults in the library, the most usual meeting spot for ghost talk. The sun had yet to set, so the room was washed with light that was just hinting of pink. Through the glass, the summer gardens were ripe, sumptuous, spears of lavender foxglove dancing over pools of white impatiens, brightened with elegant drips of hot-pink fuschia.

She spotted the soft, fuzzy green of betony, the waxy charm of begonias, the inverted cups of purple coneflowers with their prickly brown heads.

She'd missed her evening walk with Lily, she remembered, and promised herself she'd take her daughter out for a stroll through the gardens the next day.

Out of habit, she crossed to the table where a baby monitor stood beside a vase of poppy-red lilies.

Once she was assured it was on, she tuned in to the rest of the room.

"Now that we're all here," Mitch began, "I thought I should bring you up-to-date."

"You're not going to break my heart and tell us you researched during your honeymoon," David put in.

"Your heart's safe, but we did manage to find some time to discuss various theories here and there. The thing is, I had a couple of e-mails from our contact in Boston. The descendant of the Harper housekeeper during Reginald and Beatrice's reign here."

"She find something?" Harper had chosen the floor rather than one of the seats, and now folded himself from prone to sitting.

"I've been feeding her what we know, and told her what we found in Beatrice Harper's journal, regarding your great-grandfather, Harper. The fact that he wasn't her son, but in fact Reginald's son with his mistress—whom we have to assume was Amelia. She hasn't had any luck, yet, digging up any letters or diaries from Mary Havers—the housekeeper. She has found photographs, and is getting us copies."

Hayley looked toward the second level of the library, to the table loaded with books, Mitch's laptop. And the board beside it that was full of photos and copies of letters and journal entries. "What will that do for us?"

"The more visuals, the better," he said. "She's also been talking to her grandmother, who's not doing very well, although she does have some lucid moments. The grandmother claims to recall her mother and a cousin who also worked here at the time talk about their days at Harper House. Lots of talk about the parties and the work. She also recalls her cousin talking about the young master, that's how she referred to Reginald Jr. And saying the stork got rich delivering that one. That her mother told her to hush, that blood money and curses aside, the child was innocent. When she asked what she meant, her mother wouldn't speak of it, except to say she'd done her duty by the Harper family, and would have to live with it. But the happiest day of her life had been when she'd walked out the door of this house for the last time."

"She knew my grandfather had been taken from his mother." Roz reached down, touched a hand to Harper's shoulder. "And if this woman is remembering correctly, it sounds as though Amelia wasn't willing to give him up."

"Blood money and curses," Stella repeated. "Who was paid, and what was cursed?"

"There would have been a doctor or a midwife, perhaps both, attending Amelia during the birth." Mitch spread his hands. "Almost certainly they'd have been paid off. Some of the servants here might have been bribed."

"I know that's awful," Hayley said. "But you wouldn't call that blood money, would you? Hush money more like."

"Bull's-eye," Mitch told her. "If there was blood money, where was the blood?"

"Amelia's death." Logan shifted, leaned forward. "She haunts here, so she died here. You haven't been able to find any record of that, so we have to assume it was covered up. Easiest way to cover something up is money."

"I agree." Stella nodded. "But how did she get here? There's no mention of Amelia in any of Beatrice's journals. No mention of Reginald's mistress by name, or of her coming to Harper House. She wrote about the baby, and how she felt about Reginald bringing him here, expecting her to pretend she'd given birth to him. Wouldn't she have been just as outraged, and written of that, if he'd established Amelia in the house?"

"He wouldn't have." Hayley spoke quietly. "From everything we've learned about him, he wouldn't have brought a woman of her class, one he considered a convenience, a means to an end, into the house he was so proud of. He wouldn't have wanted her around his son—the one he was passing as legitimate. It'd be a constant reminder."

"That's a good point." Harper stretched out his legs, crossed them at the ankles. "But if we believe she died here, then we have to believe she *was* here."

"Maybe she passed as a servant," Stella suggested. She gestured, and her wedding ring glinted gold in the softening light. "If Beatrice didn't know her, what she looked like, Amelia might have managed to get a position in the house, so she'd be close to her son. She sings to the children of the house, she's obsessed with the children here, in her way. Wouldn't she have been even more so with her own child?"

"It's a possibility," Mitch commented. "We haven't found her through the household records, but it's a possibility."

"Or she came here to try to get him." Roz looked at Stella, at Hayley. "A mother, frantic, desperate, and not completely balanced. She sure as hell didn't go crazy after she died. I'm not willing to stretch credulity that far. Doesn't it play that she would have come here, and something went terribly wrong? We have to consider that if she came here, she might have been murdered. Blood money to cover up the crime."

"So the house is cursed." Harper lifted a shoulder. "And she haunts it until, what, she's avenged? How?"

"Maybe just recognized," Hayley corrected. "Given her due, I guess. You're her blood," she said to Harper. "Maybe it's going to take Harper blood to put her to rest."

"I have to say that sounds logical." David gave a little shudder. "And creepy."

"We're a bunch of rational adults sitting around talking about a ghost," Stella reminded him. "It doesn't get much more creepy."

"I saw her last night."

At Hayley's statement all eyes turned to her. "And you didn't tell us?" Harper demanded.

"I told David this morning," she shot back. "And I'm telling everybody now. I didn't want to say anything in front of the kids."

"Let's get this on record." Mitch rose to go to the table for his tape recorder.

"It wasn't that much of a big."

"We agreed last spring after the last two violent apparitions, that everything goes on the record." He came back to sit again, and set the recorder on the table. "Tell us."

Talking on tape made her feel self-conscious, but she related everything.

"I hear her singing sometimes, but usually when I go in to check, she's gone. You know she's been there. Sometimes I hear her in the boys' room—Gavin's and Luke's old room. Sometimes she's crying. And once I thought . . ."

"Thought what?" Mitch prompted.

"I thought I might've seen her walking outside. The night y'all left on your honeymoon, after we had the wedding party here? I woke up—had a little more wine than I should, I guess—and I had a little headache. So I took some aspirin, checked on Lily. I thought I saw someone, out the window. There was enough moonlight that I could make out the blond hair, the white dress. It appeared like she was going toward the carriage house. But when I opened the doors, to go out on the terrace and get a better look, she was gone."

"Didn't we have an agreement, starting after Mama finally decided to clue us in about nearly being drowned in the bathtub, that we put everything on record?" Anger simmered in Harper's voice. "We don't wait a damn week to make an announcement."

"Harper," Roz said dryly. "That horse is dead. Don't start beating it again."

"We had an agreement."

"I didn't know for sure." Hayley's back went up, and it reflected in her tone as she glared down at Harper. "I still don't. Just because I thought I saw a woman walking toward your place didn't mean she was a ghost. Could just as likely—more likely—have been flesh and blood. What was I supposed to do, Harper, call you over at the carriage house and ask if you were getting a bootie call?"

"Jesus Christ."

"Well, there you are." Pleased, she nodded decisively. "It's not like you never have female company over there."

"Fine, fine. Just FYI, I didn't have female company—flesh and blood variety—that night. Next time, follow through."

"Class," Mitch said mildly, and gave a professorial tap of pencil on notebook. "Can you tell us any more about what you saw, Hayley?"

"Honestly, it was only a few seconds. I was just standing there, hoping the aspirin would kick in before morning, and I caught a movement. I saw a woman—a lot of blond or light hair, and she was wearing white. My first thought was Harper got lucky."

"Oh, man," was Harper's muttered comment.

"Then I thought about Amelia, but when I went out to see better, she was gone. I only mention it because if it was her, and I guess it was, that's twice I've seen her in about a week. And that's a lot for me."

"You were the only woman in the house during that week," Logan pointed out. "She's been more likely to show herself to women."

"That makes sense." And made her feel better.

"Added to that, it was the night after Mitch and I were married," Roz said. "She'd have been miffed."

"And it's the second time we've got a firsthand report of her walking toward the carriage house. There's something there," Mitch said to Harper.

"She's not letting me know about it. So far."

"Meanwhile we keep looking. We believe she lived in this area, so our best bet is Reginald kept her in one of his properties." Mitch lifted his hands. "I'm still pursuing that avenue."

"If we find out her name, her whole name," Hayley asked him, "would you be able to research her the way you did the Harper family?"

"It'd give me a start."

"Maybe she'll tell us, if we just find the right way to ask. Maybe . . ." She trailed off when singing came through the monitor. "She's with Lily, and she's early tonight. I'm just going to go up and check."

"I'll go with you." Harper got to his feet.

She didn't argue. Even after more than a year, the sound of that sad voice sent a chill up her spine. As was her habit, she'd flicked lights on in her wing so she wouldn't have to come back up in the dark. They reassured her now, as the sun was nearly set, as did the sounds of Luke and Gavin playing in the sitting room.

"You know, if you're uneasy being over here alone, you could move into the other wing, closer to Mama and Mitch."

"Just what the newly married couple need. Me and a baby as chaperones. Anyway, I'm mostly used to it. She's not stopping." She dropped her voice to a whisper. "She almost always stops before I get to the door."

Instinctively she reached for Harper's hand as she eased open the door she always left off the latch.

It was cold, but she'd expected that. Even after Amelia was gone, the chill would linger. Yet Lily was never disturbed by it. Her breath puffed out, a little startled cloud when she heard the distinctive creak of the rocker.

That was a new one, Hayley thought. Oh boy.

She sat in the rocker, wearing her gray dress. Her hands lay quiet in her lap as she sang. Her voice was pretty, unschooled but light and tuneful. Comforting, as a voice singing lullabies should be.

But when she turned her head, when she looked toward the door, Hayley's blood ran as cold as the air in the room.

It wasn't a smile on her face, but a grimace. Her eyes bulged, and were rimmed with violent red.

This is what they do. This is what they give.

As she spoke—thought—the form began to disintegrate. Flesh melted away to bone until what sat in the chair was a skeleton that rocked in rags.

Then even that was gone.

"Please tell me you saw that." Hayley's voice trembled. "Heard that."

"Yeah." With his hand firm on hers, he drew Hayley across the room to the crib. "Warmer here. Feel it? It's warm around the crib."

"She's never done anything to scare Lily. Still, I don't want to leave, go down again. I'd just feel better if I stayed close tonight. You can tell the others what happened?"

"I can bunk up here tonight. Take one of the guest rooms."

"It's all right." She arranged Lily's blanket more securely. "We'll be all right."

He tugged her hand, gestured so that she went back out into the hall with him. "That was a first, right?"

"A definite first for me. It's going to give me nightmares."

"You sure you're going to be okay?" He touched his hand to her cheek, and it flitted through her mind that was another first. They were standing close, her hand in his, his fingers on her cheek.

All she had to do was say, no. Stay with me.

And then what? She could start something, and ruin everything.

"Yeah. It's not like she's mad at me or anything. No reason to be. We're good, we're fine. You'd better go down, fill the others in."

"You get spooked in the night, call. I'll come."

"Good to know. Thanks."

She slid her hand out of his, eased back, and slipped into her own room.

No, Amelia had no reason to be mad at her, Hayley considered. She had no boyfriend, no husband, no lover. The only man she wanted was off-limits.

"So you can relax," she murmured. "Looks like I'll be going solo for the next little while.

tHRee

HE HUNTED HER UP THE NEXT DAY, MID-MORNING. But he had to be sly about it. He knew her well enough to be sure if she thought he was trying to help, to get her mind off things, to give her any sort of break, she'd brush him off.

Hayley Phillips was the original I'm-fine-don't-worry-about-me girl.

Nothing wrong with that, Harper thought. In her place, a lot of women would have been happy to take advantage of his mother's generosity, or at least to take that generosity for granted. Hayley did neither, and he respected that. He could admire her stand—to a point. But plenty of times, to his mind, that point tripped over into just mule-headed stubborn.

So he kept it casual, even when he had to poke into two greenhouses, work his way to the main building before he found her setting up a new display of houseplants.

She was wearing one of the nursery's bib aprons over black camp shorts and a V-necked tank. There was damp soil on the apron, and on her forearm. Only repressed lust could be responsible for him finding it so absurdly sexy.

"Hey, how's it going?"

"Not too bad. Had ourselves a little run on dish gardens. Customer just came in and bagged five as centerpieces for her sorority reunion lunch. And I talked her into taking the sago palm for her own sunroom."

"Nice going. Guess you're busy then."

She glanced over her shoulder. "Not too. Stella wants to make up more dish gardens, but she's tied up with Logan, which isn't as sexy as it sounds. Big job came in, and she's locked him in the office until she gets all the details for the contract. Last I walked by, he wasn't all that happy about it."

"Ought to be at it for a while then. I was going to do some chip-budding. Could use some help, but—"

"Really? Can I do it? I can take one of the two-ways in case Ruby or Stella need me."

"I could use another pair of hands."

"Mine'll be right back. Hold on."

She dashed through the double glass doors, and was back in thirty seconds, shed of the apron and hitching a two-way to her waistband. And giving him a quick peek at smooth belly skin.

"I read up some, but I can't remember which is the chip-budding."

"It's an old method," he told her as they started out. "More widely used now than it used to be. What we're going to do is work some of the field stock, some of the ornamentals. Mid-summer's the time for it."

Heat hit like a wet wall. "This sure is mid-summer."

"We'll start on magnolias." He picked up a bucket of

water he'd left outside the door. "They never stop being popular."

They walked over gravel, between greenhouses, and headed out to the fields. "Things stay quiet last night?"

"Not a peep after that little show we were treated to. I'm hoping she doesn't plan an encore of that trick. Gross, you know?"

"She sure knows how to get your attention anyway. Okay, here's what we do first." He stopped in front of a tall, leafy magnolia. "I'm going to pick some ripe shoots, this season's wood. You want one not much thicker than a pencil with well-developed buds. See this one?"

With an ungloved hand, he reached up, gently drew a shoot down.

"Okay, then what?"

"I clip it off." He drew pruners out of his tool bag. "See here, where the base is starting to go woody? That's what we're looking for. You don't want green shoots, they're too weak yet."

After he'd cut it, Harper put the shoot in the water bucket. "We keep it wet. If it dries out, it won't unite. Now you pick one."

She started to move around the tree, but he caught her hand. "No, it's better to work on the sunny side of the tree."

"Okay." She rolled her bottom lip between her teeth as she searched, selected. "How about this one?"

"Good. Here, make the cut."

She took the pruners, and since he was close he could smell the scent she wore—always light with a surprising kick—along with the garden green.

"How many are you doing?"

"About a dozen." He stuck his hands in his pockets as he leaned in to watch her, smell her. And told himself he was suffering for a good cause. "Go ahead, pick another."

"I don't get out in the field much." She drew down another shoot, looked toward Harper and got his nod. "It's different out here. Different than selling and displaying, talking to customers."

"You're good at that."

"Yeah, I am, but being out here, it's getting your hands into the thing. Stella knows all this stuff, and Roz, she knows everything. I like to learn. You sell better the more you know."

"I'd rather ram that shoot in my eye than have to sell every day."

She smiled as she worked. "But you're a loner at heart, aren't you? I'd go crazy holed up in the grafting house day after day like you. I like seeing people, and having them talk to me about what they're looking for and why. I like selling, too. 'Here, you take this pretty thing, and give me the money.'"

She laughed as she put another shoot in the bucket. "That's why you and Roz need somebody like me, so you can squirrel away in your caves and work with the plants for hours, and I can sell them."

"Seems to be working."

"That's a dozen, even. What next?"

"Over here, what we've got is rooted shoots I got from stool-grown stock plants."

"Stooling, I know what that is." She stared down at the nursery bed and its line of straight, slim shoots. "Um, you hill the ground up to stimulate rooting, and cut them back hard in the winter, then you take the roots from the what-doyoucallit, parent plant, and plant them out."

"You have been reading up."

"I like to learn."

"Shows." And was just one more click for him. He'd never found a woman who'd interested him physically, emotionally, who shared his love of gardening. "Okay. We use a sharp, clean knife. We're going to trim off all the leaves from the budstick—the shoots we just cut. But we'll leave just a little stub, just about an eighth of an inch of the petiole—the leaf stalk."

"I know what a petiole is," she muttered, and watched Harper demonstrate before she took her turn.

Good hands, she thought. Quick, skilled, sure. Despite—or maybe because of the nicks and calluses—they were elegantly male.

She thought they reflected who he was perfectly, that combination of privileged background and working-class.

"Cut the soft tip from the top, see? Now watch." He angled around so she could see, and their heads bent close together. "We want the first bud at the base, that's where we're going to cut into the stem, just a little below there. See how you have to angle the cut, going down, then another above, behind the bud toward that first cut. And . . ." Gently, holding the chip by the leaf stalk, he held it out.

"I can do that."

"Go ahead." He slipped the bud chip into a plastic bag, and watched her work.

She was careful, which was a relief to him, and he heard her whispering his instructions to herself with every move.

"I did it!"

"Nice job. Let's get the rest."

He did seven in the time it took her to do three, but she didn't mind. He showed her how to stand astride the rootstock to remove the sideshoots and leaves from the bottom twelve inches.

She knew it was a maneuver, and really, she'd probably feel guilty about it later, but she deliberately fumbled her first attempt.

"No, you need to position it between your legs, more like this."

As she'd hoped, he came over to stand behind her, in a nice vertical spoon, his arms coming around, making her belly dance as his hands closed over her wrists.

"Bend down a little, loosen at the knees. That's it. Now . . ." He guided her hand for the cut. "Just a sliver of the bark," he murmured, and his breath breezed along her ear. "See, there's the cambium. You want to leave a lip at the base where the chip will layer."

He smelled like the trees, sort of hot and earthy. His body felt so firm pressed against hers. She wished she could turn around, just turn so they were pressed front to front. She'd only have to rise up on her toes for their mouths to line up.

It was a maneuver, and *shame* on her, but she looked over her shoulder, looked dead into his eyes. And smiled. "Is that better?"

"Yeah. Better. A lot."

As she'd hoped, his gaze skimmed down, lingered on her mouth. Classic move, she thought. Classic results.

"I'll . . . show you how to do the rest."

He looked blank for a moment, like a man who'd forgotten what he was doing in the middle of a task. She couldn't have been more delighted.

Then he stepped back, reached in his tool bag for the grafting tape.

That had been so nice, she mused. Line to line, heat to heat, for just a few seconds. Of course now she was all churned up, but it felt good, felt fine to have everything swimming around inside her.

But as penance for her calculation, she behaved herself, played the eager student as she positioned the bud chip on the stock so the cambium layers met as snugly as her body had met Harper's.

She bound the chip to stock using the tape around and over the bud as instructed.

"Good. Perfect." He still felt a little breathless, and the palms of his hands were damp enough that he wiped them on the knees of his jeans. "In six weeks, maybe two months, the chip will have united, and we'll take off the tape. Late next winter, we'll cut the top of the stock, just above this bud, and during the spring the grafted bud will send out a shoot, and we're off and running."

"It's fun, isn't it? How you can take a little something from one, a little something from another, put them together and make more."

"That's the plan."

"Will you show me some of the other techniques sometime? Like what you do in the grafting house?" Her body was angled, her head bent over the next rootstock. "Roz and Stella showed me some of the propagation techniques. I've done some flats by myself. I'd like to try something in the grafting house."

Alone with her there, in all that moist heat. He'd probably drown in a pool of his own lust.

"Sure, sure. No problem."

"Harper?" She knelt to join chip bud with rootstock. "Did you ever think, when your mama started this place, it'd be what it is?"

He had to focus, on her words, on the work, and ignore— or at least suffer through—his body's reaction to her.

Lily's mama, he reminded himself. A guest in his home. An employee. Could it be any more complicated?

Jesus, God. Help.

"Harper?"

"Sorry." He wrapped grafting tape. "I did." When he looked up, looked around, beyond the fields and nursery beds, to the greenhouses, and sheds, he calmed. "I guess I could see it because it was what I wanted, too. And I know when Mama puts her mind to something, puts her back into it, she's going to make it work."

"What if she hadn't wanted it, or put her mind to it? What would you be doing?"

"Just what I'm doing. If she hadn't decided on this I'd've started it myself. And because I wanted it, she'd've got on board, so I guess we'd have pretty much what we have here."

"She's the best, isn't she? It's good that you know that, that you understand how lucky you are. I see that between you. You don't take each other for granted. I hope Lily and I have that one day."

"Seems like you already do."

She smiled at that, and rose to go to the next rootstock. "Do you think you and Roz are the way you are with each other, to each other—and your brothers, too—because you didn't have a daddy most of your life? I mean, I think I was closer to my own daddy because it was just the two of us than I might've been otherwise. I've wondered about that."

"Maybe." His hair, a thick tangle of black, fell forward as he worked. He shook it back, momentarily annoyed he'd forgotten a hat. "I remember her and my father, how they were together. It was special. She's got something like that with Mitch—not the same. I guess it's never the same, not supposed to be. But they've got something good and special. That's what she deserves."

"Do you ever think about finding somebody? Somebody good and special?"

"Me?" His head whipped up, and he narrowly missed slicing his own finger with the knife. "No. No. Well, eventually. Why? Do you?"

He heard her sigh as she moved down the nursery bed. "Eventually."

*   *   *

WHEN THEY WERE FINISHED, AND SHE HAD GONE, Harper walked back to the pond. He emptied out his pockets, tossed his sunglasses on the grass. Then dived in.

It had been something he'd done—with or without clothes—since childhood. There was nothing like a quick dip into the pond to cool you down on a sticky summer day.

He'd been on the point of kissing her. More than, he admitted, and sank under the surface, along the lily pads and yellow flags. It had been more than a kiss—even a hot and greedy one—that had run through his mind when he'd had his hands on her.

He had to put that aside—well off to the side—as he had been for more than a year now. She looked to him for friendship. God help him, she probably thought of him as a kind of brother.

So he'd just have to keep tamping down his less than brotherly feelings until he beat out the last of the sparks. Or burned up.

Best thing for him to do was get himself back into circulation. He was spending too much time at home, and too much of that time alone. Maybe he'd go into the city tonight, make some calls, meet some friends. Better yet, make a date. Have dinner, listen to music. Charm himself into some willing female's bed.

The trouble was, he couldn't think of any particular female he wanted to be with, over dinner, with music, or in the bed. That right there, it seemed to him, illustrated his pitiful state of affairs. Or lack of them.

He just wasn't in the mood to do the dance that ended up between the sheets. He couldn't bring himself to call another woman, put on the show, go through the pretense, when the woman he wanted was sleeping in his own house.

And as far out of his reach as the moon.

He pulled himself out of the water, shook like a dog. Maybe he'd go into town though. He picked up the rest of his things, shoving them in his dripping pockets. See if any of his unattached friends felt like catching a movie, eating some barbecue, hitting a club. Something, anything, to take his mind somewhere else for a night.

BUT WHEN HE GOT HOME, HE WASN'T IN THE MOOD TO go out. He made excuses to himself: It was too hot, he was too tired, he didn't feel like the drive. What he really wanted was a cool shower and a cold beer. He was pretty sure there was a frozen pizza buried with the leftovers David was always giving him. There was a ballgame on TV.

What else did he need?

A long warm body with miles of leg and smooth skin. Luscious lips and big blue eyes.

Since that wasn't on the menu, he decided to drop the temperature of the shower to cold.

His hair was still dripping and he wore nothing but ancient cutoffs when he wandered into the kitchen for that beer.

Like the rest of the house, it was small-scale. He didn't need big, he'd grown up in big. And he liked the charm and convenience of his little rooms. He thought of the converted two-story carriage house as a kind of country cottage. The way it sat away from the main house, surrounded by the gardens with their curving paths, shaded by old trees, gave it the kind of solitude and privacy that suited him. And kept him close enough to the main house that he could be on hand if his mother needed him.

If he wanted company, all he had to do was stroll over. If he didn't, he stayed put. More often than not, he admitted, he stayed put.

He remembered when he'd decided to move in, and his biggest decorating plan had been to paint all the walls white and be done with it. Both his mother and David had been all over him like white on rice for that one.

They'd been right, he had to admit it. He liked the silvery sage walls in his kitchen and the stone gray counters, the distressed wood of the cabinets. He supposed the color had inspired him to juice the place up a little with the pieces of old pottery or china sitting around, the herbs growing on the windowsill.

It was a nice space, even if he was just eating a sandwich over the sink. He liked standing here, looking out at his own little greenhouse, and the explosion of the summer gardens.

The hydrangeas were as big as soccerballs this year, he noted, and the infusion of iron he'd given them turned them a strong, unearthly blue. Maybe he'd cut a few, plunk them down somewhere in the house.

Butterflies were massing around the garden he and his mother had planted to lure them. A flurry of colorful wings flashed over the welcoming bloom of purple coneflower, the sunny coreopsis, fragrant verbena, and the reliable asters. Backing them was the elegant dance of daylilies.

Maybe he'd cut a few of those, too, and take them over to the house so Lily could have them in her room. She liked flowers, liked when he took her walking in the gardens so she could touch them.

And her eyes, blue like her mama's, got so big and serious when he recited the names. Just like she was taking it all in, filing it away.

Christ, who'd have thought he'd be so gone on a kid?

But it was so cool the way she'd march along with her little hand in his, then stop and reach up, that pretty face turned to his, that pretty face full of light because she knew he'd swing her up. Then the way she'd hook her arm around his neck, or pat his hair. It just killed him.

It was amazing to love, to be loved in that open, uncomplicated way.

He took a pull of the beer, then opened the freezer to look for the pizza. He heard the quick knock on the front door seconds before it opened.

"Hope I'm interrupting an orgy," David called out. He strolled in, cocked his head at Harper. "What, no dancing girls?"

"They just left."

"I see they ripped your clothes off first."

"You know how it is with dancing girls. Wanna beer?"

"Tempting, but no. I'm saving myself for an exceptional Grey Goose martini. Night off, heading into Memphis to meet some people. Why don't you cover up that manly chest and come along?"

"Too hot."

"I'm driving, got AC. Go on, put on some dancing shoes. We're going to check out some clubs."

Harper pointed his beer toward his friend. "Every time I check out some clubs with you, somebody hits on me. And they're not always female."

"You heartbreaker. I'll protect you, throw myself bodily on anyone who tries to pat your ass. What're you going to do, Harp, stew around here with a beer and Kraft's mac and cheese?"

"Kraft's mac and cheese is the packaged dinner of champions. But I'm going with frozen pizza tonight. Besides, there's a game on."

"You *are* breaking my heart. Harper, we're young, we're hot. You're straight, I'm gay, which means we cover all available ground and double our chances of getting lucky. Between us we can cut a mighty swath down Beale Street. Don't you remember, Harp?" He took Harper by the shoulders, gave him a dramatic shake. "Don't you remember how once we ruled?"

He had to grin. "Those were the days."

"These are still the days."

"Don't you remember how once we puked our guts up in the gutter?"

"Sweet, sweet memories." David hitched himself up to sit on the counter, took Harper's beer for one sip. "Should I be worried about you?"

"No. Why?"

"When's the last time you had your pipes cleaned?"

"Jesus, David." He took a gulp of beer.

"Used to be a time when the nubiles were lined up three deep on the path to your door. Now the closest you come to a bang is nuking Kraft's in the mike."

It was too close to the truth for comfort. "I'm on sabbatical. I guess I got tired of it," he said with a shrug. "Besides, things have been pretty busy and intense around here for a while. The business with the Bride, especially finding out she was like my great-great-grandmother. Somebody screwed with her, messed her up. Careless, you know, callous, the way it's playing out. I don't want to be careless anymore."

"You never were." Soberly now, David boosted himself down. "How long have we been friends? Almost for fucking ever. I've never known you to be careless with anyone. If you're talking sex, you're the only person I know who stays friendly with a lover once the heat blows off. You're not careless with people, Harper. And just because Reginald was a bastard—most likely—doesn't mean you're doomed to be."

"No, I know. I'm not obsessing about it or anything. Just

sort of taking stock. Just chilling awhile until I figure out what I want for the next phase."

"You want company, I can take you up on that beer and whip up something considerably less revolting than frozen pizza."

"I like frozen pizza." He'd do it, Harper thought. He'd blow off his plans, just to hang, to be a pal. "Go, there's a martini with your name on it." He slapped a hand on David's shoulder to lead him to the front door. "Eat, drink, make Barry."

"Got my cell phone if you change your mind."

"Thanks." He opened the door, leaned on the jamb. "But while you're steaming along Beale, I'm going to be sitting in the cool, watching the Braves trounce the Mariners."

"Pitiful, son, just pitiful."

"And drinking beer in my underwear, which cannot be overstated." He broke off, felt the punch straight to the belly when Hayley and Lily came around a turn of the garden.

"Now that's a pretty sight."

"Yeah. They look good." The baby wore some sort of romper thing, pink and white stripes, with a little pink bow in her hair—dark hair, like her mother's. She looked sweet as a candy stick.

And Mama—tiny blue shorts, a yard of leg, bare feet. Some skinny little white top and wraparound shades. A different kind of candy altogether. Maybe it was sweet, but it was sure as hell hot.

He tipped up the beer to cool his throat, and Lily spotted them. She let out something between a yell and a squeal— all delight—and pulling away from Hayley made a beeline toward the carriage house as fast as her little legs could manage.

"Slow down, sweet potato." David moved forward to

scoop her up, give her a toss. She patted his face with both of her hands, gabbled at him, then reached for Harper.

"As always, I'm day-old paté when you're around."

"Hand her over," Harper hitched her onto his hip where she kicked her legs with joy and beamed at him. "Hey, pretty girl."

In response, she tilted her head to lay it on his shoulder.

"What a flirt," Hayley commented as she walked up. "Here we are having a nice walk, having a little girl-talk, she spots a couple of handsome men, and blows me off."

"Why don't you leave her with Harper, put on a party dress and drive on into Memphis with me?"

"Oh, I—"

"Sure." Harper kept his voice carefully neutral as he jiggled Lily. "She can hang with me. You can bring that Portacrib thing over and I'll put her down when she's tired."

"That's nice, I appreciate it. But it's been a long day. I don't think I'm up for a trip to Memphis."

"Fuds and duds, Lily." David leaned over to kiss her. "I'm surrounded by fuds and duds. I'm flying solo then, and I better get started. See y'all."

"I don't mind watching her if you want to get out awhile."

"No. I'm going to put her down pretty soon, then curl on up myself. Why aren't you going?"

"Too hot," he said, decided it was the easiest catchall excuse.

"Isn't it? And you're letting all the cool out. Come on, Lily."

But when she tried to take the baby, Lily squirmed away and clung to Harper like ivy to a tree. The sound she made was distinctly *da-da*.

The flush glowed on Hayley's cheeks even as she gave a weak laugh. "She doesn't mean anything. Those D sounds are the easiest to make, is all. Lots of things are da-da these days. Come on, Lily."

This time her arms circled Harper's neck like a noose, and she started to wail.

"You want to come in for a while?"

"No, no." She spoke quickly now, a tumble of words. "We were just taking a little walk, nearly done with it, and she has to have a bath before bedtime."

"I'll walk back with you." He turned his head, kissed Lily's cheek then whispered in her ear so she laughed and snuggled against him.

"She can't have everything she wants."

"She'll have to learn that soon enough." He reached behind him, and shut the door.

SHE MANAGED BATH AND BEDTIME, KEPT HERSELF distracted with Lily's needs until the baby was asleep.

She tried to read, she tried TV. Too restless for either, she plugged in a yoga tape she'd bought at the mall and gave it a spin. She went down for cookies. She put on music, then turned it off.

By midnight, she was still edgy and unsettled, so gave up and went out on the terrace to take in the warm night.

The lights were on in the carriage house. His bedroom light, she assumed. She'd never been up to the second floor, or what he called the loft. Where he slept. Where he was probably in bed right now, reading a book. Naked.

She should never have walked that way with Lily. All those directions to take, and she'd headed straight toward the carriage house. As besotted as her daughter.

God, she'd nearly melted at the knees when she'd come around that turn in the path and seen him.

Leaning against the doorjamb, wearing nothing but those ragged old cutoffs. Hard chest, golden tan, his hair all curly and damp. That lazy smile on his face as he'd taken a sip from a bottle of beer.

He'd looked so sexy—a freaking billboard for sexy, framed in that cottage doorway, surrounded by flowers, sultry in the heat. She'd been amazed she'd been able to get reasonable words out of her throat when she'd been tingling the whole time, inside and out, while they'd stood there.

And she had no business tingling around Harper. It really had to stop. Why couldn't it go back to the way it used to be? When she'd been pregnant, she'd felt comfortable around him. Even the first months after Lily's birth she'd been easy in his company. When had it started to change on her?

She didn't know, she couldn't pinpoint it. It just was.

And couldn't be. Lily wasn't the only one who couldn't have everything she wanted.

four

SHE FELT ODD AND OUT OF SORTS AT WORK. AS IF HER skin was too small, her head too heavy. Too much yoga for the novice, she decided. Too much work, not enough sleep. Maybe she should take a little vacation. She could get the time off, and she could afford a few days. She could drive back to Little Rock, visit some of her old friends and co-workers. Show Lily off.

But it would eke into the vacation fund she'd started to take Lily to DisneyWorld for her third birthday. Still, how much would it cost, really? A few hundred dollars, and the change of scene might do her good.

She swiped the back of her hand over her forehead. The air in the greenhouse felt too close, too thick. Her fingers as she tried to arrange dish gardens were too fat and clumsy. She didn't see why she got stuck with this job. Stella could've done it, or Ruby. Then she could work the counter—a monkey could work the counter this time of year, she thought irritably.

She should have had the day off. It wasn't as if they needed her. She should have been home, in the cool, relaxing for a damn change. But here she was, sweating and dirty, stuffing plants into bowls because Stella said so. Orders, orders, orders. When was she going to be able to do what she wanted, when she wanted?

They looked down on her because she didn't have the bloodline, she didn't have the education, she didn't have the fancy background that made them all so *important*. But she was just as good as they were. Better. She was better because she'd made her own way. She'd clawed her way up from nothing because—

"Hey, hey! You're breaking the roots on that ludisia."

"What?" She stared down at the plant, and her fingers went limp as Stella snatched it from them. "I'm sorry. Did I kill it? I don't know what I was thinking."

"It's okay. You looked upset. What's wrong?"

"Nothing. I don't know." She shook herself, and flushed with the shame of her own thoughts. "The heat's making me irritable, headachy, I guess. I'm sorry I haven't got these done. I can't seem to concentrate."

"It's okay. I came back to give you a hand anyway."

"I can do it. You don't have to take the time."

"Hayley, you know how I like to play in the dirt when I can. Here." She reached into the cooler under the workbench, took out two bottles of water. "Take five."

What had she been thinking before? she wondered as she took a long pull from the bottle. Nasty, petty thoughts. She didn't understand why her mind would have come up with such mean things. She didn't feel that way. But for a minute or two she had, and it made her feel ugly now.

"I don't know what's wrong with me, Stella."

Frowning, Stella laid her hand on Hayley's brow in the classic mother's gesture. "Maybe you're coming down with a summer cold."

"No, I think it's more the blahs. Not even the blues, just the blahs. They keep sneaking up on me, and I don't know why. I've got the most beautiful baby in the world. I love my job. I've got good friends."

"You can have all that, and still get the blahs." Stella took an apron off a hook, studying Hayley as she tied it on. "You haven't dated in more than a year."

"Closer to two." And that called for another long drink of water. "I've thought about it. I've been asked out a few times. You know Mrs. Bentley's son, Wyatt? He was in a few weeks ago, buying her a hanging basket for her birthday, and he was flirting pretty hard. Asked me if I'd like to have dinner sometime."

"He's pretty cute."

"Yeah, he's got that sexy jock thing going for him, and I thought about it, then I just didn't want to go to all the bother, and I edged back."

"I seem to remember you pushing me out the door when I talked about not wanting to go to all the bother when Logan first asked me out."

"I did, didn't I?" She smiled a little. "I've got such a big mouth."

Before Stella selected plants, she tightened the band that held her mass of curling red hair into a tail. "Maybe you're just a little nervous on the board? You know, taking that dive into the dating pool again."

"I've never been nervous about dating. It's one of my primary skills. I like going out. And I know if I wanted to, you or Roz, or David would take care of Lily." The knowledge brought on another stab of guilt for the resentful thoughts that had wormed into her mind. "I know she'd be fine, so that's no excuse. I just can't seem to get myself in gear."

"Maybe you just haven't met somebody who makes you want to oil the gears and get them moving again."

"I guess . . . maybe." She took another long drink, braced herself. "The thing is, Stella . . ."

When the silence dragged on, Stella glanced up from the pot she was building. "What's the thing?"

"First you gotta promise, *swear* that you won't tell anybody. Even Logan. You can't say anything."

"All right."

"You absolutely swear?"

"I'm not going to spit in my palm, Hayley. You'll have to take my word for it."

"Okay. Okay." She walked down the aisle between tables, then back again. "The thing is, I like Harper."

Stella nodded encouragement. "Sure. So do I."

"No!" Frustrated, mortified to hear herself say it out loud, Hayley set the water down and clamped her hands over her face. "God."

It took her a minute for the light to shine. "Oh," Stella said with her eyes going wide. "Oh. Oh," she repeated drawing out the syllable. Then she pursed her lips. "Oh."

"If that's the best you can do, I'm going to have to hit you."

"I'm trying to take it in. Absorb it."

"It's crazy. I know it's crazy." Hayley dropped her hands. "I know it's not right, it's not even on the table. But I . . . forget I said anything. Just highlight and hit delete."

"I didn't say it was crazy, it's just unexpected. As far as not being right, I don't follow you."

"He's Roz's son. Roz, the woman who took me in off the street."

"Oh, you mean when you were penniless, naked, and

suffering from some rare, debilitating disease? It was saintly of her to take you in, clothe you and spoon-feed you broth night after night."

"I'm allowed to exaggerate when I'm being a fool," Hayley snapped. "She did take me in, she gave me a job. She gave me and Lily a home, and here I am imagining how I can get naked and sweaty with her firstborn."

"If you're attracted to Harper—"

"I want to bite his ass. I want to pour honey all over his body then lick it off an inch at a time. I want to—"

"Okay, okay." Stella held out one hand, laid the other on her heart. "Please don't put any more of those images in my head. We'll just agree you've got the hots for him."

"Major hots. And I can't do anything about it because we're friends. Look how screwed up things got for Ross and Rachel. Of course Monica and Chandler's a different story, but—"

"Hayley."

"And I know this isn't a television show," she muttered over Stella's roll of laughter. "But you know how life imitates art? Besides, he doesn't think about me that way."

"The honey-licking way?"

Hayley's eyes went blurry. "Oh God, now I've got that image in my head."

"Serves you right. Anyway, are you sure he doesn't think of you that way?"

"He hasn't made a move, has he? It's not like there haven't been opportunities. And what if I made a move on him, and he was just, like, horrified or something?"

"What if he wasn't?"

"That could be even worse. We'd have ourselves some wild jungle sex, then after we'd both be . . ." She lifted her hands into the air, waved them wildly. "Oh God, what've I done, and all awkward with each other. And I'd have to take Lily and move to Georgia or somewhere. And Roz would never want to speak to me again."

"Hayley." Stella patted her on the shoulder. "This is just my impression, just my opinion, but I'm fairly sure Roz knows Harper has sex."

"You know what I mean. It's different when he's having sex with women she doesn't know."

"Oh yes, I'm sure she's perfectly delighted that her son has sex with strangers. Strangers to her, anyway," she added with a laugh. "And naturally she'd be appalled to learn that he might be intimate with a woman she knows and loves. Yes, that would be a real knife in the heart."

"It's a kind of betrayal."

"It's no kind of betrayal. He's a grown man, Hayley, and his choices in relationships are his own business. Roz would be the first to say so, and the first—without a doubt—to tell you she doesn't want to be one of the angles in this triangle you've formed."

"Well, maybe, but—"

"Maybe, maybe, but, but." Stella waved them all aside with such enthusiasm, Hayley had to duck and blink. "If you're interested in Harper, you should let him know. See what happens. Besides, I think he's had a crush on you from the get-go."

"He has not."

Stella shrugged. "Just my opinion, just my impression."

"Really?" The quick bump under her heart at the idea was painful and nice. "I don't know. I think if he has a crush on anybody, it's Lily. But I could think about maybe giving it a little push, see what happens."

"Positive thinking. Now, let's get these dish gardens done."

"Stella." Hayley poked a finger in the dirt. "You swear you won't say anything about this to Roz."

"Oh, for God's sake." Stella held out her palm and, mimicking the sacred rite she'd seen her sons perform, spat in it.

When offered the hand Stella held out, Hayley stared at it, and said: "Eeuuww."

IT MADE HER FEEL BETTER. HAVING SOMEBODY ELSE know what she was thinking and feeling took a weight off. Especially when that somebody else was Stella. Who hadn't been shocked, Hayley reminded herself. Surprised, sure, but not shocked, so that was good.

Just as it was good to take a couple of days and think about it. In fact, she was thinking about it, a little dreamily, when with Lily down for the night, she stretched out on the sitting room couch to unwind with some TV.

Idly, she channel surfed and decided how nice it was to have nothing to do for an hour. Still, reruns, repeats, and other summer dreck, she decided, wasn't what she wanted for a lazy hour of entertainment.

She flipped to an old black-and-white movie, something she didn't recognize. It seemed like some kind of romantic drama, where everyone wore gorgeous clothes and went dancing every night at elaborate clubs where they had orchestras and voluptuous girl singers.

Everybody drank highballs.

Why did they call them highballs? she wondered, yawning as she snuggled down. Because the glasses were tall, okay, but why were the glasses called balls? She should look it up sometime.

What would it be like to wear those incredible gowns and glide around a dance floor with everything all Art Deco and glittering? He'd be wearing a tuxedo, of course. She bet Harper looked awesome in a tux.

And what if they'd both come with someone else, but then they saw each other. Through all that silk and shine, their eyes met. And they just knew.

They'd dance, and everything else would wash away. That's the way it was in black-and-white. It didn't have to be complicated; whatever separated you could be vanquished or overcome. Then it all washed away except the two of you together as the end music swelled.

And when it did, you'd be in each other's arms, your face tipped up to his as your lips came together in that movie-perfect kiss. The kind you felt all the way down to the soles of your feet, the kind that meant you'd love each other forever.

Soft, soft kiss, so tender as his hand brushed over your hair, then deepening, heating just a bit when your arms locked around his neck. Up on your toes so your body leaned to his.

Line, angle, curve, all beautifully fitted.

Then after it faded to black, his hands moved over you, touching where it tingled and ached. Stroking over silk and skin so that your mouths met now with little gasps and moans.

The taste of that kiss was so potent, so powerful, the flavor of it streamed through your whole system, woke everything up, made everything swell.

And everywhere you'd felt cold and tired warmed again because you wanted, and were wanted.

Candles were flickering. Smoke and shadows. Flowers scented the room. Lilies, it had to be lilies. The flowers he'd brought her, bold and red and passionate. His eyes, deep brown, depthless brown, told her everything she wanted. That she was beautiful to him, and precious.

When they undressed each other, her gown melted away into a pool of glittery white against the black of his jacket.

Skin to skin, at last. Smooth and soft. Gold dust and milk. His shoulders under her hands, the length of his back, so she could feel those muscles tense as she aroused him.

The way he touched her, with such need, filled her with excitement so that when he gathered her up in his arms—oh—she was quivering for him. He laid her on the bed, the big white bed with sheets as soft as water, then sank into it with her.

His lips skimmed her throat, captured her breast so appetites quickened, and the tug, that long, liquid pull in her belly made her moan out his name.

Candlelight. Firelight. Flowers. Not lilies, but roses. His hands were smooth—a gentleman's hands. Rich hands. She stretched under them, arched, adding throaty purrs. Men liked their whores to make noise. She stroked her hand along the length of him. Ready, more than ready, she thought. But she'd tease him a bit longer. It was wives who lay passive, who let men do what they willed, to have done with it.

That's why they came to her, why they needed her. Why they paid.

She brought her shoulders off the mound of pillows, so her curling mane of golden hair spilled back. And she rolled with him, lush breasts and hips to entice, rolled him over on the bed to slither her way down, to nip and lick her way down his body to do what his cold-blooded, prim-mouthed wife would never do.

His grunts and gasps were her satisfaction.

His hands were in her hair now, gripping, twisting while she pleasured him. His body was trim, and she could gain some enjoyment from it, but had he been fat as a pig she'd have convinced him he was a god to her. It was so easy.

When she straddled him, looked down at his handsome face, saw the greedy desperation in his eyes, she smiled.

She took him into her, fast and hard and thought that nothing fit so well inside her as did a rich man's cock.

Hayley bolted up from the sofa as if she'd been shot out of a cannon. Her heart clanged, hammer to anvil, in her chest. Her breasts felt heavy as if, oh God, as if they'd been fondled. Her lips tingled. Panicked, she grabbed at her hair and nearly wept with relief when she felt her own.

Someone laughed, and had her stumbling back, rapping up against the couch and nearly spilling onto it again. The television, she saw as she crossed her arms protectively over her breasts. Just the television, sophisticated drama in black-and-white.

And oh, God, what had happened to her?

Not a dream, or not just a dream. It couldn't have been.

She dashed out of the room to check on Lily. Her baby slept, snuggled with her stuffed dog.

Ordering herself to calm, she went downstairs. But when she reached the library, she hesitated. Mitch sat at the library table, tapping away at the keyboard of his laptop. She didn't want to disturb him, but she had to check. She had to be sure. Waiting until morning just wasn't in the cards.

She stepped inside. "Mitch?"

"Hmm? What? Where?" He looked up, blinked behind his hornrims. "Hi."

"I'm sorry. You're working."

"Just some e-mail. Do you need something?"

"I just wanted to . . ." She wasn't shy, and she wasn't prudish, but she wasn't sure how to comfortably relate what she'd just experienced to her employer's husband. "Um, do you think Roz is busy?"

"Why don't I call up and see?"

"I don't want to bother her if . . . Yes, yes, I do. Could you ask her to come down?"

"All right." He reached for the phone to dial the bedroom extension. "Something happened."

"Yeah. Sort of. Maybe." To settle one point, she walked to the second level, behind the table and studied the pictures on Mitch's work board.

She stared at the copy of the photograph of a man in formal dress—strong features, dark hair, cool eyes.

"This is Reginald Harper, right? The first one."

"That's right. Roz, can you come down to the library. Hayley's here. She needs to talk to you. Right." He hung up. "She'll be right down. Do you want something—some water, some coffee?"

She shook her head. "No, thanks. I'm okay, just feeling a little weirded out. Ah, when Stella first came here, when she was living here, she had dreams. That's when it really started, right? I mean, before that there were . . . incidents. Sightings. But nothing much ever happened—at least not that Roz heard of—that was dangerous. Regarding The Bride, I mean."

"That seems to be the case. There's been a kind of escalation, which seemed to start when Stella moved in with her boys."

"And I came a few weeks after. So it was the three of us here, living in Harper House." Her skin still felt chilled. She rubbed her bare arms and wished for a sweatshirt. "I was pregnant, Stella had the boys, and Roz, well, Roz is bloodline."

He nodded. "Keep going."

"Stella had the dreams. Intense dreams, which we have to believe were somehow plugged into her subconscious by Amelia. That's not a very scientific way of putting it, but—"

"It's good enough."

"And when Stella and Logan—" She broke off as Roz came in. "I'm sorry I dragged you down here."

"It's all right. What happened?"

"Finish your thought out first," Mitch suggested. "Line it up."

"Okay, well, Stella and Logan got involved, and Amelia didn't like it. Stella's dreams got more disturbing, more pointed, and there were violent incidents, culminating in how she blocked us all out of the boys' room that night—that first night you came here, Mitch."

"I'll never forget it."

"She told us her name that night," Roz commented. "Stella got through to her, and she gave us her first name."

"Yeah. Wouldn't you say she's left Stella be pretty much since then? She'd have told us if she had dreams still, or if anything happened to her directly."

"The focus transferred to Roz," Mitch said.

"Yeah." Pleased they seemed to be traveling the same road, Hayley nodded. "And it was even more intense, right? Like waking dreams, Roz?"

"Yes, and an escalation of violent behavior."

"The closer you got to Mitch, the crazier she got. That's the kind of thing that pisses her off. She nearly killed you. She rode to the rescue, you could say, when you were in trouble, when push came to shove, but before that she attacked you. But since then, since you and Mitch got engaged, got married, she's backed off."

"Apparently, at least for the moment." Roz stepped over, ran a hand down Hayley's arm. "She's moving on you now, isn't she?"

"I think so. I think that the three of us being in the house—you and Stella and me—maybe that pushed her out of pattern." She looked toward Mitch, lifting her hands. "I don't know how to put it, exactly, but things really got rolling then, and the ball seems to pick up bulk and speed, if you get me."

"I do, and it's interesting. The three of you—three women at varying stages of life—all unattached at the point you came together. Your connection made a connection to her, we could say. And as Stella, then Roz became emotionally, romantically involved, it caused Amelia's behavior to deteriorate."

"Honey, did she hurt you?"

"No." Hayley pressed her lips together, then looked from Roz to Mitch. "I know we're supposed to, like, report anything, so Mitch has it on record. I just don't know how to say all this. At least not delicately. It's a little bit embarrassing."

"You want me to step out?" Mitch asked her. "So you can talk to Roz about it?"

"No, that's just dumb—of me, I mean. She'll just tell you anyway." To brace herself, Hayley blew out a long breath. "Okay, so I was taking an hour to relax, watch some TV upstairs in the sitting room. And there was this old movie on, and I was daydreaming, I guess. All those fabulous clothes, you know, and the beautiful lighting, and the fancy clubs where people went out to dance and all. I was imagining what it would be like, how I'd be all dressed up, and I'd see someone."

She trailed off a moment. She didn't have to say the someone was Harper. That didn't have to be relevant.

"Anyway, we'd dance, and fall in love, and have that big movie kiss? You know what I mean."

Roz smiled. "Absolutely."

"Well, then I guess I was drifting off some, and I was thinking about what happens after The End? Thinking about sex, I guess," she said and cleared her throat. "Just a fantasy thing, candlelight and flowers and a big white bed, being in love. Making love." She lowered her head, put it in her hands. "This is mortifying."

"Don't be silly. Healthy girl like you didn't think about

sex, I'd be worried." Roz gave her shoulder a little shake.

"It was nice. Romantic and exciting. Then, it changed. Or I changed. And it was calculating. I was thinking about how I'd do these things. I could feel the skin and the form and the heat. There were roses. I could smell roses, but I had lilies in the fantasy, and now there were roses, and fire-light. And his hands were different—soft and smooth. Rich, that's what I thought. And I thought the guy's wife wouldn't do what I'd do, and that's why he came to me. How he'd pay. And I felt my hair, and I could see it. Long and blond and curly. I saw it when it fell over my face, not like I was watching, but like I was there. It *was* me. And I saw him. His face."

She turned to the board and pointed at Reginald. "His face. He was inside me, and I saw his face."

She let out another long breath. "So."

After a moment of silence, Roz spoke. "I don't think it would be that unusual for your mind to weave that sort of thing together, Hayley. We all spend a lot of time thinking about these people, trying to put it all together. We know she was his mistress, we know she bore him a child, so we know they had sex. And for her, we can assume or at least speculate that it was, at least in part, a kind of business arrangement."

"You know how your body feels when you've been fool-ing around? Physically. Not just the buzz you get from a sex dream, but how you feel physically when you've been with a guy. Maybe I haven't been with one since before Lily was born, but you don't forget how it feels. And that's where I was when I woke up, or came out of it. Roz, I smelled those roses. I know how his body was shaped."

She had to take a breath, had to swallow hard. "I felt him inside me. Inside her, I guess, but it was like being her while it was happening. She liked being with someone handsome and skilled. It wouldn't have mattered if he'd been ugly as homemade sin and a dud in bed, but this was like a bonus. Rich was the bottom line—the rest was icing. I know that; because I was right inside her head. Or she was in mine. I didn't imagine it."

"I believe you," Mitch told her.

"We believe you," Roz corrected. "You're the closest to her age when she died, at least the age we think she was. Maybe she's relating to that, to you, and trying to go through you to tell us what it was like for her."

"Possibly." Mitch tipped back in the chair when Roz arched her brows at him. "It could give us more insight on her, on what happened and why. What else can you tell us about her?"

"Well, I don't think she got that much of a rush out of sex—from the power, the control, yeah, but not the rest of it. It's just what she did, and from his, um, response, she was good at what she did. Her body was a lot better than mine."

With a sheepish smile, she held her hands in front of her breasts to mime someone well-endowed. "And she was cold inside. The whole time they were doing it, she was thinking about what she'd get out of him. There was a derision—that's the best way to describe it—for the wives of men like him. I guess that's about it."

"Hardly her best side. Or maybe it is, from her point of view," Mitch considered. "She was in charge, doing what she'd chosen to do. Young, beautiful, desired by a powerful man and controlling that man through sex. Interesting."

"Creepy's what it was. And if I get to have sex, I'd like to have it with my own body. But anyway, I feel better, getting all that out. I think I'll go back up, maybe do some yoga. I don't think she's going to bother me while I'm trying to twist myself into the warrior position or whatever. Thanks for hearing me out."

"Anything else happens, I want to hear it," Roz told her.

"That's a promise."

Roz waited until Hayley was gone, then turned to Mitch. "We're going to have to worry about her, aren't we?"

"Let's not skip straight to worry." He took her hand. "Let's start with we'll keep an eye out for her."

five

❦

From Stella's kitchen window, Hayley could see the spread of the back gardens, the patio, the arbor, the treehouse Logan and the boys had built snugged into the branches of a sycamore.

She watched Logan push Lily on a red swing that hung from another branch while the boys tossed an old ball for Parker to chase.

It was, she thought, a kind of moving portrait of summer evening. The sort of lazy contentment that only comes on breathless summer days right before the kids are called in for supper and the porch light goes on. Yellow glows to chase the moths away and to shine a circle that says: We're home.

She remembered, so clearly, what it was to be a child in August, to love the heat, to rush through it to snatch every drop of the sun before it went down.

Now, she hoped, she was learning what it was to be a mother. To be on the other side of the screen door. To be the one who turned on the porch light.

"Do you get used to it, or do you still look out sometimes like this, and think 'I'm the luckiest woman in the world.' "

Stella moved over to the window, smiled. "Both. You want to sit out on the patio with this lemonade?"

"In a minute. I didn't want to talk about this at work. Not just because it's at work, but because it's still on the Harper estate. And she's on the estate. She can't come here."

"Roz told me what happened." Stella laid a hand on Hayley's shoulder.

"I didn't tell her that it was Harper. I mean when I was fantasizing, I was with Harper. I'm just not going to tell her I was fantasizing about getting naked with her son."

"I think that's a judicious edit at this point. Has anything happened since?"

"No, nothing. And I don't know whether to hope something does or something doesn't." She watched Logan field the mangled slobbery ball that rolled his way, then toss it, sending dog and boys on a mad chase while Lily bounced in the swing and clapped her hands.

"I can tell you this, if I have to star in someone's life and times, I'd rather take a turn in yours."

"I believe in being a good and true friend, Hayley, but I'm not letting you have sex with Logan."

Hayley snorted out a laugh, then gave Stella an elbow nudge. "Spoilsport, and though I wasn't going there, I bet—wow."

Stella's smile was lazy as a cat's. "You bet right."

"Anyway. I was just thinking how it would be to have someone as crazy about me as Logan is about you. Toss in a couple of great kids, a beautiful home you've made together, and who needs fantasies?"

"You'll have what you're looking for one day, too."

"Listen to me, you'd think I was the redheaded stepchild. I don't know what's wrong with me lately." She rolled her shoulders as if shrugging off a weight. "I keep catching myself doing a poor-me routine. It's not like me, Stella. I'm happy. And even when I'm not, I look for a way to make myself happy. I don't brood and bitch. Or hardly."

"No, you don't."

"Maybe I've got a thing for Harper, but a little frustration's not enough to bring me down. Next time you hear me feeling sorry for myself, give me a good smack."

"Sure. What are friends for?"

She meant it, too. She wasn't the type to sit around ticking off the negatives of her life to see if she could make them outweigh the positives. If something was wrong, something was missing, she acted. Fix the problem and move ahead. Or if the problem couldn't be fixed, she found the best way to live with it.

When her mother had left, she'd been sad and scared and hurt. But there'd been nothing she could do to bring her back. So she'd done without—and done pretty damn well, Hayley thought as she drove back to Harper House.

She'd learned how to help make a home, and she and her father had had a good life. They'd been happy; she'd been loved. And she'd been useful.

She'd done well in school. She'd gotten a job to help with expenses. She knew how to work, and how to enjoy the work. She liked to learn, and to sell people things that made them happy.

If she'd stayed in Little Rock, at the bookstore, she'd have made manager. She'd have earned it.

Then her father had died. That had blasted a hole in the foundation of her life, and had shaken her like nothing before or since. He'd been her rock, as she'd been his. Nothing had felt steady or sure when he'd died, and her grief had been a constant raw ache.

So she'd turned to a friend—that's all he'd been really, she admitted as she turned down the drive to Harper House. A nice boy, a comfort.

Lily had come from that, and she wasn't ashamed of it. Maybe comfort wasn't love, but it was a positive act, a giving one. How could she have paid that kindness back by pushing the boy into marriage, or responsibility when he'd already moved on by the time she'd realized she was pregnant?

She hadn't wallowed—or hardly. She hadn't cursed God or man, for long. She'd accepted responsibility for her own actions, as she'd been taught, and had made the choice that was right for her.

To keep the child, and raise the child on her own.

Hadn't worked out quite that way, though, she thought with a smile as she parked. Little Rock, the bookstore, the house she'd shared with her father had no longer been her comfort zones once she'd started to show. Once the looks and the questions and the murmurs had begun.

So, fresh start.

She climbed out of the car, rounded it to open the back door and unhook Lily from her car seat.

Sell everything that could be sold, pack up the rest. Positive, move forward. All she'd expected by coming here to Roz was the possibility of a job. What she'd been given was family.

Just more proof, to her mind, that good things happened

when you took steps, when you worked for them—and when you were lucky enough to find people who'd give you a chance to do your best.

"That's what we are, Lily." She hoisted Lily up, covered her face with kisses. "We're a couple of lucky girls."

She swung the diaper bag over her shoulder, bumped the car door shut with her hip. But as she started toward the house an idea bloomed.

Maybe it was time to try her luck again.

Sit around waiting for things to happen and nothing much did. But act, you either failed or succeeded. Either was better than standing still.

She strolled around the house, taking her time, just to see if she could talk herself out of it. But the idea was planted now, and she couldn't find a good enough reason to uproot it.

Maybe he'd be shocked or stunned or even appalled. Well, that would be his problem. At least she'd know *something* and stop wondering all the damn time.

As she rounded the curve in the path, she set Lily down, and let her little girl trot toward Harper's front door.

Maybe he wasn't home, out with some woman. Or worse, had some woman in *his* home. Okay, that would be bad, but she'd deal with it.

It was time she dealt with it.

Though the dark wasn't deep yet, the path lights were glowing, those pretty soft green lanterns speared at the edges of the brick to guide the way. A few early lightning bugs blinked on and off, on and off over the heads of flowers, and out beyond to the roll of grass to lose themselves in the shadows of the woods.

She drew in the perfume of heliotrope, sweet peas, roses, and the more pungent aroma of earth. All of those scents, along with the different tones of growing green would forever make her think of Harper, and this place.

She caught up with Lily, knocked. On impulse she stepped back and to the side, leaving her little girl clapping her hands at Harper's front door. Where the porch light was on, a glowing circle of yellow.

When the door opened, she heard Lily give her greeting—something between hi and hey and a cry of pleasure.

"Look what I found at my front door."

From her vantage point, Hayley could see Lily's arms go up; and Harper's come down. When he scooped her up, Lily was already babbling in her excited and incomprehensible language.

"Is that right? Just thought you'd drop by to say hi? Maybe you ought to come in and have a cookie, but we'd better find your mama first."

"She's right here." Laughing, Hayley stepped over to the door. "Sorry, but it was so cute. You know she can't walk by your place without wanting to see you, so I thought I'd knock and let her stand there on her own."

She reached out, but as usual when Harper was involved, Lily shook her head and wrapped herself around her favorite man.

"I mentioned the C word. Why don't you come in and I'll dig one out for her."

"You're not busy?"

"No. Was just thinking about getting a beer and doing some paperwork. Just as soon postpone the paperwork part of it."

"I always like coming in here." She glanced around the living room as he carried Lily back toward the kitchen. "You're pretty tidy, too, for a single straight guy."

"Comes from living with Mama, I guess." With Lily on his hip, he reached in a cupboard and got out the box of an-

imal crackers he kept on hand for her. "Now how'd these get here?"

He opened the box, let her dig one out. "Want a beer?"

"I wouldn't mind. I stopped off at Stella's after work. Ended up having burgers on the grill, but I passed on the wine. I don't like sipping when I'm driving, even just a little when I've got Lily in the car."

He offered her a beer, got one for himself. "How you doing?" When she only angled her head, he shrugged. "Word spreads. I heard about what happened. In any case, it's something we're all involved in, so word should spread."

"It's a little embarrassing to have word of my sex dreams spreading."

"It wasn't like that. Besides, nothing wrong with a good sex dream."

"I'd as soon the next one I have be all my own idea." She tipped back the beer, watching him. "You look a little like him, you know."

"Sorry?"

"Reginald, especially now that I've seen him in what you could call a more intimate situation. Something more personal than an old photograph. You've got the same coloring, and the same shape to your face—your mouth. His build's not as good as yours."

"Oh. Well." He lifted his beer, drank deep.

"He was slim, but soft. Like his hands. And he was older than you, a little gray in the hair. And some hard lines coming in around the mouth, out from the eyes. But still, very handsome, very virile."

She got Lily's sip-cup of juice and her music cube out of the diaper bag. Bribing her, she lifted her away from Harper and set her on the floor.

"You got better shoulders, and no pudge right here." She poked her finger into his belly.

"Okay."

Lily sat down with her music cube, playing with it so it switched from "This Old Man" to "Bingo."

"I noticed all that," Hayley said, "seeing as we were all naked and sweaty."

"I bet."

"I especially noticed the resemblance—the similarities and the differences because when I started out fantasizing— my own part of it—it was with you."

"It was . . . what?"

Okay, a little shocked, but more confused, she decided, and moved in. "It started with you, something like this."

She slid a hand around to the back of his neck, rose up on her toes. She stopped, her lips a whisper from his, to savor that instant when the breath catches and the heart stumbles. Then she closed the distance.

Soft, as she'd imagined it would be soft. And warm. His hair was a silky weight on the back of her hand, and his body such a pleasure to press against.

He'd gone so still, but for his heart that slammed against hers. Then she felt his hand on her back, the fist he made as he gathered her shirt in his fingers.

On the floor, Lily's music cube was a jubilant crash of sound.

She made herself ease back. One step at a time, she reminded herself. Though her belly was quivering, she did her best to take a casual sip of beer while he stared at her with those dark eyes.

"So, what do you think?"

He lifted a hand, then dropped it again. "I appear to have lost the capability for rational thought."

"When you get it back, you'll have to let me know."

She turned to gather the baby's things.

"Hayley." He reached out, grabbed her by the waistband of her jeans and tugged. "Uh-uh."

Her belly jumped, joyfully. She glanced over her shoulder. "Which means?"

"The short way of saying you don't walk in here, kiss me like that, then walk out again. Question. Was that a demonstration to catch me up with what's happening with Amelia, or was it something else?"

"I've been wondering what it would be like, so I decided to find out."

"Okay." He turned her around, glanced down to be sure Lily was still occupied, then backed her into the counter.

His hands were at her hips when his mouth met hers. As his tongue dipped in, an intimate taste, those hands slid up, cruising over her, setting off little charges under her skin.

Then he stepped back, rubbed a thumb over her tingling lips. "I've been wondering what it would be like, too. So I guess we both know."

"Looks like," she managed.

Since Lily came over to tug at his pants, Harper boosted her up on his hip. "I guess it's complicated."

"Yeah, it is. Very. We'll need to take it slow, think it all the way through."

"Sure. Or we can say screw that and I can come to your room later tonight."

"I . . . I want to say yes. I'm thinking yes," she said on a rush. "Yes is screaming inside my head and I don't know why yes isn't coming out of my mouth. It's exactly what I want."

"But." He nodded. "It's okay. We should give it a little time. Be sure."

"Be sure," she repeated, and hurried to pick up Lily's things. "I need to go, or I'll forget about a little time and

being sure, because, *man,* you sure can kiss. And I need to get Lily ready for bed. I don't want to mess things up, Harper. I so don't want to mess things up."

"We won't."

"We can't." She took Lily, though the baby cried pitifully at being pried away from Harper. "I'll see you at work."

"Sure, but I can walk you back."

"No." She hurried toward the door with Lily struggling and crying in her arms. "She'll be okay."

The crying escalated into a full-blown temper tantrum with kicking legs, stiffly arched back, and ear-piercing shrieks. "For God's sake, Lily, you'll see him again tomorrow. It's not like he's going off to war."

The diaper bag slipped off her shoulder to weigh like an anchor on her arm while her sweet baby morphed into a red-faced demon from hell. Tiny, hard-toed walking shoes punched bruises into her hip, her belly, her thighs as she struggled to cart twenty pounds of fury through the dragging summer heat.

"I'd like to've stayed, too, you know." Frustration sharpened her voice. "But we can't, that's just the way it is, so you're going to have to deal."

Sweat dripped into her eyes, blurred her vision so that for a moment, the grand old house seemed to be floating like a mirage. An illusion she'd never reach.

It would just keep swimming farther away, because it wasn't real. Not for her. She'd never really belong there. It would be better, smarter, easier if she packed up, moved on. The house and Harper were one in the same—things that could never be hers. As long as she stayed here, *she* was the illusion.

"Well, what's all this?"

She saw Roz through the shimmer of heat, the daze of

twilight, and felt her own body sway as everything snapped back into focus. A sly tongue of nausea curled in her stomach. Then Lily, tears streaming, all but launched herself out of her arms and into Roz's.

"She's mad at me," Hayley said weakly, and tears stung her own eyes as Lily wrapped her arms around Roz's neck and wept into her shoulder.

"Won't be the last time." Roz rubbed Lily's back, going into that instinctive side-to-side rocking motion as she studied Hayley's face. "What set her off?"

"She saw Harper. She wanted to stay with him."

"It's hard leaving your best guy."

"She needs a bath and bed. Should've had them already. I'm sorry we bothered you. I guess they could hear her screaming clear down to Memphis."

"You didn't bother me. She's not the first baby I've heard in a temper, and she won't be the last."

"I'll take her up."

"I got her." Roz turned to take the steps up to the second floor. "You frazzled each other out. That's what happens when babies want one thing and their mama knows they need something different. Then you end up feeling guilty because they act like it's the end of their world, and you're the one who pulled the rug out."

A tear spilled over, and Hayley rubbed it away. "I hate letting her down."

"And how did you let her down by doing what's best for her? This baby's tired," Roz said as she opened the door to the nursery, turned on the lamp. "And sweaty. She needs her bath, a nightie, and a little quiet time. Go on, get her bath started. I'll get her clothes off."

"That's all right, I can—"

"Honey, you've got to learn to share."

Since Roz was already carrying a now calm Lily away,

Hayley moved into the bathroom. She ran the water, adding the bubbles Lily liked to splash in, the rubber duck and frogs. And caught herself swallowing back tears a half dozen times.

"I got myself a naked baby," she heard Roz say. "Yes, I do. And look at that belly, just calling out to be tickled."

Lily's laughter had Hayley sniffling back more tears as Roz stepped in.

"Why don't you go have yourself a shower? You're hot and you're blue. Lily and I'll have some fun in the tub."

"I don't want you to have to do all this."

"You've been around long enough to know I don't offer to do something if I don't want to do it. Go on. Clean up, cool down."

"All right." Since she feared she'd burst into tears at any moment, she fled.

SHE WAS CLEANER, AND SHE WAS COOLER, IF NOT A great deal steadier when she came back to find Roz putting a little cotton nightgown on a sleepy Lily.

The nursery smelled like powder and sweet soap, and her baby was calm.

"And here's your mama come to give you good night kisses." She lifted Lily, and the baby stretched out her arms to Hayley. "Come on over to the sitting room when you're done putting her down."

"Okay." She held Lily close, breathing in her hair, her skin. "Thanks, Roz."

She stood where she was, holding her little girl, letting the embrace center her. "Mama's sorry, baby. I'd give you the world if I could. The whole wide world and a silver box to put it in."

There were kisses, and quiet murmurs as she laid Lily

down in the crib with her little dog to cuddle. Leaving a low light burning, she slipped out of the room and down the hall to the sitting room.

"I got us some bottled water out of your stash." Roz held one out. "That do for you?"

"Perfect. Oh, Roz, I feel so stupid. I don't know what I'd do without you."

"You'd do fine. Better with me, but then everybody does." Roz sat, stretched out her legs. Her feet were bare tonight, and her toes painted a gumdrop pink. "You keep beating yourself up because your child had herself a tantrum, you're going to be permanently black and blue before you're thirty."

"I knew she was tired. I should've brought her straight into the house instead of letting her visit Harper."

"And I bet she enjoyed the visit as much as he did. Now she's sleeping peaceful in her crib, and no harm done."

"I'm not a terrible mother, am I?"

"You're certainly not anything of the sort. That baby is happy and healthy and loved. She has a sweet disposition. She also knows what she wants when she wants it, and that's a sign of character in my opinion. She's got a right to a temper, hasn't she, same as anybody else?"

"Boy, she's sure got one. I don't know what's wrong with me, Roz." Hayley set the bottle down without drinking. "I'm emotional and bitchy one minute, on top of the world the next. You'd think I was pregnant again, except there's no possibility of that unless the Second Coming's scheduled some time soon."

"That might be your answer right there. You're young and healthy. You've got needs, and they're not being met. Sex is important."

"Maybe, but it's not easily, or safely come by for somebody in my situation."

"I know what that's like, too. You know if you're interested in dating again, you have all manner of willing baby-sitters."

"I know."

"Actually, Hayley, I think sex might be one of the keys to Amelia."

"I'm sorry, Roz, I'd do most anything to help, but I have to draw the line at having sex with Amelia. Ghost, female, psycho. That's a full three strikes."

"There's our girl," Roz said with a laugh. "Mitch and I were talking about what happened to you the other evening, sort of expanding on our theories. Sex is what Amelia used to get what she wanted in life. It was her commodity. In any case, that's our conclusion: She was Reginald's mistress. And it was how, obviously, she conceived a child."

"Well, maybe she loved him. Amelia. It's possible she was seduced by him, in love with him. We really only have Beatrice's viewpoint of her from the journals, and she wouldn't be an objective source."

"Good point, and yes, possible." Roz took a thoughtful sip of water. "But that still points to sex. Even if she was in love and being used, it came down to sex. Reginald went to her for his pleasure, and his purposes. To conceive a male heir. It's not far-fetched to assume Amelia's view of sex is far from healthy."

"Okay."

"Then we come into it, the three of us, living together in this house. Stella hears her, sees her—not that unusual as there were children involved. But there's Logan, and not just an emotional spark between them, but a sexual one. And the episodes begin to escalate. We move to me and Mitch, another sexual contact, and more escalation. Now you."

"I'm not having sex." Yet, she thought. Oh boy.

"You're thinking about it. You're considering it. As Stella was. As I was."

"So . . . you think her focus is on me, the sexual energy kind of thing being the magnet. And things will escalate again."

"I think that may be, and particularly if that sexual energy becomes tied together with genuine affection. With love."

"If I got involved with someone, emotionally, sexually, she could hurt them. Or Lily. She could—"

"Now wait." Roz laid a hand over Hayley's. "She's never hurt a child. Never in all these years. There's absolutely no reason to think she might cause Lily any harm. But you're another matter."

"She could hurt me, or try. I get that." Hayley let out a shaky breath. "So I have to make sure she doesn't. She could hurt someone else, too. You or Mitch, David, any of us. And if there was someone I cared about, someone I wanted, he'd be the most likely target, wouldn't he?"

"Maybe. But I know you can't live your life on maybes. You have a right to your life. Hayley, I don't want you to feel obligated to stay here, or to keep working at In the Garden."

"You want me to leave?"

"I don't." Roz's hand gripped tighter. "On a purely selfish level, I want you here. You're the daughter I never had, that's the God's truth. And that child in the other room is one of the brightest lights of my life. It's because of what you mean to me I'm telling you to go."

Hayley took a deep breath as she rose, first to cross to the window. To look out over the summer gardens, so bold and bright in the hazy dark. And beyond them, to the carriage house, with the porch light glowing.

"My mama left us. Daddy and I weren't enough to keep her. She didn't love us enough. When he died, I didn't even know where to write and tell her. She'll never see her granddaughter. That's a shame for her, I think. But not for Lily. Lily has you. I've got you. I'll go if you tell me to. I'll get another place, get another job. And I'll stay away from Harper House for as long as it takes. But you need to tell me something first, and I know you'll tell me the truth because that's what you do."

"All right."

She turned back, met Roz's eyes. "If you were standing here where I am, having to decide whether to leave people you love—especially when you might be able to help—to leave a place you love, work you love. And you had to decide that because maybe something might happen. Maybe you might have trouble, have to face something hard along the way. What would you do, Roz?"

Roz got to her feet. "I guess you're staying."

"I guess I am."

"David made peach pie."

"Oh my God."

Roz held out a hand. "Let's go have a big sinful slice, and I'll tell you about the flower shop I'm thinking of adding on next year."

IN THE CARRIAGE HOUSE, HARPER RAIDED HIS STASH of leftovers. And thought of Hayley while he ate some of David's fried chicken.

She'd gone and changed the playing field, and he wasn't quite sure what to do with the ball. He'd spent the last year and a half suppressing his feelings and urges when it came to Hayley, and assuming—from her attitude, from every

damn signal—that she considered him a friend. Even, God help him, a kind of surrogate brother.

He'd done his best to fill that role.

Now she'd come waltzing in, and put the moves on him. Kissed the brains right out of his head, to the tune of— what the hell was it?—"Bingo."

He was never going to be able to hear that ridiculous song again without getting hot.

What the hell was he supposed to do now, ask her out? He was good at asking women out. It was normal, but there was nothing normal about all of this, not when he'd convinced himself she wasn't interested that way. That he shouldn't be.

Add that they worked together. That she lived in the main house with his mother, for God's sake. Then there was Lily to consider. It sliced him in two, the way she'd cried for him when Hayley had taken her home. What if he and Hayley got together, and something went wrong? Would it spill over onto Lily?

He'd have to make certain it didn't, that's all. He'd have to be careful, take it slow and easy.

Which crossed out any idea brewing in the back of his mind about going over to Hayley's room after dark and letting nature take its course.

He cleaned up the kitchen, as was his habit, then went up to the loft that held his bedroom, a bath, and a small room he used as an office. He spent an hour on paperwork, ordering his mind back to the business at hand every time it drifted toward Hayley.

He switched on ESPN, picked up a book, and indulged in one of his favorite solo evening activities. Reading between innings. Somewhere in the eighth, with Boston down two and the Yankees with a runner on second, he drifted off.

He dreamed that he and Hayley were making love in Fenway Park, rolling naked over the infield grass while the game played on around them. Somehow he knew the batter had a count of three and two, even as Hayley locked those long legs around him, as he sank into her. Into that heat, into those soft blue eyes.

The crash woke him, and his dreaming mind heard the joyful crack of ball on bat. He thought home run even as he sat up, shaking his head to toss off sleep.

Jesus! He rubbed his hands over his face. Weird, very weird, even if it did combine two of his favorite activities. Sports and sex. Amused at himself, he started to toss the book aside.

The second crash from downstairs was like a bullet shot, and no dream.

He was on his feet in a fingersnap and grabbing the Louisville Slugger he'd had since his twelfth birthday as he rushed out of the room.

His first thought was that Bryce Clerk, his mother's ex-husband, had gotten out of jail and was back to cause more trouble. He'd be sorry for it, Harper thought grimly as he gripped the bat. His blood was up as he charged toward the fury of crashing and banging.

He slapped on the lights in time to see a plate come winging toward him. Instinct had him swinging for the fences. The plate shattered, shooting out shards.

Then there was utter silence.

The room he'd washed up before going upstairs looked as though it had been set upon by a particularly destructive gang of vandals. Broken dishes littered the floor along with spilled beer and the jagged remains of the bottles it had come from. His refrigerator door hung open, with all the contents pulled out. His counters and walls were covered with what looked like a nasty mix of ketchup and mustard.

There was no one there but himself. And he could see his own breath in the chill that had yet to fade out of the air.

"Son of a bitch." He scooped a hand through his hair. "Son of a goddamn bitch."

She'd used ketchup—at least he hoped it was that benign condiment rather than the blood it resembled—to write her message on the wall.

I will not rest

He studied the mess. "You're not the only one."

SIX

MITCH ADJUSTED HIS GLASSES AND LOOKED MORE closely at the photographs. Harper had been thorough, he thought, getting pictures from every angle, taking close-ups and wide angles.

The boy had a steady hand and a cool head.

But . . .

"You should've called us when this happened."

"It was one in the morning. What was the point? This is what it looked like."

"What it looks like is you pissed her off. Any ideas?"

"No."

Mitch spread the photos out, adjusting their order, while David looked over his shoulder. "You clean that shit up?" David asked Harper.

"Yeah." Temper seemed to vibrate off the blades of his tensed shoulders. "She got every damn dish in the place."

"No great loss there. They were ugly anyway. What are those?" David snatched one of the pictures up. "Twinkies? What are you, twelve? Harper." His face a picture of pity, David shook his head. "I worry about you."

"I happen to like Twinkies."

Mitch held up a hand. "Snack choices aside—"

"Twinkies are bombs of sugar and fat and preservatives." Interrupting Mitch, David tried for a pinch at Harper's waist.

"Cut it out." But the move, as designed, pushed a little humor through the wall of Harper's temper.

"Girls," Mitch said mildly. "To get back to the matter at hand. This is another change of pattern. She's never, to your knowledge, come into the carriage house, or caused you any particular trouble." He looked to Harper for confirmation.

"No." A glance at the photos he'd taken brought back the shock, the fury, and the *time* it had taken to deal with the destruction. "And this is a hell of a debut."

"Your mother's going to have to know about this."

"Yeah, yeah." Still steaming, Harper paced to the back door, scowled out at the morning haze. He'd waited, deliberately, until he'd seen his mother head out for her morning run. "I value my life, don't I? But I wanted us to go over this first, before we bring her into it." He glanced up at the ceiling, where he imagined Hayley was getting started on the day. "Or any of them."

"Strategizing to protect the womenfolk?" David said in an exaggerated drawl. "Not that I don't agree, son, but Roz isn't going to care for that." He jerked a thumb toward the ceiling. "She won't either."

"I don't want them going postal over it, that's all. If we could downplay it some. It was just dishes and kitchen crap."

"A personal attack, Harper, not on you but on your property, in your home. That's how it is, and that's how they'll see it." Mitch waved a hand at him before he could speak. "We've dealt with worse, all of us, and we'll deal with this. The important thing is to figure out why it happened."

"Maybe it's because she's crazy," Harper snapped back. "That might be a small, contributing factor."

"Takes after his mama when he's riled up," David offered. "Mean and stubborn."

"I've noticed. She's been seen walking in the direction of the carriage house in the past." Mitch leaned a hip on the table. "You saw her yourselves when you were kids. We can assume she did, at some point in her life, go there. We can assume it was after Reginald Harper brought their love child here to pass him off as his legitimate heir."

"And we can assume she was crazy as a crack monkey," David added. "From the way she looked."

"Yet, from what we know she's never bothered with the place since Harper's lived there. How long?"

"Shit, I don't know." He shrugged, drummed his fingers on the thighs of his ragged work pants. "Since college. Six, seven years."

"But she goes in now, destructively. She may be crazy, but there's a reason. Everything she's done has a root and a reason. Have you brought anything in there recently? Anything new?"

"Ah, no." But the idea made him pause and consider instead of stew. "Plants. I rotate plants, but I've done that for years. And the usual stuff, you know, groceries, CDs, clothes. Nothing particular or unusual."

"Anyone?"

"Sorry?"

"Have you had anyone over who hasn't been there before? A woman?"

"No."

"Now that's just sad." David swung an arm around Harper's shoulders. "Losing your touch?"

"My touch is still gold. Just been a little busy."

"And before it happened, you were?"

"Watching the game upstairs in the bedroom, reading. Zonked out, and the next I know it's crash, boom, bang."

He heard Lily's happy call and winced. "Damn it, here they come. Mitch, let's put those away, put this all away until—"

He broke off, cursing himself for not moving faster, when Lily ran in just ahead of Hayley. She zipped straight for him, all grins and upstretched arms.

"She heard your voice," Hayley said as he picked Lily up. "Her face just lit."

"His touch is gold," David said dryly, "with toddlers."

"It's sure her favorite way to start the morning." She went to the refrigerator for juice, and when she turned with the bottle and Lily's cup in her hands, spotted the photographs. "What's all this?"

"It's nothing. Just a little late-night adventure."

"Good God, what a mess! You have a party and not invite us?" Then she blinked, and paled as she leaned closer. "Oh. Oh, Amelia. Are you all right? Are you hurt?" She dropped Lily's cup as she swung toward him. "Harper, did she hurt you?"

"No. No." He patted the hand she was running over his face, his arm. "It's just dishes."

David bent to retrieve the plastic cup, wiggled his eyebrows at Mitch on the way up, and said, "Aha," under his breath.

"But look at your things." She snatched up a photo. "Your sweet little kitchen. What is *wrong* with her? Why does she have to be so damn mean?"

"Being dead probably ticks her off some. I think Lily wants her juice."

"All right, all right. If it's not one thing it's six others with her—Amelia, not Lily. I'm getting fed up." She poured the juice, secured the lid, then handed it to Lily. "There you are, baby. Just what are we going to do about this?" she demanded as she rounded on Mitch.

"Innocent bystander," he reminded her and held up his hands.

"We all are, aren't we? But that doesn't mean a damn to her, apparently. Bitch." She sat down, folded her arms.

"Feel better?" David asked her, and poured her some coffee.

"I don't know what I feel."

"Just dishes." Harper settled Lily in her highchair. "And according to David, ugly ones."

Hayley worked up a smile. "They weren't too ugly. I'm sorry, Harper." She touched his hand. "I'm so sorry."

"Sorry about what?" Roz asked as she came in.

"There's the bell for round two." David gestured with the coffeepot. "I think I'll make crepes."

SHE COULDN'T CONCENTRATE. HAYLEY WENT THROUGH the routine of waiting on customers, ringing up sales on automatic. When she didn't think she could stand making inane chat with another living soul, she went into Stella's office to throw herself on her mercy.

"Give me some manual labor, will you? Something hot and sweaty. Get me off the counter, please. I keep feeling this bitch attack coming on, and I don't want one to spew onto the customers."

Stella pushed back in her chair to give Hayley the once-over. "Why don't you take a break instead?"

"I stop doing, I'll start thinking. Then I'll start seeing those pictures of Harper's kitchen in my head again."

"I know it's upsetting, Hayley, but—"

"It's my fault."

"How is Harper's kitchen getting trashed your fault? And did you have anything to do with the broken vase in my living room, because no one in my house is taking responsibility. At the moment, I Dunno is taking the rap."

"I Dunno is the classic whipping boy."

"Between him and Not Me, nothing is safe, nothing is sacred."

Blowing out a breath, Hayley dropped into a chair. "All right, I will take a break, just for a minute. Can you take one, too, talk to me?"

"Sure." Stella swung away from the spreadsheet on her computer monitor.

"When I left your place last night I went to Harper's. I talked myself into taking some action, making a move, going up a step, you know? He wants to think of me as Cousin Hayley, or Lily's mama, or whatever the hell he thinks, fine. But I'll give him a taste and see what he thinks of that."

"Woo-hoo. And?"

"I laid one on him. Standing right there in his kitchen, moved in and gave him one of those here's-what-you're-missing-so-why-don't-you-come-get-it kisses."

Stella's lips quivered up into a smile. "And did he? Come and get it?"

"You could say. The kiss he gave me back was more of the since-you-opened-the-gate-I'm-galloping-right-on-in variety. He's got a really amazing mouth. I sort of figured he did, but having a couple of good samples made me realize I'd underestimated. Considerably."

"That's good, isn't it? It's what you wanted."

"It's not about what I want. Or maybe it is." She pushed back to her feet, but there was nowhere to pace in the tiny office. "Maybe that's just the point. In his kitchen, Stella. I kissed him in his kitchen, and a few hours later, she's in there wrecking the place. It doesn't take a math whiz to put that two and two together. I opened the gate, all right, but she's the one who came in."

"You're mixing metaphors. I'm not saying you're entirely wrong," she added, and stretched out from the chair to open her little cooler for bottled water. "But I am going to say it's not your fault. She's a volatile presence, Hayley, and none of us is responsible for her actions, or what happened to her."

"No, but try telling her that. Thanks," she said when Stella handed her one of the bottles.

"What we're doing is trying to find out, maybe to make it as right as it can be made, but we have to live our lives while we do."

"It's about sexual energy and emotional attachments. That's what Roz thinks, and I think she's on to something."

"You told Roz about you and Harper."

She took a long, deep drink. "No, no, I mean in general. And there isn't any 'me and Harper,' not really. Roz and Mitch think it's the sexual buzz and the developing emotions that get her stirred up, at least in part. So I've got to work off some of this buzz and these feelings."

"Even if you could, you're not taking Harper's buzz or feelings into account."

"I can take care of that. It's when they're directed at me. Otherwise, she'd've slapped at him before." Her fingers tightened on the bottle, but she caught herself before the gesture pushed water over the lip. "You can bet he's done more than kiss a woman in his kitchen in that house before last night, and she didn't get bent out of shape."

"Again, no argument. But if it does connect to you and Harper, then it must mean something. Maybe something important. The way Logan and I, the way Mitch and Roz mean something important to each other."

"I can't think about that. Not now. I just want to work off this edge. Give me something physical."

"I want all the excess stock cleared out of greenhouse one, brought around front for a display. One table for annuals, one for perennials, and marked thirty percent off."

"I'll get right on it. Thanks."

"Be sure to remember you thanked me when you collapse from heat exhaustion," Stella called out.

SHE LOADED FLATS AND POTS ON A FLATBED CART AND hauled them around to the front of the building. It took her four trips. She muscled over the tables she wanted, positioning them where they'd be most likely to catch the eye of someone driving by. Possible impulse sales, she decided.

She still had to stop from time to time, talk to customers or direct them, but for the most part, she was blessedly left alone.

The air was close and heavy, the sort that brewed itself into thunderstorms. She hoped it did. She'd relish a bitching good storm. It would suit her mood exactly.

Still, the work kept her mind busy. She played the game of identifying and reciting the name of each specimen as she unloaded. Pretty soon she might be as good as Roz or Stella at recognizing plants. And she was pretty sure by the time she finished the work, she'd be too worn out to think about anything.

"Hayley. Been looking for you." Harper's brows drew together as he got closer. "What the hell are you doing?"

"Working." She swiped a forearm over her sweaty brow. "That's what I do around here."

"It's too hot for this kind of work, and the air quality's in the toilet today. Get inside."

"You're not my boss."

"Technically I am as I'm part owner of this place."

She was a little breathless, and the damn sweat kept dribbling into her eyes. It only made her more irritable. "Stella told me to set this up, and I'm setting it up. She's my immediate supervisor."

"Of all the stupid—" He broke off, strode inside.

And straight into Stella's office. "What the hell's wrong with you, sending Hayley out in this heat hauling stock around?"

"Good God, is she still at it?" Alarmed, she pushed back from her desk. "I had no idea she'd—"

"Give me a goddamn bottle of water."

Stella grabbed one out of her cooler. "Harper, I never thought she'd—"

But he held up a hand to cut her off. "Don't. Just don't."

He marched out again, stormed outside, straight to Hayley. She took a swat at him when he grabbed her arm, but he pulled her away from the front of the building.

"Let go. What do you think you're doing?"

"Getting you into the shade for a start." He propelled her around the back, through tables and potted shrubs, between greenhouses, until he came to the shaded banks of the pond.

"Sit. Drink."

"I don't like you this way."

"Right back at you. Now drink that water, and consider yourself lucky I don't just toss you in the pond to cool you off. I expected better of Stella," he said when Hayley glugged down water. "But the fact is, even though this is

her second summer, she's a Yankee. You were born and raised down here. You know what this kind of heat can do."

"And I know how to handle it. And don't you blame Stella for anything." But she had to admit, now that she'd stopped, she felt a little queasy and light-headed. Giving in, she stretched out flat on the grass. "Maybe I overdid it. I got caught up, is all." She turned her head, looked over at him. "But I don't like being pushed around, Harper."

"I don't like pushing people around, but sometimes they need it." He pulled off his fielder's cap and waved it at her face to stir the air and cool her. "And since your color's several shades under fire engine now, I'd say you did."

It was hard to argue when it felt so good to stretch out on the grass, and so sweet to have him fanning her with his sweaty old cap.

The sun was behind him, but filtered through the high, thickly leaved branches so that it dappled over him, made him look romantic and handsome sitting in the summer shade.

All that dark hair, curling a bit at the ends from the heat and humidity. And those long, chocolate brown eyes were so . . . delicious. The blades of his cheekbones, the full, sexy shape of his mouth.

She could lie here, she thought, for hours just looking at him. The idea was foolish enough to make her smile.

"You get away with it, this once. I had a lot on my mind, and good, sweaty work helps me deal with it."

"I got another way to deal with it." He leaned down, then stopped, cocked his head when she brought her hand up between them.

"We're on the clock here."

"I thought we were on a break."

"Work environment." The work, however draining, had done the trick. She'd made her decision. It wasn't about

what she wanted, but about what was right. "Besides, I realized that sort of thing isn't a good idea."

"What sort of thing?"

"The you and me sort." She sat up, shook her hair back and made sure she smiled at him. It would drop the base out of her world if they stopped being friends. "I like you, Harper. You mean a lot to me, to Lily, and I want to stay friends. We add sex to that, sure, it'd be nice for a while, but then it'd just get awkward and sticky."

"It doesn't have to."

"Odds are." She touched his knee, gave it a brisk rub. "I was just in a mood yesterday. I liked kissing you. It was nice."

"Nice?"

"Sure." Because she knew that expression on his face—or rather the lack of expression—meant he was angry and fighting it back, she bumped up the smile several degrees. "Kissing a good-looking guy's always nice. But I've got to think beyond that kind of thing, and the best thing for me is to leave things just the way they are."

"Things aren't the way they were. You already changed that."

"Harper, a couple of smoochies between friends isn't such a big." She patted his hand, started to get up, but he clamped his fingers around her wrist.

"It was more than that."

His temper was winning, she could see it. And from the few times she'd watched it fly, she knew it was formidable. Better he was mad, she thought quickly. Better for him that he was mad or disgusted or even hurt for the short term.

"Harper, I know you're probably not used to having a woman put on the brakes, but I'm not going to sit here and argue about whether I'm going to have sex with you."

"It's more than that."

More. And that single word had her heart trembling. "It isn't. And I don't want it to be."

"What's this, some kind of game? You came to me, you moved on me. And now it's that was nice, but I'm not interested?"

"That's the nutshell. I've got to get back to work."

His voice stayed calm and cool; a dangerous sign. "I know what you felt when I had my hands on you."

"Well, for God's sake, Harper, of course I felt something. I haven't had any action in months."

His fingers tightened, then released. Let her go. "So, you were just cruising for a fuck buddy."

It wasn't her heart that bumped this time, but her belly. "I did something on impulse I realized I shouldn't have done. You want to make it crude, go ahead."

Her vision wavered, so she seemed to be looking at him through a rippling wave of heat. The anger inside her spiked up, so acute it all but scored her throat. "Men always take it down to fucking, lying and cheating and buying their way to it. And once they have, the woman's no more than a whore to be used again or tossed away. It's men who are the whores, plotting and planning their way to the next rut."

Her eyes had changed. He couldn't say how, but he knew he wasn't looking at her through them. The heat of his temper froze in fear. "Hayley—"

"Is this what you want, Master Harper?" With a sly smile, she cupped her breasts, caressed them. "And this?" She slid a hand between her legs. "What will you pay?"

He took her shoulders, gave her a quick shake. "Hayley. Stop it."

"Do you want me to play the lady? I'm so good at it. Good enough to be used to breed."

"No." He needed to stay calm, though he could feel his own fingers tremble. "I want you exactly the way you are.

Hayley." He gripped her chin, kept his eyes focused on hers. "I'm talking to you. We've got things to do around here, then you've got to go get Lily. You don't want to be late picking up Lily."

"What? Hey." Frowning, she pushed at his hand. "I said I didn't . . ."

"What did you say?" He moved his hands back to her shoulders, rubbed them gently up and down. "Tell me what you just said to me."

"I said . . . I said I did something on impulse. I said— Oh God." The color drained out of her face. "I didn't. I didn't mean—"

"Do you remember?"

"I don't know. I don't feel right." She pressed a clammy hand to her belly as nausea rolled. "I feel a little sick."

"Okay. I'm going to get you home."

"I didn't mean those things, Harper. I was upset." Her knees wobbled when he helped her to her feet. "I say stupid things when I'm upset, but I didn't mean them. I don't know where that came from."

"That's all right." His tone was grim as he took her weight to walk her around the front. "I do."

"I don't understand." She wanted to lie on the grass again, lie in the shade until her head stopped spinning.

"We'll get you home first, then we'll talk about it."

"I have to tell Stella—"

"I'll tell her. I didn't bring my car. Where are your keys?"

"Um. In my purse, behind the counter. Harper, I really feel . . . off."

"In the car." He opened the door, nudged her in. "I'll get your purse."

Stella was behind the counter when he hurried in. "Hayley's purse. I'm taking her home."

"Oh, Harper, is she sick? I'm so sorry. I—"

"It's not that. I'll explain later." He snatched the purse out of Stella's hand. "Tell Mama, tell her to come. Tell her I need her home."

Though she protested she was feeling better, he all but carried her in the house, then jerked his chin at David. "Get her something. Tea."

"What's the matter with our girl?"

"Just get the tea, David. And Mitch. Get Mitch. Come on, lie down in here."

"Harper, I'm not sick. Exactly. I just got overheated or something." But it was hard to argue with a man who plopped you down on a sofa.

"It's the 'or something' part that worries me. You're still pale." He ran his knuckles down her cheek.

"It could be because I'm completely embarrassed by what came out of my mouth. I shouldn't have said those things, Harper, even if I was mad."

"You weren't that mad." He looked around as Mitch came into the room.

"What's going on?"

"We had . . . a thing."

"Hey, baby, what's the matter?" Mitch walked to the sofa, crouched down.

"Just the heat." The sick weakness was passing, and let her work up an embarrassed smile. "Made me a little crazy."

"It wasn't the heat," Harper corrected. "And you're not the one who's crazy. Mama's on her way. We're going to wait for her."

"You didn't drag Roz away from work over this? Just how bad do you want me to feel?"

"Quiet down," Harper ordered.

"Look, I don't blame you for being mad at me, but I'm not going to lie here and—"

"Yes, you are. Lily doesn't have to be fetched for a couple hours. One of us will go get her."

Since her only response was a dropped jaw, he turned as David brought a tea tray into the room. "You can get Lily from the sitter's, can't you?"

"No problem."

"Since she's my daughter, I'm the one who picks her up, or delegates," Hayley snapped.

"Color's coming back," Harper observed. "Drink your tea."

"I don't want any damn tea."

"There now, sugar, it's nice green tea." David soothed as he set the tray down and poured. "Be a good girl now."

"I wish y'all would stop fussing and making me feel like an idiot." She sulked, but took the cup. "But since you ask, David, I will." She continued to sulk as she sipped, then cursed under her breath when she heard Roz come through the front door.

"What's the matter? What happened?"

"Harper's on some sort of rampage," Hayley said.

"Harper, you rampaging again?" Roz rubbed her hand over his arm as she brushed by him to study Hayley. "When are you going to grow out of these things?"

"Roz, I'm sorry for all this trouble," Hayley began. "I got a little overheated and wonky, is all. I'll put in extra time tomorrow to make up for today."

"Oh good, then I won't have to fire you. Now somebody tell me what the hell's going on."

"First, she was working herself up to a good case of heat exhaustion," Harper told her.

"I overdid just a little, which isn't the same as—"

"Didn't I tell you to quiet down once already?"

She set the cup down with a snap of china on china. "I

don't know where you get off taking that tone with me."

The glance he sent her was as mild, and as formidable, as his tone. "Since it's not working, I'll just tell you to shut the hell up. I got her into the shade, got some water in her," he continued. "We talked a couple minutes, then we had an argument. In the middle of it, it wasn't her talking anymore. It was Amelia."

"No. Just because I said things I shouldn't have—"

"Hayley, it wasn't you saying them. She sounded different," he told Mitch. "Different tonal quality, you could say. And the accent was pure Memphis. Not a trace of Arkansas in it. And her eyes, I don't know how to explain it exactly. They were older. Colder."

Everything inside Hayley sank and shivered. "It's not possible."

"You know it is. You know it happened."

"All right." Roz sat beside Hayley. "What did happen, Hayley, from your point of view?"

"I wasn't feeling quite right—the heat. Then Harper and I got into an argument. He just pushed my buttons, that's all, and I slapped back. I said things. I said . . ."

Her hand shook, groped for Roz's. "Oh God, oh God. I felt—away, detached. I don't know how to say it. And at the same time, I was filled with all this rage. I didn't know what I was saying. It was like I stopped saying anything. Then he was saying my name, and I was irritated. For a minute I couldn't remember. My—my brain felt a little dull, like it does when you first wake up from a nap. And I felt a little queasy."

"Hayley." Mitch spoke gently. "Has this happened before?"

"No. I don't know. Maybe." She closed her eyes a moment. "I've been having these thoughts, these moods, that

don't seem like me. A lot of bitchiness, but it just seemed like I was feeling bitchy, that's all. God, what am I going to do?"

"Stay calm," Harper advised. "And we'll figure it out."

"Easy for you to say," she shot back. "You're not possessed by a psychopathic ghost."

seven

"A LITTLE LIKE OLD TIMES," STELLA COMMENTED AS she settled down in the upstairs sitting room with Roz and Hayley. And a bottle of cool white wine.

"I should be getting Lily her supper."

Roz poured the wine, then chose one of the sugared green grapes from the platter David had put together. "Hayley, you not only know she'll be fed, but that she'll handle all those men just fine."

"And it's good practice for Logan. We're thinking maybe we'll try to have a baby."

"Really?" For the first time in hours Hayley felt pure pleasure. "I think that's great. You'll make a beautiful baby, and Gavin and Luke would just love having another brother or a sister."

"Still in the talking stage, but we're leaning toward the acting on it stage."

"Feeling better?" Roz asked Hayley.

"Yeah. A lot. Sorry I cracked on you."

"I think we can make allowances. And give you some leeway. You didn't want to talk about what Mitch called the trigger—what you and Harper were arguing about. You needed your panic time and your weepy time, and you've had them."

"And then some. Nothing clears men out of the room faster than female hysterics."

"Which, I believe, was something you wanted anyway." Roz raised her brows and popped another grape. "You didn't want to discuss this with Mitch. Not what you argued about, or what you said to Harper—or rather what Amelia said."

Rather than meet Roz's eyes, Hayley kept hers fixed on the platter as if the cure for cancer was coded in among the glossy grapes and strawberry flowers. "I don't see what's important about what was said. The important thing is it happened. I think we should all—"

"That's enough nonsense." Roz's voice was mild as May. "Everything's important, every detail. I haven't pushed Harper on this, but I will. I'd prefer to hear it from you and it's been each one of us most intimately involved with this thing. So suck up your pride or whatever it is, Hayley, and spill it."

"I'm sorry. I took advantage of you."

"And how did you do that?"

Hayley took a bracing gulp of wine. "I hit on Harper."

"And?"

"And?" That stumped her for a minute. "You took me into your home, me and Lily. You treat us like family. More than. You—"

"And don't make me regret it by putting strings around it that I never tied on. Harper's a grown man, and makes

his own decisions about a number of things, including the women in his life. If you hit on him I have no doubt he knew how to block or hit back."

As Hayley remained silent, Roz settled back with her wine, tucked her legs up, sipped. "And unless I don't know or understand my son as well as I think, I'd bet on the latter."

"It happened in the kitchen. I made it happen. Just kissing," Hayley said quickly when she realized how it sounded. "I mean Lily was right there and it was the first time . . ."

"The kitchen," Roz murmured.

"Yes, yes. You see?" She shuddered. "And that same night, she tore his kitchen apart. So I realized this wasn't something that could happen just because I've got the . . . because I'm attracted to Harper. I told him that I wasn't interested after all, and I probably hurt his feelings. But it's better his feelings get hurt than something else happen."

"Mmm-hmm." Roz nodded as she watched Hayley over the rim of her glass. "I don't imagine he took it well."

"Not exactly, so I was like, what's the big deal." She set her glass down so she could gesture freely with both hands. "Then he said something deliberately crude, and it upset me. Because it wasn't like that. It was just a kiss—well, two," she corrected. "But it wasn't like we stripped down naked and had monkey sex on the kitchen floor."

"Difficult when Lily was there," Roz commented.

"Yeah, but even so, I'm not like that, even though I got pregnant with Lily the way I did. And it might seem like I'm a big ho, but—"

"It doesn't seem," Stella cut in. "Not for a minute. We all know what it is to need someone. Whether for the moment, or for more. Personally, I don't care to hear you talking about a friend of mine that way, or to intimate that I would."

Roz smiled, stirred herself to lean forward and tap her glass to Stella's. "Nice."

"Thanks."

"I forgot where I was," Hayley said after a moment.

"You were arguing with Harper," Stella said helpfully. "You big ho."

It made her laugh, settled her down. "Right. We were arguing, then it happened, the way I said. I sort of faded back, and there were these things coming out of my mouth I didn't put there. About how men are all liars and cheats, and just want to fuck you, and treat you like a whore. It was ugly, and it wasn't true. Especially not about Harper."

"The first thing you have to remember is it wasn't you saying it," Stella reminded her. "And the second is, it fits with what we know of her, and the pattern of her behavior. Men are the enemy, and sex is a trigger."

"During the argument, before Amelia's participation, Harper said something to make you feel cheap."

Hayley picked up her glass again, looked at Roz. "He didn't mean it the way I took it."

"Don't make excuses for my boy." Roz angled her head. "If he was perfect, he wouldn't be mine. The point is, you felt that way, and she moved in."

"Roz, I want you to know, I'm not going to pursue this thing with Harper. This personal thing."

"Is that so?" Roz raised her eyebrows. "What's wrong with him?"

"Nothing." Blinking, Hayley looked to Stella for support and got a smile and a shrug. "Nothing's wrong with him."

"So you're attracted to him, nothing's wrong with you, but you've dumped him before things really got started. Why is that?"

"Well, because he's . . ."

"Mine?" Roz finished. "Then what's wrong with me?"

"Nothing!" At her wit's end, Hayley spread a hand over her face. "I can't even believe how embarrassing this is."

"I expect you and Harper to work this out, and to leave me entirely out of the equation. I will make one observation, as his mother. If he knew you were showing him the door in order to protect him from possible future harm, he'd turn right back around and kick that door in. And I'd applaud the action."

"You won't tell him."

"It's not my place to tell him. It's yours." She pushed to her feet. "Now I'm going downstairs, and I'll discuss this with Mitch over our dinner. Meanwhile, I think you have another hour coming—for sulking time. After that, I expect you to straighten up."

Stella gestured with her glass as Roz walked out, then took a slow, satisfying sip. "She's just frigging terrific, isn't she?"

"You weren't a lot of help," Hayley complained.

"Actually, I was. I agreed with everything she said there at the end, but I didn't mention it. Seems to me, keeping my mouth shut was helpful. Hey, you're doing really well with this sulking hour," she added. "And you're only a couple minutes into it."

"Maybe you should shut up again."

"I love you, Hayley."

"Oh, shit."

"And I'm worried about you. We all are. So we're going to figure this out. Go team and all that. In the meantime you've got to decide what's best for you in regards to Harper. You can't let Amelia drive the train."

"It's tough when she's already highjacked it and put on the engineer's hat. She was inside me, Stella. Somehow."

Stella got up, moved to the couch to sit beside Hayley, to drape her arm over her friend's shoulders.

"I am seriously freaked," Hayley whispered.

"Me, too."

SHE FELT LIKE SHE WAS TIPTOEING ON EGGSHELLS. Only the eggshells were sharp as razor blades. She questioned everything she did or thought or said.

It all seemed like her, she decided as she undressed for bed. She'd tasted the pasta salad, the garden-fresh tomatoes at dinner. It was her head that had throbbed with a tension headache, and her hands that had tucked Lily into the crib.

But just how long could she go on being so hyper-aware of every single action, every breath she took without going a little loopy herself?

There were things she could do, and she was going to start doing them the next day. The first order of business was to weigh down her credit card with the purchase of a laptop. The Internet was probably full of information on possession.

That's what they'd call what had happened to her. Possession.

What she knew about it came out of books, novels mostly. To think she'd enjoyed having her spine tingled with those kind of stories once. Maybe she could take some of the things she'd read and apply it to her situation. Though the one that came first to her mind was Stephen King's *Christine.* She was a woman not a classic car, and come to think of it, the solution of smashing the car to bits didn't seem very practical. Besides, it hadn't really worked anyway.

There was *The Exorcist,* but she wasn't Catholic—and that dealt with demons. Still, she'd be willing to try a priest if things got any worse. In fact, the minute her head spun a three-sixty, she was heading for the nearest church.

She was probably overreacting, she decided, and slipped on a tank and cotton shorts. Just because it happened once didn't mean it would happen again. Especially now that she was aware. She could stop it from happening, probably. Willpower, strength of self.

She needed to do more yoga. Who knew that yoga wasn't the cure for possession? .

No, what she was going to do was get some air. The thunderstorm she'd wanted was just starting to lash. The wind was up, and shimmers of lightning were buzzing light against the windows. She'd throw open the terrace doors, let the wind pour in. Then she'd read something light, a nice romantic comedy, and turn her head off for sleep.

She walked to the doors, gave them a big, dramatic yank.

And screamed.

"Jesus! Jesus!" Harper grabbed her before she could let out the next peal. "I'm not an ax murderer. Chill."

"Chill? Chill? You're skulking around, scare my hair white, and I'm supposed to chill?"

"I wasn't skulking. I was just about to knock when you opened the doors. I think you may have cracked my eardrum."

"I hope I did. What are you doing out there? It's just about to storm."

"A couple of things. The first was I saw your light and wanted to see if you were okay."

"Well, I was before you gave me a damn heart attack."

"Good." His gaze drifted down, up again. "Nice outfit."

"Oh stop." Annoyed, she folded her arms over her chest. "It's no less than I might wear running around the yard with the kids."

"Yeah, I've noticed you running around the yard. The second is I was thinking about what happened this afternoon."

"Harper, I haven't been able to think about anything

else for hours." Weary of it, she pushed a hand through her hair, then pressed it to her temple. "I just don't think I *can* think about it any more tonight."

"You don't have to, you just have to answer a question." When he started to step inside, she gave him a good, solid shove back.

"I didn't ask you in. And I don't think it's a good idea for you to be in here when I'm not really dressed."

His eyebrows lifted as he leaned comfortably on the doorjamb. Like he owned the place, she thought. Which, of course, he did.

"Let me point out that you've been here for about a year and a half. During that time I've somehow managed to restrain myself from jumping you. I think I can continue that policy for another few minutes."

"You're feeling pretty snarky, aren't you?"

"I'd say what I'm feeling is pissed off. Especially if you're going to be a drama queen and insist we have this conversation with me standing out here and you standing in there."

The first fat drops began to fall, and he lifted his eyebrows again. Exactly the way his mother did.

"Oh, all right, come in then. No point in you standing out there getting soaked like an idiot."

"Gee, thanks so much."

"And leave those doors open." She jabbed a finger at them because the gesture made her feel more in charge. "Because you're not staying."

"Fine." The wind whipped in through them, chased by a charge of thunder. And he stood, thumbs hooked in the front pockets of ratty jeans, his hip cocked.

She wondered, even through the irritation, why she didn't drool.

"You know," he began, "after I more or less—mostly

less—calmed down about everything, replayed it in my head some, the way you do, something interesting occurred to me."

"You going to make a speech or ask your question?"

He inclined his head, an action that managed to look regal despite the jeans, T-shirt, and bare feet. "You've done a lot of swiping at me since you came here. I've tolerated it pretty well, for certain reasons. I'm about done with that now. But to get back to my point. The interesting thing that occurred to me was timing. Here's how it plays for me. You come over, make your move, I make one back. We have a moment, a couple of them. You want to take it slow, I get that. Then the next time we're together, you're all about now you're not really interested after all, it was just an impulse, no big, and let's just be pals."

"That's right. And if your question is have I changed my mind—"

"It's not. Between those two interludes, I get a visit from our resident crazy, who happens to decide to trash my place. My kitchen to be exact, the scene of interlude one. So my question is, how much did that event play into your role in interlude two?"

"I don't know what you're talking about."

"Well now you're just lying, straight to my face."

Her expression went to pitiful. She could actually feel it move across her face and settle in. "I wish you'd go away, Harper. I'm tired, and I have a headache. It hasn't been the easiest day for me."

"You pulled back because you figured she didn't like us together. Enough that she fired what we could call a warning shot."

"I pulled back because I pulled back. And that should be enough."

"It would be, would have to be, if that were true. If that

was all. I'm not going to push myself on you, on any woman who doesn't want me. I've got too much pride for that, and I was raised better."

He straightened, took another step toward her. "And those are the exact same reasons I don't walk away from a fight anymore than I let somebody stand in front of me if there's trouble."

He angled his head again, rocked on his heels. "So don't even think about getting in my way on this, Hayley, about stepping aside from something to protect me from her."

She cupped her elbows. "You say you won't push, but I feel pushed, so—"

"I've wanted you since the first minute I saw you."

Her arms went limp, simply fell to her sides. "You have not."

"The first moment—it was like being blasted with light. Went straight through me." With his eyes on hers, he tapped a fist on his chest. "I think I stuttered. I could hardly speak."

"Oh God." She pressed a hand to her heart, hoping that would hold it in place. "That's a lousy thing to say to me."

"Maybe." His lips twitched, his eyes warmed. "I'll just follow it up with some lousy behavior then." He reached out, drew her against him.

"Harper, this really isn't something we should—" It was some move, or so she would think when she could think again. With a subtle shift, a tiny bump, they were fitted together. Angle to angle, line to line so that every inch of her body felt the jolt.

"Oh," she murmured. "Uh-oh."

A smile flickered at the corners of his mouth, then that mouth was on hers. Hot and warm and sweet, like liquid sugar. The kiss was a slow, irresistible seduction, a drugging of the senses, as his hands cruised over her, a light and

lazy touch. A touch, she thought mistily, of a man confident enough to take his time—sure enough that he had
plenty of it.

And his lips rubbed silkily over hers until she'd have
sworn she felt her own shimmer.

It was like being gradually, skillfully, thoroughly
melted, body and will, heart and mind, until what choice
was there really, but surrender?

She moaned for him, that soft, helplessly pleasured
sound. And she yielded, degree by erotic degree, until the
fingers that had gripped his shoulders went lax.

When he eased back, her eyes were blurred, her lips
parted.

"Hayley?"

"Mmm."

"That's not the response of a woman who isn't interested."

She managed to get her hand on his shoulder again, but
it wasn't much of a push. "That wasn't really fair."

"Why not?"

"Because . . . that mouth." She couldn't stop her gaze
from dropping down to it. "You should need a license to
kiss that way."

"Who says I haven't got one?"

"Well, in that case. Do it again, would you?"

"Was planning on it."

It was the same rush with the wind spewing in through
the door, and his mouth lighting small, sparkling fires inside her. Little tongues of heat, she thought, that were going to lick their way through her until she simply
dissolved.

"Harper." She said it with the kiss, shuddering at the
sensation of their lips moving together.

"Hmm?"

"We really have to stop this." She couldn't resist nipping that sexy bottom lip of his, just a little. "Sometime."

"Later is good. Let's say next week."

She had to laugh, but it came out shaky, then ended on a gasp as his mouth slid from hers to find some magic point just under her ear.

"That's good, that's . . . exceptional. But I really think we need to wait, just a . . . Oh." She let her head fall back as his cruising mouth found yet another magical spot. "That's so . . ."

She turned her head to give him better access, and her heavy eyes blinked clear. Widened. "Harper."

When she jerked in his arms, he just shifted his grip. "What? It's not next week yet."

"Harper. Oh God, stop. Look."

Amelia stood in the doorway, the storm raging at her back. Behind her, *through* her, Hayley could see trees whipping in the wind and the bruised fists of clouds that smothered the sky.

Her hair was matted and wild, her white gown streaked with mud that dripped, it seemed to drip, into a filthy pool over her bare and bloodied feet. She carried a long, curved blade in one hand, a rope in the other. And her face was a mask of bitter rage.

"You see her, don't you? You see her." Hayley shuddered now from fear and cold.

"Yeah, I see her." In one easy move, he changed his stance so Hayley was behind him. "You're going to have to get over it," he said to Amelia. "You're dead. We're not."

The force of the blow lifted him off his feet, shot him back five feet to slam against the wall. He tasted blood in his mouth even as he shoved clear again.

"Stop! Stop!" Hayley shouted. Force of will and fear had her pushing against the freezing wind toward Harper.

"He's your great-great-grandbaby. He comes out of you. You sang to him when he was a boy. You can't hurt him now."

She started forward, with no clear idea what she would do if she reached Amelia. Before Harper could yank her back, a gust of wind knocked her off her feet and sent her sprawling. She thought she heard someone scream, in rage or grief. Then there was nothing but the sound of the storm.

"Are you crazy?" Harper dropped down beside her to prop her up.

"No, are you? You're the one whose mouth's bleeding."

He swiped the side of his hand over it. "You hurt?"

"No. She's gone. At least she's gone. Christ, Harper, she had a knife."

"Sickle. And yeah, that's a new one."

"It can't be real, right? I mean, she's not corporeal, so the rest of it isn't real either. She couldn't slice us up with it. You think?"

"No." But he wondered if she could make you imagine you were cut, or do yourself some kind of harm defending yourself.

She stayed on the floor, getting her breath back, leaning on him as she stared through the open doors. "When I first came here, when I was pregnant, she'd come to my room sometimes. It was a little spooky, sure, but there was something comforting, too. The way it seemed she was just looking in on me, seeing if I was okay. And this sense I got, this wistfulness, from her. And now she's—"

She was on her feet and running the instant she heard the singing come through the baby monitor.

She was fast; Harper was faster and got to Lily's door two strides ahead of her. Quick enough to throw out an arm and block her. "It's okay, it's all right. Let's not wake her up."

Lily slept in the crib, curled under her blanket with her stuffed dog. In the rocking chair, Amelia sang. She wore

her gray dress, her hair in neat coils, and her face was calm and quiet.

"It's so cold."

"It's not bothering the baby. It never bothered me as a kid. I don't know why."

In her chair, Amelia turned her head to look over. There was sorrow on her face, grief, and, Hayley thought, regret. She continued to sing, low and sweet, but her gaze was on Harper now.

When the song was done, she faded away.

"She was singing to you," Hayley told him. "Some part of her remembers, some part of her knows, and she's sorry. What must it be like, to be insane for a hundred years?"

Together, they crossed to the crib where Hayley fussed with the blanket.

"She's okay, Hayley. Lily's just fine. Come on."

"Sometimes I don't know if I can take it, this roller-coaster ride through the haunted house." She pushed at her hair as they walked back to Hayley's bedroom. "One minute she's knocking us around, and the next, she's singing lullabies."

"Dead lunatic," he pointed out. "Still, maybe it's a way of telling us she might come after you or me, but she won't hurt Lily."

"What if I do? What if she does what she did at the pond, and makes me hurt Lily, or someone else?"

"You won't let that happen. Sit down a minute. You want something? Water or something?"

"No."

He eased her down so they sat on the side of the bed. "She never hurt anybody in this house. Maybe she wanted to. Maybe she even tried, but she never did." He took her hand, and because it still felt chilled, rubbed it between both of his. "That's one thing that would've gotten passed

down. A crazy woman attacking a Harper, or even a servant. It would've been reported, and she'd have been taken away, put in jail or an asylum."

"Maybe. What about the sickle, and the rope? That says: I'm gonna tie somebody up and slice them to ribbons."

"Nobody ever got sliced to ribbons in Harper House." He rose to move over and close her terrace doors.

"That you know about."

"Okay, that I know about." He sat again. "We'll pass this on to Mitch. He can look into police records maybe. It's an avenue."

"You've got this calm surface," she said after a moment. "It's deceptive, seeing as there are all these little hot pockets under it. Shows me I don't know you as well as I thought I did."

"Back at you."

She sighed, looked down at her hands as they sat on the side of her bed together. "I can't just sleep with you. I thought I could—at first. Then I thought, I can't go jumping on that. I do and he's going to get hurt. She's going to hurt him." She looked up. "You were right about that."

He only smiled. "Duh."

She gave his arm a swat. "Think you're so clever and smart."

"Only because I am. You can ask my mama, when she's in a good mood."

"You're easy to be around, except when you're not." She studied him, trying to take in all the new things she was learning. "I like that, I guess, finding all those under-the-surface pockets. And God knows you're nice to look at."

"How big a fall are you building me up for?"

"It's not—" She shook her head, rose to wander the room. "I've got all these feelings stored up, and all these needs. It'd be so easy to set them loose on you."

"I don't recall putting up a fight."

"I didn't know you looked at me, not that way. Knowing you did, you do, just adds to everything. I've never been kissed like that in my life, and I've been kissed pretty good now and then. If she hadn't come in here when she did, it's likely we'd be in bed right now, going where that kiss was leading."

"That's no way to make me feel fonder of my great-great-grandmother."

"I'm not feeling so fond of her myself. But it gave me time to think instead of just want." Ordering herself to be sensible, for both of them, she sat on the arm of a chair. "I'm not shy about sex, and I think if you and I were somewhere else, in some other sort of situation, we could be lovers without all these extra complications."

"Why do people always think being lovers shouldn't be complicated?"

She frowned, then shook her head. "Well, that's a question. A good one. I don't know."

"Seems to me," he began, crossing to her. "That there are flings, and that's uncomplicated by design. Nothing wrong with it. But being lovers, going into it thinking about more than a night or two, that should have weight. You've got weight, you've got some complications."

"You're right, I can't say you're not. But there's a lot to consider before we take a step like this. I think we need to be sure it's the right thing for both of us before we take that step. There are things we don't know about each other, and maybe we should."

"How about dinner?"

She stared up at him. "You're hungry?"

"Not now, Hayley. I'm asking you for a date. Have dinner with me. We'll go into the city, have a meal, listen to some music."

Her shoulders relaxed and the tight coil in her belly loosened. "That'd be good."

"Tomorrow?" he said as he drew her to her feet.

"If your mama or Stella can mind Lily, tomorrow's fine. Ah, we'll need to tell them about what happened. About Amelia."

"In the morning."

"It's a little awkward, explaining how you were in here, and what we were doing when—"

"No." He took her face in his hands, laid his lips on hers. "It's not. You going to be all right now?"

"Yeah." She looked over his shoulder to the doors he'd shut. "Storm's passing, you should go now, in case it decides to rain some more."

"I'll bunk in Stella's old room."

"You don't have to do that."

"We'll both sleep easier that way."

SHE DID FEEL BETTER, EVEN THOUGH IT DIDN'T EXactly cajole sleep to imagine him just down the hall. Or to imagine how easy it would be to tiptoe down there, slide into bed beside him.

She had no doubt they'd both sleep a lot easier *that* way.

It was hell being responsible and mature.

Even a bigger hell to realize she cared about him more than she'd bargained for. But that was good, wasn't it? she thought as she tossed and turned. She wasn't a slut who hopped into bed with a guy just because he was good-looking and sexy.

Some people might think differently, because of Lily, but it hadn't been that way. She'd cared for Lily's father. She'd liked him. Maybe she'd been careless, but it hadn't been cheap.

And she'd wanted the baby. Maybe not at first, she admitted. But after the panic and pity, the anger and denial, she'd wanted the baby. She'd never wanted anything in her life as much.

Her beautiful baby.

She'd taken nothing from the father, had she? The spineless, selfish bastard who'd used her grief to have his way. That hadn't been stupid. She'd been smart not to tell him, to go away, keep her child to herself. Only hers. Always.

But she could have more, couldn't she? She was thinking about this all the wrong way. Why should she work? Sweat and slave, settle for a room in the great house. She could have it all. Her child would have it all.

He wanted her. She could play this well. Oh yes, who knew better how to play a man. He would come begging before she was done, and she would bind him to her.

When it was done, Harper House would be hers, hers and her child's.

At last.

eight

∽

In the propagation house, Hayley watched Roz set a ceanothus cutting in a rockwood plug. "Are you sure you don't mind watching Lily?"

"Why would I mind? Mitch and I will spend the evening spoiling her rotten while you aren't around to run interference."

"She loves being with you. Roz, I feel so weird about everything."

"I don't know why you'd feel weird about going out on a date with Harper. He's a handsome, charming young man."

"Your young man."

"Yes." Roz smiled as she dipped another cutting in rooting compound. "Aren't I lucky? I also have two other handsome, charming young men, and wouldn't be the least surprised if they had dates tonight."

"It's different with Harper. He's your first, he's your partner. I'm working for you."

"We've been over this, Hayley."

"I know." Just as she knew that impatient tone. "I'm not able to wind myself through it as easy as you, I guess."

"You might if you'd relax, go out, and have a good time." Roz glanced up before sliding the cutting into the plug. "Wouldn't hurt to try to catch a quick nap beforehand, either. See if you can deal with those circles under your eyes."

"I didn't sleep well."

"Not surprising, considering."

The music in the propagation house today was some sort of complicated piano, drenched in romance. Hayley had more skill identifying plants than classical composers, so she just let the music drift around her as she worked.

"I kept having weird dreams, at least I think I did. I can't remember any of them clearly. Roz, are you afraid?"

"Concerned. Here, you do the next one." She stepped back so Hayley could take over. "And angry, too. Nobody slaps at my boy—except me. And if I get the opportunity, I'll tell her so, in no uncertain terms. That's good," she said with a nod as Hayley worked. "This kind of hardwood cutting needs a dry rooting medium or you get rot."

"She may have gotten that sickle and the rope out of the carriage house. I mean all those years ago. Maybe she tried to use them and someone stopped her."

"There are a lot of maybes, Hayley. Since Beatrice didn't mention Amelia again in any of her journals, we may never know all of it."

"And if we don't we may never get her out. Roz, there are people, paranormal experts, who you can hire to clean houses." She glanced up, knitted her brows. "I don't know why you smile at that. It's not such a strange idea."

"I just had an image of a bunch of people running around the house armed with buckets and brooms, and that ray gun sort of thing Bill Murray used in *Ghostbusters*."

"Proton streams—and I have no idea why I know that. But really, Roz, it's a fringe science and all that, but there are serious and legitimate studies. Maybe we need outside help."

"If it comes to that, we'll see about it."

"I looked up some sites on the Internet."

"Hayley."

"I know, I know, just a contingency."

They both looked over as the door opened. Mitch came in, and something about the look on his face had Hayley holding her breath.

"I think I found her. How soon can you wrap things up here and come home?"

"An hour," Roz decided. "But for God's sake, Mitchell, don't leave it at that. Who was she?"

"Her name was Amelia Connor. Amelia Ellen Connor, born in Memphis, May 12, 1868. No death certificate on record."

"How did you—"

"I'll get into all that at home." He flashed her a wide grin. "Rally your troops, Rosalind. See you there."

"Well, for heaven's sake," she muttered when he walked out. "Isn't that just like a man? I'll finish up here, Hayley. You go tell Harper and Stella to finish up whatever they're doing. Let me think," she said as she pressed fingers to her temple. "Stella can get in touch with Logan if she wants him there, and she'll need to leave Ruby in charge, see that she closes today. Looks like we're taking off a couple hours early."

* * *

AMELIA ELLEN CONNOR. HAYLEY CLOSED HER EYES and thought the name as she stood just inside the foyer of Harper House. Nothing happened, no ghostly revelations or appearances, no sweep of sudden knowledge. She felt a little foolish because she'd been sure *something* would happen if she concentrated on the name while standing inside the house.

She tried saying it out loud, quietly, but got the same results. She'd wanted to be found, Hayley thought. She'd wanted to be acknowledged. All right then.

"Amelia Ellen Connor," she said aloud. "I'm acknowledging you as the mother of Reginald Edward Harper."

But there was nothing but silence in answer, and the scent of David's lemon oil and Roz's summer roses.

Deciding she'd keep the failed experiment to herself, she headed to the library.

Roz and Mitch were already there, with Mitch hammering away at his laptop.

"Says he wants to get some things down while they're fresh in his mind," Roz told her with some exasperation whipping around the edges of her voice. "Stella's in the kitchen with David. Her boys are with their grandparents today. Logan'll be along when he's along. I imagine the same goes for Harper."

"He said he'd come. He just had to finish . . ." She lifted her shoulder. "Whatever."

"Have a seat." Roz waved a hand. "Dr. Carnegie seems determined to keep us in suspense."

"Iced tea and lemon cookies," David announced and he wheeled in a cart just ahead of Stella. "You cracked him yet?" He nodded toward Mitch.

"No, but it's not going to take much more to push me to do just that. Mitch!"

"Five minutes."

"It's such a simple name, isn't it?" Hayley shrugged when Roz looked at her. "Sorry, I was just thinking. Amelia, that's sort of flowy and feminine. But the rest. Ellen Connor. It's solid and simple. You sort of expect the rest to be flowy, too, or a little exotic. Then again, Amelia means industrious—I looked it up."

"Of course you did," Roz said fondly.

"It doesn't sound like that's what it should mean. I think Ellen's a derivative of Helen, and makes me think Helen of Troy, so it's actually more sort of feminine and exotic when you come down to it. And none of that's important."

"Interesting, as always though, to see how your mind works. And here's the rest of our happy few."

"Ran into Harper out front." Logan walked over to kiss Stella. "Sweaty, sorry. Came straight from the job." He picked up a glass of iced tea David had poured and drank every drop.

"So what's the deal?" Harper zeroed in on the cookies, took three, then plopped into a chair. "We've got her name, so what, drum roll?"

"It's pretty impressive Mitch could find her name with the little we had to go on," Hayley shot back.

"Not saying otherwise, just wondering what we do with it."

"First, I'd like to know how he came by it. Mitchell," Roz said with growing impatience. "Don't make me hurt you in front of the children."

"So." Mitch pushed back from the keyboard, took off his glasses to polish them on his shirt. "Reginald Harper owned several properties, including houses. Here in Shelby County, and outside it. Some were rented, of course, investment properties, income. I did find a few, through the old ledgers, that were listed as tenanted through certain periods, but generated no income."

"Cooking the books?" Harper suggested.

"Possibly. Or these residences might have been where he installed mistresses."

"Plural?" Logan took another glass of tea. "Busy boy."

"Beatrice's journal speaks of women, not woman, so it follows. It also follows, as we find him a shrewd, goal-oriented type that as he wanted a son, whatever the cost, he maintained more than one candidate until he got what he was after. But the journals also indicate Amelia was local, so I concentrated on the local properties."

"I doubt he'd list a mistress as a tenant," Roz said.

"No. Meanwhile, I've been scouring the census lists. A lot of names, a lot of years to cover. Then a little lightbulb goes off, and I narrowed it to the years Reginald held those local properties, and before 1892. Still a lot to cull through, but I hit in the 1890 census."

His gaze scanned the room, landed on the cart. "Are those cookies?"

"Jesus, David, get the man some cookies before I have to kill him. What did you hit in 1890?"

"Amelia Ellen Connor, resident of one of Reginald's Memphis houses. One that generated no income from the later half of that year, through March of 1893. One, in fact, he'd listed as untenanted during that period."

"Almost certainly has to be her," Stella said. "It's too neat and tidy not to be."

"She knows her neat and tidy," Logan commented. "In spades."

"If it's not our Amelia, it's one hell of a coincidence." Mitch tossed his glasses onto the table. "Reginald's very careful bookkeeper noted on Reginald's books a number of expenses incurred during the period the property was supposedly empty, and Amelia Connor listed it as her residence on the census. In February of 1893, considerably

more expenses were noted dealing with refurbishing in preparation for new tenants, paying tenants. The house was sold, if you're interested, in 1899."

"So we know she lived in Memphis," Hayley began, "at least until a few months after the baby was born."

"More than that. Amelia Ellen Connor." He slipped his glasses back on and read his notes. "Born 1868 to Thomas Edward Connor and Mary Kathleen Connor née Bingham. Though Amelia listed both her parents as deceased, that was only true of her father, who died in 1886. Her mother was alive, and very possibly well, until her death in 1897. She was employed by the Lucerne family as a housemaid at a home on the river, called—"

"The Willows," Roz finished. "I know that house. It's older than this one. It's a bed-and-breakfast now, a very lovely one. It was bought and restored oh, twenty years ago at least."

"Mary Connor worked there," Mitch continued, "and though she listed no children for the census, a check of vital records shows she had a daughter—Amelia Ellen."

"Estranged, I suppose," Stella said.

"Enough that the daughter considered her mother dead, and the mother didn't acknowledge the daughter. There's another interesting bit. There's no record of Amelia having a child, just as there's no record of her death."

"Money can grease wheels or muddy them up," Hayley added.

"What's next?" Logan wondered.

"I'm going to go back over old newspapers, again, keep looking for any mention of her death—unidentified female, that sort of thing. And we'll keep trying to find information through the descendants of servants. I'll see if the people who own The Willows now will let me have a look at any documents or papers from that time."

"I'll smooth the way," Roz offered. "Old family names grease wheels, too."

SHE WAS OUT ON A DATE FOR THE FIRST TIME IN . . . it was really too sad to think about how long. And she looked pretty good, if she did say so herself. The little red top showed off her arms and shoulders, which were nicely toned between hauling Lily, yoga, and digging in the dirt.

There was a great-looking guy sitting across from her in a noisy, energetic Beale Street restaurant. And she couldn't keep her mind on the moment.

"We'll talk about it," Harper said, then picked up the glass of wine she'd ignored and handed it to her. "You'll feel better getting it out than working so hard not to say anything."

"I can't stop thinking about it. Her. I mean she had his baby, Harper, and he just took it. It's not so hard to see why she'd have this hard-on about men."

"Devil's advocate? She sold herself."

"But, Harper—"

"Hold on. She came from a working-class family. Instead of opting to work, she opted to be kept. Her choice, and I got no problem with it. But she traded sex for a house and servants."

"Which gives him the right to take her child?"

"Not saying that, by a long shot. I'm saying it's unlikely she was a rosy-cheeked innocent. She lived in that house, as his mistress, for what, more than a year before she got pregnant."

She wasn't ready to have it all taken down to its lowest level. "Maybe she loved him."

"Maybe she loved the life." He jerked a shoulder.

"I didn't know you were so cynical."

He only smiled. "I didn't know you were so romantic. More than likely, the truth of it hits somewhere in the middle of cynicism and romance, so we'll split the difference."

"Seems fair. I don't always like being fair though."

"Either way it falls, we know this is one screwed-up individual, Hayley. It's pretty likely she was screwed up before this happened. That doesn't mean she deserved it, but I'm betting on a hard edge. It takes one, doesn't it, to list your own mother as dead when she's living a few miles away?"

"Yeah. It doesn't paint a nice picture. I guess part of me wants to see her as a victim, like the heroine, when it's just not that cut and dried."

Deliberately she sipped her wine. "Okay, that's enough. That's all she gets for tonight."

"Fine with me."

"I just have to do one thing."

Harper reached in his pocket. "Here, use my phone."

Laughing, she took it. "I know she's fine with Roz and Mitch. I just want to check."

SHE ATE CATFISH AND HUSH PUPPIES AND DRANK TWO glasses of wine. It was amazing how liberating it was to sit as long as she liked, to talk about whatever came to mind.

"I forgot what this was like." Simply because she could, Hayley lounged back in her chair. "Eating a whole meal without interruptions. I'm glad you finally asked me out."

"Finally?"

"You've had plenty of time," she pointed out. "Then I wouldn't have had to make the first move."

"I liked your first move." He reached over, took her hand.

"It was one of my better ones. Harper." Relaxed, she eased forward, her eyes on his. "Were you really thinking about me that way all this time?"

"I put a lot of effort into not thinking about you that way. It worked some of the time."

"Why did you? Put a lot of effort into it, I mean."

"It seemed . . . rude," was the best he could think of, "to imagine seducing a houseguest, especially a pregnant one. I helped you out of the car once—the day of your baby shower."

"Oh God, I remember." It made her laugh even as she covered her face with her free hand. "I was so awful to you. I felt so hot and fat and miserable."

"You looked amazing. Vital. That was my first impression of you. Light and energy, and well, sex, but I tried to tramp that one out. But that day, when I helped you out, the baby moved. I felt it move. It was . . ."

"Scary?"

"Powerful, and yeah, a little scary. I watched you give birth."

She went still, and flushed to the tips of her ears. "Oh, oh God, I forgot about that." She squeezed her eyes shut. "Oh no."

He grabbed her hands, pulled them toward him to kiss. "It was impossible to describe. After I got over the get-me-the-hell-out-of-here stage, it was just staggering. I saw her born. I've been in love with her ever since."

"I know." Embarrassment faded as her heart swam up into her eyes. "That I know. You never ask about her father."

"It's not my business."

"If we take this any further, it should be. You should at least know. Could we maybe take a walk?"

"Sure."

THEY TURNED AWAY FROM THE LIGHTS AND ACTION of Beale Street and wandered toward the river. Tourists

flocked there as well, to stroll through the park or stand and watch the water, but the relative quiet made it easier for her to go back in her mind, and take him with her.

"I didn't love him. I want to say that right off because some people still like to think poor girl, some guy got her in trouble then didn't stand by her. And they think your heart's been broken by some asshole. It wasn't like that."

"Good. It'd be a shame if Lily's father was an asshole."

The laugh bubbled up, made her shake her head. "You're going to make this easier. You've got a way of doing that. He was a nice guy, a grad student I met when I was working at the bookstore back home. We'd flirt with each other, and we hit it off, went out a couple of times. Then my father died."

They crossed the little bridge over the replica of the river, wandered past the couples sitting at stone tables. "I was so lost, so sad."

He slid his arm around her shoulder. "I think if anything happened to my mother, it would be like being blinded. I've got my brothers to hold on to, but I can't imagine the world without her."

"It's like that, like you just can't see. What to do next, what to say next. No matter how kind people are—and they were, Harper, a lot of kind people—you're in the dark. People loved my father, you just had to. So there were neighbors and family and friends, the people I worked with, that he worked with. But still, he was so much the center of my life, I felt alone, just isolated in this void of grief."

"I was a lot younger when my father died, and I guess in some ways it's easier. But I know there's a stage you have to go through, the one where you can't believe anything's ever going to be right again, or solid again."

"Yes, exactly. And when you get through it, start to feel again, it hurts. This guy, he was there for me. He was very

sweet, very comforting, and that's how one thing led to another."

She tilted her head to meet his eyes. "Still, we were never more than friends. But it wasn't a fling, it was—"

"Healing."

Her heart warmed. "Yes. He went back to school, and I got on. I didn't realize I was pregnant at first. The signs didn't filter through my head. And when I did . . ."

"You were scared."

She shook her head. "I was *pissed*. I was so mad. Why the hell had this happened to me? Didn't I have enough to deal with? It wasn't like I'd slept around, it wasn't like I hadn't been responsible, so what the hell was this? A joke? God, Harper, I wasn't all soft and shivery. I was enraged. I got around to panic at some point, but I bounced back pretty quick to mad."

"It was a tough spot, Hayley. You were alone."

"Don't pretty it up. I didn't want to be pregnant. I didn't want a baby. I had to work, I had to grieve, and it was about damn time somebody up there gave me a freaking break."

They moved toward the river, and she kept her voice down as she looked out toward the water. "Now I was going to have to get an abortion, and that meant I'd have to figure out how to get some time off work, and pay for it."

"But you didn't."

"I got the literature, and I found a clinic, and then I started thinking maybe it'd be better if I had it then gave it up for adoption. Signed up with one of those agencies. You read so much about these infertile couples pining for a baby. I thought maybe that would be something positive I could do."

He brushed a hand down her hair, spoke softly. "But you didn't do that either."

"I got literature on that kind of thing, started research-

ing. And all the time I was going back and forth, cursing
God and so on, I was wondering why this guy wasn't coming back in the store, or calling me. Part of my thinking
when I was a little calmer was that I had to tell him, he had
to know. I didn't get pregnant by myself, and he'd better
take some responsibility, too. Somewhere in all that thinking, it got real. I was going to have a baby. If I had a baby,
I wouldn't be alone. That was selfish thinking, and the first
time I realized I was leaning toward keeping it. For me."

She breathed deep and faced him. "I decided to keep the
baby because I was lonely. That, then, was the heaviest
weight on the scale."

He didn't say anything for a moment. "And the grad
student?"

"I went to see him, to tell him. Tracked him down at college, all ready to say, oops, look what happened, and here's
what I've decided to do so step on up."

A breeze fluttered her hair, and she let it go. Let the
damp warm air breathe over her face. "He was glad to see
me, a little embarrassed, I think, that he hadn't kept in
touch. The thing was, he'd fallen in love with somebody.
Big sunbursts of love," she said, throwing her arms out to
illustrate. "He was so happy and excited, and when he
talked about her he just sent off waves of love."

"So you didn't tell him."

"I didn't tell him. What was I supposed to do? Say, gee,
that's nice, glad you found someone who makes your world
complete. How do you think she'll feel about the fact that
you knocked me up? Too bad you screwed up the rest of
your life because you were being a friend to me when I
needed one. On top of that, I didn't want him. I didn't want
to marry him or anything, so what was the point?"

"He doesn't know about Lily?"

"Another selfish decision, maybe with a little unselfish

best-for-him worked in. I wrestled with it later, when the pregnancy got more real, when I started to show and feel the baby kick around inside me. But I stuck with what I'd done."

She paused a moment. It was harder than she'd known it could be to finish it out, to go on when he was quiet, when the quality of his listening was so complete.

"I know he has a right to know. But that's what I did, and what I'd do again. I heard he married that girl in April, and they moved up to Virginia where his people are from. I think, whatever the reasons were, I did the right thing for all of us. Maybe he'd love Lily, or maybe she'd just be a mistake to him. I don't want to know. Because she was a mistake for me for those first few months, and I hate knowing that. I didn't start to love her, really love her, until I was about five months gone, and then it was like . . . oh, it was like everything in me opened up, and she was filling it. That's when I knew I had to leave home. Give us both a new start, clean slate."

"It was brave, and it was right."

It was so simple, his response, and nothing like what she'd prepared for. "It was crazy."

"Brave," he repeated. He stopped, by deliberate design, next to a patch of small yellow lilies. "And right."

"Turned out right. I was going to name her Eliza. That was the name I had picked out for a girl. Then you brought those red lilies into the room, and they were so beautiful, so bright. When she was born, I thought, she's so beautiful, so bright. She's Lily. So . . ." She let out a long breath. "That's the big circle, from the beginning around to the end."

He leaned down, touched his lips to hers. "The thing about circles? You can keep widening them."

"Is that a way of saying you weren't so bored by my personal soap opera you might want to do this again?"

"One thing you've never done is bore me." He linked his hand with hers so they could continue walking. "And yeah, I'd like to do this again."

"Away from the house. Away from her."

"We can do that. The thing is, Hayley, we live there. We work there. We can't avoid her."

TOO TRUE, HAYLEY THOUGHT WHEN SHE WALKED INTO her bedroom. All the drawers on her dresser hung open. Her clothes from there, from the closet, were all heaped on the bed. She crossed over, lifted a shirt, a pair of jeans. No damage, she noted, so that was something.

There'd been nothing amiss in Lily's room when she'd checked, and that was even more important. Curious, she walked to the bathroom. All of her toiletries had been shoved into a pile on the counter.

"Your way of reminding me this isn't really my place?" she wondered aloud. "That I may be told to pack up and go any time? Maybe you're right. If and when, I'll handle it, so all you managed to do was give me an hour's annoying work before I go to bed."

She began to put away the creams and colognes, the lipsticks and mascaras. Discount brands mostly, with a couple of splurges tossed in. And maybe she did wish she could afford better, just for the fun of it.

The same went for the clothes, she admitted as she went into the bedroom to deal with them. What was wrong with wishing she could afford really good fabrics or designer labels?

It wasn't like she was obsessed with it.

Still, wouldn't it be wonderful to be hanging up fabulous dresses instead of knockoffs and discount rack. Silks and cashmere. It would feel so good against her skin.

Roz had all those incredible clothes, and walked around in old shirts half the time. More than. What was the point in having so much, then taking it for granted? Leaving it hanging when someone else could use it. Use it better, too. Someone younger who knew how to live. Who deserved it, who'd *earned* it instead of just having everything handed to her.

And all those jewels, just going to waste, sitting in a safe when they'd look so beautiful around her throat. Sparkling.

She should just take them, take a few pieces here and there. Who'd know the difference?

Everything she wanted was right here for the taking, so why not . . .

She dropped the shirt she'd been holding. Holding, she realized in front of her the way a woman holds some lovely gown. Swaying in front of the mirror. And thinking of theft.

Not me. Shaking, she stared at her own reflection.

"Not me," she said aloud. "I don't need what you need. I don't want what you want. Maybe you can get inside me, but you can't make me do something like that. You can't."

She dumped the rest of her clothes in a chair, then lay down on the bed fully dressed. And slept with the lights on.

NINE

~

She was glad to be working the counter, grateful to the steady trickle of customers who kept her busy. Amelia didn't appear to be interested in her when she was working. At least not so far.

She'd made a list, documenting every incident she remembered clearly for Mitch's files. She'd noted down the locations: the pond, her bedroom, the nursery. She wasn't absolutely sure, but she thought there had been other times her thoughts weren't really hers. In the garden at Harper House, when she'd been daydreaming at work.

Once it was down on paper, she decided, it didn't seem that enormous.

At least not during the day, when people were around.

She looked over as a new customer came in. Young, good shoes, good haircut. Healthy disposable income, Hayley decided, and hoped to help her dispose of some.

"'Morning. Can I help you find something today?"

"Well, I . . . I'm sorry, I think I've forgotten your name."

"It's Hayley." She narrowed her focus while keeping her expression pleasant. Swingy, streaky blond hair, narrow face, pretty eyes. A little bit shy.

Then her own eyes popped wide. "Jane? Roz's cousin Jane? Holy cow, look at you."

The woman flushed. "I . . . got my hair cut," she told her, and fluffed a hand over the flattering swing.

"I'll say. You look great, totally great."

The last time she'd seen Jane, she'd helped Roz and Stella move the woman's few possessions out of the over-stuffed, overheated city apartment ruled by Clarissa Harper. The woman they'd smuggled out—along with journals Clarissa had nipped out of Harper House—had been dull and dowdy, like a pencil sketch that barely showed up on the paper.

Now her plain, dishwater blond hair had been lightened, highlighted, and shortened to a sassy length that didn't drag down her long, thin face.

Her clothes were simple, but the cotton shirt and breezy cropped pants were a far cry from the dumpy skirt she'd been wearing when she'd made her escape.

"I've gotta say: Wow. You look like you've been on one of those makeover shows. You know, like *What Not to Wear*. And oh boy, what just came out of my mouth was really rude."

"No, it's okay." Her smile spread even as her blush deepened. "I guess I feel made over. Jolene—you know Jolene, Stella's stepmother?"

"Yeah, she's terrific."

"She helped me get the job at the gallery, and the day before I started, she came to my new apartment. She just . . . highjacked me. She said she was my fairy god-

mother for the day. Before I knew it, I was getting my hair cut, and they were putting aluminum foil in what was left of it. I was too terrified to say no."

"Bet you're glad you didn't."

"I was in a daze. She dragged me out of there to the mall, and said she was going to start me off with three outfits, top to toe. After that, she expected me to fill out the rest of my wardrobe in a like manner."

Her smile wreathed from ear to ear even as her eyes went damp. "It was the most wonderful day of my life."

"That's the sweetest story." Hayley teared up as Jane did. "You deserved a fairy godmother after being kicked around by that wicked witch. You know, historically fairy tales were women's stories, passed orally in a time when women didn't have many rights."

"Um. Oh?"

"Sorry, trivia head. It's just that this is all such a girl thing, I guess. I've got to get Stella."

"I didn't want to interrupt anything. I just hoped to see Cousin Rosalind, and thank her."

"We'll get her, too." Hayley hurried over to Stella's office door. "But Stella's really going to want to see this." She poked her head in without knocking. "You've got to come out here a minute."

"Is there a problem?"

"No, just take my word and come out here."

"Hayley, I've still got half a dozen calls to make before I . . ." She trailed off, automatically putting on her greeting-the-public face when she spotted Jane. "Sorry. Is there something—Oh my God. It's Jane."

"New and improved," Hayley said, then winced. "Sorry."

"Don't be. That's just how I feel."

"Jolene said she'd given you the Jo Special." Delighted,

Stella walked a circle around Jane. "Boy, didn't she just. I love your hair."

"So do I. Your stepmother, she's been so good to me."

"She's enjoyed every minute of it. I've had reports, but I have to say, a picture's worth a thousand. I hope you're doing as well as you look."

"I love my job. I love my apartment. I really love feeling pretty."

"Oh." Stella's eyes filled.

"Same thing happened to me," Hayley said as she got a two-way from behind the counter. "Roz," she said into it, "we need you at checkout."

She clicked it off on Roz's staticky complaint about being busy.

"I don't want to drag her away from her work."

"She'll want to see you. And I want to see her see you. God, this is fun!"

"Tell us what else you've been up to," Stella said.

"Work's number one. I really love it, and I'm learning so much. I've made a couple of friends there."

"Male types?" Hayley wondered.

"I'm not ready for that yet. But there is this man in my building. He's very nice."

"Is he cute? Shoot, customer," Hayley grumbled as one came in through the back with a loaded cart. "Don't talk about anything sexy while I'm busy."

"I thought I'd be embarrassed to see the two of you again." Jane turned to Stella as Hayley waited on the customer.

"Why?"

"That time, when I met you, I was so whiny and horrible."

"You were not, you were scared and upset. For good reason. You were taking a big step, letting us in so Roz could get those journals."

"They belonged to her. Clarissa didn't have the right to take them from Harper House."

"No, she didn't. But it was still a big step for you, to let Roz get them back, to move out, start a new job, a new life. I know how scary that is. So does Hayley."

Jane glanced over her shoulder to where Hayley rang up sales and chatted with her customer. "She doesn't look like she'd be scared of anything. That's what I thought when I met her, and you. That the two of you would never be afraid to stand up for yourselves, never let yourselves get pushed around like I did."

"We all get scared, and we don't always do something so radical and positive about it."

Roz came in, the only sign of irritation the slap of her gardening gloves on her thigh. "Is there a problem?"

"Absolutely not." Stella gestured. "Jane wanted to see you."

Roz's brows lifted, and her smile spread slowly. "Well, well, well. Jolene is a woman of her word. Aren't you just blooming." She stuck her gloves in her back pocket, then lost her breath as Jane threw arms around her. "I'm glad to see you, too."

"Thank you. Thank you so much. I'll never be able to tell you."

"You're welcome."

"I'm so happy."

"I can see that. Feel it, too."

"Sorry." Sniffling, Jane released her. "I didn't intend to do that. I wanted to come, to thank you, and to tell you I'm doing a good job at work. I got a raise already, and I'm making something of myself."

"I can see that, too. I don't have to ask if you've been well. I'm happy for you. And, however small it might be of me, I'm downright delighted to see you looking so pretty,

so excited about your life because that must just burn Cousin Rissa's bony ass."

Jane gave a watery laugh. "It does. It has. She came to see me."

"What'd I miss, what'd I miss?" Hayley demanded as she hurried over. "Go back and repeat all the good stuff."

"I think we're just getting to it." Roz angled her head. "So Rissa got her broom out of storage and came to see you?"

"In my apartment. I guess my mother gave her my address, even though I asked her not to. It was about a month ago. I looked through the peephole and saw her. I almost didn't answer the door."

"Who could blame you?" In support, Hayley patted Jane's back.

"But I thought, I can't just sit here like a rabbit hiding in my own apartment. So I opened the door, and don't you know she walked right in, sniffed the air, ordered me to fetch her some sweet tea, then sat down."

"Bless her heart," Roz drawled. "Her ego never withers."

"What floor's that apartment on again?" Hayley squinted as she tried to remember. "Third or fourth, as I recall. She'd've made a nice splat if you'd tossed her out the window."

"I wish I could say I did, but I went and got the tea. I was just quaking. When I came back with it, she said I was an ungrateful, wicked girl, and I could cut off my hair, get myself into some rathole of an apartment, fool some brainless ninny into giving me a job I was certainly unqualified to handle, but it didn't change what I was. She said a number of uncomplimentary things about you, Roz."

"Oh, tell."

"Well, um. Scheming harlot for one."

"I always wanted to be called a harlot. People just don't use the word enough these days."

"That's what started getting my back up. I thought maybe she was entitled to call me ungrateful, because I was." Jane fisted her hands on her hips, jutted her chin in the air. "My apartment's not a rathole, it's just sweet, but with her tastes it might seem like it, and she didn't know Carrie—my boss?—so she might think she's brainless to give me a chance. But she had some nerve calling you names when she's the one who stole from you."

Jane squared her shoulders, gave a decisive nod. "And I said so."

"To her face." Hooting out a laugh, Roz framed Jane's face in her hands. "I couldn't be more proud."

"Her eyes almost bugged out of her head. I don't know where the words came from. I don't have much of a temper, but I was so *mad*. I just cut loose on her, said all the things I hadn't hardly let myself think when I was living with her, and waiting on her hand and foot. How she was mean and spiteful and no one had an ounce of affection for her. How she was a thief and a liar, and she was lucky you hadn't called the police on her."

"Get you." Hayley gave her an elbow nudge. "That's better than tossing her out the window."

"And I wasn't even done."

"Keep right on going," Hayley prompted.

"I said I'd beg on the street before I'd come back and be her whipping girl. Then I told her to get out of my apartment." Jane threw out an arm and pointed. "I gestured, just like this? Sort of over the top, I guess, but I was wound up. She said I'd regret it. I think she might've said I'd rue the day, but I was so stirred up I didn't pay much mind. And she left."

She blew out a breath, waved a hand in front of her face. "Whew."

"Why, Jane, you're a Trojan." Roz took her hand, gave it a squeeze. "Who'd have thought?"

"It didn't end there, exactly. She tried to have me fired."

"That bitch." Hayley's face darkened. "What did she do?"

"She went to Carrie, told her I was a woman of loose morals, how I'd had an affair with a married man, and that I'd stolen from her when she'd graciously taken me into her home. Said she felt it was her Christian duty to warn Carrie about me."

"I've always thought there were special front row seats in hell for Christians such as Clarissa," Roz commented.

"When Carrie called me into her office and told me she'd been there, what she'd said, I was sure I was going to be fired. Instead she asked me how I'd stood living with that horrible old crow. That's what she called her. And the fact that I had told her I had a lot of patience and fortitude, which she thought were good qualities in an employee. Since I had them and had proven I was willing to work hard and learned fast, she was giving me a raise."

"I like Carrie," Hayley decided. "I'd like to buy her a drink."

"THERE'S NOTHING BETTER THAN A HAPPY ENDING." Unless, Hayley decided, it was sitting in the shade on the glider, sipping a cold drink while Lily played on the grass. And Harper swung beside her.

"It's always a happy ending when Cousin Clarissa gets the heave-ho. She used to terrorize me when I was a kid, whenever she came around. Before Mama booted her out."

"Know what Jane said she called your mama?"

"No." The relaxed expression on his face settled into cold stone. "What?"

"A harlot."

"A . . ." The stone broke into a huge, rolling laugh that

had Lily clapping her hands. "A harlot. God, Mama would *love* that."

"She did. You really know her, don't you? It was just such a good morning. Pushed all the bad stuff away awhile. Seeing somebody who'd discovered themselves the way Jane has, or is, I guess. The one time I met her before? She was practically invisible. Now's she's, well, she's pretty hot."

"Yeah? How hot?"

She laughed, elbowed him. "Never you mind. One cousin at a time."

"Exactly what kind of cousins are we anyway? I've never figured it out."

"I think your daddy and mine were third cousins, which makes us fifth. At least, I think. Maybe we're fourth cousins once removed. It could be third cousins, twice removed. I can never get it just right in my head. And there's half blood in there, too with my great-grandmother's second marriage—"

It was probably just as well he stopped her mouth with his. "Kissing cousins covers it," he decided.

"Works for me." Because it did, she leaned in to take his mouth again.

Lily interrupted with a few squawks and babbles, tugging on Harper's legs until he hauled her up. Curling her arm around his neck, she pushed Hayley back.

"Well, I guess that shows me." Amused, Hayley leaned in again, and Lily pushed her back and wrapped tighter to Harper.

"Girls are always fighting over me," he said. "It's a curse."

"I bet. That one you were with last New Year's Eve looked like she could scratch and bite."

He smiled at Lily. "I don't know what she's talking about."

"Oh, yes, you do. The blonde with about a yard of hair and perfect Victoria's Secret breasts."

"Yeah, the breasts are coming back to me."

"That's a terrible thing to say!"

"You started it. Amber," he said with a chuckle as he lifted the baby high over his head to make her laugh.

"Of course. She looked like an Amber."

"She's a corporate lawyer."

"She is not."

"God's truth." He held up a hand like a man taking an oath. "Beautiful doesn't have to mean bimbo, of which you are living proof."

"Good save. Were you serious—and forget that spilled out. I hate when women, or men for that matter, poke into past relationships."

"You showed me yours. Not serious. She didn't want serious, neither did I. She's focused on her career right now."

"You ever been serious?"

"I've approached the parameter of serious a few times. Never crossed over into the zone." He sat Lily between them, snugging her in so she could swing.

Better leave it at that, Hayley told herself. Leave it comfortable with the three of them lazing on the glider with the bees humming in the hazy heat and the flowers bursting through it with bold summer colors.

"This is the best part of summer," she told him. "Evening shade. It seems like you could sit where you are for hours, without a single important thing to do."

"Don't want to get away from here awhile?"

"Not tonight. I wouldn't want to leave Lily two nights running."

"I was thinking we could take her to get some ice cream after dinner."

Surprised, she looked over. Then wondered why she'd

been surprised he'd suggest it. "She'd love that. So would I."

"Then it's a date. In fact, why don't we go out, get a burger and finish it off with ice cream?"

"Even better."

STEAMY JULY MELTED INTO SWELTERING AUGUST, days of white skies and breathless nights. It seemed almost normal, almost peaceful as day blended into day.

"I'm starting to wonder if just finding out her name was enough." Hayley potted up pink and yellow pentas. "Maybe the fact we worked to find it, and how she's Roz's great-grandmother's, satisfied her, calmed her down."

"You think she's done?" Stella asked her.

"I still hear her singing in Lily's room, almost every night. But she hasn't done anything mean. Every once in a while I feel something, or sense something, but it fades away. I haven't done anything weird lately, have I?"

"You were listening to Pink the other day, and talking about getting a tattoo."

"That's not weird. I think we should both get tattoos—a flower theme. I'd get a red lily, and you could get a blue dahlia. I bet Logan would think it was wicked sexy."

"Then let him get the tattoo."

"Just a little one. A girly one."

"I think girly tattoo is an oxymoron."

"Absolutely not," Hayley protested. "Flowers, butterflies, unicorns, that kind of thing. I bet I could talk Roz into getting one."

The idea had Stella tossing back her red curls and laughing. "Tell you what, you talk Roz into getting a tattoo and . . . Nope, I still won't join the party."

"Historically, tattoos are ancient art forms, back to the Egyptians. And they were often used to control the super-

natural. Since we've got some heavy supernatural going on, it would be like a talisman, *and* a personal statement."

"My personal statement will be refusing to let some guy named Tank carve a symbol—girly or otherwise—into my flesh. Just call me fussy. Those look good, Hayley. Very sweet."

"Customer wanted sweet, and the yellow and pink are her daughter's wedding colors. These'll make nice center-pieces for the wedding shower. I think I'd shoot for something a little bolder, a little punchier myself. Maybe jewel tones."

"Something you're not telling me?"

"Hmm?"

"Bride colors on your mind?"

"Oh, no." She laughed and set a completed pot aside. "No, nothing like that. We're just, Harper and me, we're just taking it slow. Really, really slow," she added with a huff of breath.

"Isn't that what you wanted?"

"Yeah, I did. I do. I don't know." She blew out another breath, fluttering her bangs. "It's smarter. It's more sensi-ble to take things really easy. There's a lot at stake most people don't have to consider. Like our friendship, and the work, and our connection to Roz. We can't just jump into the sack because I've—we've got an itch."

"But you want to jump into the sack."

Hayley slid her eyes over to Stella's. "I was thinking more dive in, headfirst."

"Why don't you just tell him, Hayley?"

"I made the first move. He's got to make this one. I sure as hell hope he picks up speed pretty soon."

"I'M TRYING NOT TO RUSH HER." IN THE KITCHEN, Harper drained the better part of a can of Coke. He rarely

broke for lunch, but early afternoon meant there would be no one in the house but David.

"You've known her going on two years, Harp. That's not just not rushing, that's standing still."

"It was different before. We've only just started seeing each other this way. She said she wanted slow. I think it's killing me."

"I don't think people actually die from sexual frustration."

"Good. I'll be the first. I'll be written up in medical journals posthumously."

"And I'll be able to say I knew him when. Here, eat."

Dubiously, Harper poked at the sandwich David set in front of him. "What is this?"

"Delicious."

Without much interest, Harper picked up the sandwich. "What is this?" he asked again after a sampling bite. "Lamb? Cold lamb?"

"With a touch of nectarine chutney."

"That's . . . pretty damn good. Where do you come up with—no, no, stay on target." He took another bite. "I'm good at reading women, but I can't get a handle on her, on this. It's never been important before—not this way—so I keep clutching."

With his own sandwich, David slid across from him. "It is good you came to me, young student, for I am the master."

"I know. I thought about just walking over one night, maybe with a bottle of wine, knock on her terrace door. The direct approach."

"It's a classic for a reason."

"But she's nervous about Amelia, about having any sort of, you know, encounter, in the house. At least that's my take."

"Is encounter code for hot sex?"

"Damn you, you're too clever for my pitiful ruses. Any-

way, I could have her and Lily over for dinner, and after the baby was asleep—a little wine, a little music." He shrugged and felt he was riding around the same circle again.

"There's also a reason why fine hotels have room service and Do Not Disturb signs."

"Room service?"

"Work with me, Harp. You take her out to dinner—fancy dinner. Let's try the Peabody. They have lovely rooms, lovely service, fine food—in-room dining."

Chewing thoughtfully, Harper played it out in his head. "I take her out to dinner—in a hotel room? Don't you think that's a little . . . brilliant," he decided after a moment.

"Yes, I do. Wine, candles, music, the works, all in the elegant privacy of a hotel suite. You'll be bringing her breakfast in bed the next morning."

Harper licked chutney off his thumb. "I'd need a two-bedroom suite for that. Lily."

"Your mama, Mitch, and I would be more than happy to entertain the charming Lily for a night. And to show your amazing forethought—or mine—I'll pack an overnight bag for Hayley. You'll just have to get the room, take her things in, arrange the service, set the scene. Then sweep her up there and off her feet.

"This is a good idea, David. I should've thought of it myself, which just shows how messed up in the head she's got me. I've got to get back, talk Stella into juggling the schedule so I can pull this off. Thanks."

"I'm always here to serve the course of true love, or at least hot hotel sex."

SHE WORE HER RED DRESS. IT WAS THE NICEST SHE had, and she liked the way it looked on her. But she wished

he'd given her time to go out and get something new. All their other dates had been casual.

He'd seen her in this dress. The fact was, he'd seen her in everything she owned.

Still, she had great shoes. Roz's cast-off Jimmy Choo's that probably cost three times what the dress did. And worth every penny, Hayley decided as she turned in front of the full-length mirror. Just look what they did for her legs. Sexy instead of skinny, she decided.

Maybe she should wear her hair up. Lips pursed, she scooped it off her neck, angling her head this way and that to check the effect.

"What do you think?" she asked Lily, who was sitting on the floor busily putting a pile of little toys in Hayley's oldest purse. "Up or down? I think I can pull the up-do off, if I keep it sort of tousled. Then I could wear those cool earrings. Let's try it."

When a man said he wanted to take you out to a special dinner, she decided as she pinned and re-pinned, the least you could do was pull out all the stops, appearance-wise.

Right down to the underwear. At least that was new—and purchased recently with the idea that eventually he'd see her in it.

Maybe tonight, if they could extend the evening a little. He could come back here with her. She'd just have to block Amelia out of her mind. Block the idea that Harper's mama was right in the other wing. That her own daughter was in the next room.

Why the hell did it have to be so complicated?

She wanted him. They were both young, free, unattached, healthy. It should be simple.

Becoming lovers should have weight. She remembered Harper's words. Well, the situation had weight. It was time she started thinking of that as a plus instead of a minus.

"I'm the one making it weird, Lily. I can't seem to help it. But I'm going to try."

She put on the earrings, long, flashy gold dangles, considered a necklace and rejected it. The earrings made the show. "Well." She stepped back to do a little turn for her daughter. "What do you think? Does Mama look pretty?"

Lily's response was a mile-wide grin as she dumped everything out of the purse.

"I'll take that as a yes," Hayley said, then turned back to the mirror for one last check.

The breath left her body so fast her head went light.

She wore a red dress, but not the thin-strapped, short-skirted number she'd had for more than two years.

It was long and elaborate, cut low so that her breasts rose up to be framed by the silk with a cascade of rubies and diamonds spilling down over the exposed flesh.

Her hair was piled high in an elaborate confection of shining gold curls with a few arranged to frame a striking face with lush red lips and smoldering gray eyes.

"I'm not you," she whispered. "I'm not."

She turned deliberately away, crouched to pick up scattered toys with trembling fingers. "I know who I am. I know who she is. We aren't the same. We aren't alike."

Chilled with a sudden panic, she spun back again, more than half afraid she'd see Amelia step out of the glass, and become flesh and blood. But she saw only herself now, with her eyes too wide and dark against her pale cheeks.

"Come on, baby." She grabbed Lily, and at the baby's wail of protest, snatched up the old purse, then her own evening bag.

She made herself walk at a reasonable pace, and slowed even that as she approached the stairs. Roz would see the shock on her face, and she didn't want to talk about it. Just

for one night she wanted to continue the illusion of normal.

So she took her time, got her breath back, got her features under control. She strolled into the main parlor with Lily on her hip and a smile on her face.

ten

HEAT LIGHTNING SIZZLED IN THE SKY, BROODY BURSTS, as they drove into Memphis. The traffic was as sulky as the night, but Harper seemed immune to it. They might have limped into the city, but the air was cool in the car, and Coldplay simmered out of the speakers.

Every so often he'd take his hand off the wheel to lay it over hers. A casually intimate gesture that made her heart sigh.

She'd been right to say nothing of that vision, or apparition, whatever it had been, in her bedroom mirror. Tomorrow was soon enough.

"I've never had dinner here," she said when he pulled into the hotel's lot. "I bet it's wonderful."

"One of Memphis's finest jewels."

"I've been in the lobby. You can't come to Memphis

without seeing the Peabody's duck walk. It'd be like not seeing Graceland or Beale Street."

"You forgot Sun Records."

"Oh! Isn't that the coolest place?" She shot him a stern look. "And don't think I don't know you're laughing at me."

"Maybe a chuckle. Not an outright laugh."

"Well, anyway, the Peabody's got an awesome lobby. You know they've been doing that duck walk for over seventy-five years."

"Is that a fact?"

She gave him a little shove as they walked toward the hotel. "I guess you know all there is to know about the place, being a native."

"Finding out more all the time." He led her into the lobby.

"Maybe we could have a drink in here before dinner, by the fountain." She imagined something cool and sophisticated to mirror the way she was feeling. A champagne cocktail or a cosmopolitan. "Is there time?"

"We could, but I think you'll like what I have in mind even better." He walked with her toward the elevators.

She glanced back over her shoulder with some regret. All that gorgeous marble and colored glass. "Is there a dining room upstairs? They don't have one on the roof, do they? I've always thought roof-top dining was so elegant. Unless it rains. Or it's windy. Or it's too hot," she added with a laugh. "I think roof-top dining's really elegant in the movies."

He only smiled, nudged her inside ahead of him. "Did I tell you that you look beautiful tonight?"

"You did, but I don't mind certain kinds of repetition."

"You look beautiful." He touched his lips to hers. "You should always wear red."

"And look at you." She ran her fingers down the lapels

of his dark jacket. "All duded up in a suit. The rest of the women in the restaurant won't be able to eat for envying me my good luck."

"If that's the case, we might just have to give them a break." He took her hand as the doors opened, then led her into the hallway. "Come with me."

"What's going on?"

"Something I hope you'll like." He stopped at a door, took out a key. He unlocked the door, opened it, gestured. "After you."

She stepped inside, her breath catching as she saw the spacious room. Her hand fluttered up to her throat as she crossed the black and white checkerboard tiles into a parlor where candles flickered, and red lilies speared lavishly out of glass vases.

The colors were deep and rich, long windows adding the sparkling lights of the city. In front of one, a table was set for two, and a bottle of champagne sat in a gleaming silver bucket.

There was music playing, slow, soft Memphis blues. Stunned, she turned a circle, saw the spiral staircase that led to a second level.

"You . . . you did this?"

"I wanted to be alone with you."

Her heart was still in her throat as she turned to face him. "You did this for me?"

"For both of us."

"This beautiful room—just for us. Flowers and candles, and God, champagne. I'm overwhelmed."

"I want you to be." He stepped to her, took both her hands. "I want tonight to be special, memorable." And brought them to his lips. "Perfect."

"It's sure off to a good start. Harper, no one's ever gone to so much trouble for me. I've never felt more special."

"It's just the start. I ordered dinner already. It'll be up in about fifteen minutes. Plenty of time for us to have that drink. How do you feel about champagne?"

"I feel like I couldn't settle for anything less right now. Thank you." She leaned to him, took his mouth for a long, warm kiss.

"I'd better open that bottle, or I'll forget the lineup of events."

"There's a lineup?"

"More or less." He walked over to lift the bottle from the bucket. "And just so you can relax, I gave Mama the number here. She's got that, your cell, mine, and I made her promise to call if Lily so much as hiccups."

He popped the cork as she laughed. "All right. I'll trust Roz to keep it all under control."

She did a little spin, just couldn't help herself. "I feel like Cinderella. Minus the evil stepsisters, and well, the pumpkin. But other than that, me and Cindy, we're practically twins."

"If the shoe fits."

"I'm going to wallow in this, Harper, I may as well just tell you that. I don't know how sophisticated I can be when I just want to jump up and down, go racing around to look at everything. I bet the bathrooms are amazing. Do you think that fireplace works? I know it's too hot for a fire, but I don't care."

"We'll light it. Here." He handed her a glass, tapped his to it. "To memorable moments."

She held the moment, the glow of it. "And to men who make them happen. Oh, wow," she said after the first sip. "This is really good. Maybe I'm dreaming."

"If you are, I am, too."

"That's all right then."

He touched her, skimming his fingers over the back of

her neck, exposed by her upswept hair. Then with the lightest of pressure eased her toward him. The knock on the door brought on a wry grin.

"Prompt service. I'll get it. Once they've set up dinner, we'll be completely alone."

HE MADE IT ALL HAPPEN, SHE MUSED. THE BIG PICture, the tiny details so the evening unfolded for her like the pages of a storybook. And because of him, she was sitting in an elegant suite, sipping champagne with the romance of candlelight, the shimmer of firelight. Flowers scented the air. There was a lovely meal she could barely taste through the anticipation bubbling in her throat.

Tonight, they would make love.

"Tell me what it was like for you, growing up," she asked him.

"I liked having brothers, even when they pissed me off."

"You're close. I can see that whenever they come to visit. Even though they live away from Memphis, the three of you are like a team."

He topped off her glass. "Did you wish for sibs when you were a kid?"

"I did. I had friends and cousins to play with, but I did. A sister especially. Somebody to tell secrets to in the middle of the night, or even to fight with. You had all that."

"As kids, it was like having a personal gang, especially when David came along."

"Bet the four of you drove Roz crazy."

He grinned, lifted his glass. "We did our best. Summers were long, the way they're supposed to be when you're a kid. Long, hot days, and the yard, the woods, they were the whole world. I remember how it smelled, all green and thick. And this time of year, how you'd hear the cicadas all night."

"I used to leave my window open a little ways at night so I could hear them better. I bet y'all got in plenty of trouble."

"Probably more than our share. You couldn't slip much by Mama. She had this radar, it was a little scary. I remember how she'd be in the garden, or in the house doing something, and I'd come around and she'd just know I'd been doing something I shouldn't've been doing."

She propped an elbow on the table, cupped her chin in her hand. "Name something."

"The most baffling, at least at the time, was when I was with a girl the first time." He drenched one of the strawberries in whipped cream, held it out for her to bite. "I came home having had my first sample of paradise in the backseat of my much-loved Camaro, about six months after my sixteenth birthday. She came into my room the next morning, and put a box of Trojans on my dresser."

With a shake of his head, he polished off the berry. "She said, and I remember this very well, that we'd already talked about sex and responsibility, about being safe and smart and careful, so she assumed that I had used protection, and would continue to do so. Then she asked if I had any questions or comments."

"What did you say?"

"I said, 'No ma'am.' And when she walked out the door, I pulled the covers up over my head and asked God how the hell my mama came to know I'd had sex with Jenny Proctor in my Camaro. It was both mystifying and humiliating."

"I hope I'm like that."

His eyebrows lifted as he coated another berry. "Mystified and humiliated?"

"No. As smart as your mama. As wise as that with Lily."

"Lily's not allowed to have sex until she's thirty, and married a couple of years."

"Goes without saying." She bit into the berry he offered,

mmm'd over it. "What happened to Jenny Proctor?"

"Jenny?" He got a look on his face, a kind of half smile that told her he was looking back. "Why, she just pined away for me. She was forced to go to California to college, and stay out there and marry a screenwriter."

"Poor thing. I shouldn't have any more," she said when he topped off her glass again. "I'm already half buzzed."

"No point in doing things halfway."

Angling her head, she sent him a deliberately provocative look. "Is part of the lineup you talked about getting me loose on champagne so you can have your way with me?"

"It was on the schedule."

"Thank God. Is that event coming up soon, because I don't think I can sit here and look at you much longer without having you touch me."

His eyes darkened as he rose, held out a hand for hers. "Here was my plan. I was going to ask you to dance, so I could get my arms around you, something like this."

She slid into them. "I haven't found a single flaw in your plan so far."

"Then I was going to kiss you, here." He brushed his lips over her temple. "And here." Her cheek. "And here." And her mouth, sinking in slowly and deeply until that meeting of lips was the center of the world.

"I want you so much." She pressed against him, burrowed in. "It takes me over. Take me over, Harper. I'll go crazy if you don't."

He circled her toward the steps, stopped at the base and looked into her eyes. "Come upstairs, and be with me."

With her hand in his, she started up, then let out a breathless laugh. "My knees are shaking. I can't even tell if it's from nerves or excitement. I've imagined myself with you so many times, but I never imagined I'd be nervous."

"We'll go slow. No rush."

Her heart was beginning to trip and stumble, but there was one more thing. "Um, I'm using something—birth control—but I think we should . . . I didn't bring any of those Trojans."

"I'll take care of it."

"Should've figured you'd thought of everything."

"Be prepared."

"Were you a Boy Scout?"

"No, but I dated a few former Girl Scouts."

It made her chuckle, and nearly relax again. "I think . . ."

She trailed off as she stepped into the bedroom. There were candles waiting to be lit, and the lamp on low. The bed was already turned down, with a single red lily resting on the pillow.

The romance of it saturated her.

"Oh, Harper."

"Wait." He walked around the room to light the candles, to turn off the lamp. Then he picked up the flower and offered it. "I brought you these because it's how I think of you, how I've thought of you since the beginning. I've never thought of anyone else the same way."

She stroked the petals over her cheek, breathed in their fragrance, then set the lily aside. "Undress me."

He lifted a hand, nudged the thin strap from her shoulder, laid his lips there. In turn, with her heart beating thickly, she slid the jacket off his.

Then her mouth found his as her fingers opened the buttons of his shirt, as his drew down the zipper at the back of her dress. His hands cruised over her back, and hers spread over his chest. When her dress slithered to the floor, she stepped out of it—then held her breath as he eased back and just looked at her.

She wore flimsy scraps of red that shimmered in the candlelight against her smooth pale skin. And high, high

heels with long, long legs. Desire, already impossibly strong, clutched at his belly.

"You're amazing."

"I'm skinny. All angles, no curves."

He shook his head, reached out to trace a finger over the subtle curve of her breast. "Delicate, like a lily stem. Would you take your hair down?"

With her eyes on his, she reached up to pull out the pins, then skimmed her fingers through it. And waited.

"Amazing," he repeated. Taking her hand, he drew her to the bed. "Just sit," he said, then knelt in front of her to slip off her shoes.

His lips trailed up her calf and had her clutching the edge of the bed. "Oh God."

"Let me do the things I've thought about doing." His teeth grazed the back of her knee. "All of them."

There was no thought to deny him, and no words that could surface through the flood of sensation. His tongue slid along her thigh, that mouth burning tiny brands into her flesh even as his hands traveled up, tracing her breasts with his fingers until they ached over her thundering heart.

She shuddered out his name, falling back on the bed as he came to her.

She could hold him close now, touch as she was touched. Taste as she was tasted. The pleasure filled her— the glide of his hands, the heat of his lips, the catch of his breath as they rolled together to find more.

No rush, he'd told her, but he couldn't slow his hands. They wanted to take, and take more. Her breasts in his hands, in his mouth, small and firm and satin smooth, and when he feasted on them she bowed up, exposing the long, slender line of her throat.

At last, she was his.

Her nails bit into his back, scraped down his hips. Tiny

thrilling pains. Then she was over him, her mouth as greedy as his, and her quick, gasping breaths roaring in his head like a storm.

Candlelight sheened over her skin, skin going damp with the heat they fueled through each other. The gold of those flickering lights glowed in the deepening blue of her eyes as he slid his hand over her, found her hot. Found her wet.

The orgasm was like a burst of light, a stunning flash that blinded her, set her body on fire then left it to glow. She felt herself slide toward oblivion, then come back into the bright, bright world of swimming sensations. Her body was awake, alive.

Then his mouth found her and sent her spinning beyond pleasure. It was a roiling heat that built and built, then gushed through her so that she was weak and wavery when he dragged her to her knees.

He looked at her, into her it seemed, so deep she thought he must see everything she was. And his mouth took hers in a kiss that made her heart tremble.

So this was love, she thought. This utter trust and surrender of self. This complete gift of heart that left you open, defenseless. And full of joy.

She touched her hand to his cheek, her lips curving as she shifted, as she wrapped her legs around him. "Yes," she said, and took him into her. "Yes," then arched back with a moan as the beauty swamped her.

He lowered his brow to her shoulder, barely able to breathe as she closed around him. But he drew her back to him, heart against heart. Not close enough, he thought. It could never be close enough.

Her arms locked around him, her mouth found his as they rocked themselves toward the edge, and over.

*   *   *

There was probably something more relaxing than sprawling on a big bed, limbs tangled with your lover's after mind-melting sex. But Hayley figured it was probably illegal.

In any case, she'd take this shimmery afterglow.

As far as romantic nights, this one left everything else she'd experienced in the dust. Gliding on it, she curled her body a little closer to his, and smiled dreamily when his hand stroked over her back.

"That was wonderful," she murmured. "You're wonderful. Everything's wonderful. I feel like if I stepped outside right now, this light inside me would blind the entire population of Memphis."

"If you stepped outside right now, you'd be arrested." His hand slipped lower. "Better just stay right here with me."

"You're probably right. Mmm, I feel so loose." She stretched like a cat. "I guess I was pretty blocked up, you know? Self-servicing isn't nearly as satisfying as . . . Oh God, I can't believe I said that."

His shoulders were already shaking as he snorted out a laugh. He hooked an arm firmly around her before she could roll away. "Happy to be . . . at your service."

She buried her face against his shoulder. "Things just jump out of my mouth sometimes. It's not like I'm a sex maniac or anything."

"Well, now you've shattered my dreams."

She cuddled closer, tipped her head up. "It's nice being here like this. I mean just like this," she said, and feathered her fingers through his hair. "All soft and warm, snuggled up in bed. I wish we could just stay, and tonight would just go on and on."

"We can stay, and when tonight stops going on, we can have breakfast right here in bed."

"That sounds amazing, but you know I can't. Lily—"

"Is sound asleep in the Portacrib we moved into my mother's sitting room earlier today." When her eyes widened, he pressed a kiss to her forehead. "Mama was practically rubbing her hands together with glee at the prospect of keeping her overnight.

"Your mama . . ." She pushed up on her elbow. "God, did everybody know about this but me?"

"Pretty much."

"Roz knows we're . . . that's just very strange. But I don't think I should—"

"Mama said to remind you she managed to raise three boys, keep them all alive and out of jail."

"But . . . I'm a terrible mother. I want to stay."

"You're not a terrible mother. You're an awesome mother." He sat up as she did, took her shoulders. "You know Lily's fine, and you know Mama loves having her."

"I do. I do know that, but . . . what if she wakes up and wants me? Okay," she said with a sigh when he just lifted his eyebrows. "If she wakes up, Roz'll handle it. And Lily loves spending time with her, and Mitch. I'm being a cliché."

"But you're such a pretty one."

She looked around the room. Beautiful, sumptuous—absolute freedom. "We can really just stay?"

"I'm hoping you will."

She bit her lip. "I don't have any . . . things, you know? Not even a toothbrush. A hairbrush. I don't have my—"

"David packed you a bag."

"David . . . well, that's all right then. He'd know what I'd want." She felt giddy little bubbles rising up in her throat. "We're just staying?"

"That's the plan. If it's okay with you."

"If it's okay with me?" she repeated, and a gleam came into her eyes as she launched herself at him. "Let me show you what I think about that."

* * *

LATER, SHE CAME RUSHING OUT OF THE BATHROOM. "Harper, did you see these robes? They're so big and soft." She stood rubbing a sleeve against her cheek. "There are two of them, one for each of us."

Lazily, he opened one eye. The woman, he thought, was proving to be insatiable. Praise Jesus. "Nice."

"Everything in here is wonderful."

"Romeo and Juliet suite," he murmured, almost drifting.

"What?"

"The suite. It's the Romeo and Juliet suite."

"Really, but that's . . ." Her brows drew together. "Well, if you think about it, they were a couple of teenage suicides."

On a laugh, he opened his eyes. "Trust you."

"I never saw it as being romantic. Tragic is what it was—and plain stupid. Not the play," she corrected, turning a circle to swirl the robe. "It's brilliant, but those two? Oops, she's dead, I'll drink this poison. Oops, he's dead, I'll stab myself in the heart. I mean, *Jesus,* and I'm babbling."

"What you are," he said, staring at her, "is fascinating."

"I get pretty opinionated about books. But whoever it's named for, the suite's downright awesome. It just makes me want to dance all around it, buck-ass naked."

"I knew I should've brought a camera."

"I wouldn't mind." Holding the robe up like a cape, she swirled once more. "I think it'd be sexy if we took naked pictures of each other. Then when I'm old, and all brittle and wrinkled up, I'd look at myself and remember being young."

She bounced onto the bed. "You got any naked pictures of yourself?"

"Not so far."

"Look at you." She tickled his knee. "You're embarrassed."

"Not entirely." Oh yeah, he thought, she was fascinating. "You got any?"

"Never trusted anybody enough before. And I've got this bony build. But you didn't seem to mind it."

"I think you're beautiful."

He meant it, and wasn't that a miracle? She could see it in his eyes. She'd felt it in his touch. "I feel beautiful tonight." She rose, wrapping the white robe around her. "All plush and lush and decadent."

"Let's order dessert."

She stopped twirling. "Dessert? But it's almost two in the morning."

"They have this amazing invention called twenty-four-hour room service."

"All night? I'm such a rube. But I don't care." She plopped back down on the bed. "Can we eat it up here? In bed?"

"The rules attached to twenty-four-hour room service are if you order after midnight, you're required to eat in bed. Naked."

She grinned wickedly. "Rules are rules."

They lay belly-down, facing each other, with a plate of chocolate-soaked cake between them.

"Probably going to be sick," she said as she ate another mouthful. "But it's so good."

"Here." He stretched out an arm, managed to grab one of the glasses on the floor. "Wash it down."

"I can't believe you ordered another bottle of champagne."

"You can't do naked chocolate cake without champagne. It's declassé."

"If you say so." She drank, then forked up more cake and held it out for him. "You know . . ." She wagged the fork at him. "On the date-o-meter you're going to have to go a ways to top this one. I don't think I can settle for any-

thing less than, oh, a wild weekend in Paris or maybe a quick jet to Tuscany to make love in a vineyard."

"How about a sun-and-sex-soaked sojourn to Bimini."

"Sex-soaked sojourn." She gave a tipsy giggle. "Say that five times fast." On a moan, she rolled over to her back. "If I eat another bite, I believe I'll regret it for the rest of my life."

"Can't have that." He set the plate aside. Then easing forward, closed his mouth over hers in a lingering upside-down kiss.

"Mmm." She rubbed her lips together when he lifted his head. "You taste very potent."

"Got a nice chocolate high going here."

She smiled as he slid down to her, as his hands trailed over her breasts, her torso, her belly. Then gasped when his lips nibbled away.

"Oh my God, Harper."

"I forgot to mention this part of late-night dessert." He shifted, reached out. Swirling a finger through cream and chocolate, he smeared it lightly onto her breast. "Oops. I'd better get that off."

SHE FELT SO SMUG AND COSMOPOLITAN, STEPPING OUT of the elevator into the lobby with her overnight bag. It was nearly noon, and she was just wandering into the day. She'd had breakfast in bed. The fact was, she thought, she'd had about everything in bed that was available in the State of Tennessee.

She imagined even her toenails were glowing as a result.

"I'm going to check out." He nipped a little kiss on her lips. "Why don't you sit down?"

"I'm going to walk around. Look at everything. And I want to pick up a few things in the gift shop."

"Be right back."

She let out a happy sigh. She wanted to remember everything. The people, the fountain, the tidy bellmen, the shiny displays of art and jewelry.

She bought a little quacking duck for Lily, and a silver frame as a thank-you gift for Roz. Then there were the sweet duck-shaped soaps, and the pretty yellow cap that would look so cute on Lily. And . . .

"No man in his right mind turns his back on a woman in a gift shop," Harper said from behind her.

"I can't help it. Everything's so pretty. No," she said when she saw him reach for his wallet. "I'm getting these." She set all her items on the counter, then picked up a canister once it was rung up. "This is for you."

"Duck soap?"

She inclined her head. "To commemorate our stay. We had the best time," she told the clerk.

"I'm glad you enjoyed the hotel. Are you here on business or pleasure?"

"Just pleasure." Hayley gathered the bag. "Just lots and lots of pleasure." She tucked her free hand into Harper's as they strolled back into the lobby. "We'd better get home before Lily forgets what I look like and . . . oh man, just *look* at that bracelet."

The display showcasing a local jeweler glittered and shone, but all Hayley could see was the delicate bracelet with sizzling white diamonds framing gleaming ruby hearts.

"It's drop dead, isn't it? I mean it's elegant, even delicate, and the heart shapes make it romantic, but something about it just says: Hey, I'm an important piece. Maybe because it's an estate piece. Antique jewelry has such a— what's the word I want. Panache," she decided.

"Nice."

"Nice," she said and rolled her eyes at him. "Such a guy. What it is, is stunning. Some of the other pieces in there have bigger stones, more diamonds, whatever, but this is the one that stands out. To me, anyway."

He scanned the name and address of the store. "Let's go get it."

"Sure." She laughed up at him. "Why don't we pick up a new car on the way, too?"

"I like my car. The bracelet would suit you. Rubies would be your stone."

"Harper, paste is my stone."

She tugged his hand, but he continued to study the bracelet. The longer he looked at it, the more clearly he could see it on her. "I'll just talk to the concierge."

"Harper." Distressed now, she stepped back. "I was just looking. That's what we girls do—we look in shop windows."

"I want to buy it for you."

It was more than distress now, and closer to panic. "You can't buy me something like that. It probably costs—I can't even guess."

"Then let's find out."

"Harper, just wait. Just . . . I don't expect you to buy me expensive jewelry. I don't expect you to do things like this." She gestured to encompass the hotel. "It was the most incredible night of my life, but it's not why—Harper, it's not why I'm with you."

"Hayley, if it was why you were with me, you wouldn't be. Last night was for us, and it meant every bit as much to me as it did to you. I've got enough of my mother in me that you should know if I do something like this, it's because I want to. I want to buy this for you, and if it's not out of my range, that's what I'm going to do." He kissed her forehead. "Just hang here a minute."

Speechless, she watched him walk to the concierge desk.

And on the drive home, she continued to be speechless at the way the ruby hearts in their diamond frames glittered on her wrist.

eLeven

SHE FRETTED FOR THE REST OF THE AFTERNOON, AND lavished attention on Lily. It was a strange and, she imagined, strictly maternal sort of juggling act to balance the fact that she'd missed her baby girl with the fact that she'd had the most wonderful time without her.

Guilt, she thought, came in many forms. By the time Roz got in from work, Hayley had built up a sputtering head of guilt.

"Welcome home." Roz stretched her back, eyed Hayley who stood in the foyer. "Did you have a good time?"

"Yes. Wonderful. Beyond wonderful. I should start out saying you raised the most incredible man."

"That was the goal."

"Roz, I can't thank you enough for keeping Lily that way." Unconsciously, she covered the bracelet on her wrist with her other hand. "It was more than I could expect."

"I enjoyed it. We all did. Where is she?"

"I wore her out," Hayley said with a weak smile. "All but kissed the skin off her bones. She's taking a quick nap. I got you a gift."

"Isn't that sweet." Taking the box, Roz strolled into the parlor to open it. And beamed when she found the frame, already spotlighting a picture of her with Lily. "I love this shot. I'm going to put this on the desk in my sitting room."

"I hope she didn't give you any trouble last night."

"Not a bit. We had ourselves a fine time."

"I—we—Harper. Hell. Can we sit down a minute?"

Obligingly, Roz sat on the sofa, propped her feet on the table. "I wonder if David's made any lemonade? I could drink a gallon."

"I'll go get you some."

Roz waved toward a seat. "I'll get my own in a minute. Tell me what's on your mind."

Hayley sat, stiff-backed, her hands folded in her lap. "I got to know the mothers of some of the guys I dated. We always got along okay. But I never . . . it's so surreal to be good friends with the mother of a man I'm . . . romantically intimate with."

"I'd think, all in all, that would be a bonus."

"It's not that it isn't. I suppose it would be less surreal if I'd gotten to know you, gotten to be friends with you *after* things became—"

"Romantically intimate."

"Yeah. I don't know how to talk to you about it, exactly, because the relationships are all tangled together. But I wanted to say, to tell you, that you raised an amazing individual. I know I did that, but I want to say it again. Harper went to so much trouble, took such care to give me something special. There aren't many like that, at least in my experience."

"He's a very special man. I'm glad you see that, and appreciate it."

"I do. He had this beautiful suite, and flowers and candles. Champagne. No one's ever done anything like that for me. I don't just mean the lavishness, you know? I'd've been fine with a plate of ribs and a motel room. And how crude is that," she muttered, closing her eyes.

"Not crude. Honest. And refreshing."

"What I mean to say is no one's ever taken that time, that care to plan a whole evening with me in mind."

"It's a disconcerting thrill to be swept off your feet."

"Yes." Relief poured through her. "Yes, exactly. My head's still spinning. I wanted you to know that I'd never take advantage of his nature, his consideration."

"He bought you that bracelet."

Hayley jolted, clamped a hand over it. "Yes. Roz—"

"I've been admiring it since I came in. And watching you rub your hand over it, guiltily. As if you'd stolen it."

"I feel like I did."

"Oh, don't be ridiculous." Roz's eyebrows drew together as she waved a hand. "You'll irritate me."

"I didn't ask for it. I told him not to. All I did was admire it in the window, and the next thing you know he's making arrangements with the concierge and the jewelry store. He wouldn't tell me how much it cost."

"I should hope not," she said staunchly. "I raised him better."

"Roz, these are real stones. It's an antique. It's a real antique."

"I've been on my feet most of today. Don't make me get up to get a closer look at it."

Emotions in turmoil, Hayley stepped over, held out her wrist. Roz simply tugged her down on the sofa. "That is a

beauty, and certainly suits you. How many ruby hearts are there?"

"I wouldn't count them," she began, then lowered her head at Roz's bland stare. "Fourteen," she confessed. "With ten little diamonds around here, and two between each heart. God, I'm crass."

"No, you're a girl. And one with excellent taste. Don't wear that to work, no matter how much you want to. You'll get it dirty."

"You're not upset?"

"Harper is free to spend his money as he sees fit, and has the good sense to spend it with some discrimination. He gave you a lovely gift. Why don't you just enjoy it?"

"I thought you'd be mad."

"Then you underestimate me."

"I don't. I don't." Tears swam into her eyes as she burrowed against Roz. "I love you. I'm sorry, I'm so twisted up. I'm so happy. I'm so scared. I'm in love with him. I'm in love with Harper."

"Yes, honey." Roz curled an arm around Hayley, and patted gently. "I know."

"You know." Sniffling, Hayley reared back.

"Look at you." Smiling a little, Roz brushed Hayley's hair away from her damp cheeks. "Sitting here crying, happy, scared tears. The kind a woman sheds over some man she's realized she's crazy about, and doesn't know quite how the hell it happened to her."

"I didn't really know until last night. I knew I liked him, that I cared about him, but mostly I thought I wanted to bang him. Then . . . Oh God, oh God, I actually said that." Mortified, she pressed the heels of her hands against her eyes and rubbed. "See why this is surreal? I just told Harper's mother I wanted to bang him."

"I admit, the situation is a bit unique. But I think my sensibilities can handle it."

"It all just opened up inside me last night, everything opened up and poured through. I've never felt like that." Hayley pressed a hand to her heart, and the rubies glittered. "I've never been in love before, not all the way in love. And I thought, when it happened, that this is it, this is how it feels when you fall. Don't tell him." She gripped Roz's hand. "Please don't tell him."

"It's not for me to tell him. It's for you, when you're ready. Love's a gift, Hayley, to be taken and received freely."

"Love's a lie, an illusion created by weak women and conniving men. An excuse for the middle class to breed and their betters to ignore so they can marry within their own station and build more wealth."

Roz felt the shudder run through her, and her breath back up in her lungs. But she straightened, continued to look in the eyes that were no longer only Hayley's. "Is that how you justified the choices you made?"

"I lived very well on my choices." She lifted her arm, smiled as she trailed a finger over the bracelet. "Very well. Better than those I came from. She was content to serve on her knees. I preferred serving on my back. I could have lived here."

She rose, wandering the room. "I should have. So now I am here. Always."

"But you're not happy. What happened? Why are you here, and so unhappy?"

"I made life." She whirled, cupping a hand over her belly. "You know the power of that. Life grew in me, came from me. And he took it. My son." She looked around, those eyes darting. "My son. I came for my son."

"He's gone now, too." Roz rose slowly. "Long ago. My grandfather. He was a good man."

"A baby. My baby. Little boy, sweet, small. Mine. Men, men are liars, thieves, cheats. I should have killed him."

"The child?"

Those eyes glittered, bright and hard as the diamonds on her wrist. "The father. I should have found a way to kill him, all of them. Burned the house to the ground around them, and sent us all to hell."

There was a chill, and the pity Roz had once felt couldn't chip through the ice of it. "What did you do?"

"I came, I came in the night. Quiet as a mouse." She tapped a finger to her lips, then began to laugh. "Gone." She turned a circle, holding her arm high so the rubies and diamonds flashed. "All gone, everything gone. Nothing left for me." Her head cocked, her gaze turned to the monitor, and Lily's waking cries.

"The baby. The baby's crying."

Her head lolled as she slid to the floor.

"Mitch! David!" Roz rushed across the room to drop down beside Hayley.

"Got a little dizzy," Hayley murmured, passing a hand over her face. Then she looked around, groped for Roz's hand. "What? What?"

"It's all right. Just stay down a minute. David." Roz glanced over her shoulder when both men hurried into the room. "Get us some water and the brandy."

"What happened?" Mitch demanded.

"She had a spell, an episode."

"Lily. Lily's crying."

"I'll get her." Mitch, touched Hayley's shoulder. "I'll go get her."

"I remember. I think. Sort of. My head hurts."

"All right, sweetie. Let's get you onto the couch."

"Little queasy," Hayley managed when Roz helped her to her feet. "I didn't feel it coming, Roz. Then it was . . . it was stronger that time. It was more."

David brought both water and brandy, and sitting on Hayley's other side, put a glass of water in her hand. "Here now, baby doll, sip some water."

"Thanks. I'm okay, feeling better. Just a little shaky."

"You're not the only one," Roz said.

"You talked to her."

"We had quite the conversation."

"You asked her questions. I don't know how you held it together like that."

"Have a little brandy," Roz suggested, but Hayley wrinkled her nose.

"I don't like it. I feel better, honest."

"Then I'll have your share." Roz picked up the snifter and took a healthy swallow as Mitch came in with Lily.

"She'll want her juice. She likes a little juice when she gets up from a nap."

"I'll get her some," Mitch told Hayley.

"No, I'll take her in. I'd like to do something normal for a few minutes." She got to her feet, reaching for Lily as Lily reached for her. "There's my baby girl. We'll be right back."

Roz got to her feet when Hayley left the room. "I'm going to call Harper. He'll want to know about this."

"I'd like to know about this myself," Mitch reminded her.

"You'll want your notebook and tape recorder."

"WE WERE JUST SITTING THERE TALKING. I WAS TELLING Roz what a wonderful time I'd had last night, and showing

her the bracelet. And—sorry Harper—but I was telling her I felt guilty about you buying it for me. And I guess I got emotional." She sent a pleading look at Roz, clearly begging confidence. "And then she was just there. Like a bang. I'm a little bit vague on it. It was like hearing a conversation—like when you hold a glass to a wall to hear what people are saying in the next room. All sort of tinny and echoing."

"She was amused, in my opinion, in a nasty sort of way," Roz began, and took them through it.

"She was accustomed to receiving gifts for sex." Mitch scribbled in his notebook. "So that's how she'd equate the bracelet Hayley's wearing. She wouldn't understand," he continued, hearing the quiet sound of distress she made, "generosity, or the pleasure of giving for the sake of the gift. When something was given to her, it was an exchange. Never a token of affection."

Hayley nodded and continued to sit on the floor with Lily.

"She came here," he continued. "By her own words she came here at night. She wanted to cause harm to Reginald, perhaps the entire household. Maybe even planned to. But she didn't. We could assume harm came to her here. She said she was here, always."

"Died here." Hayley nodded. "Remains here. Yes. It felt like that. Like I could almost, almost, see what was in her head while it was happening. And that's what it felt like. She died here, and she stays here. And she thinks of the child she had as a baby still. She's the way she was then, and in her mind—I think—so is her son."

"So she relates to, is drawn to, children," Harper finished. "Once they grow up, they're no real substitute for hers. Especially if they happen to grow up into men."

"She came to help me when I needed it," Roz pointed out. "She recognizes the blood connection. Acknowledges

it, at least when it suits her. Hayley's heightened emotions brought her out. But then she answered questions, she spoke intelligently."

"So I'm a kind of conduit." Hayley fought back another shudder. "But why me?"

"Maybe because you're a young mother," Mitch suggested. "Close to the age she was when she died, raising a child—something that was denied her. She made life. It was stolen from her. When life is stolen, what's left?"

"Death," Hayley said with a shudder. She stayed where she was when Lily ran over to Harper and lifted her arms to be held. "She's getting stronger, that's how it felt. She likes having a body around her, having her say. She'd like more. She'd like . . ."

She caught herself twisting the bracelet, and stared down at it. "I forgot," she whispered. "Oh God, I forgot. Last night, when I was dressing, checking myself out in the mirror. She was there."

"You had one of these experiences last night?" Harper demanded.

"No. Or not like this one. She was there, instead of me, in the mirror. I wasn't—" She shook her head impatiently. "I was me, all the way, but the reflection was her. I didn't say anything because I just didn't want to go around about it last night. I just wanted to get out awhile, then everything . . . it went out of my mind until now. She wasn't like we've seen her before."

"What do you mean?" Mitch sat, pencil poised.

"She was all dressed up. A red dress, but not like what I was wearing. Fancy gown, low-cut, off the shoulders. Ball gown, I'd guess. She wore a lot of jewels. Rubies and diamonds. The necklace was . . ." She trailed off to stare at the bracelet in speechless shock.

"Rubies and diamonds," she repeated. "She was wear-

ing this. This bracelet. I'm sure of it. When I saw it at the hotel, I was so pulled toward it. I couldn't see anything else in the display. She was wearing this, on her right wrist. It was hers. This was hers."

Mitch left his seat to crouch on the floor by Hayley and examine the bracelet. "I don't know anything about dating jewelry, about eras along this avenue. Harper, did the jeweler give you a history?"

"Circa 1890," he said tightly. "I never thought twice about it."

"Maybe she pushed you to buy it for me." Hayley shoved to her feet. "If she—"

"No. I wanted to give you something. It's as simple as that. If it makes you uncomfortable to have it, or weirds you out, we can keep it in the safe."

Utter trust, she remembered. That was love. "No. It wasn't an exchange, it was a gift." She crossed to him, kissed him lightly on the lips. "So screw her."

"That's my girl."

Lily batted her hand on his cheek until he turned his face to hers, then she bumped her mouth to his.

"Or one of them," he added.

By evening, she was calm again. Calmer still when she settled down in the rocking chair with Lily. She prized these moments, when the room was quiet and she could rock her baby to sleep. Sing to her, and though her voice was no prize, Lily seemed to like it.

This was what Amelia craved, maybe what she craved most under the madness. Just these moments of unity and peace, a mother rocking her child to sleep with a lullaby.

She would try to remember that, Hayley promised herself, whenever she got too frightened or too angry. She

would try to remember what Amelia had lost, what had been stolen from her.

She tried "Hush, Little Baby," because it pleased her she knew all the words. And Lily's head was usually heavy on her shoulder by the time the song was finished.

She was nearly there when a movement at the doorway had her heart bumping her ribs. Then it stilled when Harper smiled in at her. In the same rusty, sing-song voice she was using for the lullabye, she warned him.

"She won't go down if she sees you in here."

He nodded, lingered another moment, then slipped away.

Humming, she rose to walk to the crib, tucking Lily in with her stuffed dog within cuddling reach. "When you're three, Mama'll get you a real puppy. Okay, when you're two, but that's my final offer. 'Night, baby."

Leaving the night-light glowing, she left the baby sleeping. Harper turned from the terrace doors when she came in.

"That was a pretty picture, you and Lily rocking in the chair. Mama says she used to rock me and my brothers to sleep in that chair."

"It's why it feels so good. A lot of love's sat in that rocker."

"It's cooler tonight, at least a little cooler. Maybe we could sit out for a while."

"All right." She picked up her bedside monitor, and went with him.

In front of the rail, there was a trio of huge copper pots, greening softly in the weather. She'd been charged with selecting and planting the flowers in them this year, and was always thrilled to see the thriving mix of color, shape, and texture.

"I don't mind the heat, not this time of day anyway." She leaned down to sniff a purple bloom. "The sun goes

down a little more, the lightning bugs'll come out, and the cicadas'll start singing."

"Gave me a scare when Mama called earlier."

"Guess so."

"So here's the thing." He ran a hand absently along her arm. "You shouldn't stay here after tonight. You can move on over to Logan's tomorrow. Take some time off," he continued as she turned to stare at him.

"Time off?"

"The nursery's the same as Harper House, as far as this goes. Best you steer clear of both for a while. Mitch and I'll see what we can do about tracing the bracelet, for what that's worth."

"Just pack up and move to Stella's, quit work."

"I didn't say quit. Take some time off."

There was such patience in his voice, the sort of patience that raised her hackles like fingernails on a blackboard.

"Some time."

"Yeah. I talked to Mama about that, and to Stella about you staying with them for a while."

"You did? You talked to them about it."

He knew how a woman sounded when she was getting ready to tear a strip out of him. "No point getting your back up. This is the sensible thing to do."

"So you figure the *sensible* thing is for you to make decisions for me, talk them over with other people, then present them to me on a platter?" Deliberately she took a step back, as if to illustrate she stood on her own feet. "You don't tell me what to do, Harper, and I don't leave this house unless Roz shows me the door."

"No one's kicking you out. What's the damn big deal about staying with a friend for a while?"

It sounded so reasonable. It was infuriating. "Because

this is my home now. This is where I live, and the nursery is where I work."

"And it'll still be your home, still be where you live and where you work. For Christ's sake, don't be so pigheaded."

The lash of temper delighted her. It meant she could lash right back. "Don't you swear at me and call me names."

"I'm not—" He bit off the rest of the words, rammed his hands in his pockets to stride up and down the terrace while he fought with his temper. "You said she was getting stronger. Why the hell would you stay here, risk what happens to you, when all you have to do is move a couple miles away? Temporarily."

"How temporarily? Have you figured that out, too? I'm supposed to just sit around at Stella's, twiddling my thumbs until you decide I can come back?"

"Till it's safe."

"How do you know when it'll be safe, if it'll ever be safe. And if you're so damn worried, why aren't you packing up?"

"Because I . . ." He cleared his throat, turned to glare out at the gardens.

"That was a wise move. Choking back any comment that resembled because you're a man. But I saw it on your face." She gave him a hard shove. "Don't think I didn't see what almost came out of your mouth."

"Don't tell me what almost came out of my mouth, and don't put words into it. I want you somewhere I don't have to worry about you."

"Nobody's asking you to worry. I've been taking care of myself for a lot of years now. I'm not so stupid, or so *pig*-headed that I'm not concerned about what's been going on. But I'm also smart enough to consider that maybe I'm the last push. Maybe I'm what's going to finish this. Roz *talked* to her, Harper. Next time maybe there'll be answers

that tell us just what happened, and what needs to be done to make it right."

"Next time? Listen to yourself. I don't want her touching you."

"It's not your decision, and I'm no quitter. Do you know me so little you'd think I'd just, yes, Harper, and trot along like a nice little puppy?"

"I'm not trying to run your life, goddamn it, Hayley. I'm just trying to protect you."

Of course, he was. And he looked so aggrieved, so frustrated, she had to sympathize. A little. "You can't. Not this way. And the only thing that you're going to accomplish by making plans around me that don't include talking to me first is piss me off."

"There's a news flash. Just give me a week then. Just do this for a week and let me try to—"

"Harper, they took her child away. They drove her mad. Maybe she was heading there anyway, but they sure as hell gave her the last push over the edge. I've been part of this for over a year now. I can't walk away from it."

She lifted her hand, stroked the bracelet she continued to wear. "She showed me this. Somehow. I'm wearing what was hers. You gave it to me. It means something. I have to find out what that is. And I, very much, need to stay here with you." She softened enough to touch his cheek. "You had to know I'd stay. What did your mother say when you said you were going to tell me to go to Stella's?"

He shrugged, walked back to the terrace rail.

"Figured that. And Stella, I imagine said the same."

"Logan agreed with me."

"I bet he did." She moved to him now, wrapped her arms around him, rested her cheek on his back.

He had a good, strong back. Working man, prince of the

castle. What a fascinating combination of both he was. "I appreciate the thought, if not the method. That help any?"

"Not so much."

"How about it's nice that you care enough about me to try to boss me around?"

"It's not bossing you around to—" He broke off with a curse and a sigh when he turned to see her grinning at him. "You're not going to budge."

"Not an inch. I think some of the Ashby blood, even as diluted as it is in me, must have stubborn corpuscles. And I want to be a part of finding the answers to all this, Harper. It's important to me, maybe more important now that I've shared a kind of consciousness with her. Boy, that sounds pretty woo-woo, but I don't know how else to say it."

"How about she invades you?"

Her face sobered. "All right, that's fair. You're still mad, and that's fair, too. I guess I don't mind knowing you're worried enough about me to be mad."

"If you're going to be reasonable about this, it's just going to piss me off more." He laid his hands on her shoulders, rubbed. "I do care about you, Hayley, and I am worried."

"I know. Just remember I care about me, too, and worry enough to be as careful as I can be."

"I'm going to stay with you tonight. I'm not budging about that."

"Good thing that's just where I want you. You know . . ." She slid her hands up his chest, linked them around his neck. "If we start fooling around, she might do something. So I think we ought to test that." She rose on her toes, played her lips over his. "Like an experiment."

"In my line of work I live for experiments."

"Come on inside." She stepped back, caught both his hands in hers. "We'll set up the lab."

* * *

LATER, WHEN THEY LAY TURNED TOWARD EACH OTHER in the dark, she brushed at his hair. "She didn't seem to be interested this time."

"You can't predict a ghost who should be haunting an asylum."

"Guess not." She snuggled closer. "You're a kind of scientist, right?"

"Kind of."

"When scientists are experimenting, they usually have to try more than once, maybe with some slight varieties, over a course of time. I've heard."

"Absolutely."

"So." She closed her eyes, all but purring at the stroke of his hand. "We'll just have to try this again, at some opportunity. Don't you think?"

"I do. And I think I hear opportunity knocking right now."

She opened her eyes, laughed into his. "They don't call that opportunity where I come from."

twelve

DAVID TURNED THE MAP UPSIDE DOWN, AND RAN A fingertip down a line of road. "We're like detectives. Like Batman and Robin."

"They weren't detectives," Harper corrected. "They were crime fighters."

"Picky, picky. All right, like Nick and Nora Charles."

"Just tell me where I turn, Nora."

"Should be a right in about two miles." David let the map lay on his lap and shifted to enjoy the scenery. "Now that we're so hot on the trail of the mysterious jewels, just what are we going to do if and when we find out where the bracelet originally came from?"

"Knowledge is power." Harper shrugged. "Something like that. And I've had enough of sitting around waiting for something to happen. The jeweler said it came from the Hopkins estate."

"Cream cheese."

"What? You're hungry?"

"Cream cheese," David repeated. "You spread it on smooth and thick. 'My girlfriend really loved the bracelet. She's got a birthday coming up soon, and since it was such a hit with her, I wondered if you had any matching pieces. Something from the same estate? That's the Kent estate, isn't it?' Guy practically fell over himself to give you the information, even if he did try to sell you a couple of gaudy rings. Ethel Hopkins did not have flawless taste. You should've sprung for the earrings, though. Hayley would love them."

"I just bought her a bracelet. Earrings are overkill at this point."

"Your right's coming up. Earrings are never overkill," he added when Harper made the turn. "About a half mile down this road. Should be on the left."

He pulled into a double drive beside a late-model Town Car, then sat tapping his fingers on the steering wheel as he studied the lay of the land.

The house was large and well-kept in an old, well-to-do neighborhood. It was a two-story English Tudor with a good selection of foundation plants, an old oak, and a nicely shaped dogwood in the front. The lawn was trimmed and lushly green, which meant lawn service or automatic sprinklers.

"Okay, what have we got here?" he queried. "Established, upper middle class."

"Ethel's only surviving daughter, Mae Hopkins Ives Fitzpatrick," David read from the notes he'd taken from the courthouse records. "She's seventy-six. Twice married, twice widowed. And you can thank me for digging that up so quickly due to my brilliant observation of Mitch's methods."

"Let's see if we can charm our way in, then get her to tell us if she remembers when her mother came by the bracelet."

They went to the door, rang the bell, and waited in the thick heat.

The woman who opened the door had a short, sleek cap of brown hair, and faded blue eyes behind the lenses of fashionable gold-framed glasses. She was tiny, maybe an inch over five feet, and workout trim in a pair of blue cotton pants and a crisp white camp shirt. There were pearls around her throat, whopping sapphires on the ring fingers of either hand, and delicate gold hoops in her ears.

"You don't look like salesmen to me." She spoke in a raspy voice and kept a hand on the handle of the screened door.

"No, ma'am." Harper warmed up his smile. "I'm Harper Ashby, and this is my friend David Wentworth. We'd like to speak with Mae Fitzpatrick."

"That's what you're doing."

Genetic good luck or, more likely, a skilled plastic surgeon, Harper thought, had shaved a good ten years off her seventy-six. "I'm pleased to meet you, Miz Fitzpatrick. I realize this is an odd sort of intrusion, but I wonder if we might come in and have a word with you?"

The color of her eyes might have been faded, but the expression of them was sharp as a scalpel. "Do I look like the simpleminded sort of woman who lets strange men into her house?"

"No, ma'am." But he had to wonder why a woman who claimed good sense would believe a screened door was any sort of barrier. "If you wouldn't mind then, if I could just ask you a few questions regarding a—"

"Ashby, you said?"

"Yes, ma'am."

"Any relation to Miriam Norwood Ashby?"

"Yes, ma'am. She was my paternal grandmother."

"I knew her a little."

"I can't really claim the same."

"Don't expect so, as she's been dead some time now. You'd be Rosalind Harper's boy then."

"Yes, ma'am, her oldest."

"I've met her a time or two. First time being at her wedding to John Ashby. You have the look of her, don't you?"

"I do. Yes, ma'am."

She slid her eyes toward David. "This isn't your brother."

"A family friend, Miz Fitzpatrick," David said with a full-wattage smile. "I live at Harper House, and work for Rosalind. Perhaps you'd feel more at ease if you contacted Miz Harper before you speak to us. We'd be happy to give you a number where you can reach her, and wait out here while you do."

Instead she opened the screen. "I don't believe Miriam Ashby's grandson is going to knock me unconscious and rob me. Y'all come in."

"Thank you."

The house was as neat and well-tended as its mistress, with polished oak floors and muted green walls. She let them into a generous living room that was furnished in a contemporary, almost minimalistic style.

"I suppose you boys could use a cold drink."

"We don't want to put you to any trouble, Miz Fitzpatrick," Harper told her.

"Sweet tea's simple enough. Have a seat. I'll be with you in a minute."

"Classy," David commented when she left the room. "A bit pared down, but classy."

"The place, or her?"

"Both." He took a seat on the sofa. "Ashby-Harper is a very slick entree. Charm wouldn't have worked on her."

"Interesting she knew my grandmother—she's some younger—and that she was invited to my mother's wedding. All these little intersections. I wonder if one of her ancestors knew Reginald or Beatrice."

"Coincidence is only coincidence if you don't have an open mind."

"Living with a ghost tends to leave it gaping." Harper got to his feet as Mae came back with a tray of glasses. "Let me get that for you. We very much appreciate your time, Miz Fitzpatrick." He set the tray on the coffee table. "I'll try not to take up too much of it."

"Your grandmother was a kindhearted woman. While I didn't know her intimately, your grandfather and my first husband had a small business venture together many years ago. A real estate venture," she added, "that was satisfactorily profitable for all involved. Now, why has her grandson come knocking on my door?"

"It has to do with a bracelet from your mother's estate."

She angled her head with polite interest. "My mother's estate."

"Yes, ma'am. It happens that I bought this bracelet from the jeweler who acquired it from the estate."

"And is there something wrong with the bracelet?"

"No. No, ma'am. I'm hoping you might remember some of the history of it, as I'm very interested in its origins. I'm told it was made sometime around 1890. It's made up of ruby hearts framed in diamonds."

"Yes, I know the piece. I sold it and several others recently as they weren't to my taste and saw no reason to have them sitting in a safety deposit box as they had been since my mother's death some years ago." She sipped her tea as she watched him. "You're curious about its history?"

"Yes, ma'am, I am."

"But not forthcoming with your reasons."

"Oddly enough, I have reason to believe it—or one very like it—was in my family. When I discovered that, I found it interesting and thought satisfying my curiosity would be worth a little time in trying to trace it back."

"Is that so? Now, that I find interesting. The bracelet was given by my grandfather to my grandmother in 1893, as an anniversary gift. It's possible that there was more than one made, in that same design, at the time."

"Yes, possibly."

"There is, however, a story behind it, if you'd like to hear it."

"I really would."

She held out the plate of cookies she'd brought out with the tea, waited until each of the men had taken one. Then she settled back with a hint of a smile on her face. "My grandparents did not have a happy marriage, my grandfather being somewhat of a scoundrel. He enjoyed gambling and shady deals and the company of loose women— according to my grandmother, who lived to the ripe age of ninety-eight, so I knew her quite well."

Rising, she walked to an étagère and took down a photo framed in slim silver.

"My grandparents," she said, passing the photo to Harper. "A formal portrait taken in 1891. You can see, scoundrel or not, he was quite handsome."

"Both are." And, Harper noted, the style of dress, hair, even the photographic tone was similar to the copies of photographs Mitch had pinned to his workboard.

"She's a beauty." David glanced up. "You favor her."

"So I've been told. Physically, and in temperament." Obviously pleased, she took the photo, replaced it. "My grandmother claimed two of the happiest days of her life

were her wedding day, when she was too young and foolish to know what she was getting into, and the day she became a widow—some twelve years later, and could enjoy life without the burden of a man who couldn't be trusted."

She sat again, picked up her tea. "A handsome man, as you saw for yourselves. A charming man, by all accounts, and one who had considerable success with the gambling and the shady deals. But my grandmother was a moral sort of woman. One who managed to bend those morals, just enough to enjoy the results of her husband's successes, even as she decried them."

She set down her tea, sat back, obviously relishing her role. "She told the story, often, of discovering—during one of my grandfather's drunken confessions that the anniversary gift—the ruby hearts—had come from a somewhat less than reputable source. He had acquired it in a payoff of a gambling debt from a man who bought jewelry and so forth on the cheap from those unfortunate or desperate enough to have to sell their possessions quickly. Often, more likely, from those who had stolen those possessions and used him as a fence."

She smiled broadly now, no doubt relishing the thought. "It had belonged to a wealthy man's mistress, and was stolen from her by one of the servants after she had been cut off by him. The story, as my grandmother claimed it was told to her, was that the woman had gone raving mad, and had subsequently vanished."

She reached for her tea, sipped. "I always wondered if that story was true."

HARPER WENT TO HIS MOTHER FIRST, AND KNELT DOWN beside her in the gardens at home. Absently, he began to help her weed.

"I heard you took some time off today," she began.

"I had something I wanted to do. Why aren't you wearing a hat?"

"I forgot it. I was only going to come out for a minute, then I got started."

He pulled off the ballcap he wore, tugged it down over her head. "Do you remember how so many times after school, if I was working out here when you came home, you'd sit down beside me, help me weed or plant and tell me your troubles, or your triumphs of the day?"

"I remember you were always here to listen. To me, to Austin and Mason. Sometimes to all three of us at once. How'd you do that?"

"A mother's got an ear for the voices of her children. Like a conductor for each separate instrument in his orchestra, even in the middle of a symphony. What are your troubles, baby boy?"

"You were right about Hayley."

"I make being right a policy. What was I right about exactly?"

"That she wouldn't move over to Logan's because I asked her to."

Under the bill, Roz's eyebrows arched. "Asked her?"

"Asked her, told her." He shrugged. "What's the difference when you've got the person's welfare in mind?"

She let out a husky laugh, patted her dirty hands on his cheeks. "Such a man."

"A minute ago I was your baby boy."

"My baby boy is such a man. I don't see that as a flaw. An amusement sometimes—such as now—a puzzlement now and then, and on rare occasions a damned irritation. Are you fighting? It didn't seem to me you were at odds when you came down to breakfast together this morning."

"No, we're all right. If you don't like me sleeping with her in the house, I get that."

"So you'll respect the sanctity of our home and sleep with her elsewhere?"

"Yeah."

"I slept with men I wasn't married to in Harper House. It's not a cathedral, it's a home. Yours as much as mine. If you're having sex with Hayley, you might as well have it comfortably. And safely," she added with a direct look.

Even after all these years, it made his shoulders hunch. "I buy my own condoms these days."

"I'm glad to hear it."

"And that isn't what I wanted to get into. I traced the bracelet back to Amelia."

Those eyes widened as she sat back on her heels. "You did? That was fast work."

"Fast work, coincidence, lucky break. I'm not sure where it falls. It came from the estate of an Esther Hopkins. She's been dead a few years now, apparently, and her daughter decided to go ahead and sell some of the things she didn't like, or care to keep. Mae Fitzpatrick. She said she knew you."

"Mae Fitzpatrick." Roz closed her eyes and tried to flip through the vast mental files of acquaintances. "I'm sorry, it doesn't seem familiar."

"She was married before. Wait a minute . . . Ives?"

"Mae Ives doesn't ring bells either."

"Well, she said she'd only met you a couple of times. Once was when you married Daddy. She was at your wedding."

"Is that a fact? Well, that's interesting, but not all that surprising. I think between my mama and John's we had everybody in Shelby County and most of Tennessee at the wedding."

"She knew Grandma Ashby."

He sat on the garden path with her and told her of the conversation he'd had with Mae Fitzpatrick.

"Amazing, isn't it," she mused. "All those little angles and curls, and how they fit together."

"I know. Mama, she had it figured. Too well-bred to say it right out, but she put it together, about Reginald Harper being the wealthy protector who'd cast his mistress off. She's likely to talk about it."

"And you think that bothers me? Honey, the fact that my great-grandfather had mistresses, that he kept women, tossed them aside, and lived a life generally rife with infidelity isn't a reflection on me, or you. His behavior isn't our responsibility, which is something I sincerely wish Amelia would realize."

She dug out more weeds. "As to the rest of his behavior, which is beyond deplorable, it's not our fault either. Mitch is writing about it. Unless you and your brothers feel strongly that all of this should be kept as closely within the family as possible, I want him to do this book."

"Why?"

"It's not our fault, it's not our responsibility. That's all true," she said as she sat back to look at him. "But I feel that airing all of this is somehow giving her her due. It's a way to acknowledge an ancestor who, no matter what she did, what she became, was treated shabbily at best, monstrously at worst."

She lifted her hand, pressed her soil-streaked palm to his. "She's our blood."

"Does that make me heartless because I want her gone, I want her ended for what she nearly did to you, for what she's doing now to Hayley?"

"No. It means Hayley and I are closer to your heart. That's enough for today." She swiped her hands on the

thighs of her gardening pants. "We're going to boil in this wet heat if we stay out much longer. Come on inside with me. Let's sit in the cool and have a beer."

"Tell me something." He studied the house as they walked down the path. "How did you know that Daddy was the one?"

"Stars in my eyes." She laughed, and despite the heat hooked an arm through his. "I swear, stars in my eyes. I was so young, and he put stars in my eyes. But that was in-fatuation. I think I knew that he was mine when we talked for hours one night. I snuck out of the house to meet him. God, my daddy would have skinned him alive. But all we did was talk, hour after hour, under a willow tree. He was just a boy, but I knew I'd love him all of my life. And I have. I knew because we sat there, almost till dawn, and he made me laugh, and made me think and dream and trem-ble. I never thought I'd love again. But I do. It takes noth-ing away from your father, Harper."

"Mama. I know." He closed a hand over hers. "How did you know with Mitch?"

"I guess I was too cynical for those stars, at least at first. It was slower, and scarier. He makes me laugh and think and dream and tremble. And there was a time during that longer, slower climb that I looked at him, and my heart warmed again. I'd forgotten what it was like to feel that warmth inside the heart."

"He's a good man. He loves you. He watches you when you come into a room, when you walk out of one. I'm glad you found him."

"So am I."

"With Daddy? What willow was it?"

"Oh, it was a big, beautiful old tree, way back, beyond the old stables." She paused, looked toward the ruin, ges-tured. "John was going to come back sometime soon after,

carve our initials in the trunk. But that next night lightning struck it, split it right in two, and—Oh my God."

"Amelia," he said softly.

"It had to be. It never occurred to me before this, but I remember there hadn't been a storm. The servants were talking about the tree and the lightning hitting it when there hadn't been a storm."

"So even then," he said, "she took her shots."

"How mean, how petty of her. I cried over that tree. I fell in love under it, and cried when I watched the groundskeepers clear away the wood and pull the trunk out."

"Don't you wonder if there were other things? Small, violent acts we passed off as nature or some strange quirk, all while we thought of her as benevolent?"

He studied the house now, thought of what it was to him—and what had walked there long before he was born. "She's never been benevolent, not really."

"All that hate and anger stored up. Trapped."

"Leaking now and again, like water through a crack in a dam. It's coming faster and harder now. And we can't put it back in, Mama. What we have to do is empty it out, draw out every drop."

"How?"

"I think we're going to have to break the dam, while we're the ones holding the hammer."

IT WAS TWILIGHT WHEN HAYLEY WANDERED THROUGH the gardens. The baby was asleep, and Roz and Mitch were taking monitor duty. Harper's car was there, so he was *somewhere*. Not in the carriage house, because she'd knocked, then poked her head in and called.

It wasn't as if they were joined at the hip, she reminded herself. But he hadn't stayed for dinner. He'd said he'd had

something to do, that he'd be back before dark.

Well, it was nearly dark, and she was just wondering.

Besides, she liked walking in the gardens, in the gloaming. Even under the circumstances. It was soothing, and she could use a little soothing after running the story he'd told her about the bracelet over and over in her head.

They were getting closer to the answers, she was sure of it. But she was no longer sure it would all end quietly once they had them.

Amelia might not be content to give up her last links with this world and pass on—she supposed that was the term—to the next.

She liked inhabiting a body. If you could call it inhabiting. Sharing one? Sliding through one? Whatever it was, Amelia liked it, of that Hayley was sure. Just as she was sure it was something as new for Amelia as it was for herself.

If it happened again—*when,* she corrected, ordering herself to face facts. When it happened again, she was going to fight to stay more aware, to find more control.

And wasn't that what she was doing out here alone, in the half light? No point in pretending to herself this wasn't a deliberate move. A sort of dare. *Come on, bitch.* She wanted to see what she could handle, and how she would handle it when no one else was around to run interference. Or be hurt.

But nothing was happening. She felt completely normal, completely herself.

And was completely herself when sounds out of the shadows made her jump. She stopped, caught in the crosshairs of fight or flight, ears straining. The rhythmic, repetitive sound made her frown as she inched forward.

It sounded . . . but it couldn't be. Still her heart beat like wings as she crept closer, envisioning a ghostly figure digging a grave.

Amelia's grave. It could be. This could be the answer, at last. Reginald had murdered her, then buried her here on the property. She was going to be shown the grave—on unconsecrated ground. They could have it blessed or marked or—well, she'd look up what was done in cases like this.

Then the haunting of Harper House would be over.

She picked her way quietly around the ruins of the stables, edging as close to the building as she dared. Her palms sprang damp, and her breath seemed to rattle in her throat.

She turned the corner of the building, following the sound, prepared to be terrified and amazed.

And saw Harper, his T-shirt stripped off and tossed to the ground, digging a hole.

The letdown had the breath expelling from her lungs in a frantic whoosh.

"Harper, for Christ's sake, you scared me brainless. What are you doing?"

He continued to spear the blade of the shovel into the ground, tossing the dirt into the pile beside it. Though she was still jittery, she cast her eyes skyward, then marched to him.

"I said—" He jumped a clean foot off the ground when she poked a finger in his back. And even as she yelped in response, he whirled, cocking the shovel over his shoulder like a bat. He managed to check his swing, cursed a blue streak as she stumbled back and fell hard on her ass.

"Jesus, God almighty!" He dragged the headset down to his shoulders. "What the hell are you doing, sneaking around in the dark?"

"I didn't sneak, I called you. If you didn't play that headset so loud you could hear a person when they said something. I thought you were going to brain me with that shovel. I thought . . ."

She began to giggle, tried to snuff it back. "You should've

seen your face. Your eyes were this big." She held up her hands, curling her fingers into wide balls, then dissolved into laughter when he snarled at her.

"Oh, oh, I'm going to wet my pants. Wait." She squeezed her eyes, bounced quickly in place while more giggles bubbled. "Okay, okay, back in control. The least you could do is help me up after you knocked me down."

"I didn't knock you down. Damn near though." He offered a hand, pulled her up.

"I thought you were Reginald, digging Amelia's untimely grave."

Shaking his head, he leaned on the shovel and stared at her. "So you came on around to what, give him a hand?"

"Well, I had to see, didn't I? What in the world are you doing, digging a hole out here in the dark?"

"It's not dark."

"You said it was dark when you yelled at me. What are you doing?"

"Playing third base for the Atlanta Braves."

"I don't see why you're being pissy. I'm the one who fell down and nearly wet her pants."

"Sorry. Did you hurt yourself?"

"No. You planting that tree?" She finally focused in on the slim, young willow. "Why are you planting a tree, Harper, back here and at this time of night?"

"It's for Mama. She told me this story today, about how she snuck out of the house to meet my father one night, and that they sat under a willow that used to be back here, and talked. That's when she fell in love with him. The next day it got hit by lightning. Amelia," he said and dug out another shovelful of dirt. "She didn't put it together before, but you've got to figure the odds. So I'm putting one in for her."

She stood silently for a moment while he eyeballed the hole, then the rootball, then dug some more.

"That's the sweetest thing. That just coats my heart with sweetness, Harper. Can I help, or is it something you want to do alone?"

"Hole's about right. You can help me put it in."

"I never planted a tree before."

"See, you want the hole about three times as wide as the rootball, but no deeper. Get the sides of the hole loose so the roots have room to spread."

He picked up the tree, set it in the hole. "How's that look to you?"

"It looks right, like you said."

"Now you peel the burlap back, from the main stem, then we'll see the original soil line, at least we will if you turn on that flashlight over there, because it is getting dark. Took me a while to get everything I needed for this."

She turned it on, crouched down and aimed. "How's that?"

"Good. See?" He tapped a finger on the mark at the base. "That's the soil line, and we've got the right depth here. We've just got a little bit of roots that need pruning off. Hand me those."

She got the clippers, passed them to him. "You know digging a hole for a tree sounds the same as digging a grave."

He flicked her a look. "Have you ever heard anybody digging a grave?"

"In movies."

"Right. We're going to fill the hole, but we do it little by little and firm the soil down as we do. I don't have any spare gloves. Here."

"No." She waved him back when he started to pull off his work gloves. "A little dirt won't hurt me. Am I doing this right?"

"Yeah, that's good. You just keep filling and firming,

hilling it up toward the base and leaving a kind of shallow moat around the edge of the hole."

"I like the way it feels. The dirt."

"I know what you mean." When they'd finished to his satisfaction, he took out his knife, trimmed off the exposed burlap, then pushed to his feet. "We'll give it plenty of water, pour it into the rim around the mound, see?"

He hauled up one of the buckets he'd filled, nodded when she lifted the other.

"There, you planted a tree."

"Helped plant one anyway." She stepped back, reached out a hand for his. "It looks lovely, Harper. It'll mean a lot to her that you thought to do this."

"It meant something to me to do it." He gave her hand a squeeze, then bent to pick up his tools. "Probably should've waited until next spring, but I wanted to do it now. A kind of nose-thumbing. Go ahead and knock them down, we'll just put them back up. I wanted to do it now."

"You're so angry with her."

"I'm not a kid, charmed by lullabies anymore. I've seen her for what she is."

Hayley shook her head, shivered a little in the close evening air. "I don't think any of us have seen her for what she is. Not yet."

thirteen

THE GRAFTING HOUSE WAS MORE THAN A WORK SPACE for Harper. It was also part playhouse, part sanctuary, and part lab. He could, and often did, lose himself for hours inside its warm, music-filled air, working, experimenting, or just reveling in being the only human among the plants.

A lot of times he preferred the plants to humans. Though he wasn't altogether sure what that said about him, he wasn't all that concerned about it.

He'd found his passion in life, and considered himself fortunate that he could make a living doing something that made him completely happy.

His brothers had to leave home to find theirs. It was the bonus round for him that he'd been able to stay where he loved, and do what he loved.

He had his home, his work, his family. Throughout his adult life he'd had women he'd liked and enjoyed. But none

of them had ever made him think, had ever nudged him to consider the next step on the rung of what he'd thought of vaguely as The Future.

He hadn't worried about that either. His vision of marriage was reflected in what he knew his parents had together. Love, dedication, respect, and tempering it all, like an alloy in steel, an unwavering friendship.

He understood his mother had found that a second time, with Mitch. Not so much lightning striking twice as a true and perfect graft that united to make a new and healthy plant.

In his mind, nothing less strong, less important was worth the time or risk.

So he'd enjoyed the women who'd passed through his life, and had never pictured any of them as The One.

Until Hayley.

Now, so much of his world had changed, while other parts of it remained, comfortably, the same.

He'd flipped on Chopin for his plants' enjoyment today. And had P.O.D rocking the party on his headset.

The space might not appear efficient with its groupings of plants in various stages of growth, the buckets of gravel or wood chips, the scatter of tapes and twine, clothespins and labels. There were scraps of burlap, piles of pots, bags of soil, tangles of rubber bands. Trays of knives and clippers. But he knew where to find what he wanted when he needed it.

There might have been times he couldn't put his hands on a pair of matching socks, but he could always put them on the tool he needed.

He walked along, airing the tents and cases that housed his plants, as he did every morning. A few minutes without their covers would dry off any surface moisture that might have condensed on his rootstocks. Fungal disease was always a worry. Still, too much air might dry out the union.

As he aired them, he checked specimens for progress, for any signs of disease or rot. He was particularly pleased with the camellia he'd cleft-grafted over the winter. His specimens would take another year, perhaps two to flower, but he believed they'd be worth the wait.

The work required his passion, but it also required his patience, and his faith.

He made notes to be transcribed to his computer files. There was active, steady growth in the astrophytum seedlings he had protected under a bottle cloche, and the nurse grafts of his clematis looked strong and healthy.

Making the rounds once more, he retented the plants. He'd need to check the pond later to study the water lilies and irises he'd hybridized. A side and personal experiment he hoped would prove rewarding.

Plus, it would give him an excuse to take a cooling dip in the heat of the day.

But for now, he had several cultivars to see to.

He gathered the tools he'd need, then selected a healthy rootstock from his pot-grown lantana, made the oblique cut, then matched it with a scion of viburnum. The girths were similar enough that he was able to use the simple slant of each cut to place them together so the cambiums on each side met truly.

Using elastic bands, he kept the pressure light and even as he bound them together. Judging the graft good, he used grafting wax to seal the joining. He set it in a seed tray, covered the roots and graft with moist soil—his mother's mix—then labeled.

Once he'd repeated the process several times, he tented the tray, and swiveled to his computer to log in the work.

Before he started on the next house specimens, he switched his music to Michelle Branch and pulled a Coke from his cooler.

By the time he'd finished, Michelle had played through and his morning's work was completed.

He gathered a bag of tools and supplies, left his headset behind, and went out to check his field-grown and water plants.

There were a few customers wandering around, scouting out the discounted stock under shade screens or poking into the public greenhouses. He knew if he didn't make his escape quickly, one of them might catch him.

He didn't mind talking plants or directing a customer toward what they were looking for. He just preferred keeping his mind in the game, and right now that game was checking his field plants.

He made it past the portulaca before someone called his name. Should've kept the headset on, he thought, but turned, readying up his customer smile.

The brunette had a curvy little body, which he'd had occasion to see naked several times. At the moment, she was showing it off in belly-baring shorts and a brief top designed to make a man give thanks for August heat.

With a delighted laugh, she bounced up on her toes, clamped her arms around his neck and gave him a loud smack of a kiss. She still tasted of bing cherries, and brought back a flood of equally sweet memories.

Instinctively he gave her a hard hug before stepping back to get a better view. "Dory, what're you doing in town? How've you been?"

"I've been terrific, and I just moved back. Just a couple weeks ago. Got a job with a PR firm here. I got tired of Miami, missed being home, too, I guess."

She'd probably changed her hair from the last time he'd seen her. Women were forever changing their hair. But since he wasn't absolutely sure, he fell back on the standard: "You look great."

"Feel the same. And look at you, all buff and tan. I was going to call you but I wasn't sure you were still living in that sweet little house."

"Yeah, still there."

"I was hoping. I always loved that place. How's your mama, and David, and your brothers, and oh, just everybody." She gave a bubbling laugh, threw out her arms. "I feel like I've been living on Mars for the past three years."

"Everybody's good. Mama got married a few weeks ago."

"I heard. My mama caught me up with some of the local news. I heard you haven't."

"Haven't what? Oh, no."

"I was thinking you and I could do some catching up." Dory trailed a finger down his chest. "I'd love to see your place again. I could pick up some Chinese, a bottle of wine. Like the old days."

"Ah, well . . ."

"A kind of welcome-home and thank-you for you helping me pick out some houseplants for my new place. You'll do that, won't you, Harper? I'd like a few nice ones."

"Sure. I mean, sure I'll help you pick out some plants. But—"

"Why don't we go inside, out of this heat. You can tell me what you've been up to while you help me out. But save some of the good stuff for later."

She took his hand, squeezing it as she tugged him with her. "I've missed seeing you," she continued. "We barely had a chance to talk when I was up for a few days last year. I was going out with that photographer then, remember? I told you."

"Yeah." Vaguely. "And I'm—"

"Well, that is so over. I don't know why I wasted a year of my life on a man so self-centered. It was always about him, you know what I mean? What made me think I

wanted to hook up with the artistic, broody type?"

"I—"

"So I shook him and the sand out of my shoes, and here I am."

Inside, she turned and slid her hands in the back pockets of his jeans. An old habit of hers that brought on another memory flash. "I really have missed the hell right out of you. You're glad to see me, aren't you, Harper?"

"Sure. Sure, I am. The thing is, Dory, I'm seeing somebody."

"Oh." Her full bottom lip pouted. "Some serious somebody?"

"Yeah."

"Oh well." She left her hands in his pockets another moment, then drew them out. Gave his ass a little pat. "I guess I figured it would take a lot of luck on my part for you to be flying solo. How long have you been seeing her?"

"Depends. What I mean is, I've known her awhile, but we've only started . . . we've only been involved recently."

"Looks like I should've gotten here sooner. We're still friends, right? Good friends."

"We always were."

"That's what I remembered, and I guess what I missed with Justin, the photographer. We never managed to be friends, and we sure as hell weren't anything close to friends when it fell apart. You, on the other hand. I was telling another friend of mine not long ago how I've never been dumped as sweetly as I was with you."

She laughed, rose on her toes to kiss him lightly. "You're a rare one, Harper."

She stepped back, and seconds later, Hayley came through the glass doors. "I'm sorry, am I interrupting? Is there something I can help you with?"

"No, thanks. Harper's giving me a hand." Dory patted

hers on his arm. "I'm clueless about plants, so I came to the expert."

"Hayley, this is Dory. We went to college together."

"Is that right?" She smiled, widely. "I don't think I've seen you in here before."

"I haven't been, for a long time. I've just moved back from Miami. New job, fresh start, you know how it goes."

"Don't I just," Hayley purred with that wide smile still in place.

"I decided I'd come see Harper, and catch up, and get a few plants to liven up my new apartment. Wait till you see it, Harper, it's a big step up from the hole I rented off-campus back in the day."

"Anything would be. I hope you got rid of that futon."

"I burned it. Harper hated that thing," she said to Hayley. "Even offered to buy me a bed, but all I had was this tiny little place—just one room. If I had three people over, we were so crammed together we were halfway to an orgy."

"Those were the days," Harper said, and made Dory laugh.

"Weren't they? Well, you'd better show me what I'm going to need, or I'll keep you talking the rest of the day."

"I'll just leave y'all alone." Hayley backed out the doors.

She got back to work, but made certain she wasn't on checkout duty when Dory was ready to pay for the plants Harper selected for her. But she could hear Dory laugh—a particularly grating laugh, in her opinion—as she stocked shelves across the room.

Harper leaned on the counter through the process, she noted out of the corner of her eye. And just look how he wore that lazy smile of his while they talked about mutual friends and the good old days.

And damn if that Dory didn't keep touching him. Little pats and pokes in between her hair flips. The steam began

to rise from her belly up to her throat as Harper pulled the cart of potted plants out to Dory's car.

Hayley decided she really needed to check the stock of the shelves by the window. And if a person happened to look out while they were working, it wasn't spying. It was glancing.

Enough of a glance that she saw Harper lean down and exchange a liplock with his college buddy.

Bastard.

Then he waved her off before strolling around the side of the building like he wasn't a low-life cheating scum. Worse, the sort that did his low-life cheating right in front of her face.

You'd think he'd have the courtesy, the good breeding, to at least do it behind her back.

Well, that was just fine. She wasn't going to let it matter. She wasn't going to give a single wrinkled, balled-up damn.

And she wasn't going outside to kick him in his two-timing balls either. She was just going out to see if any customers needed her assistance.

That's what she got paid for. Not for flirting, not for spending half the day reminiscing. And certainly not for kissing customers before she waved bye-bye.

She was nearly to the grafting house when she saw him out in the field. He was already crouched down, examining grafts on the magnolias she'd helped him graft and plant weeks before.

He flicked her a glance and a smile as she approached. "Take a look. These are coming along. Couple of weeks we can remove the tape."

"If you say so."

"Yeah, they're looking good. I need to check some of the other ornamentals. I think we're going to have some

nice weeping pears and cherries for next season. Have I shown you the fruiting pears I did? The dwarfs?"

"No. Did your friend get what she was after?"

"Hmm. Yeah." He rose, walked across to check the balance of the canopies on his weepers. "Kept it simple," he said absently as he studied the tree. "Low maintenance. What I did here was use *pyrus communis* for stock—three-year-olds, and grafted three pendulas. You gotta make sure you get the spacing right, so you produce a nice shape."

"And you know all about shapes."

"Yeah. I like chip-budding these. I did these two springs ago, and these this spring. See how they develop?"

"I see how a lot of things develop. I was surprised you didn't go with her, carry the plants to her door."

"Who? Oh, Dory?" He flipped Hayley an absent look as sarcasm sailed, visibly, over his head. "She'll be able to handle it. A couple trips."

He continued to walk, continued to examine.

"Here? For these weeping cherries, I used a semi-dwarfing rootstock. Should make a nice specimen tree for smaller spaces. 'Round October, I'm going to take some ripe shoots from the Colt stock. What you do is bundle them, and drop them root-end down in a trench in the nursery bed, and hill 'em up so they're about three-quarters buried. Then next spring, we'll lift the bundles, plant the cuttings, and by summer they'll be ready to use for rootstocks."

"That's all just fascinating, Harper. Did you spend all that time with Dory lecturing her on how to make a damn rootstock?"

"Huh." His distraction was evident on his face as he glanced around. "She's not interested in this kind of work. She's in public relations."

"Private ones from what I saw."

"What?"

"I was about to come back and suggest the two of you get a room. You ought to know better than to make out in one of the retail areas."

This time his mouth dropped open. "*What?* We weren't. We were just—"

"Those doors are glass, Harper, in case you've forgotten. I saw you, and you ought to have more respect for your workplace than to fool around in one of the public areas during working hours. But as you're the boss, I guess you can do what the hell you like."

"My mother's the boss, and I wasn't fooling around anywhere. Dory and I are old friends. We were just—"

"Kissing, touching, flirting, making dates. It's unprofessional, in my opinion, to do that during work hours. But it's downright rude to do it in front of me."

"Behind your back would be better?"

Because it echoed her own nasty thoughts, her eyes went hot, searing like suns. "Let me just say, fuck you, Harper."

Since it was as good an exit line as she could think of when her brain was ready to explode, she turned on her heel. And spun right back when he grabbed her arm.

He didn't look distracted now, she noted. He looked ice-cold mad. "I wasn't flirting or making dates."

"Just kissing and touching then."

"I kissed her because she's a friend, a good one, who I haven't seen in a while. I kissed her the way you kiss a friend. Which is nothing like this, for instance."

He gave her a yank that threw her off balance so her body collided with his. Then was scooped up, pulled in. He got a fistful of her hair, gave it a quick tug. And had his mouth crushed to hers.

Not sweetly, not warmly, but with the stark heat of raw temper. She struggled, shocked that she was clamped so

hard and tight she couldn't fight her way free. A thread of
fear snaked through her anger, and began to tighten just before he let her go.

"That's how I kiss women I don't feel friendly toward."

"You think you have the right to treat me that way?"

"As much as you do to accuse me of doing something,
of being something I'm not. I don't cheat and I don't lie,
and I'm not going to apologize for my behavior. If you
want to know something about my relationship with Dory,
or anyone else, past or present, then ask. But don't come
tearing into me with accusations."

"I saw—"

"Maybe you saw what you were ready to see. That's on
you, Hayley. Now I've got work. If you've got any more to
say about this, then say it after hours."

He strode off toward the pond, leaving her no choice, as
she saw it, but to storm away in the opposite direction.

"THEN HE HAD THE NERVE, THE *NERVE* TO SNAP AT ME
and act like I was in the wrong." Hayley paced back and
forth on Stella's front porch while Lily raced over the lawn
after Parker. "Acting like I've got a dirty mind or that I'm
some crazy jealous witch because I have a reasonable and
legitimate complaint about him slobbering all over another
woman. And in front of my face."

"Before you said she was slobbering over him."

"It was mutual slobbering. And when I walked in on
them, after seeing all this going on through the door, he
acts like it's nothing. He doesn't even have the grace to
look embarrassed or nervous."

"So you said." Twice, Stella thought, but she understood
the nature of female friendship and didn't mention the repetition. "Sweetie, we've both known Harper for some time

now. Don't you think he would've looked embarrassed if he'd been caught doing something he shouldn't?"

"I guess I just don't mean enough to him for it to embarrass him."

"Now stop. That's not true."

"It feels true." Hayley slumped to the steps. "It feels awful."

"I know." Sitting beside her, Stella wrapped her arm around her shoulders. "I know it does. I'm so sorry you were hurt."

"He doesn't even care."

"Yes, he does. Maybe what you saw hit you wrong because of the way you feel about him."

"Stella, he *kissed* her."

"He's kissed me, too."

"It's not the same."

"If you hadn't met me before, and you saw him kiss me, what would you think?"

"Before or after I mentally ripped your lungs out through your nose?"

"Ouch. I'm not saying it didn't look bad, but that you might have, possibly, misinterpreted. I'm saying that because I know Harper, and because of his reaction."

"You're saying I overreacted."

"I'm saying, if I were you, I'd want to find out for sure."

"He slept with her. Okay, okay," she muttered when Stella stared at her. "Before, and before is before, blah blah. But she was so pretty. She had a great body, and those dark, exotic eyes. And this sheen, you know, this polish. Oh, hell."

"You're going to go talk to him."

"I guess."

"Want me to keep Lily while you do?"

"No." Hayley let out a long sigh. "She needs her supper

soon, and besides, if I take her with me we're not as likely
to yell at each other."

"All right. You can call me if you want, let me know how
it goes. Or you can just come back over. I'll break out the
Ben and Jerry's."

"Way I'm feeling, I'll need a full quart."

SHE HAD LILY'S HAND IN HERS WHEN SHE KNOCKED
on the door of the carriage house. He hadn't been long out
of the shower, she noted when he answered. His hair was
still damp. But if the grim set of his face was any barome-
ter, it hadn't cooled him off.

"I'd like to talk to you." She said it briskly. "If you have
the time."

He simply bent down to pick up Lily who'd already
wrapped her arms around his leg. He turned, without a
word for Hayley, and carried the baby back toward the
kitchen. "Hey, pretty girl. Look what we got here."

One-handed, he opened a cupboard, took out a couple
of plastic bowls, then rooted through a drawer for a big
plastic spoon. He set them, and Lily, on the floor where she
immediately went to town banging.

"Want a drink?" he said to Hayley.

"No, no, I don't. I want to ask you—"

"I'm having a beer. You want any milk or juice for Lily?"

"I didn't bring her sippy cup."

"I have one."

"Oh." The fact that he did threw her off, made her heart
start to melt. "She could have a little juice. You have to di-
lute it."

"I've seen the routine." He fixed the juice, handed it to
Lily, then got out a beer. "So?" He took a long gulp.

"I wanted to ask—No, I wanted to say that I know we

haven't made any sort of commitment to each other. But sleeping with someone is a form of commitment to me, enough of one that it's insulting to see the person I'm sleeping with kissing and flirting with another woman. And I don't find that unreasonable."

He took another pull, slowly, thoughtfully. "You know if you'd put it that way to begin with, you wouldn't have insulted me, or pissed me off. I'm going to repeat that I was flirting with Dory, but not the way you mean."

"If you come on to all women the way—"

"Or coming on to her. And be careful or you'll piss me off again. If you want to know what was going on, why don't you ask?"

"I don't like being in this position."

"Well, neither do I. If that's the way you want to leave it, I need to throw something together for dinner. I missed lunch."

"Fine." She started to bend down for Lily, then stopped. "Why are you so hard?"

"Why are you so mistrustful?"

"I *saw* you. She had her arms around you. She put her hands in your damn pockets and felt your ass. You weren't exactly fighting her off, Harper."

"Okay, you've got a point. It was something she used to do, and I didn't think much about it when she did it today. I was thinking more how I was going to tell her I couldn't pick things up with her, couldn't see her beyond the friendship thing because I was with somebody else."

"How long does it take to say that?"

"A little longer than it might otherwise if a woman's got her hands on your ass." She opened her mouth, but the way his eyebrows shot up had her closing it again, and waiting. "Right or wrong, Hayley. But I did tell her, before you came through the door."

"Before? But . . . you didn't even miss a beat, Harper. And the two of you were all . . ." She waved a hand, trying to find the phrase. "Touchy. And you kissed her when you went out to the car."

His eyes narrowed. "You were watching us."

"No. Yes. So what?"

"Too bad you didn't manage to slip a listening device on me, then this conversation wouldn't be necessary."

She folded her arms and met his insult straight-on. "I'm not apologizing for my behavior either."

"Fine. First, why should I have missed a beat? I wasn't doing anything to feel guilty about. Next, Dory's a touchy kind of person. She makes contact with people, which is probably why she's good in PR. And yeah, I kissed her before she left. I'll probably kiss her next time I see her. I like her. We have a history. We met in high school, ended up in college together—and ended up being an item for about a year. In college, Hayley, for Christ's sake. When we stopped being an item, we stayed friends. If you can manage to whip some of the green out of your vision, you'd probably end up being friends with her, too."

"I don't like being jealous. I've never really been jealous before, and I don't like it."

"If you'd heard our conversation out by her car, you'd have heard her tell me that she hoped you and I would come into the city, have drinks, so she could get to know you. She said it was good to see me, and good to see me happy. I said pretty much the same, and I kissed her goodbye."

"It's just . . . you looked like a couple."

"We're not. That's what you and I are. That's what I feel," he said when she only stared at him. "That's what I want. I don't know what I've done to make you doubt me, or that."

"You've never actually said . . ."

He stepped to her, caught her face in his hands. "I don't want to be with anyone but you. You're the only one, Hayley. Is that clear enough?"

"Yeah." She laid her hand on his, turned her head so that her lips pressed to his palm.

"So we're good now?"

"It looks like. Um, you told her you were seeing someone. I mean me?"

"I didn't have to. When you walked back out, she punched me in the arm. She said, 'She's taller than me, she's thinner than me, and she's got better hair.' What is it about your breed and hair?"

"Never mind that. What else did she say?"

"That it was bad enough I was blowing her off, but it had to be over somebody who looked like you. I figured it for some sort of twisted girl compliment."

"A nice one. Now I feel guilty. I bet I would like her, and that's just a little bit irritating." She brooded a minute, then beamed. "But I'll get over it. I'm not going to apologize, exactly, because—hey, hands on your ass. But I'll offer to cook you dinner."

"Sold," he said without hesitation.

"Got anything in mind?"

"Nothing. Surprise me. Us," he corrected and scooped Lily up to hang her upside down. "I'll get shortie here out of your hair. We have some havoc to wreak in the other room."

And just like that, she thought, her life was back on level. With the sounds of growling from Harper, and wild giggles from Lily rolling out of the living room, Hayley opened the refrigerator to examine the contents.

Pitiful, she decided. A total guy assortment of beer, soft drinks, bottled water, what appeared to be an ancient fried chicken leg, two eggs, a stick of butter and a small, moldy hunk of cheese.

She opened the freezer, and hit the payload. Several carefully labeled containers of leftovers. David to the rescue. But it was a shame she couldn't actually cook something, impress Harper.

Who's pitiful? He flaunts another woman in your face and you grovel. Now cooking for him, like a servant. Women are nothing but servants to men. Their conveniences.

He lies as all men lie, and you believe because you're weak and foolish.

Make him pay. They should all pay.

"No." She said it softly when she found herself standing in front of the open freezer door. "No. Those weren't my thoughts. And I won't have them in my head."

"You say something?" Harper called out.

"No. No," she said more calmly.

There was nothing to say. Nothing to think. She would put a meal together and they'd eat. Like a couple. Or even, just a little bit, like a family.

The three of them. Only the three of them.

fourteen

FEELING SO SETTLED WAS JUST A LITTLE SPOOKY TO Harper's mind. They'd taken to having dinner together in the evenings. Sitting together in the kitchen, Lily strapped in the highchair he'd carted over from the main house, he and Hayley at the table with a meal, and conversation seemed so easy it made him nervous.

They were drifting into something solid, like a boat sailing toward shore in a light wind. He wasn't sure whether when they hit it, they'd end up bruised and battered or safe and sound.

Did she seem edgy, too, under the casual? he wondered. Or was he projecting his own jitters?

It was all so normal, this eating together at the end of the day, talking about work or Lily's latest accomplishment. Yet twined through the respite was an intensity, a feeling. A here we are, and here we'll stay—at least for the night.

How much did he, did both of them, want to keep the "at least" in the mix?

"I was thinking," he began, "that if things are slow inside tomorrow, I could show you how to hybridize."

"I know a little. Roz walked me through a snapdragon."

"I was thinking a lily. They're a good specimen for it, and we could try one. I was thinking we could try for a mini, something in a kind of candy pink. And name it for Lily."

Her face switched on to glow. "Really? Like create a new specimen, for her? Oh, Harper, that would be so awesome."

"I thought pink—but a strong pink—and we could try for a hint of red blushing the petals. Red's your color, so it'd be like Hayley's Lily. I was thinking."

"You're going to make me cry."

"Spend some time hand-pollinating and you might just cry. It's not an instant-gratification deal."

"I'd really like to try."

"Then we'll work on it. What do you think of that, shortie?" he asked Lily. "Want your own flower?"

She picked up a green bean with two delicate fingers and dropped it with some care on the floor.

"I bet she likes the flower more than her vegetables. That's her signal she's done." Hayley rose. "I'll clean her up."

"I could do it. Give her a bath."

With a laugh, Hayley removed the highchair tray. "Ever given a toddler a bath?"

"No, but I've had a few. Just fill up the tub, dump her in, hand her the soap. Then go back and dry her off after I've had another beer. Just kidding," he said when Hayley's eyes bugged out. He unstrapped Lily, hitched her up. "Your mama thinks I'm a bath moron. We'll show her."

"Oh, but—"

"Stay with her at all times. Don't even turn your back.

Warm water, not hot. Blah, blah, blah," he continued as he walked away. Over his shoulder, Lily happily waved bye-bye.

She checked on them three times, but tried to be subtle about it.

By the time she'd finished dealing with the kitchen, Lily was running around, all pink and powdered and wearing nothing but her Huggies. Some men, she decided, were natural with children. Harper seemed to be one of them.

"What's next on her agenda?"

"I usually let her play for another hour or so, tires her out. Then maybe we'll read a book—or part of one—if she'll sit still long enough. Harper, don't you want to get rid of us?"

"No. I'm hoping you'll stay. I can set that portable deal up in the spare room. We'll hear her if she wakes up. Then you could be with me." He took Hayley's hands, leaned in to take her lips. "I want you to be with me tonight."

"Harper . . ." She eased away, then hurried after Lily. "Wait," she said, and stopped in the living room when Lily made a beeline for a pile of plastic trucks and cars. "Where'd they come from?"

"They were mine. Some things you keep."

She imagined Harper as a little boy, playing with his trucks and making engine noises, much as her baby was doing now. "Harper, this is so hard."

"What's hard?"

"Not falling dead stupid in love with you."

He said nothing for a moment, then turned her around to face him. "What if you did?"

"That's what I don't know. See, that's what I don't know." Her voice hitched, and she swallowed to even it out. "There's a lot tangled up in this. We only started being with each other a few weeks ago, and there's all this stuff

happening. I don't know what you want, what you're looking for."

"I'm still figuring it out."

"That's fine for you, Harper. I mean it really is, it's just
fine. But what if I love you? I love you, and you figure out
what you want is a trip to Belize and six months bumming
on the beach? I've got Lily to consider. I can't—"

"Hayley, if I wanted to be a beach bum, I think I'd know
it by now."

"You know what I'm talking about."

"Okay, yeah. What if I fall for you, what if I love you
and you decide you want to go back to Little Rock with
Lily and open your own nursery?"

"I couldn't—"

He held up a hand. "Sure you could. It's the kind of risk
people take when they get involved this way. Maybe you'll
fall, and maybe the other person won't want what you're
looking for."

"So we're sensible? Take it a day at a time."

"We could. We could do that."

"What if I don't want to be sensible?" she fired back.
"What if I want to stand here right now and tell you I'm in
love with you? What are you going to do about it?"

"I'm not sure since it's pissing you off."

"Of course I'm pissed off." She threw up her arms. "I'm
in love with you, damn it, Harper, and you want to be sensible, take it a day at a time. And from where I'm standing
your way just sucks sideways."

He considered himself a fairly laid-back sort of man, al-
beit one with a dangerous temper, which he was careful to
control most of the time. How, he wondered, had he fallen
so completely for a women whose moods tended to bounce
around like a pinball?

Proved, he supposed, that there was no logic in love.

"Instead of going off, you should listen. I said we could be sensible. We could take it a day at a time. But since I'm in love with you right back, I'm not so crazy about that idea either."

"You go around doing romantic stuff, movie-time romantic stuff. And then the sweet things like giving my little girl a bath, and I'm supposed to stay sensible? I mean, what do you expect, Harper, what do you expect when you . . ."

She caught her breath, then took a long one while he just looked at her, that lazy half smile on his face. "What was that part after how I should listen?"

"I said I was in love with you right back."

"Oh. Oh." She crouched when Lily brought her one of the trucks. "That's nice, honey. Why don't you go get it?" She rolled the truck across the room, got back up. "You're not saying that because I'm being bitchy?"

"Generally, my policy doesn't include telling a woman I'm in love with her when she's being bitchy. Fact is, I haven't said it to anyone before, because it's the kind of thing that has weight. Should have weight. So you're the first."

"It's not because you're so stuck on Lily?"

He cast his eyes to heaven. "For Christ's sake."

"I'm picking it apart." She held her hands up, wagged them. "I hear myself. I'm just breathless. You make me so happy I've been miserable."

"Yeah, I can see how that works. Completely not."

"I've been so scared." On a laugh, she threw her arms around him. "I was so scared that I'd fall for you, then we'd end up being friends like that woman who came into the nursery the other day. I'm not going to be friends with you, Harper, if this doesn't work out." She reared back, then pressed her mouth hard to his. "I'm going to hate you forever."

"Good. I think."

She sighed, long and deep, as she laid her cheek to his. "What do we do now?"

"Since it's a first for me, I'd like to ride on it awhile. It's some pretty heady stuff. More immediately, I'd say we'll play with Lily. Tire her out good, so that after you put her to bed I can take you to mine."

"I like that plan."

BY THE TIME SHE'D SETTLED LILY DOWN, HARPER HAD music on. She knew he was rarely without it. Though it was just dusk, he had candles flickering in his bedroom. And flowers—a touch she'd rarely seen in another man, but had come to expect from him.

"She okay?" he asked her.

"Fine. She goes down pretty easy, doesn't always stay that way through the night though."

"Then we should take advantage of the quiet." He slid his hands down her arms, then back up the sides of her body. "I love making love with you. Touching you. Watching you when I touch you. The way your body moves with mine."

"Maybe we're just in lust."

"I've been in lust." His lips cruised over her jaw. "Is that what this feels like to you?"

"No." She turned her head so their lips could meet. "Not just."

"I think about you. How you look, how you sound, how you feel. And here we are."

She linked her arms around his neck as he lowered her to the bed. His hands glided down, up, then palmed over her breast.

"You are perfect. Perfect, perfect." He nibbled his way down, then nipped lightly at her nipple through her shirt until she quivered under him.

Then he tugged her shirt down, and took flesh.

More than arousal, she thought even as her body bowed up in response. There was joy fizzing through the excitement, like the bubbles in champagne. He loved her. Harper with the patient hands and ripping temper loved her.

Whatever happened, she was loved. And the love that rose so full and strong inside her was welcomed. There was no gift she treasured more.

To show him, and how she needed to show him, she poured herself into a kiss on a flood of that love.

She surrounded him with it so he felt his heart ache from the brilliance. He loved. It had never come to him before, this stunning surge of emotion that filled heart and soul, gut and mind. This woman, the one who moved with him, merged with him, was the one who sparked it.

He savored the scent and flavor of her skin as the sky deepened to night and a whippoorwill began to sing in the apple tree outside his window.

Inside, the air went soft and thick, throbbing with the sounds of sighs. He felt her rise, tremble, and tremble on the peak, then float down on a moan that was his name. Her skin quivered where he touched and his own warmed as her hands glided over him.

Her lips. He could sink into them until pleasure swirled and shimmered in his mind like mists.

When she rolled over him, rose over him, he could see her face in the candlelight. The glow of it framed by her dark hair, the delicate blue of her eyes deepened with passion.

Her lips reclaimed his, soft, soft even as the kiss deepened. Then the throaty hum as she took him into her. He closed his eyes, riding the sensation as she closed around him.

"This is what you want," she whispered. "What you all want."

The change was like a finger snap, the cold like a sheath of ice. He looked at her, and everything inside him stilled.

"No."

"To penetrate. To bury yourself."

"Stop." Even as she rocked, arousal mixing with horror, he gripped her hips to hold her still.

"Tell her anything. Love. Promises. Lies. As long as you get between her legs." Her thighs clamped him, long, lean vises. Hayley's body, he knew, but not Hayley. Revulsion rose in his throat.

"Stop." He reached up, and what was inside her laughed.

"Shall I make you come? Shall I ride you like a pony until you—"

He shoved her back, and she continued to laugh, sprawled naked in the flickering light.

"Leave her alone." He hauled her back. "You've got no right to her."

"As much as you. More. We're the same, she and I. The same."

"No. You're not. She doesn't look for the easy way. She's warm and strong and honest."

"I could have been." Something else came into her eyes then. Regret, grief, need. "I can be. And I know better than she does what can be done with this body." She pressed it to his, began to whisper erotic suggestions in his ear.

With sick panic burning in his belly, he shook her. "Hayley. Damn it, Hayley. You're stronger than her. Don't let her do this." And though it was still something else that looked at him, though her lips were cold, so cold, he kissed her. Gently. "I love you. Hayley, I love you. Come back to me."

He knew when she did, the instant. And gathered her hard and close while she shivered. "Harper."

"Ssh. It's okay."

"She was— Oh God. It wasn't me. I didn't mean those things. Harper—"

Comfort, he thought, wasn't the answer, not here, not now. "It's you I want." His lips skimmed over her face, and his hands began to stroke her warm once more. "Just you, just me. We won't let her touch this. Look at me."

He gripped her hands in his, and plunged into her. "Look at me," he repeated. "Stay with me."

The cold became heat, the horror became joy. She stayed with him. Linked.

SHE COULDN'T SPEAK, EVEN WHEN HIS HEAD WAS pillowed on her belly and the whippoorwill had given way to the cicadas. So much churned inside her she couldn't separate the shock from the fear, the fear from the shame.

He brushed a kiss over her flesh, then rose.

"I'm going to get us some water, and I'll look in on Lily."

She had to choke back words now. Pleas that he not leave her alone, even for a moment. But that was foolish, and impossible. She couldn't be watched every minute. More, she couldn't bear the idea that he might feel he had to watch her, waiting for Amelia to use her again.

She sat up, drawing her knees up to rest her brow on them.

She stayed that way when he came back, sat on the bed beside her.

"Harper. I don't know what to say."

"It wasn't your fault, let's just get that out of the way. And you pushed her out, or pushed through her, whatever the hell."

"I don't know how you could stand to touch me after."

"You think I'd let her win? You think I'd let her beat us?"

The barely restrained fury in his voice had her lifting

her head. "You . . . you were inside me when she— It's so creepy."

"Here." He nudged the water on her. "Creepy for both of us," he agreed. "And a little incestuous for me. Jesus. Nothing like getting really close to your great-great-grandmother."

"She wasn't thinking of you that way. I don't know if that helps." Fighting off a shudder, she handed the water back to him. "She was . . . I felt like she was seeing him. Reginald. She was—I was—all turned on, you know, then it was like this spit of rage spewing up through that. But the kind that makes it more, sort of more exciting. Darker. Then it was all blurred together. Her and me, him and you. And I was so wound up I couldn't get a grip on anything. Then you said you loved me, you kissed me and I could hold on to that."

"She tried to use us. We didn't let her." He set the water aside before easing her back so he could lie beside her and draw her close. "It's going to be okay."

But even lying beside him, held firm and safe in his arms, she couldn't quite believe it.

It was awkward, but Harper felt Mitch should know about any incident involving Amelia. Even if that incident had happened in bed with Hayley.

At least it was a man-to-man sort of thing. If his mother had to have the information, Harper would just as soon have it filtered through his stepfather.

"How long did it last?" Mitch asked.

"Maybe a couple of minutes. Seemed longer, considering the situation, but probably around that."

"She wasn't violent."

"No. But you know . . ." He had to pause a moment and

give his attention fully to the work board in the library. "Rape's not always violent, but it's still . . . Anyway, that's what it felt like, to me. Like a kind of rape. Like a power thing. Got you by the dick, so I'm in charge."

"It fits the kind of personality profile we've been building. She wouldn't get that while what's between you and Hayley is sexual, sex for the sake of sex isn't the driving force. Must've shaken you up."

Harper only nodded. There was still a coating of that raw sickness in his belly. "How much more do we need to know before we can stop this?"

"I wish I could tell you. We have her name, her circumstance. We know your bloodline comes down through her. We know her baby was taken, and we're assuming without her consent. Or that after she gave it, she changed her mind. We know she came here, to Harper House, and we have to believe she died here. Maybe if we find out how, but that's no guarantee."

He'd never counted on guarantees, not in his life or in his work. His father had died when he'd been seven, which had put paid to any sort of traditional family warranty. His work was a series of experiments, calculated risks, learned skills, and sheer luck. None of those guaranteed success.

Harper considered failure a postponement at worst, and another step in the process at best.

But things were considerably different when it involved the woman he loved, and her welfare, her well-being.

He was reminded of that when he found her watering flats.

She wore the cotton shorts and tank that was a kind of summer uniform around the nursery. Her feet were tucked into thin, backless canvas shoes that could take a soaking, and her face was shaded by the bill of one of the nursery's gimme caps.

She looked entirely too sad and thoughtful. The thoughtful part was proven right when she jumped nearly a foot off the ground when he said, "Hey."

"God, you scared me."

"That's what you get for taking side-trips when you're on the clock. Speaking of which, I'm going to start that hybridizing, and could use an assist."

"You still want to do that?"

"Why wouldn't I?"

"I thought maybe when you thought things through, you'd want to keep your distance for a while."

He simply stepped up to her, cautiously nudging the watering wand aside and kissed her. "Guess you're wrong."

"Guess I am. Lucky for me."

"Just come on over when you're done. I already let Stella know I was stealing you for a while."

He spent the time setting up for the work, lining up the tools, the plants he wanted to use. He logged the species, the cultivar, the name and characteristics of the desired plant in his files.

Since headphones wouldn't be an option as he wouldn't be working alone, he switched Beethoven for Loreena McKennitt. He figured his plants would like it fine, and he'd be a lot happier.

When Hayley came in, he was digging out a Coke, so he pulled out two.

"This is pretty exciting."

He handed her the can. "Tell me what you know about hybridizing first."

"Well, it's like you have a mama and a daddy, the parents. Two different plants—they can be the same type or two different . . . What is it?"

"Genera."

"Right. So you want ones with stable characteristics and

you cross them by hand-pollinating. Like pollen from one, seed from the other—like sex."

"Not bad. We're going to use this miniature I've been screening as a parent plant. And this variegated will be the other, the seed parent. See I've had it protected with a bag—that keeps insect pollinators from messing with it, and we're going to remove the stamens now, before it can self-pollinate. I potted these up, brought them in last winter so they could develop."

"You've been thinking about doing this for a while."

"Yeah, since she was born, more or less. Anyway, we work with the pollen parent today. You know how?"

"Roz did it before. I really just watched."

"This time, you try it. I cut this one already, just above the node, see? It's been in water and it's fully open now. See how the anthers are split? They're ready for pollen."

"So, you did the foreplay."

"One of my little skills."

She gave an exaggerated roll of her eyes. "Tell me about it."

"You go next."

"Oh man. I have to pull the petals off, right?"

"Quick, gentle twists, work inward until you see the anthers."

"Here goes."

"That's good," he said as he watched her. "Just be careful to leave the anthers intact. Yeah, nice work, good hands."

"I'm nervous. I hate screwing up."

"You're not." Her fingers were quick and precise as they twisted the petals away. "And if you do, we'll pick another."

"Is that right? Is that okay?"

"What do you see?"

She bit her lip. "The little anthers are all naked."

"Next step." He picked up a clean camel-hair brush.

"You need to collect the pollen. Use this, brush it over the anthers. We'll store it in this dish, keep it dry. See, it's fluffy, so it's ripe. I'll label the dish."

"This is fun. You wouldn't believe how totally I sucked in high school chemistry."

"Just needed a better lab partner. All mine aced. Now we're going to prep the seed parent. See this?" He held up the lily he'd chosen. "We don't want her fully open. We're looking for well-developed but with immature anthers— before self-pollination can happen. We take petals and anthers off her."

"Strip her right down."

"So to speak. No fragments left, they can cause rot fungi, then you're screwed. What we're after is nice exposed stigmas."

"You do that part. Then it's like a team."

"Okay." He twisted off the petals, then reached for his tweezers, skillfully plucking out the anthers. "Now she waits until tomorrow for the pollen. That gives her stigmas time to get sticky. Then we'll transfer the ripe pollen onto the stigmas. You can use a brush, but I like using my finger. There."

He stepped back.

"That's it?"

"That's the first one. Let's do the next. We've got a good dozen seed parents on here. I think we'll try a couple of pollen parents on her. See what we get."

They took turns with the steps. A nice, companionable rhythm, Hayley thought, and a satisfying one. "How did you pick the plants to work with?"

"I've been scoping them out awhile, tracking growth habits and form, color patterns."

"Since she was born."

"Yeah, pretty much."

"Harper, you know how I said if things don't work out with us, I'll hate you for the rest of my life?"

"Yeah, I got that."

"Well, I will, but I'll suck it in—mostly—because I know you love her. You really do."

"She's got me wrapped. I gotta admit. Tomorrow, we'll pollinate, label, log. Then we'll keep an eye on her. Probably take about a week before we see the ovary swelling, if we're successful here."

"Swelling ovaries. Takes me back."

He grinned, kept working. "Couple weeks more, the pod should be formed, then it takes about a month more for the seed to ripen. We'll know it has when the top begins to split."

"Yeah, déjà vu."

"Cut it out. That's just weird."

He moved to his computer, his long fingers tapping keys as he input data. "What we'll do is take the seeds, dry them and plant them late fall. I like to do it that way so it won't germinate until spring."

"We plant them outside?"

"No, in here. Mama's potting soil, four-inch pots, then we put them out. When they're big enough, we'll put them in nursery beds. It'll take another year before they bloom and we see what we've really got."

"Fortunately, I know nothing about a two-year pregnancy."

"Yeah, women get by with nine little months. Blink of an eye."

"You try it, pal."

"I'm a fan of the way things work. So. I've got the records logged, and if things work out, we should eventually see some new flowers, and some of them should have characteristics of each parent." He glanced over the work, nod-

ded. "We'll get what we're after, or if not exactly, hopefully something close enough that we can do another generation, or try a different parent."

"In other words, this could take years."

"Serious hybridizing isn't for weenies."

"I like it. And I like that it's not an overnight kind of deal. You have all this anticipation. And maybe you won't get exactly what you had in mind, but something else. Something, not necessarily better, but just as beautiful."

"Now you're talking the talk."

"I feel good." She stepped back from the worktable. "I was having such a bad day. I kept thinking about what happened last night, circling around and around it, and just feeling sick about the whole thing."

"It wasn't your fault."

"I know—in my head. But somewhere in there I wondered if we'd be able to be easy together again—or at least this soon. If you'd be, I don't know, uncomfortable and I'd be jittery. It seemed like the chance we had to just be in love might've been spoiled."

"Nothing's changed for me."

"I know." They stood side-by-side at the workbench and she tilted her head onto his shoulder. "And I feel calmer knowing it."

"I better let you know I told Mitch what happened."

"Oh." She sucked in a breath, winced. "I guess it had to be done, and better you than me. Was it awful?"

"No. Just a little weird. We spent a lot of time talking about it without making any eye contact."

"I'm not going to think about it," Hayley decided. "I'm just not." She turned just enough to kiss him. "I'd better get on with the work I really get paid for. I'll see you back home."

* * *

As SHE HUMMED HER WAY THROUGH THE REST OF THE day, Stella passed by, then stopped to put her hands on her hips. "Hybridizing certainly agrees with you."

"Feel great. Step two tomorrow."

"Well, good. You looked a little draggy this morning."

"Didn't sleep very well, but I've got my second wind, and then some." She glanced around to be sure no one was within hearing distance. "We're in love." Grinning, she used the index fingers of both hands to draw a heart in the air. "Me and Harper. Together."

"Wow. News flash."

With a laugh, Hayley continued hauling bags of potting soil from cart to shelf. "I mean really in love. So we said the L word to each other."

"I'm happy for you." She gave Hayley a hug. "Seriously."

"I'm happy for me, too. But there's this . . . I have to tell you about this thing that happened." Cautious, Hayley took another look around, and related the incident to Stella in undertones.

"My God. Are you all right?"

"It was awful, so awful, it still makes my stomach churn. I didn't know how we'd get past it. That was almost worse than the experience itself. But we have. We did. I can't imagine how he must've felt, but he didn't pull back from me."

"He loves you."

"He does. He really does." Miracles everywhere, she thought. "Stella, I always believed I'd fall in love one day, but I never knew it could be like this. Now that I know, I can't imagine not keeping it. You know?"

"I do. You should be happy. You should know this other thing is separate from that. And you and Harper should enjoy this bliss stage because it's very precious."

"I feel like everything in my life has been leading up to

this, to him. The good and the bad. I can take the bad because I know we've found something in each other that really matters. I guess that sounds lame, but—"

"It does not. It sounds happy."

fifteen

THE SECONDHAND LAPTOP WAS A GOOD BUY, AND US-
ing it made Hayley feel she was doing something active.
An hour or two in research mode may not have garnered
her a great deal of new information, at least as applied to
her situation, but it assured her she wasn't alone.

There were a lot of people out there who at least believed they'd had experience with ghosts and hauntings.
She was already documenting an essential piece of advice
from every website she'd visited. But at least with the computer she could type her reports instead of scrawling them
in a notebook.

And it was fun to be able to e-mail friends back in Little Rock.

Of course she got caught up in surfing the web, much as
she got caught up when scanning books. There was just so
much information, so many interesting things. And one in-

variably led to another so that if she wasn't careful, she'd be up past midnight hunched over the keyboard.

She had her chin propped on her elbow, her mind focused on an on-line report from Toronto of a ghost baby crying, when a hand brushed her shoulder.

She didn't jump, held back a scream. Instead she closed her eyes and spoke in a nearly normal tone. "Please tell me that's a real hand."

"I hope it is as it's attached to my wrist."

"Roz." Hayley let out her breath slowly. "Points for me, right, for not jumping up to cling to the ceiling like a cartoon cat."

"That might've been entertaining." She narrowed her eyes to read the screen. "Ghosthunters dot com?"

"One of many," Hayley told her. "And really, there's some pretty cool stuff. Did you know that one of the traditional ways to discourage ghosts from coming into a room was to stick pins or hammer iron nails around the door? It's like they'd get caught on them and couldn't get in. Of course, if you did it while they were already in, then they couldn't get out."

"I catch you nailing anything into my woodwork, I'll skin you."

"Already figured that. Plus I don't see how it could work." She scooted around, away from the screen. "They say you should talk to the ghost, politely, just ask it to leave. Like: Hey, sorry about your bad luck being dead and all that, but this is my house now and you're disturbing me, so I wonder if you'd mind just moving on."

"I'd say we've tried variations of that."

"Yeah, no go." When Roz sat on the sofa in the sitting room, Hayley understood she hadn't come by just to chat about Amelia. Nerves began to drum. "Of course, they say you should document everything, but Mitch already has us

doing that. And take photographs. You can hire a ghost hunter, but I don't guess you want a bunch of strangers in the house."

"You guess right."

"Or you can ask a minister or a priest to bless the house. That couldn't hurt."

"You're afraid."

"More than I was, yeah. But I know this stuff"—she tapped the screen—"isn't really helpful because what we're doing, what we always planned to do was find out who, what, why. And if we did manage just to boot her out, we wouldn't know it all. But I like, well, harvesting information."

"You and Mitch, peas in a pod. Have you documented what happened the other night, with you and Harper?"

"Yes." Heat burned her cheeks. "I haven't, ah, given it to Mitch yet."

"It's very personal. I wouldn't like sharing that sort of personal experience with an outsider."

"You're not. I mean, he's not. Neither of you."

"Anyone, no matter how you love them, is an outsider when it comes to the bed, Hayley. I want you to know I understand that. I also want you to know you've got no need to walk on eggshells with me about this. I waited a couple of days, hoping it wouldn't be quite as touchy a subject."

"I know Harper went to Mitch about it, and I knew Mitch would tell you. I just couldn't, Roz. If it'd been anybody but Harper—not that I'd be with anybody but Harper . . . And I'm already messing this up."

"You're not."

"It's . . . Harper's yours."

"Yes, he is." She propped her feet on the table, her most habitual position. "I knew when he fell in love with you, though you didn't know, and I doubt he did."

"I think maybe it was the night we stayed at the Peabody."

Roz shook her head. "That's romance, and valuable. But that wasn't when. Who held your hand when Lily was born?"

"Oh." Hayley lifted a hand to her throat as it filled. "He did. Harper did, and I think he was almost as scared as I was."

"When I saw, and I understood, my heart ached. Just for a moment. You'll know what I mean when it's Lily's turn. And if you're lucky, as I'm lucky, you'll watch your child fall in love with someone you can love, and respect and admire, be amused by, feel close to. So when your heart aches, it's with happiness, and gratitude."

Tears spilled down her cheeks. "I don't know how I could get any luckier than I already am. You've been so good to me. No, please don't brush it off," she said when Roz shook her head. "It means so much to me. When I came here, I thought I was so smart and strong, so ready. If she kicks me out, I thought, I'll just keep going. I'll find a job, get an apartment, have this baby. I'll be fine. If I'd known what it takes—not just the hours, the effort, but the love and the worry that just fills you up when you have a child, I'd've thrown myself at your feet and begged for help. But all I had to do was ask."

"I gave you a job and a place to stay because you're family, and because of the situation you were in. But that's not why you're still here. You earned your place at In the Garden, and your place in this house. Make no mistake, if you hadn't, I'd have shown you the door."

"I know." And knowing it made Hayley grin. "I wanted to prove myself to you, and I'm proud that I did. But, Roz, because I have Lily, I know what Harper means to you. And part of the reason I'm scared, more scared than I was, is I'm afraid The Bride might hurt him."

"Why do you think that?"

"She saw Reginald in him. Maybe one of the reasons she's moved on to me is because of the feelings that I developed for Harper. When I first met him, I remember thinking, wow, if I was in the market, I'd be all over that one."

When Roz laughed, Hayley flushed. "See what comes out of my mouth?" she demanded. "Jesus, you're his *mother*."

"Forget that a minute. Keep going."

"Well, see I wasn't in a place in my head, or anywhere else, where I could think seriously about a man, a relationship. I just thought he was hot, then as I got to know him, sweet and funny and smart. I liked him a lot, and I got irritated now and then that he was so cute and I was pregnant and cranky and not at my best. After Lily, I tried to think of him as kind of a brother, or a cousin. Well, he is a cousin, but you know what I mean."

"The way you think of David or Logan, or my other sons."

"Yeah. I really tried to put Harper in that same slot. And there was so much to do and learn, that it was easy to ignore that little low tickle that was going on inside me. You know the one."

"Thank God I do," Roz said with feeling.

"Then it wasn't so easy, and the feelings for him kept getting stronger. It seems to me, when I started to admit them to myself, started to imagine how it could be with him, that's when Amelia started slipping in."

"And the stronger your feelings, the stronger and more demonstrative her objections."

"I'm worried that she'll hurt him, through me. Not seeing Harper, but Reginald. I'm worried I won't be able to stop her."

Roz frowned. "Seems that you're not giving Harper enough credit for being able to handle himself."

"Maybe not. But she's awful strong, Roz. Stronger than she was, I think." Remembering the sensation of having her

self pushed aside, Hayley inhaled, exhaled, deeply. "And it seems to me she's had a lot of time to think about payback."

"Harper's stronger than she thinks. And so are you."

SHE HOPED ROZ WAS RIGHT. AS SHE LAY SLEEPLESS, with Harper beside her, she hoped she had the grit and the brains to combat the vengeance of a vindictive spirit. Worse, one she felt some sympathy for.

But Harper wasn't responsible for what had happened to her. No one who lived at Harper House now was responsible. There had to be a way, some way, for her to make Amelia understand that. To show her that Harper was not only the child she'd once sung to, but a good, caring man. And nothing like Reginald.

What had he been like, really? Reginald Harper. A man so obsessed with having a son, he would deliberately impregnate a woman not his wife. Whether or not Amelia had consented—and that they couldn't know—it had been a selfish and hurtful act on his part. Then to take the child, to force his own wife to accept it as her own. He couldn't have loved. Not his wife, not Amelia, certainly not the child.

It was no wonder Amelia despised him, and with her spirit or mind, or heart, shattered, that she'd grouped all men along with him.

What had it been like for her? For Amelia?

SHE SAT AT HER DRESSING TABLE, CAREFULLY ROUGing her cheeks by gaslight. Pregnancy had stolen her color. Just one more indignity, after the horrible sickness morning after morning, the widening of her waist, the incessant fatigue.

And yet, there were benefits. So many she hadn't counted

on. She smiled as she added color to her lips. How could she have known Reginald would be so pleased? Or so generous.

She lifted her arm to study the ruby and diamond hearts that circled her wrist. A bit delicate for her taste, really, but you couldn't fault the glimmer.

And he'd hired another maid, given her carte blanche for a new wardrobe to accommodate her changing body. More jewels. More attention.

He visited her three times a week now, and never came empty-handed. Even if it was only to bring her chocolates or candied fruit when she mentioned craving sweets.

How fascinating to know that the prospect of a child could make a man so biddable.

She imagined he'd been very solicitous of his wife, in turn. But then she'd plagued him with girls rather than the son he coveted.

She would give him a son. And in giving, would reap the benefits for the rest of her life.

A bigger house to start, she decided. Clothes, jewels, furs, a new carriage—perhaps a small country house as well. He could afford it. Reginald Harper would spare no expense for his son, even his bastard son, she was sure.

As the mother of that son, she would never have to seek out another protector, never have to flirt and seduce and bargain with the men of wealth and position, offering sex and comfort in exchange for the mode of life she craved. Deserved. Earned.

She rose from the dressing table, and hair shining gold, jewels glittering white and red, gown sweeping silver, she turned in the chevel glass.

This was her exchange now. This bulge of the belly. Look how odd and awkward, how fat and unfashionable she looked, despite the gown. And yet, Reginald doted. He would stroke that bulge, even during passion. And in pas-

sion, he was kinder, gentler than she'd ever known him to be. She could almost love him during those times, when his hands were tender instead of demanding. Almost.

But love was not part of the game, and a game was all it was. This bartering pleasure for style. How could she love what was so weak, so deceitful, so arrogant? A ridiculous notion, as ridiculous as feeling pity for the wives they betrayed with her. Women who folded their thin lips and pretended not to know. Who passed her on the street with their noses in the air. Or women like her mother who slaved for them for pennies.

She was meant for bigger things, she thought, and lifted a heavy crystal decanter to stroke scent on her throat. She was meant for silks and diamonds.

When Reginald arrived, she would pout, just a little. And tell him of the diamond broach she'd seen that afternoon. How she would pine without it.

Pining wasn't good for the child. She imagined the broach would be hers within a day.

She gave a light laugh, a little turn.

Then stopped, went still. Her hand trembled as she lifted it to press over her belly.

It had moved.

Inside her a flutter, a stretch. Little wings beating.

The glass reflected her as she stood in her shimmering gown, her fingers spread over the slight bulge as if she would guard what was inside.

Inside her. Alive. Her son.

Hers.

HAYLEY REMEMBERED IT VIVIDLY. EVEN IN THE morning there was nothing of the fragmented or misty quality of a dream.

"It was, I think it was, a kind of a bid for sympathy. More for empathy." She held her cup in both hands as she sipped coffee in the breakfast nook.

"How so?" Mitch had his tape recorder and notebook as she'd requested. "Did she speak directly to you at some point?"

"No, because it wasn't her, it was me. Or it was both of us. I wasn't dreaming so much as I was there. I felt, I saw, I thought. She wasn't just showing me, but reliving. If that makes sense."

"Eat your eggs, sweetie-pie," David urged her. "You look peaked."

She scooped some up obediently. "She was beautiful. Not like the way we've seen her, really. Vibrant and drop-dead—excuse the term. There was so much going through her head—my head—I don't know. Irritation about the changes in her body, the inconvenience, plots and plans to get more out of Reginald, surprise at his reaction to her condition, disgust for men like him, for their wives, envy, greed. It all just kept rolling around in a big mass."

She paused, breathed. "I think she was already a little bit crazy."

"And how was that a bid for sympathy?" Harper asked her. "Why would you feel sorry for someone like that?"

"It was the change. It was feeling the baby move. I felt it, too. That shock of feeling, the sudden realization that there's life inside you. And there's this wave of love along with it. In that moment, the baby was hers. Not a ploy or an inconvenience, but her child, and she loved it." She looked at Roz.

"Yes."

"So she was showing me. I loved my child, wanted it. And the man, the kind of man who'd use a woman like me, took it from me. She was wearing the bracelet. The heart

bracelet. And I did feel for her. I don't think she was a good person, certainly not a nice one, and even then, before the rest happened, I don't think she was balanced. But she loved the child, wanted it. I think what she showed me was real, and she showed me because I'd understand it more than anyone else. Yeah, I felt sorry for her."

"Sympathy is fine," Mitch said. "But you can't let down your guard. She's using you, Hayley."

"I know, and I won't. I can feel for her, but I don't have to trust her."

DAYS PASSED, AND SHE WAITED FOR THE NEXT MOVE, the next experience, but August boiled quietly toward September. The most wrenching experience was having her ancient car break down between work and the sitter's, and finally having to accept it was time to replace it.

"It's not just the money," she told Harper as she strolled Lily through the used-car lot. "It's one of my last links to childhood, I guess. My daddy bought that car, secondhand. I learned to drive with it."

"It'll go to a good home."

"Hell, Harper, it's going on the scrap heap, and we both know it. Poor, pitiful old thing. I know I've got to be sensible, too. I can't be hauling Lily around in an unreliable car. I'll be lucky if that salesman who took it off for appraisal doesn't come back and say I owe him just for dumping it on him."

"Just let me handle it."

"I will not." She stopped by a hatchback, kicked its tires. "You know what I hate? I hate that a lot of car salesmen and mechanics and that whole breed treat women who come in like brainless bimbos just because they don't have a penis. Like all the automotive data and know-it-all is stored in their dicks."

"Jesus, Hayley." He had to laugh, even as he winced.

"It's true. So, I've done my research. I know what I want and how much I should have to pay. He doesn't want to deal with me, then I'll just take my business elsewhere."

She stopped by a sedan, braced one hand on the fender and waved the other in front of her face. "God almighty, it's hot. Feel like every fluid in my body's boiled away."

"You look a little pale. Why don't we go inside, sit down for a minute?"

"I'm okay. Just not resting well. Even when I sleep, I feel like I'm on alert, like the first few weeks after Lily was born. Makes me draggy and irritable. So if I end up snapping at you, try to bear with me."

He rubbed the small of her back. "Don't worry about it."

"I appreciate you coming with me today, I really do. But don't feel like you've got to step in."

"Ever bought a car?"

She sent him a sidelong, annoyed look as she continued to push Lily's stroller. "Just because I haven't, doesn't mean I'm some rube down from the hills. I've bought lots of other things, and I can guarantee I know more about negotiating prices than you. Rich boy."

He grinned. "I'm just a working gardener."

"You may work for a living, but you've got a few silver spoons tucked away for rainy days. Now here's what I'm after."

She stopped to study a sturdy-looking five-door Chevy. "It's got plenty of room, but it's not big and bulky, and it's clean. It's bound to get better mileage than my old car and it's not flashy."

She frowned over the listed price. "I'll just get him to come down a bit, and it'll be in my range. Sort of."

"Don't tell him you—"

"Harper."

"Backing off." He shook his head, stuck his hands in his pockets.

And had to saw his tongue in half when the salesman came out, big smiles, and announced the meager offer on the trade-in.

"Oh, is that all?" Hayley widened her baby blues and fluttered her lashes. "I guess sentiment doesn't count, does it? But maybe, maybe you could just ease that up, a little bit, depending on what I buy. This one's pretty. I like the color."

Playing him, Harper realized, noting how she'd bumped up her accent. He went along for the ride as the salesman steered her toward a couple of pricier options, watched her chew her lip, flash her smile, and steer him right back to what she wanted.

Guy's toast, he decided as she finagled the price down, took Lily out of the stroller to sit with her behind the wheel. Harper concluded nobody could resist the pair of them.

Two hours later, they were driving off the lot with Lily dozing in her carseat and Hayley beaming behind the wheel.

" 'Oh, Mr. Tanner, I just don't know a thing about cars. You're so sweet to help me out this way.' " Harper shook his head. "When we were sitting in there doing the paperwork I wanted to warn him to lift up his feet. It was sure getting deep."

"He made a nice sale, got his commission, and I got what I went in for. That's what counts." But she let out a hoot of laughter. "I liked when he tried to bring you into it, showed you under the hood and you just scratched your head like you were looking at a cruise missile or something. I think we made him feel good, like he was giving me what I needed for the price I could pay. And that counts, too. Next time I have to buy, I'd go right back to Mr. Tanner."

"Didn't hurt for you to tear up a couple times."

"That was real. I was sad to sell that old heap—and don't think these car payments aren't going to sting some." More, she thought, it had put an ache in her throat when Mr. Tanner had assumed they were a family.

"If you need some help—"

"Don't go there, Harper." But she reached over to pat his hand, to show she appreciated the offer. "We'll be fine, Lily and me."

"Why don't I take you out to lunch to celebrate then?"

"That's a deal. I'm starving."

They had looked like a family, she thought. A normal young family buying a secondhand car, having lunch in a diner, treating the baby to a cup of ice cream.

But putting them there was rushing it, for all of them. They were a man and a single mother who were romantically involved. Not a unit.

At home, she decided to take advantage of the rest of her day off by curling up with Lily for an afternoon nap.

"We're all right, aren't we, baby?" she murmured as Lily played with her mother's hair, her big eyes heavy, her pretty mouth going slack. "I'm doing right by you? I'm sure trying."

She snuggled down a little closer. "I'm so tired. Got a million things I ought to be doing, but I'm so tired. I'll get them all done sooner or later, right?"

She closed her eyes, started to calculate her finances in her head, juggling funds, changing weekly deposits. But her brain wouldn't focus.

It drifted back to the used-car lot, and Mr. Tanner shaking hands with her before she drove off. How he'd smiled at her and wished her and her charming family well.

Drifted to sitting out on her terrace with Harper, drinking cold wine in the heat-soaked night.

Dancing with him in the shimmering romance of the suite at the Peabody.

Working with him in the grafting house.

Watching him lift Lily onto his shoulders.

It should be easier to be in love, she thought sleepily. It should be simpler. It shouldn't make you want more when love was everything.

She sighed once, and told herself to enjoy what she had, and let the rest come.

And the pain was like knives in the belly, shocking, sharp, and horrid. Her whole body fought against them, and she screamed at the sensation of being ripped in two.

The heat, the pain. Unbearable. How could something so loved, so desired, punish her this way? She would die from it, surely she would die. And never see her son.

Sweat streamed off her, and the utter weariness was nearly as severe as the pain.

Blood and sweat and agony. All for her child, her son. Her world. No price too dear to pay for giving him life.

And as the pain sliced her, sent her tumbling toward the dark, she heard the thin cry of birth.

Hayley woke drenched in sweat, her body still radiating from the pain. And her own child blissfully asleep in the protective crook of her arm.

She eased free, fumbled for the bedside phone.

"Harper? Can you come?"

"Where are you?"

"In my room. Lily's sleeping right here. I can't leave her. We're all right," she said quickly. "We're fine, but something just happened. Please can you come?"

"Two minutes."

She made a wall of pillows around the baby, but knew even then she couldn't leave the room. Lily might roll off somehow, or certainly climb over and fall. But she could

pace, even on her weakened legs she could pace.

She flung open the doors even as Harper ran up the steps.

"They told her it was stillborn." She swayed, and her knees nearly folded. "They told her her baby was dead."

SIXTEEN

IN THE PARLOR WHERE THE LIGHT WAS SOFT THROUGH gauzy curtains and the air was sweet with roses, Harper stood by the front window with his fists balled in his pockets.

"She was wrecked," he said with his back to the room. "She just sort of folded up when I got there, and even when she pulled it together, she looked sick."

"She wasn't hurt." Mitch held up a hand when Harper whirled. "I know how you feel. I do. But she wasn't physically harmed, and that's important."

"This time," he shot back. "It's out of hand. All of this is fucking out of hand."

"Only more reason for us to stick together, and stay calm."

"I'll be calm when she's out of the house."

"Amelia," Logan asked, "or Hayley?"

"Right now? Both."

"You know she can stay with us. And if I were in your shoes, I'd want to pack her up and haul her out. But from what I gather, you tried that once and it didn't work. If you think you've got a better shot at it now, I'll carry her suitcase."

"She won't budge. What the hell is wrong with these women?"

"They feel connected." David spread his hands. "Even when they see Amelia at her worst, they feel attached. Engaged. Right or wrong, Harp, there's a kind of solidarity."

"And it's her home," Mitch added. "As much as yours now, or mine. She won't walk out of it and leave this undone. Any more than you, or I, or any of us." He glanced around the room. "So we finish it."

Logic, even truth, didn't settle Harper's anger, or his worry. "You didn't see her after it happened."

"No, but I've got the gist from what you told me. She matters to me, too, Harper. To all of us."

"All for one, great. I'm for it." His gaze shifted to the parlor doors, and his mind traveled upstairs, to Hayley. "But she's the one on the line."

"Agreed." Mitch leaned forward in his chair to draw Harper's attention back to him. "Let's look at what happened for a minute. Hayley was taken through childbirth, and a traumatic aftermath when Amelia was told the baby was dead. And she went through this while she was napping with Lily. But Lily wasn't disturbed. That tells me that there's no intent to harm or even frighten the baby. If there were, how long do you think it would take Hayley to head out that door?"

"That may be true, but to get whatever it is she wants, Amelia's going to keep using Hayley, and using her hard."

"I agree." Mitch nodded. "Because it works. Because

this way she's feeding us information we might not ever be able to find. We know now that not only was her child taken from her, but that she was told, cruelly, that it was dead. It's hardly a wonder that her mind, which already seemed to be somewhat imbalanced, shattered."

"We can assume she came here for him," Logan suggested. "And died here."

"Well, the kid's dead, too. Dead as she is, dead as disco." Harper slumped into a chair. "She's not going to find him here."

UPSTAIRS, HAYLEY WOKE FROM A LIGHT DOZE. THE curtains were pulled so the light was dim but for a thin chink. She saw Roz sitting, reading a book in that narrow spear of light.

"Lily."

Roz set the book aside and rose. "Stella has her. She took her and the boys over to the other wing to play so you'd have some quiet. How are you feeling?"

"Exhausted. A little raw inside yet." But she sighed, comforted when Roz sat and stroked her hair. "It was harder than when I had Lily, rougher and longer. I know it was only a few minutes, really, but it seemed like hours. Hours and hours of pain and heat. Then this awful muzzy feeling toward the end. They gave her something, and it made her kind of float away, but it was almost worse."

"Laudanum, I imagine. Nothing like a shot of opiate."

"I heard the baby cry." Struggling to relax, Hayley curled on her side, tilting her head up to keep Roz in her line of sight. "You know how it is, no matter what's gone on in those hours before, everything inside you rising up when you hear your baby cry the first time."

"Hers." Roz took Hayley's hand. "Not yours."

"I know, I know, but for that instant he was mine. And that horrible tearing grief, that crazy disbelief when the doctor said it was stillborn, that was mine, too."

"I've never lost a child," Roz told her. "I can't even imagine the pain of it."

"They lied to her, Roz. I guess he paid them, too. They lied, but she knew. She heard the baby cry, and she *knew*. It drove her crazy."

Roz shifted on the bed, angling so she could rest Hayley's head on her lap. And sat in silence, staring at that thin lance of light through the curtains.

"She didn't deserve it," Hayley started.

"No. She didn't deserve it."

"Whatever she was, whatever she did, she didn't deserve to be treated that way. She loved the baby, but . . ."

"But what?"

"It wasn't right, the way she loved it. It wasn't a healthy sort of thing. She wouldn't have been a good mother."

"How do you know?"

"I felt . . ." Obsession, she thought, hunger. Impossible to describe the vastness of it. "It had to be a boy, you see? A girl wouldn't have mattered to her. A girl wouldn't have been just a disappointment, but an outrage. And if she'd had the boy and kept it, she would've twisted it. Not on purpose, but he wouldn't have been the man he was. He wouldn't have been the one who loved his dog and buried it with a marker, and loved your grandmother. And none of this would be the way it is."

She turned her head so that she could look up at Roz. "You, Harper. Nothing would be the same. But it doesn't make it right. It still doesn't make what happened right."

"Wouldn't it be nice if everything balanced in the

world? If right came out on top and wrong was punished. It sure would be simple."

Hayley's lips curved. "Then Justin Terrell, who cheated on me in tenth grade, would be fat and bald and asking people if they want fries with that instead of being part owner of a successful sport's bar and bearing a strong resemblance to Toby McGuire."

"Isn't that just the way?"

"Then again, maybe I'd go to hell for not telling Lily's biological father about her."

"Your motives were pure."

"Mostly. I guess doing what's best isn't always doing what's right. It was best for that baby to be raised here, at Harper House."

"Not the same thing, Hayley. No one's motives were pure, or even mostly, in that case. Lies and deceit, cold cruelty, and selfishness. I shudder to think what might have become of that child had it been a girl. You feeling better now?"

"Lots."

"Why don't I go down, fix you something to eat? I'll bring you food on a tray."

"I'll go down. I know Mitch wants to record all this. I know Harper's probably told him by now, but it's better if I give it to him firsthand. And I think I'll feel better yet when I do."

"If you're sure."

She nodded as she pushed herself up on the bed. "Thanks for sitting with me. It felt good knowing you were here while I slept."

She glanced in the mirror, winced. "I'm going to put on some makeup first. I may be possessed by a ghost, but I don't have to look like one."

"That's my girl. I'll go let Stella know you're up and around."

HAYLEY FIGURED SHE OWED ROZ ANOTHER ONE WHEN she realized everything had been arranged so that just she and Mitch would sit in the library to document the experience.

It was easier, somehow, to talk only to him. He was so smart and scholarly, in a studly kind of way. Sort of Harrison Fordish, in hornrims she decided.

With the leading edge of the fatigue and the shock dulled by a little sleep and a lot of TLC, she felt steadier, and more in control.

In any case, she loved this room. All the books, all those stories, all those words. Gardens outside the windows, big cozy chairs inside.

When she'd first come to Harper House she'd sometimes tiptoe down at night, just to sit in this room—her favorite of all of them—and marvel.

And she liked the way Mitch approached the whole Amelia project. With his work boards, his computer, his files and notes, he made it all rational, doable, grounded.

She studied the board now, with its long lists and columns that comprised Harper's family tree.

"Do you think, after all this is over, you could do a family tree for me?"

"Hmm?"

"Sorry." She glanced back at him, waved a hand. "Mind's wandering."

"It's okay, you've got a lot on it." He put down his notebook, focused his attention on her. "Sure I can do that. You give me the basics you know—father's full name, date and place of birth, your mother's, and we're off and running."

"I'd really like that. It'd be interesting. Harper and I cross a couple generations back, sort of over to the side. Is he awful mad at me?"

"No, honey. Why would he be?"

"He was upset. He wanted to scoop me and Lily right up and haul us to Stella's. I wouldn't go. I can't."

Mitch doodled on a pad. "If I could've gotten Roz out of this house a few months ago, I'd have done it—even if it had taken dynamite."

"Did you fight about it?"

"Not really." Amusement danced in his eyes. "But then I'm older, wiser, and more in tune with the limitations a man faces when dealing with a stubborn woman."

"Am I wrong?"

"That's not for me to say."

"It is if I'm asking you."

"Rock and hard place, kid. That's where you've shoved me." He pushed back, took off his glasses. "I understand exactly how Harper feels and why, and he's not wrong. I respect how you feel and why, and you're not wrong either. How's that?"

She managed a wry smile. "Smart—and no help at all."

"Just another benefit of that older and wiser phase of life. But I'm going to add one thing as a potentially over-protective male. I don't think you should spend a lot of time alone."

"Good thing I like people." When his cell phone rang, she rose. "I'll go on, let you get that."

Because she'd seen Harper outside, she went out the side door. She hoped Stella wouldn't mind a little more time on Lily patrol. She wandered the path toward where he worked in the cutting garden.

Summer still had her world in its sweaty clutches, but the heat was strong and vital. Real. She'd take all the real-

ity she could get. Mammoth blue balls of hydrangeas weighed down the bushes, daylilies speared up with their elegant cheer, and passionflowers twined their arbor in bursts of purple.

The air was thick with fragrance and birdsong, and through it rode the frantic wings of butterflies.

Around the curve Harper stood, legs spread, body slightly bent as his quick, skilled fingers twisted off dead-heads, then dropped them in a bag knotted to his belt. At his feet was a small, shallow basket where daisies and snapdragons, larkspur and cosmos already lay.

It was, somehow, so sweepingly romantic—the man, the evening, the sea of flowers—that her heart floated up to her throat and ached there.

A hummingbird, a sapphire and emerald whir, arrowed past him to hover over the feathery cup of a deep red blossom of monarda and drink.

She saw him pause to watch it, going still with his hand on a stem and his other holding a seed head. And she wished she could paint. All those vivid colors of late summer, bold and strong, and the man so still, so patient, stopping his work to share his flowers with a bird.

Love saturated her.

The bird flew off, a small, electric jewel. He watched it, as she watched him.

"Harper."

"The hummingbirds like the bee balm," he said, then took his sheers and clipped a monarda. "But there's enough for all of us. It's a good spreader."

"Harper," she said again and walked up to slide her arms around him, press her cheek to his back. "I know you're worried, and I won't ask you not to be. But please don't be mad."

"I'm not. I came out here to cool off. It usually works. I'm down to irritated and worried."

"I was set to come out here, argue with you." She rubbed her cheek over his shirt. She could smell soap and sweat, both healthy and male. "Then I saw you, and I just don't want to argue. I just don't want to fight. I can't do what you want when everything inside me pulls the other way. Even if it's wrong, I can't."

"I don't have any choice about that." He clipped more flowers for the basket, deadheaded others. "And you don't have any say about this. I'm moving in. I'd rather you and Lily shift over to my place, but it makes more sense for me to move into your room for now since there are two of you and one of me. When this is over, we'll reevaluate."

"Reevaluate."

"That's right." He'd yet to look at her, really look, and now moved off a few paces to cut more blooms. "It's a little hard to figure out where we're going, what we're doing under the circumstances."

"So you figure we'll live together, under the circumstances, and when those circumstances change, we'll take another look at the picture."

"That's right."

Maybe she did feel like arguing. "Ever heard of asking?"

"Heard of it. Not doing it. At the nursery, you work with Stella, Mama, or me, at all times."

"Who suddenly made you the boss of me?"

With steady hands, unerring eye, he just kept working. "One of us will drive back and forth with you."

"One of you coming with me every time I have to pee?"

"If necessary. You've got your mind set on staying, those are the terms."

The hummingbird whizzed back, but this time she wasn't caught by its charm. "Terms? Somebody die and make you king? Listen, Harper—"

"No. This is how it's going to be. You're determined to

stay, see this through. I'm just as determined you'll be looked after. I love you, so that's the end of it."

She opened her mouth, closed it again, and took a calming breath. "If you'd said that—the I love you part—right off, I might've been more open to discussion."

"There is no discussion."

Her eyes narrowed. He'd yet to stop what he was doing and face her fully. "You sure can be a hard-ass when you put your mind to it."

"This didn't take much effort." He reached down, gathered the flowers in the basket, tucking their stems into a casual bouquet. Now he turned, and those long brown eyes met hers. "Here."

She took them, frowned at him over them. "Did you cut these for me?"

The slow, lazy smile moved over his face. "Who else?"

She blew out a breath. He'd added nicotiana to the bouquet, and when she inhaled, she drew in its rich perfume. "It's exasperating, I swear, how you can be pushy one minute and sweet the next. They're really pretty."

"So are you."

"You know, another man might've started off with the flowers, the flattery, and the I-love-yous to soften me up for the rest. But you go at it ass-backwards."

His gaze stayed on hers, steady. "I wasn't worried about softening you up."

"I get that. You're not waiting for me to say, all right, Harper, we'll do this your way. You're just going to make sure I do."

"See how quick you catch on?"

She had to laugh, and clutching the flowers in one hand gave in and linked her arms around his neck. "In case you're interested, I'm glad you're going to be staying with

me. Next time I have my spine tingled, I'd as soon you be there."

"I will be."

"If you've got more work to do out here—"

She broke off when Logan strode down the path. "Sorry. Something's up," he said. "Better come on back in."

HAYLEY FELT THE EXCITEMENT, LIKE A HUM IN THE AIR when they stepped back into the library. She took a quick scan first, saw Lily playing cars with Gavin and Luke on the floor by the fireplace David had filled with flowers for the summer months.

Spotting her mother, Lily began to jabber and interrupted her game to come over and show off her dump truck. But the minute Hayley lifted her, Lily stretched out her arms for Harper.

"Everybody's second choice when you're around," Hayley commented as she passed her over.

"She understands I know the fine points of Fisher-Price. It's all right," he added. "I've got her. What's up?" he asked his mother.

"I'm going to let Mitch explain. Ah, David, we can always count on you."

He wheeled in a cart with cold drinks, and finger food for the kids. "Gotta keep body and soul together." He winked at the boys. "Especially around this house."

"Y'all get what you want," Roz ordered. "And let's get settled."

While the wine looked tempting, Hayley opted for the iced tea. Her stomach wasn't quite a hundred percent yet. "Thanks for looking out for my girl," she said to Stella.

"You know I love it. It always amazes me how well the

boys play with her." Stella brushed a hand down Hayley's arm. "How're you feeling?"

"A little off yet, but okay. You know what this is about?"

"Not even a glimmer. Go on and sit. You look worn out."

As she did, Hayley grinned. "You're getting a little southern in your accent. Yankee southern, but it's starting to creep in. Kinda cute."

"Must come from being outnumbered." Because she was concerned with how pale Hayley looked still, she sat on the arm of the chair.

"How long you going to keep us dangling?" Logan complained, and Mitch stood in front of the library table.

Like a teacher, Hayley thought. Sometimes she forgot he'd been one.

"Y'all know I've been in contact for several months with a descendant of the housekeeper who worked here during Reginald and Beatrice Harper's time."

"The Boston lawyer," Harper said and sat on the floor with Lily and her truck.

Mitch nodded. "Her interest has been piqued, and the more she's looked for information, the more people she's spoken with, the more invested she's become."

"Added to that Mitch has been doing a genealogy for her—gratis," Roz added.

"Tit for tat," he said. "And we needed some of the information anyway. Up till now she hasn't been able to find a great deal that applied to us. But today, she got a hit."

"You're killing us here," Stella commented.

"A letter, written by the housekeeper in question. Roni—Veronica, my contact, found a box full of letters in the attic of one of her great-aunts. It's considerable to sort through, to read through. But today, she found one written by Mary Havers to a cousin. The letter was dated January 12, 1893."

"A few months after the baby was born," Hayley added.

"That's right. Most of the letter deals with family business, or the sort of casual conversational observations that you'd expect—particularly in an era when people still wrote conversational letters. But in the body of the letter . . ." He held up papers. "She faxed me copies. I'm going to read the pertinent parts."

"Mom!" Luke's aggrieved voice wailed out. "Gavin's looking at me with the *face*."

"Gavin, not now. I mean it. Sorry," Stella apologized. She took a deep breath and determined to ignore the whispered argument from behind her. "Keep going."

"Just hold on one minute." Logan rose, walked over to crouch and have a conversation with the boys. There was a cheer, then they scrambled up.

"We're going to take Lily out to play," Gavin announced, and puffed out his chest. "Come on Lily. Wanna go outside?"

Clutching her truck, she deserted Harper, waved byebye, and took Gavin's hand. Logan closed the door behind them. "We're going out for ice cream later," he said to Stella as he walked back to his seat.

"Bribery. Good thinking. Sorry, Mitch."

"No problem. This was written to Mary Havers's cousin, Lucille."

Leaning back on the library table, Mitch adjusted his glasses, and read.

" 'I should not be writing of this, but I am so troubled in my heart and in my mind. I wrote to you last summer of the birth of my employers' baby boy. He is a beautiful child, Master Reginald, with such a sweet nature. The nurse Mister Harper hired is very competent and seems both gentle with him and quite attached. To my knowledge, the mistress has never entered the nursery. The nurse re-

ports to Mister Harper, and only Mister Harper. Below-stairs Alice, the nurse, tends to chatter, as girls often do. More than once I have heard her comment that the mistress never sees the child, has never held him, has never asked of his welfare.' "

"Cold bitch," Roz said quietly. "I'm glad she's not a blood ancestor. I'd rather have crazy than cruel." Then she lifted a hand. "Sorry, Mitchell. I shouldn't interrupt."

"It's okay. I've already read this through a couple times, and tend to agree with you. Mary Havers contin-ues," he said.

" 'It is not my place to criticize, of course. However, it would seem unnatural that a mother show no interest in her child, particularly the son who was so desired in this house. It cannot be said that the mistress is a warm woman, or naturally maternal, yet with her girls she is somewhat involved in their daily activities. I cannot count the number of nurses and governesses who have come and gone over the last few years. Mrs. Harper is very particular. Yet, she has never once given Alice instructions on what she ex-pects regarding Master Reginald.

" 'I tell you this, Lucy, because while we both know that often those abovestairs take little interest in the details of the household, unless there is an inconvenience, I suspect there is something troubling in this matter, and I must tell someone my thoughts, my fears.' "

"She knew something wasn't right," Hayley interrupted. "Sorry," she added with a glance around the room. "But you can hear it, even in what she doesn't say."

"She's fond of the baby, too." Stella turned her wine-glass around and around in her hands. "Concerned for him. You can hear that, too. Go on, Mitch."

"She writes, 'While I told you of the baby's birth, I did not mention in previous correspondence that there was no

sign in the months before that Mrs. Harper was expecting. Her activities, her appearance remained as ever. We who serve are privy to the intimate details of a household and those who live in it. It is unavoidable. There was no preparation for this child. No talk of nursemaids, of layettes, there was no lying-in for Mrs. Harper, no visits from the doctor. The baby was simply here one morning, as if, indeed, the stork had delivered him. While there was some talk belowstairs, I did not allow it to continue, at least in my presence. It is not our place to question such matters.

" 'Yet, Lucille, she has been so separate from this child it breaks the heart. So, yes, I have wondered. There can be little doubt who fathered the boy as he is the image of Mister Harper. His maternity, however, was another matter, at least in my mind.' "

"So they knew." Harper turned to his mother. "She knew, this Havers, and the household knew. And nothing was done."

"What could they do?" Hayley asked, and her voice was thick with emotion. "They were servants, employees. Even if they'd made noise about it, who would listen? They'd have been fired and kicked out, and nothing would have changed here."

"You're right." Mitch sipped from his glass of mineral water. "Nothing would have changed. Nothing did. She wrote more."

He set down his glass, turned the next page. " 'Earlier today a woman came to Harper House. So pale, so thin was she, and in her eyes, Lucy, was something not only desperate but not quite sane. Danby—' That was the butler at the time," Mitch explained. " 'Danby mistook her for someone looking for employment, but she pushed into the house by the front door, something wild in her. She claimed to have

come for the baby, for her baby. For her son she called
James. She said she heard him crying for her. Even if the
child had cried, no one could hear in the entrance hall as he
was tucked up in the nursery. I could not turn her away,
could not wrest her away as she ran wildly up the stairs, calling for her son. I do not know what I might have done, but
the mistress appeared and bade me show the woman up to
her sitting room. This poor creature trembled as I led her in.
The mistress would allow me to bring no refreshment. I
should not have done what I did next, what I have never
done in all my years of employment. I listened at the door.'"

"So she did come here." There was pity in Stella's voice
as she laid a hand on Hayley's shoulder. "She did come for
her baby. Poor Amelia."

" 'I heard the cruel things the mistress said to this unfortunate woman,'" Mitch continued. " 'I heard the cold
things she said about the child. Wishing him dead, Lucy,
God's pity, wishing him and this desperate woman dead
even as she, who called herself Amelia Connor, asked to
have the child returned to her. She was refused. She was
threatened. She was dismissed. I know now that the master
got this child, this son he craved, with this poor woman, his
lightskirt, and took the baby from her to foist it on his wife,
to raise the boy here as his heir. I understand that the doctor and the midwife who attended this woman were ordered to tell her the child, a girl child, was stillborn.

" 'I have known Mister Harper to be coldly determined
in his business, in his private affairs. I have not seen affection between him and his wife, or from him for his daughters. Yet I would not have deemed him capable of such a
monstrous act. I would not have believed his wife capable
of aligning herself with him. Miss Connor, in her ill-fitting
gray dress and shattered eyes, was ordered away, was
threatened with the police should she ever come back, ever

speak of what was spoken of in that room. I did my duty, Lucille, and showed her from the house. I watched her carriage drive away. I have not been easy in my mind since.

"'I feel I should try to help her, but what can I do? Is it not my Christian duty to offer some assistance, or comfort at the very least, to this woman? Yet my duty to my employers, those who provide the roof over my head, the food I eat, the money which keeps me independent, is to remain silent. To remember my place.

"'I will pray that I come to know what is right. I will pray for this young woman who came for the child she birthed, and was turned away.'"

Mitch set the pages down. And there was silence.

Tears slid down Hayley's cheeks. Her head was lowered, as it had been during the last page of Mitch's recital. Now she lifted it, and with her eyes shining with tears, smiled.

"But I came back."

SEVENTEEN

"HAYLEY."

"Don't." Mitch stepped forward as Harper sprang off the floor. "Wait."

"I came back," Hayley repeated, "for what was mine."

"But you weren't able to get to the child," Mitch said.

"Wasn't I? Didn't I?" In the chair Hayley lifted her arms, held her palms up. "Aren't I here? Didn't I watch him, didn't I sing him to sleep, night after night? And all the others who came after? They were never rid of me."

"But that's not enough now."

"I want what's mine! I want my due. I want . . ." Her eyes darted around the room. "Where are the children? Where are they?"

"Outside." Roz spoke quietly. "Playing outside."

"I like the children," Hayley said dreamily. "Who would have guessed? Such messy, selfish creatures. But so sweet,

so soft and sweet when they sleep. I like them best when they sleep. I would have shown him the world, my James. The world. And he would never have left me. Do you think I want her pity?" she said in a sudden rage. "A house-keeper? A *servant*? Do you think I want pity from her? Damn her and the rest of them. I should have killed them in their sleep."

"Why didn't you?"

Her gaze shifted, latched on Harper. "There are other ways to damn. So handsome. You are so like him."

"I'm not. I'm yours. The great-grandson of your son."

Her eyes clouded, and her fingers plucked at the thighs of her pants. "James? My James? I watched you. Sweet baby. Pretty little boy. I came to you."

"I remember. What do you want?"

"Find me. I'm lost."

"What happened to you?"

"You know! You did it. You're damned for it. Cursed with my last breath. I will have what's *mine*." Hayley's head fell back, and her hand clutched at her belly before her body shuddered. "God." She breathed out audibly. "Intense."

Harper grabbed her hands, knelt in front of her. "Hayley."

"Yeah." Her eyes were blurred, her face white as paper. "Can I have some water?"

He brought her hands up, pressed his face into them. "You can't keep doing this."

"Just as soon not. She was pissed. Thanks," she said to David as he handed her a glass of water. She drank it down like a woman dying of thirst. "Pissed, then sad, then pissed again—all sort of over the top on the emotional scale. The letter got to her. Well, it got to me."

She turned to Mitch with her hands still caught in Harper's. "I felt so sorry for her, and for the housekeeper. I

could see it. You know, how you do when you're reading a book. The house, the people. I could imagine what it would be like if somebody had Lily, and I couldn't do anything to get her back. 'Course the first thing I'd've done was clock Beatrice. The bitch. I guess I was getting pretty worked up, in my head, and she just sort of slid in."

Her fingers tightened on Harper's. "She's twisted up about you. Mostly, she's just twisted altogether, but she remembers you as a baby, as a little boy, she feels love for you because you're her blood. But you're his, too. And you resemble him, sort of. At least that's how it seems to me. It's confusing when it happens."

"You're stronger than she is," Harper told her.

"Saner anyhow. Way."

"You did great." Mitch set his tape recorder aside. "And I'd say you've had enough for today."

"It's been a busy one." She worked up a smile as she looked around the room. "Did I wig everybody out?"

"You could say that. Look, why don't you go up, stretch out," Stella suggested. "Logan will go out, check on the kids. Right?"

"Sure." He stepped over to Hayley first, gave her head a pat. "Go on up, beautiful, take a load off."

"I think I will, thanks." Harper straightened, took her hand to bring her to her feet. "I don't know what I'd do without you guys, I really don't."

Roz waited until they were out of the room. "This is wearing on her. I've never seen her look so tired. Hayley's a bundle of energy most times. Hell, she wears me out just watching her."

"We've got to finish this." Logan walked to the door, opened it. "And soon," he said before he went outside.

"What can we do?" Stella spread her hands. "Waiting and watching doesn't seem like enough. I don't know about

the rest of you, but seeing that happen, seeing it, shook me right down to the bone."

"I could go to Boston, help Veronica sort through the papers." Mitch shook his head. "But I'm just not comfortable leaving right now."

"Safety in numbers?" Roz reached out a hand for his, squeezed. "I feel the same. To tell the truth, at this point I don't like David spending so much time alone in the house."

"She doesn't bother me." He'd poured a glass of wine and lifted it now in a half toast. "Maybe because I'm not a blood-related male. Add gay to that and I'm not of much interest to her. You can factor in that she'd see me as a servant. That puts me bottom of the feeding chain."

"A lot she knows," Roz replied. "But that's logical, from her point of view, and does a lot to relieve my mind. Find her. She's said that before."

"Her grave," Mitch put in.

"I think we're all agreed on that." Roz walked over, helped herself to a sip of David's wine. "And how the hell are we supposed to do that?"

LATER, WHEN THE HOUSE WAS QUIET AND LILY SLEPT in her crib, Hayley couldn't settle. "One minute I'm ready to drop, and the next I'm all revved up. I must be really annoying."

"Now that you mention it." With a grin, Harper pulled her down on the sofa beside him. "Why don't we watch the game. I'll raid the kitchen for junk food."

"You want me to sit here and watch baseball?"

"I thought you liked baseball."

"Yeah, but not enough to zone out in front of the TV."

"Okay." He heaved an exaggerated sigh. "I'm about to

make the ultimate sacrifice for my breed. Pick a DVD. We'll watch a movie, even if it's a chick flick."

She eased back. "Really?"

"But you have to make the popcorn."

"You mean you'll sit here and watch a girlie movie without making snide comments?"

"I don't remember agreeing to the second part."

"You know, I like action flicks."

"Now we're talking."

"But I'd love to watch something romancey, with a couple of good weep scenes. Thanks!" She pressed her lips noisily to his, then jumped up. "I'm loading the popcorn with butter." At the door, she stopped and beamed back at him. "I feel better already."

SHE'D NEVER HAD SO MANY UPS AND DOWNS IN HER moods in all of her life. From manic energy to exhaustion, from joy to despair. She ran the gamut, it seemed, every day. And under the swings, the spurts, and the tumbles was an edgy anticipation of what happens next. And when.

When she spiraled down, she struggled to remind herself of what she had. A beautiful child, a wonderful man who loved her, friends, family, a good interesting job. And still, once the spiral began, she couldn't seem to control the fall.

She worried there was something physically wrong with her. A chemical imbalance, a brain tumor. Maybe she was going as crazy as The Bride.

Feeling harassed and overtired, she swung into Wal-Mart on her morning off to pick up diapers, shampoo, a few other basics. She could only thank God to be able to snatch this little window of alone time. Or alone with Lily time, she corrected, as she strapped her daughter in the shopping cart.

At least nobody felt they were obliged to watch her when she was away from Harper House or work. And watching was what they did. Like hawks.

She understood why, God knew she appreciated the concern and care. But that didn't stop her from feeling smothered. She could barely start to brush her teeth without whoever was hovering offering to spread the paste on the brush for her.

She wandered down aisles, listlessly picking up what she needed. Then she detoured into cosmetics, thinking a new lipstick might cheer her up. But the shades seemed too dark or too light, too bold or too dull. Nothing suited her.

She looked so pale and wan these days, she decided if she put anything bright on her lips they'd look as though they walked into the room a foot ahead of her.

New perfume maybe. But every tester she sniffed made her feel slightly queasy.

"Just forget it," she muttered, and glanced back at Lily who was trying to stretch out her arm to reach a spin rack of mascaras and eye pencils.

"Not for a long time yet, young lady. It's fun being a girl though, you'll see. All these toys we get to play with." She chose one of the mascaras herself, tossed it in the cart. "I just can't seem to gear myself up for it right now. We'll just go on, get your diapers. And maybe if you're good, a new board book."

She turned down another aisle, reluctant to leave. Once she did, she'd need to take Lily to the sitter's, go to work. Where somebody would be attached to her hip for the rest of the day.

She wanted to do something normal, damn it. More, she wanted to *feel* like doing something. Anything.

And an absent glance to her right stopped her in her tracks.

Something that was both panic and nausea, with a help-ing of dull realization spurted into her belly. It continued to rise as she did hasty calculations in her head.

While everything inside her sank, Hayley closed her eyes. She opened them again, looked into Lily's happy face. And reached for the home pregnancy test.

SHE DROPPED LILY OFF, KEPT A SMILE PLASTERED ON her face until she walked out the door to her car. Afraid to do otherwise, she kept her mind blank while she drove home. She wouldn't think, she wouldn't project. She would just go home, take the test. Twice. When it came out nega-tive, which of course it would, she'd hide the packages somewhere until she could dispose of them without anyone knowing she'd had a panic attack.

She wasn't pregnant again. She absolutely couldn't be pregnant again.

She parked, and made certain the boxes were buried at the bottom of her bag and well hidden. But she'd taken two steps into the house when David appeared like some magic genie.

"Hi, sugar, want a hand with that?"

"No." She gripped the bag to her chest like a cache of gold. "No," she repeated more calmly. "I'm just going to take these things up. And I have to pee, if that's all the same to you."

"It is. I often have to pee myself."

Knowing her tone had been nasty, she rubbed a hand over her face. "I'm sorry. I'm in a mood."

"Something else I often have." He pulled an open tube of Life Savers from his pocket, thumbed out a cherry cir-cle. "Open up."

She smiled, obeyed.

"Let's see if that sweetens your mood," he said as he popped the candy into her mouth. "Can't help worrying about you, honey."

"I know. If I'm not back down in fifteen minutes, you can call out the cavalry. Deal?"

"Deal."

She hurried up, then dumped the contents of the bag on her bed—for God's sake, she'd forgotten the diapers. Cursing, she snatched both pregnancy tests and bolted to the bathroom.

For a moment she was afraid she wouldn't be able to pee. Wouldn't that just be her luck? She ordered herself to calm down, took several long breaths. Added a prayer.

Moments later, with the sweetness of cherry candy still on her tongue, she was staring at the stick with PREGNANT reading clear as day in its window.

"No." She gripped the stick, shook it as if it were a thermometer and the action would drop things back down to normal. "No, no, no, no! What *is* this? What are you?" She looked down at herself, rapped a fist lightly below her navel. "Some kind of sperm magnet?"

Undone, she sat on the toilet lid, buried her face in her hands.

THOUGH SHE MIGHT HAVE PREFERRED TO CRAWL INTO the cabinet under the sink, curl up in the dark, and stay there for the next nine months, she didn't have much time to indulge in a pity fest. She washed her face, slapping on cold water to eradicate the signs of her bathroom crying jag.

"Yeah, crying's going to make a difference," she berated herself. "That'll do the trick, all right. It'll change everything so when you look at that *stupid* test again the damn stick will read: Why no, Hayley, you're not pregnant.

You just needed to sit on the toilet and bawl for ten minutes. Idiot."

She sniffled back what felt like another flood of tears and faced herself in the mirror. "You played, now you pay. Deal with it."

A quick makeup session helped. The sunglasses she grabbed out of her purse helped more.

She buried the home pregnancy test boxes in the bottom of her underwear drawer, jumpy as a drug addict hiding his stash.

When she went out, David was already halfway up the stairs.

"I was about to get my bugle."

She stared at him. "What?"

"To call the cavalry, honey. You were longer than fifteen."

"Sorry. I got . . . Sorry."

He started to smile and brush it off, then shook his head. "Nope, not going to pretend I don't know you've been crying. What's the matter?"

"I can't." Even on those two words her voice shook, broke. "I'm going to be late for work."

"Somehow the world will keep turning. What you're going to do is sit right down here in my office." Taking her hand, he tugged until she sat on the steps with him. "And tell Uncle David your troubles."

"I don't have troubles. I'm *in* trouble." She didn't mean to tell him, to tell anyone. Not until she had time to think, to deal. To bury her head in the sand for a few days. But he draped an arm around her shoulders to hug her, and the words leaped out of her mouth.

"I'm pregnant."

"Oh." His hand stroked up and down her arm. "Well, that's something my secret horde of super chocolate truffles won't fix."

She turned her head, pressed her face to his shoulder. "I'm like some sort of fertility bomb, David. What am I going to do? What the hell am I going to do?"

"What's right for you. You're sure now?"

Sniffling, she boosted her butt off the steps, tugged the stick out of her pocket. "What's that say in there?"

"Mmm. The eagle has landed." Gently, he caught her chin in his hand, lifted her face. "How are you feeling?"

"Sick, scared. Stupid! So damn stupid. We used protection, David. It's not like we were a couple of lust-crazed teenagers in the back of a Chevy. I think I have some sort of *über*eggs or something, and they just spit on barriers and *suck* the sperm in."

He laughed, then gave her another squeeze. "Sorry. I know it's not funny to you. Let's calm down here and take a look at the big picture. You're in love with Harper."

"Of course I am, but—"

"He's in love with you."

"Yes, but— Oh, David, we're just getting started on that. On being in love, on being together. Maybe I let myself imagine how it might be down the road some. But we haven't made any plans about the long-term. We haven't talked about it at all."

"That's why sooner comes before later, honey. You'll talk now."

"How can any man in the world not feel trapped when a woman comes up and tells him she's pregnant?"

"You manage to get that way all by yourself?"

"That's not the point."

"Hayley." He drew back, tipped her sunglasses down her nose so he could look into her eyes. "That's exactly the point. With Lily, you did what was right for you, and what you felt in your heart was right for the father, and for the baby. Right or wrong—and personally I think it was

right—but either way, I think it was brave. Now you've got to be brave again, do what's right for everybody concerned. You've got to tell Harper."

"I don't know how. I get sick thinking about it."

"Then you might love him, but you're not giving him credit for being the man he is."

"I am, that's the trouble." She stared back down at the stick and the word in that window seemed to scream in her head. "He'll stand up. How will I know if he did because he loves me, or because he feels responsible?"

David leaned over, kissed her temple. "Because you will."

IT ALL SOUNDED GOOD. IT SOUNDED REASONABLE, logical, and adult. But it didn't make it any easier to do what she was about to do.

She wished she could delay it, just ignore it all for a few days. Even pretend it would go away. And that was small and selfish and childish.

When she reached the nursery, she slipped into one of the employee bathrooms to take the second test. She glugged down most of a pint of water, turned the spigot on for good measure. She started to cross her fingers, but told herself not to be a complete ass.

Still, she read the results with eyes squinted half shut.

It didn't change the outcome.

Well, still pregnant, she thought. There was no crying this time, no cursing fate. She simply tucked the stick back in her pocket, opened the door, and prepared to do what needed to be done next. She had to tell Harper.

Why? Why did he have to know? She could go away now, she thought. Pack up and go. The baby was *hers*.

He was rich, he was powerful. He would take the child

and toss her aside. Take her son. For the glory of the great Harper name he would use her like a vessel, then rip away what grew in her.

He had no right to what was hers. No right to what she carried inside her.

"Hayley."

"What?" She jolted like a thief, then blinked at Stella.

She was standing among the shade plants, surrounded by hostas green as Ireland. Yards away from the restroom.

How long had she been standing there, thinking thoughts not her own?

"Are you all right?"

"A little turned around." She drew in a long breath. "I'm sorry I'm late."

"It's all right."

"I'll make it up. But I need . . . I have to talk to Harper. Before I get started I need to talk to him."

"In the grafting house. He wanted to know when you got in. Hayley, I wish you'd tell me what's wrong."

"I need to talk to Harper first." Before she lost her nerve, or her mind.

She hurried away, walking quickly between the tables of plants, across the asphalt skirt, past the greenhouses. Business was picking up, she noted, after the high summer slump. Temperatures were easing off, just a little, and made people think about their fall plantings. Stella's boys were going back to school. Days were getting shorter.

The world didn't stop just because she had a crisis on her hands.

She hesitated outside of the grafting house, struck by the fact that her mind—so full a moment before—was now a complete blank.

There was only one thing to do, she decided. That was to go in.

The house was warm and full of music. It so well suited him, full of plants in various stages of growth and development, smelling of soil and green.

She didn't know the music that played, something with harps and flutes. But she knew whatever it was wouldn't be playing through his headphones.

He was down at the far end, and it seemed like the longest walk of her life. Even when he turned, saw her, and flashed a grin.

"Hey, just who I wanted to see." He made a come-ahead gesture with one hand as he drew his headset off with the other. "Take a look."

"At what?"

"Our babies."

Since he shifted to the plants, he didn't see her jerk in response. "They're right on schedule," he continued. "See, the ovary sections have already swelled."

"They're not the only ones," she mumbled, but moved forward to stand beside him and study the plants they'd grafted a few weeks before.

"See? The pods are fully formed. We give them another three, four weeks for the seeds to ripen. The top'll split. We'll gather the seeds, plant them in pots. Keep 'em outdoors, exposed. And in the spring, they'll germinate. Once they're about three inches, we'll plant them out in nursery beds."

It wasn't procrastinating to stand there talking about a mutual project. It was . . . polite. "Then what?"

"Usually we'll get blooms the second season. Then we'll study and record the differences, the likenesses, the characteristics. What we're hoping for is at least one—and I'm banking on more—mini with a strong pink color, and that blush of red. We get that, we've got Hayley's Lily."

"If we don't."

"Pessimism isn't the gardener's friend, but if we don't, we'll have something else cool. And we'll try again. Anyway, I thought you might want to work with me on a rose, for my mother."

"Oh, um . . ." If it was a girl, should they name her Rose? "That'd be nice. Sweet of you."

"Well, it's Mitch's idea, but the guy couldn't grow a Chia Pet. He wants to try for a black. Nobody's ever managed a true black rose, but I thought we could play around and see what we came up with. It's the right time of year— time to wash down, disinfect, air and dry out this place. Hygiene's a big for this kind of work, and roses are pretty fussy. They're time-consuming, too, but it'd be fun."

He looked so excited, she thought, at the idea of starting something new. Just how would he look when she told him they already had?

"Um, when you do all this, you pick the parents—the pollen plant, the seed plant. Deliberate selection, for specific characteristics."

Her blue eyes, Harper's brown. His patience, her impulse. What would you get?

"Right. You're trying to cross them, to create something with the best—or at least the desired characteristics—of both."

His temper, her stubbornness. Oh God. "People don't work that way."

"Hmm." He turned to his computer, keying data into a file. "No, guess not."

"And with people, they can't always—or don't always— plan it all out like this. They don't always get together and say, hey, let's hybridize."

He shot a laugh over his shoulder. "Now that's a line I never thought to use in a bar, picking up a girl. I'd put it in the file, but since I've already got a girl, it'd be wasted."

"You never used a line on me," she told him. "Anyway, hybridizing's about creating something, a separate something. Not just about the fun and games."

"Hmm. Hey, did I show you the viburnum? Suckering's been a problem, but I'm pretty happy with how it's coming along."

"Harper." Tears wanted to spurt and spill again. "Harper, I'm sorry."

"It's not a big," he said absently. "I know how to deal with suckering."

"I'm pregnant."

There, she thought. She said it. Fast and clean. Like ripping a bandage off a wound.

"You said what?" He stopped typing, slowly swiveled on his stool.

She didn't know how to read his face. Maybe it was because her own vision seemed blurry and half blind. She couldn't read the tone of his voice, not with the roaring going on in her ears.

"I should've known. I should have. I've been so tired, and I missed my period—I just forgot about it—and I've been queasy on and off, and so damn moody. I thought, I didn't think. I thought it was what was happening with Amelia. I didn't put it together. I'm sorry."

The entire burst came out in a disjointed ramble that she could barely comprehend herself. She dropped into silence when he held up a hand.

"Pregnant. You said you were pregnant."

"God, do I have to spell the word out for you?" Not sure if she wanted to weep or rage, she yanked the test stick out of her pocket. "There, read it yourself. P-R-E—"

"Hold it." He took the stick from her, stared at it. "When did you find out?"

"Just today, now. A little while ago. I was in Wal-Mart, getting some things. I forgot Lily's diapers and bought mascara. What kind of a mother am I?"

"Quiet down." He rose, took her shoulders and nudged her onto the stool. "You're all right? I mean it doesn't hurt or anything."

"Of course it doesn't hurt. For Christ's sake."

"Look, don't crawl up my ass." He scrubbed a hand over the back of his neck as he studied her. Much, she thought, as he did his plants-in-progress. "It's my first day on the job. How much are you pregnant?"

"Pretty much all the way."

"Damn it, Hayley, I mean how far along, or whatever you call it?"

"I think about six weeks. Five or six."

"How big is it in there?"

She dragged a hand through her hair. "I don't know. About as big as a kernel of rice."

"Wow." He stared at her belly, laid a hand on it. "Wow. When does it start to move around? When does it get, like, fingers or toes?"

"Harper, can we focus here?"

"I don't know any of this stuff. I want to know. You need to go to the doctor, right?" He grabbed her hand. "We should go now."

"I don't need to go to the doctor now. Harper, what are we going to do?"

"What do you mean what are we going to do. We're going to have a baby. Holy shit!" He plucked her right off the stool and a half a foot off the ground. The face he tilted up to hers was split with a dazzled grin. "We're going to have a baby."

She had to brace her hands on his shoulders. "You're not mad."

"Why would I be mad?"

Now she felt dizzy, overwhelmed, shaken to the core. "Because. Because."

He lowered her, slowly, back onto the stool. And now his voice was careful and cool. "You don't want the baby."

"I don't know. How can I think about what I want? How can I think at all?"

"Pregnancy affects brain waves. Interesting."

"I—"

"But, okay, I'll do the thinking. You go to the doctor so we're sure everything's okay in there. We get married. And next spring we have a baby."

"Married? Harper, people shouldn't get married just because—"

Though he leaned back against the worktable, he still managed to hedge her in. "In my world, where the sky's blue, people who love each other and are having babies get married all the time. Maybe this is a little ahead of our regularly scheduled program, but it's the kind of bulletin you pay attention to."

"We had a regularly scheduled program?"

"I did." He reached over to tuck her hair behind her ears, then tugged gently at the ends. "I want you, you know I do. I want the baby. We're going to do this right, and that's the way it's going to be."

"So you're ordering me to marry you."

"I had planned to charm you into it, at some point a little farther down the road. But since the timing's changed— and pregnancy's jammed your power of thought—we're going this way."

"You're not even upset."

"No, I'm not upset." He paused a moment as if taking stock. "A little scared, a lot awed. Man, Lily's going to love this. Baby brother or sister to torment. Wait till I tell my

brothers they're going to be uncles. What till I tell Mama she's going to be a . . ."

"Grandmother," Hayley finished and nodded, subversively pleased to see a flicker of doubt in his eyes at last. "Just how do you think she's going to feel about that?"

"I guess I'll find out."

"I can't—just can't take all this in." She pressed the heels of her hands to her temples as if it would stop her head from spinning. "I don't even know what I'm feeling." Dropping her hands in her lap, she stared at him. "Harper, you don't think this is a mistake?"

"Our baby's not a mistake." He gathered her in, felt her breath give a hitch as she struggled with tears. "But it's one hell of a surprise."

eighteen

HE WENT IN AND OUT OF A DAZE FOR THE REST OF THE day. There was a lot to be considered, worked out, planned. The initial steps were crystal to him, as clear and precise as the initial steps in any graft.

They would get Hayley into the doctor, get her and the baby checked out. He'd start reading up on baby stuff—womb stuff—so that he understood the process, got sharper images in his head of what was going on in there.

They'd get married as soon as possible, but not so fast it had to be something rushed and cold and practical. He didn't want that for Hayley, or when he thought it through, for himself.

He wanted to get married at Harper House. In the gardens he helped tend, in the shadow of the house where he'd grown up. He wanted to make his promises to Hayley there, and he realized, to make them to Lily there, and

to this new child who was now the size of a grain of rice.

This was what he wanted, what he had, somehow, been moving toward all of his life. It was something he'd never thought about before, and knew now as surely as he knew his own name.

Hayley and Lily would move into the carriage house. He'd speak to his mother about adding on to it, giving it more space while staying true to the heart and the traditional style.

More space for their children, he thought, so that they, too, could grow up in Harper House, with its gardens, its woods, its history that would be theirs as it was his.

He could see all of that, he could *know* all of that. But what he couldn't see was the child. The child he'd helped create.

A grain of rice? How could something so small be so huge? And already be so loved?

But now there was a step that had to be taken before the others.

He found his mother in the garden, adding a few asters and mums to one of her beds.

She wore thin cotton gloves, soiled with seasons of work. Cropped cotton pants, the color of bluebonnets that were already smudged with the greens and browns of the task she performed. Her feet were bare, and he could see the backless slides she'd stepped out of before she'd knelt at the border.

When he'd been a child, he'd believed her to be invincible, almost supernatural. She knew everything whether you wanted her to or not. She'd had the answers when he'd needed them, had given him hugs—and the occasional licks. Some of which he'd still like to dispute.

Most of all she'd been there, unfailingly been there. In the best times, in the worst, and all the times between.

Now, it would be his turn.

She tilted her head up as he approached, absently brushed the back of her hand over her brow. It struck him how beautiful she was, her hat tipped over her eyes, her face serene.

"Had a good day," she said. "Thought I'd extend it and fluff up this bed. Gonna rain tonight."

"Yeah." Automatically he glanced up at the sky. "Hoping for a nice soaker."

"Your mouth, God's ear." She squinted against the sun as she studied him. "My, don't you have your serious face on. You gonna sit down here so I don't get a crick in my neck?"

He crouched. "I need to talk to you."

"You usually do when you have your serious face on."

"Hayley's pregnant."

"Well." She set down her trowel, very carefully. "Well, well, well."

"She just found out today. She thinks about six weeks. She got the symptoms—I guess you call them symptoms—mixed up with everything else that's going on."

"I can see how that might happen. Is she all right?"

"A little upset, a little scared, I guess."

She reached up, took off his sunglasses, looked into his eyes. "How about you?"

"I've been taking it in. I love her, Mama."

"I know you do. Are you happy, Harper?"

"I'm a lot of things. Happy's one of them. I know this isn't how you'd hoped I would do things."

"Harper, it doesn't matter what I hoped or want." Carefully she selected a blue aster, set it in the hole she'd already dug. Her hands worked, tucking it in, patting the earth as she spoke. "What matters is what you and Hayley want. What matters is that little girl, and the child you've started."

"I want Lily. I want to marry Hayley and make Lily

mine, legally. I want this baby. And I know it might seem like I've just dropped a pill into a glass of water. Pow, instant family, but . . . Don't cry. Please don't cry."

"I'm entitled to cry when my firstborn tells me he's making me a grandmother. I'm damn well entitled to a few tears. Where the hell is my bandanna?"

He pulled it out of her back pocket, handed it to her.

"I've got to sit all the way down a minute." She plopped down on her butt, wiped her eyes, blew her nose. "You know this day's going to come. From the moment you hold your child in your arms, you know. It's not your first thought, even a conscious one, but it's there, this knowledge that the thread's spinning out. Life cycles. Women know them. And gardeners. Harper."

She opened her arms to him. "You're going to be a daddy."

"Yeah." Because he could, he always could, he pressed his face to the strong line of her neck.

"And I'm going to be a grandmama. Two for one." She drew back, kissed his cheeks. "I love that little girl. She's already ours. I want you and Hayley to know I feel that way. That I'm happy for you. Even if you did manage to do this so the new baby arrives during our busiest season."

"Oops. Didn't think of that."

"I forgive you." She laughed, then pulled off her gloves so she could take his hands, flesh to flesh. "You asked her to marry you?"

"Sort of. Mostly I told her she was going to. And don't give me that look."

Her eyebrows stayed raised, her eyes steely. "It's exactly the look you deserve."

"I'm going to take care of it." He looked down at their joined hands, then lifted hers, one by one, to his lips. "I love you, Mama. You set the bar high."

"What bar is that?"

He looked back up, into her eyes. "I couldn't settle for anybody I loved or respected less than I love and respect you."

Tears swam again. "I'm going to need more than that bandanna in a minute."

"I'm going to give her the best I've got. And to start, I'd like to have Grandmama's rings. Grandmama Harper's engagement and wedding rings. You said once when I got married—"

"That's my boy." With her lips curved, she kissed him lightly. "That's the man I raised. I'll get them for you."

ONE OF THE OTHER THINGS HE'D NEVER IMAGINED was how he'd propose to a woman. To *the* woman. A fancy dinner and wine? A lazy picnic? A giant WILL YOU MARRY ME? on the scoreboard screen at a game.

How weak was that?

The best, he decided, was the place and the tone that suited them both.

So he took her for a walk in the gardens at twilight.

"I don't feel right about your mother riding herd on Lily again. I'm pregnant, not handicapped."

"She wanted to. And I wanted an hour alone with you. Don't—don't go there. God, it's getting so I can see what's going on in your head. I'm crazy about Lily, and I'm not going to spend time telling you what's so damn obvious."

"I know. I know you are. I just can't settle into all this. It's not like I went jumping into bed all over two states. But here I am, for the second time."

"No, this time is different. This is the first time. See that flowering plum?"

"I can only tell—or tell sometimes—when they're blooming."

"This one." He stopped, reached up to touch one of the glossy green leaves. "My parents planted this right after I was born. We'll plant one for Lily, and we'll plant one for this baby. But see this one? It's got nearly thirty years on it now, and they planted it for me. I always felt good about that. Always felt this was one of my places, right here. We'll be making other places, you and me, but we'll start here, with one that already is."

He took the box out of his pocket, watched her lips tremble open, her gaze shoot up to his face. "Oh my God."

"I'm not getting down on one knee. I'm not going to feel like an ass when I do this."

"I think it had something to do with him pledging his loyalty. I mean that's why guys started the one-knee thing."

"You'll just have to take my word on mine. I want this life we've started. Not just the baby, but what we've started together. You and me, and Lily, and now this baby. I want to live that life with you. You're the first woman I've loved. You'll be the last."

"Harper, you—you really do take my breath away."

He opened the box, smiled a little when he saw her eyes widen. "This was my grandmother's. Kind of an old-fashioned setting, I guess."

"I—" She had to swallow. "I prefer the word *classic,* or *heirloom.* Or let's get real, woo-hoo. Harper, Roz must—"

"It was promised to me. Given to me to give to you, to the woman I want to spend my life with. I want you to wear it. Marry me, Hayley."

"It's beautiful, Harper. You're beautiful."

"I'm not done."

"Oh." She gave a nervous laugh. "I can't imagine there's more."

"I want you to take my name. I want Lily to take my name. I want the whole package. I can't settle for less."

"Do you know what you're saying?" She laid a hand on his cheek. "What you're doing?"

"Exactly. And you better answer me soon, because I'd hate to spoil this romantic moment by wrestling you to the ground and shoving this ring on your finger."

"It's not going to come to that." She closed her eyes for a moment, thought of flowering plums, of generations of tradition. "I knew you'd ask me to marry you when I told you I was pregnant. You're built that way, to do what's right. What's honorable."

"This isn't—"

"You had your say." She shook her head fiercely. "I'm having mine. I knew you'd ask, and part of the reason I felt sick about all this was because I was afraid I wouldn't know for sure. That you'd ask because you felt it was what you had to do. But I do know, and that's not why. I'll marry you, Harper, and take your name. So will Lily. We'll love you all of our lives."

He took the ring out of the box, slid it on her finger.

"It's too big," he murmured as he lifted her hand to kiss.

"You're not getting it back."

He closed his hand over hers to hold the ring in place. "Just long enough to have it sized."

She managed a nod, then threw herself into his arms. "I love you. I love you, I love you."

With a laugh, he tipped back her head to kiss her. "I was hoping you'd say that."

*   *   *

She felt a little awkward going in with Harper to make the announcement to his mother and Mitch, to have David serving champagne. She was allowed half a glass, and had to make due with that for both toasts.

One on the engagement, and one for the baby.

Roz gathered her into a hug, and whispered in her ear. "You and I have to talk. Soon."

"Oh. I guess so."

"How about now? Harper, I'm going to steal your girl for a few minutes. There's something I want to show her."

Without waiting for a response, Roz hooked an arm through Hayley's and led her out of the room and toward the stairs.

"You giving any thought to the sort of wedding you want?"

"I—no. It's so much."

"I'm sure it is."

"Harper . . . he said something about getting married here."

"I was hoping. We could use the ballroom if you want something splashy. Or the gardens and terrace if you want something more intimate. Y'all discuss it and let me know. I'm dying to dive in, and I plan to be very opinionated, so you'll have to watch me like a hawk."

"You're not mad."

"I'm surprised you'd say such a thing to me."

"I'm trying to put myself in your place," Hayley said as they climbed the stairs. "And I can't quite get there."

"That's because you've got your own place. I like having mine to myself." She turned toward her wing.

"I didn't get pregnant on purpose."

At the entrance to her bedroom, Roz paused, looked Hayley squarely in her swimming eyes. "Is that what's go-

ing on in your head? Me thinking this is calculated on your part."

"No—not exactly. A lot of people would."

"I'm pleased to say I'm not a lot of people. I'm also a superior judge of character, with only one major stumble in my illustrious career. If I thought less of you, Hayley, you wouldn't be living in my home."

"I thought . . . when you said we had to talk."

"Oh, that's about enough of this business out of you." Roz walked over to the bed, opened the box that sat on it. She lifted out what looked like a pale blue cloud.

"This was Harper's blanket, what I had made for him right after he was born. I had one made for each of my boys, and they're one of the things I saved to pass on. If you have a girl, you'll use something of Lily's or want something new and feminine. But I hope, if you have boy, you'll use this. In either case, you should have this now."

"It's beautiful."

Roz held it against her cheek a moment. "Yes, it is. Harper is one of the great loves of my life. There's nothing I want more on this earth than his happiness. You make him happy. That's more than enough for me."

"I'll be a good wife to him."

"You damn well better be. Are we going to sit down and have a cry now?"

"Oh yeah. Yeah, that'd be good."

WHEN SHE LAY BESIDE HIM IN THE DARK, SHE LIS-tened to the steady, drumming rain.

"I don't know how I can be so happy and so scared at the same time."

"I'm right there with you."

"This morning, it felt like everything crashed down on my head, like a whole bookcase, and every book smacked me with the hard edge. Now it turns out it was flowers falling, and I'm covered in all these soft petals and perfume."

He took her hand, the left, the one where her thumb kept rubbing along her third finger. The ring was in its box on the dresser. "I'll get it to the jeweler tomorrow."

"I don't know how I'm going to feel about being married to somebody who reads my mind." Then she rolled over onto him, tossed back her hair. "I think I can read yours, too. And it goes something like this."

She lowered her lips to his.

Soft and smooth, that's how she felt with him. Lovely and loose. And most of all, loved. Whatever tried to darken her heart, whatever brewed in the night, she could, she would, hold off and have this time with him.

Safe, secure. Seduced.

She could trust him to hold her, as he did now, with their bodies warm, their lips tender. She could trust herself to be strong with the taste of him teasing her tongue.

They moved together, slow and easy, while the rain drummed musically on the stones of the terrace. Her heart drummed, too. Pleasure and anticipation. She knew him so well. Friend and partner, now lover. Husband.

Overcome, she laid her cheek on his. "I love you, Harper. It seems like I've already loved you forever."

"We've still got forever."

He brushed his fingers over her face, her cheeks, her temples, into her hair. He could see her in the gloomy dark, the shape of her, the gleam of her eyes. Witchy and mysterious in this storm light, but nonetheless his. He could look at her and see the long roll of the future. Touch her, and know the simple beauty of the now.

He sampled her lips, skin, the long line of her throat, the subtle curve of her breast. Her heart beat under it, steady as the rain. And quickened as his mouth possessed.

Slowly, guided by her sighs, he took his hands and lips over her. The narrow torso, so white, so delicate in the dim light, and the jump of muscles as he passed, the quivers, told him she was roused.

He laid his lips, gently, so gently, on her belly, and laid his cheek there just a moment, in wonder of what grew in her. Her hand brushed over his hair, stroked.

"Its middle name has to be Harper," she murmured. "Boy or girl, whatever we choose for the first name, it's important we pass the Harper name on."

He turned his head to press another kiss over their child. "How about Cletis? Cletis Harper Ashby."

He fought to keep his lips from curving against her skin when her hand stilled. "That's a joke, right?"

"Little Cletis, or Hermione, if it's a girl. You just don't see enough Hermiones these days."

He kissed his way back up until his lips hovered over hers.

"You'd be sorry if I fell in love with those names and insisted on them. Wouldn't be so funny then, would it?"

"Maybe Clemm." He dropped little kisses at the corners of her mouth. "Or Gertrude."

Her fingers drilled into his ribs. "Looks like I'm going to have to be sure I'm the one filling out the birth certificate. Especially since I'm thinking we'll stick with flower names. Begonia's my personal favorite."

"But what if it's a girl?"

She grabbed both of his ears and pulled, then gave up on a laugh.

And was laughing when he slipped inside her.

* * *

SHE WAS SO WARM, SO CONTENT, SNUGGLED UP BESIDE him, drifting off to sleep. The patter of rain was music, a lullabye to float away to dreams on.

She imagined herself walking toward him, her long white dress shimmering in the sunlight, lilies, bold and red lying in the crook of her arm, like a child. He would wait for her, wait to take her hand, to make promises. Take the vows that meant forever.

Till death do you part.

No. She shifted with the quiver under her heart. She wanted no mention of death on the day they married. No promises tied to it.

Death brought shadows, and shadows blocked the sun.

Empty promises. Words spoken by rote and never meant to be kept. Clouds over the sun, and the rain turning her white gown to dull, dingy gray.

It was cold, bleak. But there was such heat in her. Hate was a furnace, rage the fire that stoked it.

How strange, how extraordinary that she should feel so alive, so viciously *alive* at last.

The house was dark. A tomb. They were all dead inside. Only her child lived, and would always, ever. Endless. She and her son would live forever, be together until the end of days while the rest rotted.

This was her vengeance. Her only task now.

She had given life. She had grown it inside her own body, had pushed it into the world with a pain akin to madness. It would not be stolen from her. It was hers to keep.

She would bide in that house with her son. And she would be the true mistress of Harper House.

After this night, she and James would never be parted again.

The rain drenched her as she walked, humming her tune as the hem of her soaked nightdress waded through mud.

They would play in the gardens in the bright spring. How he would laugh. Flowers blooming, birds singing, only for them. Tea and cakes, yes, tea and cakes for her precious boy.

Soon, very soon now, an endless spring for them.

She walked through the rain, wading through the crawl of fog. Now and then she thought she heard some sound—voices, laughter, weeping, shouting.

Now and then, she thought she saw some movement out of the corner of her eye. Children playing, an old woman sleeping in a chair, a young man planting flowers.

But they were not of her world, not of the world she sought.

In her world, they would be the shadows.

She walked the paths, or trod over the winter beds, her feet bare and filthy. Her eyes mad moonbeams.

She saw the silhouette of the stables. What she needed would be there, but so would others. Servants, rutting stablehands, dirty grooms.

Instead, she tapped a finger on her lips, as if for silence, but a rolling laugh escaped. Maybe she should burn the stables, set a fire that would rise up in the sky. Oh, how the horses would scream and the men run.

A toasty blaze on an ice-cold night.

She felt that she could light fires with a thought. And thinking, whirled to face Harper House. She could burn it to ash with her mind. Every room bursting with heat. And he, the great Reginald Harper, and all who had betrayed her would perish in the hell she created.

But not the child. No, no, not the child. She pressed both hands to her mouth, banished the thought before the spark flew. It was not the way for her son.

He must come with her. Be with her.

She walked toward the carriage house. Her hair, tan-

gled around her face, dripped into her eyes, but she walked unhurried.

No locks here, she thought at the wide doors. Who would dare trespass on Harper land?

She would.

The door creaked as she pulled it open. Even in the gloom, she could see the shine of the carriages. No dull wheels for the great master. Big, glossy carriages to carry him and his whore-wife, his mewling daughters, wherever they chose to go.

While the mother of his son, the creator of *life,* drove in a stolen wagon.

Oh, he would pay.

She stood in the open doorway, swaying as her mind rolled in circles, buzzing rings of rage and confusion and terrible love. She forgot where she was, what she was, why. Then the purpose looped around once more.

Could she risk a light? Dare she? She must, she must. She couldn't see in the dark.

Not yet.

Though her fingers shook with cold as she lighted a lamp, she didn't feel it. The heat still burned through her, and made her smile as she saw the hank of rope.

There now, that would do, that would do nicely.

She left the lamp burning, the door open as she walked back out into the rain.

WHEN HARPER TURNED, REACHED FOR HER, SHE wasn't there. He half woke, stretching his arm out farther, expecting to meet her skin.

"Hayley?"

He murmured her name, pushed onto his elbow. His first

thought was that she'd gone in to Lily, but he heard nothing from the bedside monitor.

It took him a few seconds longer to realize what he did hear.

The rain was too loud. Pushing up quickly he saw the terrace doors were open. He rolled out, grabbing his jeans.

"Hayley!" He dragged on his jeans, bolted for the door. He saw nothing but the rain and the dark.

Rain pelted him, his heart constricted to an ice chip in his chest. On a panicked oath, he rushed back inside, and into Lily's room.

The baby slept, peacefully. Her mother wasn't there.

He strode back to the bedroom, grabbed the monitor, and, shoving it in his back pocket, went out to find her.

Calling for her, he bolted down the steps. The carriage house, he thought. He'd always believed Amelia had gone there. The night he'd seen her in the garden when he'd been a child, he'd been sure that's where she'd been going.

Her gown had been wet and muddy, he remembered as he ran. As if she'd been in the rain.

He knew his way, even in the dark. There was no turn of the path that wasn't familiar to him. He saw his front door hanging open, felt a trip of relief.

"Hayley!" He slapped on the light as he rushed in.

The floor was wet, and muddy footprints crossed the room, into the kitchen. He knew the house was empty even before he called for her again, before he ran through it, heart thundering, looking for her.

This time he grabbed the phone, speed-dialing as he ran back out.

"Mama, Hayley's gone. She went outside. I can't find her. She's—oh Jesus, I see her. Third floor. She's on the third floor terrace."

He tossed the phone aside and kept running.

She didn't turn when he shouted her name, but continued to cross the terrace like a wraith. His feet skidded on wet stone, and flowers were crushed as he leaped off the path into beds to cut to the stairs leading up.

Lungs burning, heart screaming, he bounded up.

He reached the third level as she flung open a door.

She hesitated when he called out to her, and slowly turned her head to face him. And smiled. "Death for life."

"No."

He made the last leap, grabbed her arm and jerked her inside out of the rain. "No," he said again, and wrapped his arms around her. "Feel me. You know who I am. You know who you are. Feel me."

He tightened his grip when she struggled. Held her close and warm even as her head whipped from side to side and her teeth snapped like a wild dog's.

"I will have my son!"

"You have a daughter. You have Lily. Lily's sleeping. Hayley, stay with us."

And swept her up in his arms when her body sagged.

"I'm cold. Harper, I'm cold."

"It's all right. You're all right." He carried her across the wide ballroom with its ghostly dust sheets as rain lashed windows.

Before he reached the door, Mitch shoved it open. After one quick glance, Mitch let out a breath. "Your mother went to check on Lily. What happened?"

"Not now." With Hayley shivering in his arms, Harper moved by Mitch. "We'll deal with it later. She needs to get warm and dry. The rest will have to wait."

NINETEEN

HE HAD HER BUNDLED IN A BLANKET FROM NECK TO toe, and sat behind her on the bed drying her hair with a towel.

"I don't remember getting up. I don't remember going out."

"Are you warm enough?"

"Yeah." Except for the sheen of ice inside her bones. She wondered if any heat would ever reach that deep in her again. "I don't know how long I was out there."

"You're back now."

She reached back, laid a hand over his. He needed warmth and comfort as much as she did. "You found me."

He pressed a kiss to her damp hair. "I always will."

"You took Lily's monitor." And that, she thought, meant even more. "You remembered to take it. You didn't leave her alone."

"Hayley." He wrapped his arms around her, pressed his cheek to hers. "I won't leave either of you alone." Then laid a hand on her belly. "Any of you. I swear it."

"I know. She doesn't believe in promises, or faith, or love. I do. I believe in us, with everything I've got." She turned her head so her lips could brush his. "I didn't always, but I do now. I have everything. She has nothing."

"You can feel sorry for her? After this? After everything?"

"I don't know what I feel for her. Or about her." It felt so wonderful to be able to lean her head back, rest it on his good, strong shoulder. "I thought I understood her, at least a little. We were both in a kind of similar situation. I mean, getting pregnant, and not wanting the baby at first."

"You're nothing alike."

"Harper, erase the personalities, and your feelings for just a minute. Look at it objectively, like you do at work. Look at the situation. We were both unmarried and pregnant. Not loving the father, not wanting to see our lives changed, burdened even. Then coming to want the baby. In different ways, for different reasons, but coming to want the baby so much."

"Different ways and different reasons," he repeated. "But all right, I can see that, on the surface, there's a pattern."

The door opened. Roz came in with a tray. "I'm not going to disturb you. Harper, you see that she drinks this." After setting the tray at the foot of the bed, Roz skirted around to the side. She took Hayley's face in her hand, kissed her cheek. "You get some rest."

Harper reached out, took Roz's hand for a moment. "Thanks, Mama."

"You need anything, you call."

"She didn't have anyone to take care of her," Hayley said quietly when the door closed behind Roz. "No one to care about her."

"Who did she care about? Who did she care for? Obsession isn't caring," he added before Hayley could speak. He eased away to get up, pour the tea. "What was done to her sucked big-time. No argument, no debate. But you know what? There aren't any heroes in her sad story."

"There should be. There should always be heroes. But no." She took the tea. "She wasn't heroic. Not even tragic, like Juliet. She's just sad. And bitter."

"Calculating," he added. "And crazy."

"That, too. She wouldn't have understood you. I think I know her well enough now to be sure of that. She wouldn't have understood your heart, or your honesty. That's sad, too."

He walked to the doors. He was getting the soaker he'd wished for and could stand there, watch the earth drink in the rain.

"She was always sad." He reached inside, beyond his anger and found the pity. "I could see it even when I was a kid, and she'd be in my room, singing. Sad and lost. Still I felt safe with her, the way you do when you're with someone you know cares about you. She cared, on some level, for me, for my brothers. I guess that has to count for something."

"She still cares, I feel that. She just gets confused. Harper, I can't remember."

She lowered the cup, and emotion swam into her eyes. "Not like I could the other times it happened. I could see, at least a part of me could. I don't know how to explain. But this time, it's mixed up, and I can't see. Not all of it. Why was she going into the ballroom? What did she do there?"

He wanted to tell her to relax, not to think. But how could she? Instead he came back, sat by her. "You went to

the carriage house. You must have. The door was open, and I could see where you'd walked back to the kitchen. The floor was wet."

"That's where she went that night, the night she died here. She had to have died here that night. Nothing else makes sense. We saw her that time, you and me. Standing out on the terrace, wet and muddy. She had a rope."

"There could've been rope in the carriage house. Probably was."

"Why would she need a rope to get the baby? To tie up the nursemaid?"

"I don't think that's why she wanted rope."

"She had that sickle thing, too." Bright and gleaming, she remembered. Sharp. "Maybe she was going to kill anyone who tried to stop her. But the rope. What would she do with rope besides tie somebody up?"

Her eyes widened and she set the cup down with a rattle when she read the look in his eyes.

"Oh my God. To kill herself? To hang herself, is that what you're thinking? But why? Why would she come all the way out here? Why would she drag herself through the rain, and hang herself in the ballroom?"

"The nursery was on the third floor back then."

What little color had come back into her cheeks drained again. "The nursery."

No, she thought as the image played in her mind, she might never be truly warm again.

ON HER DAYS OFF, HAYLEY WAS USED TO THE HOURS flying by. The time was so crowded with chores— shopping, laundry, organizing what had gotten disorganized during workdays, caring for Lily and the myriad

tasks that turned up—she barely remembered what it was like to have what those who didn't have full-time jobs and a toddler called free time.

Who knew she liked it that way?

Finding herself with time on her hands left her feeling broody and restless. But when the boss ordered you to take the day off, there was no arguing. At least not when the boss was Rosalind Harper.

She'd been banished to Stella's house for the day without even Lily as a distraction. She'd been told to rest, and she'd tried. Really she had. But her usual delight in reading didn't satisfy her; the stack of DVDs Stella had handed her didn't entertain, and the quiet, empty house kept her counting the minutes rather than lulling her into a nap.

She passed some of the time roaming the rooms, rooms she'd helped paint. Stella and Logan had turned it into a home, mixing Stella's flair for detail and style with Logan's sense of space. And the boys, of course, she thought as she paused outside of the room Gavin and Luke shared with its bunk beds and shelves loaded with comic books and trucks. It was a home created with children in mind, lots of light and color, the big yard that bumped right up to kiss the woods. Even with the elegance of gardens—and how could the landscaping be anything but beautiful here—it was a yard where kids and a dog could romp around.

She picked up Parker—the dog had been her only company through the day—and nuzzled him as she walked back downstairs.

Would she be as clever as Stella with a home and family? As loving and smart and sane?

She'd never planned it this way. Stella was the one for plans. She'd just cruised along, happy enough with her job at the bookstore, helping her father tend the little house

they shared. Now and again she'd thought about taking a few extra classes in business—to prepare for the vague dream of opening her own bookstore. One day.

She'd thought about falling in love—one day. Most girls did, she imagined. But she hadn't been in any hurry for it, for the big love, and what followed. Permanency, home, kids. The whole minivan, soccer-mom routine had been distant as the moon in her head. Years off. Light-years off.

But things had happened that had pushed her in directions she'd never expected to go. So here she was, not yet twenty-six, pregnant with her second child, working in a field she'd known next to nothing about two years before.

And so stupidly in love she was all but breathing valentines.

Just to ice that cake, a cryptic and certainly psychopathic spirit had decided to borrow her body from time to time.

When Parker wiggled, she set him down, then followed him into the kitchen where he parked himself by the back door and stared holes through it.

"Okay, okay, out you go. Guess I'm not the most sparkling company today."

She let him out, and he pranced across the yard, into the woods as if he had an appointment to keep.

She wandered out herself. It was a pretty day. The rain had freshened things, cooled the air a little. She could take a walk, do some weeding. Or she could stretch out on the patio chaise and see if being outdoors was more conducive to napping.

Without much hope, she cocked the chair back, thought about going back in for a book. And was asleep in minutes.

SHE WOKE A LITTLE FUZZY IN THE BRAIN TO THE SOUND of snoring. Baffled, she pressed a hand to her mouth, but the

sound continued. There was a light cotton throw tossed over her, and the table umbrella had been cocked to shade her.

The snoring came from Parker who was flopped on his back beside her chaise, his feet straight up in the air so he looked like a toy dog that had been knocked off its perch.

Her life might've been strange at the moment, but she didn't think a dog could have moved the umbrella or brought her a blanket.

Even as she cleared sleep from her throat and pushed herself up, Stella came out the back door bearing two glasses of iced tea.

"Nice nap?" she asked.

"I don't know. I slept through it. Thanks," she added as she took a glass of tea. "What time . . . Wow." She blinked at her own watch. "I was out for almost two hours."

"Glad to hear it. You look better."

"I hope to God. Where are the kids?"

"Logan picked them up after school. They like going to jobs with him. Gorgeous out, isn't it? The perfect day for drinking tea on the patio."

"Everything okay at the nursery? This kind of weather brings people in."

"And it did. We were busy. Look at those crepe myrtles. I love this yard," she said with a sigh.

"You and Logan have done an amazing job. I was thinking that before. What a good team you are."

"Turns out. Who'd have thought a cranky disorganized know-it-all and an anal-retentive overachiever could find true love and happiness?"

"I did. Right from the start."

"I suppose you did. Smartie. Have you eaten?"

"I wasn't really hungry."

Stella wagged a finger. "Somebody in there might be. I'm going to fix you a sandwich."

"Don't fuss, Stella."

"PB and J?"

With a shake of her head, Hayley gave in. "No fair. You know my weaknesses."

"Sit right there. The fresh air's good for you. I'll be back in a minute."

True to her word, Stella was back not only with the sandwich, but a sprig of purple grapes, bite-size wedges of cheese. And a half a dozen Milano cookies.

Hayley looked at the plate on her lap, then up at Stella. "Will you be my mommy?"

With a laugh, Stella sat on the chaise at Hayley's feet. And began to rub them in a way that had every muscle in Hayley's body sighing in relief. "One of my favorite things about being pregnant was getting pampered once in a while."

"Missed that the first few months the first time out."

"So, you'll make up for it with this one." Stella patted Hayley's leg. "How you feeling—gestating-wise?"

"Good. Tired, you know, and up and down on the emotional scale, but pretty good. Better now," she added after another bite of the sandwich. "And I hate admitting that— a long nap, comfort food, it's doing the job. I'm going to take care of myself, Stella, I promise. I was careful carrying Lily, and I'll be careful this time, too."

"I know you will. Besides, nobody's going to give you a choice."

"I get . . ." She moved her shoulders restlessly. "Funny when everybody's worried about me."

"Then you'll have to get funny, because we can't help it. Not with everything that's going on."

"Last night, it was so . . . I've used all the words before. Strong, strange, bizarre, intense. But this was the most of all of them. Stella, I didn't tell Harper everything. I couldn't."

"What do you mean?"

"I didn't tell him what I felt. He'd wig, the way guys do. I'm counting on you not to."

"Tell me what's going on."

"It's a feeling—and I don't know if it's just stress or if it's real. But I feel. Stella, she wants the baby. This baby." Hayley pressed a hand to her belly.

"How—"

"She can't. No power on this earth, no power anywhere, is strong enough to push me aside. You know, because you've had a child inside you. Harper, he'd freak."

"Explain this to me, so I don't."

"She gets mixed up is the best way I can explain it. From the here and now, to back in her own time. She wavers back and forth. When she's in the now, she wants what I have. This child, the life, the body. Even more, wealth and privilege. She wants the sensations and the payoff. Do you understand?"

"All right, yes."

"She's much more frightening, much more selfish when her mind's in the now. When it's back, when she's caught up in what happened to her, it's like it *is* happening. Then she's just angry and vindictive, so she wants someone to pay for what happened to her. Or she's sad, and pitiable, and she just wants it all to stop. She's tired. Harper thinks she committed suicide."

"I know. We talked a little."

"He thinks she hanged herself in the nursery. Right there while the baby slept. She could've done it. She was lost and crazy enough to have done it."

"I know that, too." Stella rose, walked to the edge of the patio to look out over the yard. "I've been having dreams again."

"What? When?"

"Not here, not at night. Daydreams, you could say. At

work. On Harper ground. Images like before of the dahlia. The blue dahlia. Only it's monstrous. That's how she wants me to see it. Petals like razors, waiting to slice your fingers to ribbons if you touch it. It's not growing out of a garden this time." She turned back; met Hayley's eyes. "But out of a grave. Unmarked, black dirt. The dahlia is the only thing that grows there."

"When did they start?"

"A few days ago."

"Do you think Roz has had them, too?"

"We'll need to ask her."

"Stella, we have to go up to the old nursery."

"Yes." She walked back, took the hand Hayley held out to her. "We will."

IT WAS EASY TO TALK WITHOUT MEN WHEN THE AN-nounced activity was wedding planning. Men, Hayley noted, scattered like ants when terms like guest lists and color schemes were mentioned.

So they were able to sit on Stella's patio in the balm of the evening with Lily being passed from one pair of arms to another, or playing in the grass with Parker.

"I didn't think it would be so easy to chase Harper off," Hayley complained. "You'd think he'd want some input into the wedding plans. He's getting married, too."

Roz and Stella exchanged amused looks before Roz reached over, patted Hayley's hand. "Sweet, foolish child."

"I guess it doesn't matter, since that's not what we're doing. But still." Annoyed with herself, Hayley waved her hands. "Anyway. Amelia's been messing with you, too."

"Twice," Roz confirmed. "Both times when I was alone in the propagation house. I'd be working, and then I'd be somewhere else. It's dark, too dark to tell where, and cold.

Very cold. I'm standing over an open grave. When I look down I see her, looking back at me. Her hands are clasped over the stem of a black rose. Or it looks black in the dark."

"Why didn't you tell us?" Stella demanded.

"The same could be asked of you. I intended to tell you, and did tell Mitch. But we've had a few major distractions."

Hayley hauled Lily onto her lap and admired the thick plastic bracelet she played with. "I know that when this first started and I suggested a seance everybody thought it was a joke. But maybe we should try it. The three of us have this connection to her. Maybe if we tried, really tried to communicate, she'd tell us what she wants."

"I'm not pulling out the turban and crystal ball anytime soon," Roz said, definitely. "In any case, I don't think she knows. By that, I mean she wants to be found—and I think she means her grave, or her remains. But she doesn't know where it is."

"We can't be a hundred percent certain it's on Harper property," Stella put in.

"No, we can't. Mitch is doing all he can to find death records, burial records. We don't think there are any for her."

"A secret burial." Hayley nodded. "But she always wants us to know what happened to her. It still pisses her off." She shrugged, smiled a little. "It's one of the things I get, pretty loud and clear. If she was killed, or killed herself, in the house, we need to find out."

"The nursery," Roz stated. "It was still in use when I was born."

"You stayed up there when you were a baby?" Hayley asked.

"So I'm told. At least for the first few months, with the nursemaid. My grandmother didn't approve, Grandmama Harper. Apparently she'd only used it when they were entertaining. She used her considerable influence on my par-

ents until they moved me to a room on the second floor. I never used it for my boys."

"Why?"

Roz pursed her lips and thought over Hayley's question. "First, I didn't want them that far away from me. And yes, I didn't like the feel of the room. Something I couldn't explain, and didn't think about that much at the time."

"The furniture in Lily's room came from there."

"Yes. Once Mason was out of the crib, I had everything taken back up. I took to storing the boys' things in there when they outgrew them. We don't use the third floor as a rule. It's too costly to maintain, and more space than we can practically use. Though I have had parties in the ballroom in the past."

"I'd never been up there," Hayley commented. "Which is strange now that I think about it, because I like going through houses, seeing how they look, picturing them the way they were, that kind of thing. But I never even thought of going up there in all the time I've lived in the house. Stella?"

"No, and you're right, it is odd. The boys had the run of the house for more than a year. You'd think I'd have had to chase them down from there at some point. But I don't think they ever went up either. Even if they did it in secret, Luke would've spilled. He always does."

"I think we should." Hayley looked from one to the other. "I think we have to."

"Tonight?" Stella asked.

"I don't think I can stand to wait. It's driving me crazy."

"If that's what we're going to do, we'll all do it together. The six of us," Roz said. "Not the children. David can keep them downstairs. You have to be sure, Hayley. At this point it seems, of all of us, you're the closest to her."

"I am sure. But not just me, which is something else I

wanted to bring up. Harper. Her feelings for him, about him." A little chilled, Hayley rubbed her arms. "They're awfully mixed, and potent. She loves him—the child of the child of the child sort of thing. And she hates him—a man, a Harper man, Reginald's blood."

She looked at Stella, at Roz. "That combination of feelings, it's powerful. I think maybe more powerful because of the way Harper and I feel about each other."

"Love, sex, kinship, vengeance, grief." Roz nodded. "And insanity."

"His feelings about her are pretty mixed, too." Hayley let out a breath. "I don't know if that matters, but I think all of it, at this point, everything's important. I think we must be getting close to the end of it."

"Hallelujah," Stella announced.

"I know. I want this over. I want to really plan a wedding, and plan for this baby. I want to sit here with the two of you and talk about flowers and music and the kind of dress I'm going to wear."

Roz covered Hayley's hand with hers. "We will."

"Last night, before it happened, it was like I was imagining it, seeing myself in a long white dress and the flowers . . . But I guess that's out." She gave a half shrug as she patted her belly. "I don't guess I'm entitled to a long white dress."

"Honey." Roz gave Hayley's hand a quick squeeze. "Every bride's entitled to a long white dress."

FOOD CAME FIRST, A FAMILY MEAL, THE KIND OF RITUAL that brought them all together where flowers were set and children chattered. Roz had said such things were important, and Hayley could see the purpose of it.

This is who we are, it seemed to say. What we are and

what we'll be regardless of trouble. Maybe because of it.

She'd been given this, this family. A mother, a sister, a lover, brothers and friends. A child who was loved by them, and another child to come.

Whatever it took to keep it whole and safe, she would do.

So she ate. She talked and listened, helped wipe up spills, and buried her nerves under the treasure of normality.

There was talk of flowers and books, of school and books. And here was the talk of wedding plans she'd pined for.

"I guess Hayley told you we'd like to get married here, if that suits you, Mama."

"That's what I like to hear." Roz set her fork aside. "In the gardens? We'll insist the weather stay fine, and have tents as a backup. I intend to roll up my sleeves regarding the flowers. I insist you give me my head there. You'll want lilies, I expect."

"Yes. I want to carry red lilies."

"Bold colors then, toss the pastels. I can work with that. I know you don't want anything too formal, and since we've had two weddings already this year, I think we can iron out the details without much pain and suffering."

"Step away now," Logan advised Harper. "Save yourself. Just say, 'That sounds fine.' And if they give you two choices in anything, don't fall into the trap. Just say, 'They're both great,' and tell her to pick."

"He thinks he's being funny," Stella said dryly. "I'm not kicking him under the table because he's right."

"How come everybody's getting married?" Gavin demanded. "How come we always have to wear ties?"

"Because they like to torture us," Logan told him. "It's the way of women."

"They should have to wear ties, too."

"I'll wear a tie," Stella offered. "You wear high heels."

"I know why people get married," Luke piped up. "So they can sleep in the same bed and make babies. Did you and Mitch make a baby yet?" he asked Roz.

"We already made our quota some time ago. And on that note." Roz pushed away from the table. "I think it's time for you boys to help David clear this up so you can have ice cream in the kitchen."

"All right, troops. Fall in. You, too, Private." Before Hayley could deal with it herself, David moved over to take Lily out of the high chair. "Just because you're short, doesn't mean you can skate out of KP. She likes to help me load the dishwasher," he said to Hayley. "We're fine."

"I just need to talk to you for one minute in the kitchen."

"Clear and stack, gentlemen," he ordered, then carried Lily out of the dining room. "We got this end covered," he said to Hayley. "You don't need to worry."

"No, that's not it. I know Lily's fine with you. It's about the wedding. I need to ask you for something."

He set Lily down, gave her a pot and a spoon to bang. "What do you need?"

"I know this might sound sort of strange, but I think you get to tailor a day like your wedding day to suit you best, don't you?"

"If not that day, what day?"

"That's right. So I was wondering, I was hoping, you'd give me away."

"What?" David's face went utterly blank. "Me?"

"I know you're not old enough to be my daddy, or anything. But I wasn't thinking about it that way. I was thinking how you're one of my best friends, and Harper's, too. How we're like family. And how a day like that's about family. I don't have my daddy, or any blood kin I love the way I love you. So I want you to walk me down the aisle—so to speak—and give me to Harper. It would mean a lot to me."

His eyes went misty as he wrapped his arms around her. "That's the sweetest thing," he crooned. "The damnedest sweetest thing."

"Will you?"

He drew back. "I would be honored." Taking both her hands, he turned them over, kissed her palms. "Extremely."

"Whew. I thought you might think it was silly."

"Not even close. I'm so proud, and touched. And, honey, if you don't go on now, I'm going to embarrass myself in front of my troops."

"Me, too." She sniffled. "Okay. We'll talk about all of it later on." She crouched down to kiss Lily's head, and was largely ignored. "You be good, baby girl."

"Hayley." David drew a breath as she stopped at the door. "Your daddy? He'd be proud, too."

The best she could manage was a nod as she left him.

She brushed away tears as she followed the voices in the parlor, then paused when she heard the temper in Harper's.

"I don't like this idea, not one bit. And I like less the fact that the three of you were off plotting this on your own."

"We womenfolk," Roz said with a sarcasm that dripped so heavy Hayley could feel its weight outside the room.

"The fact that you are women isn't any of my doing," he shot back. "But the fact that *my* woman is pregnant is. I don't take chances on this."

"All right, you have a valid point. But what do you intend to do with her for the next seven, eight months, honey?"

"Protect her."

"You do make it hard to argue."

"Arguing isn't going to help." Mitch's voice of reason cut between them. "We can discuss and debate, and we're unlikely to be in full agreement on all points. But we do have to come to some decisions."

Hayley straightened her spine, and stepped into the room. "I'm sorry. Hard not to overhear. Harper, I was going to ask if we could go outside so I could talk to you, but I think what I have to say needs to be said here, to everyone."

"I've got some things to say you might rather hear in private."

She only smiled. "There'll be plenty of time for you to yell at me in private. A lifetime of it. I know you kept it buttoned till now because of the kids. But I'd like you to hear me out before you say anything more."

She cleared her throat and moved farther into the room. "Earlier today, when I was alone, I was wondering how I'd gotten here. I'd never figured on moving away from where I grew up, having a couple of kids before I figured out where I really wanted to go, really wanted to do. Getting married, having babies, that was going to be later, after I'd made something of myself, had some fun. Here I am, living in another state. I've got a daughter not yet two and another baby on the way. I'm getting married. I'm working in a field I never thought about being in before. How'd I get here? What am I doing here?"

"If you're not happy—"

"Please, just listen. I asked myself that. I've still got choices. There are always choices. So I asked myself, is this what I want, is this where I want to be, what I want to do? And it is. I love you. I didn't know I had all this in me."

She kept her eyes on Harper's, only on Harper's and crossed her hands over her heart. "I didn't know I could love a child the way I do Lily. I didn't know I could love a man the way I love you. If I had every choice in the world, this is the one I'd pick. Being with you, with our children, in this place. Because you see that's one more thing, Harper. I love this house, I love this place. As much as you

do. What it is, what it stands for, what it'll be to our children, and theirs."

"I know. My mind traveled that same road. That's why you're the one for me.

"I can't walk away from here. Please don't ask me to do that. I can't walk away from this house, this family, the work I've come to love. The only way I can stay is to try to do this thing, to settle this. Right a wrong, or at least understand it. Maybe I was meant to. Maybe we found each other because *we* were meant to. I don't know if I can do it if you're not with me." She scanned the room. "All of you."

Then she looked at Harper. "Be with me, Harper. Trust me to do what's right. Trust us to do it."

He stepped to her, rested his brow on hers. "I am with you."

twenty

"THERE'S NO GUARANTEE ANYTHING WILL HAPPEN."
Mitch slipped a spare tape in his pocket.

"I think I can make it happen. What I mean . . ." Hayley
moistened her lips. "I think I can draw her. She wants
this—a part of her does, and has for a century."

"And the other part?" Harper asked.

"Wants revenge. When it comes down to it, she'll probably be more inclined to hurt you than me."

"And she can hurt us," Roz pointed out. "We've seen
that."

"So we go up there armed with cameras and tape
recorders." Logan shook his head.

"We happy few," Mitch stated.

"Well, she's raised the stakes." Logan took Stella's
hand. "Since none of us are willing to fold, let's ante up."

"We stay together," Roz said as they started up the

stairs. "No matter what. We've never really confronted her as a group before. I think there's strength in that."

"She always had the upper hand, she always moved first." Harper nodded. "Yeah, we stay together."

When they reached the third floor, Roz turned toward the ballroom. Going with instinct, she stepped forward, pushed the double pocket doors open.

"There were lovely parties here. I remember creeping up at night to watch the dancing."

She reached in to switch on the light. It showered down on the shrouded furniture, and the lovely pattern of the maple floor. "I nearly sold those chandeliers once." She looked up at the dazzling trio of them dripping down from ornate plaster medallions. "Couldn't bring myself to do it, even though it would've made day-to-day living easier. I gave my own parties here, once upon a time. I believe it's time I did so again."

"She came in this way, that night. I'm sure of it." Though her hand was already in Harper's, Hayley tightened her grip. "Don't let go."

"Not a chance."

"She came in the terrace doors. They weren't locked. She could've broken the glass if they had been. She came in, and oh . . . Gilt and crystal, the smell of beeswax and lemon oil. The rain dripping, dripping from the gutters. Turn on the lights."

"I have," Roz said quietly.

"No, she turns on the light. Harper."

"Right here."

"I can see it. I can see it."

The fog rolled in the doors behind her, smoking damp over the glossy floors. Her feet were caked with mud, with blood where she'd trod on stones, and left streaks of that mud, of that blood, where she walked.

Alive still. Heart beating blood.

This, this is how they lived at Harper House. Grand rooms lit by sparkling chandeliers, gilt mirrors on the walls, long, polished tables and potted palms so lush they smelled of the tropics.

She had never been to the tropics. She and James would go one day, one day they'd go and stroll on sugar sand by warm blue water.

But no, but no, their lives were here, in Harper House. They had cast her out, but she would be here. Always here. To dance in this ballroom, lit by crystal drops.

She swayed, a partnerless waltz, her head tilted up flirtatiously. The blade in her hand shooting light from its keen edge.

She would dance here, night after night if she chose. Drink champagne, wear fine jewels. She would teach James to waltz with her. How handsome he would be, wrapped in his soft blue blanket. How sweet a picture they would make. Mother and son.

She must go to him now, go to James, so they could always be together.

She wandered out. Where would the nursery be? In the other wing, of course. Of course. Children and those who tended them didn't belong near grand ballrooms, elegant withdrawing rooms. Smell the house! How rich its perfume. Her son's home. And hers now.

The carpet was soft as fur on her feet. And even so late, even when the house was in bed, the gaslights glowed on low.

Spare no expense! she thought. Money to burn.

Oh, she should burn them all.

At the stairs she paused. They would be sleeping down there, the bastard and his whore. The sleep of the rich and

the privileged. She could go down, kill them. Hack them to pieces, bathe in their blood.

Idly, she rubbed her thumb over the curved blade of the sickle, had blood welling red. Would their blood run blue? Harper blood. It would be so lovely to see it, spilling out of their white throats, pooling regally blue on their linen sheets.

But someone might hear. One of the servants could hear, and stop her before her duty was done.

So quiet. She tapped a finger to her cheek, stifled a laugh. Quiet as a mouse.

Quiet as a ghost.

She walked to the other wing, easing doors open if they were closed. Peeking inside.

She knew—it was her mother's heart speaking, she thought—as her trembling hand reached for the latch on the next door. She knew her James slept inside.

A low light burned, and with it she could see the shelves of toys and books, the rocking chair, the small bureaus and the chests.

And there, the crib.

Tears spilled out of her eyes as she crossed to it. There he lay sleeping, her precious son, his dark hair clean and sweet, his plump cheeks rosy with health.

Never had there been a more beautiful baby than her James. So pretty and soft in his crib. He needed to be tended, and rocked, and sung to. Sweet songs for her sweet son.

She'd forgotten his blanket! How could she have forgotten his blanket? Now she would have to use what another had bought him when it came time to carry him off with her.

Gently, so gently, she brushed her fingers over his soft hair and sang his lullaby.

"We'll be together always, James. Nothing will ever part us again."

Sitting on the floor, she went to work.

She used the blade to hack through the rope. It was difficult to form the noose, but she thought she did well. Well enough. Discarding the sickle, she carried a chair, positioned it under the ceiling lamp. And sang softly as she tied the rope to the arms of the lamp.

It held on a strong, testing pull and made her smile.

She pulled out the gris-gris she had in a bag looped around her neck by a ribbon. She'd memorized the chant the voodoo queen had sold her, but she struggled with the words now as she sprinkled the gris-gris in a circle around the chair.

She used the blade to slice open her own palm. And let the blood from her hand drip over the gris-gris, to bind the work.

Her blood. Amelia Ellen Connor. The same blood that ran in her child. A mother's blood, potent magic.

Her hands shook, but she continued to croon as she went to the crib. For the first time since he'd been born, she lifted her child into her arms.

Bloodied his blanket, and his rosy cheek.

Ah, so warm, so sweet! Weeping with joy she cuddled the child against her damp and filthy gown. When he stirred and whimpered, she hugged him only closer.

Hush, hush, my precious. Mama is here now. Mama will never leave you again. His head moved, his mouth sucking as if in search of a nipple. But when with a sob of joy, she tugged her gown below her breast, pressed him there, he arched and let out a cry.

Hush, hush, hush. Don't cry, don't fret. Sweet, sweet baby boy. Sawing her arms back and forth to rock him, she moved to the chair. Mama has you now. She'll never, never let you

go. Come with Mama, my darling James. Come with Mama now where you will never know pain or grief. Where we will waltz in the ballroom, have tea and cake in the garden.

She climbed, awkward with his weight, with his wiggles, onto the chair. Even as he wailed, she smiled down at him, and slipped the noose around her neck. Softly singing, she slipped the smaller noose around his.

Now, we're together.

The connecting door opened, a spill of light that had her turning her head, baring her teeth like a tiger protecting her cub.

The sleepy-eyed nursemaid shrieked, her hands flying to her face at the sight of the woman in the filthy white gown, and the baby in her arms, screaming with fear and angry hunger, with a rope around his neck.

"He's mine!"

As she kicked the chair away, the nursemaid sprang forward.

Screams gave way to the cold, and the dark.

Hayley sat on the floor of what had been the nursery, weeping in Harper's arms.

SHE WAS STILL ICY, EVEN IN THE PARLOR WITH A BLANKet over her legs, and the unseasonable fire Mitch had set to blaze in the hearth.

"She was going to kill him," she told them. "She was going to kill the baby. My God, my God, she meant to hang her own child."

"To keep him." Roz stood, staring at the fire. "That's more than madness."

"If the nurse hadn't come in when she did. If she hadn't heard him crying and come in quickly, she would've done it."

"Selfish woman."

"I know, I know." Hayley lifted her hands, rubbed her shoulders. "But she didn't do it to hurt him. She believed they'd be together, and happy, and, oh Jesus. She was broken, in every possible way. Then at the end, when she lost again . . ." Hayley shook her head. "She keeps waiting for him. I think she must see him in every child who comes to Harper House."

"A kind of hell isn't it?" Stella asked. "For madness."

She'd never forget it, Hayley thought. Never. "The nurse, she saved the baby."

"I haven't been able to trace her," Mitch put in. "They had more than one nursemaid during his babyhood, but the timing of this points to a girl named Alice Jameson—which also jibes with Mary Havers's letter to Lucille. Alice left the Harper employ in February of 1893, and I haven't found anything more on her."

"They sent her away." Stella closed her eyes. "That's what they'd have done. Paid her maybe, or just as likely threatened her."

"Both would be my guess," Logan said.

"I'll push on it, do what I can to find her," Mitch promised, and Roz turned to smile at him.

"I'd appreciate it. I wouldn't be here without her, nor would my sons."

"It wasn't what she wanted us to know," Hayley said quietly. "Or not all of it. She doesn't know where she is. Where she's buried. What they did with her. She won't be able to leave, to rest, to pass over, whatever it is, until we find her."

"How?" Stella spread her hands.

"I have an idea on that." Roz scanned faces. "One I think's going to hit this group about fifty-fifty."

"What's the point?" Harper objected. "So Hayley can see her try to hang a baby again?"

"So she, or one of us, can see what happened next. Hopefully. And by we, I mean myself, Hayley, and Stella."

For the first time since they'd started upstairs, Harper released Hayley's hand. He shoved off the couch. "That's a damn stupid idea."

"Don't take that tone with me, Harper."

"It's the only tone I've got when my mother goes crazy. Did you see what just happened up there? The way Hayley walked from the ballroom to the old nursery? The way she talked as if she was watching it happen, and like she was part of what was happening?"

"I saw perfectly well. That's why we have to go back."

"I've got to side with Harper on this, Roz." Logan gave an apologetic shrug. "I don't see sitting down here while three women go up there alone. I don't give a rat's ass if it's sexist."

"I expected as much. Mitch?" Her eyebrows winged up when he sat, frowning at her. "Well, you're about to surprise me again."

"You can't seriously agree with her on this?" Harper whirled around to his stepfather.

"The hell of it, Harper, is that I am. I don't like it, but I see where she's going, and why. And before you take my head off, consider this: They'll do it later, at some point when none of us is around."

"What happened to staying together?"

"It's a man who used her, abused her, stole her child, cast her off. She's been poking at me and Stella again. She won't trust you. Maybe we can convince her to trust us."

"And maybe she'll toss you off the third floor terrace."

"Harper." Roz crossed to him, her smile as thin as a blade. "Anybody gets tossed out of this house, it's going to be her. That's a stone promise. My sympathy for her is at an end. You still have it." She looked over at Hayley. "And

that's fine, probably an advantage. But mine is over. What she would have done if not for intervention is unforgivable to me. I will have her out of this house. Can you go back?" she asked Hayley.

"Yes, I can. I want it done. I don't think I'll ever have another easy moment until it is."

"You're asking me to risk you."

"No." Hayley rose to go to Harper. "To believe in me."

"YOU KNOW HOW, IN THE MOVIES, THE STUPID, USU-ally scantily clad blonde, goes down in the basement alone when she hears a noise, especially if there's a slasher-type killer running around?"

Roz laughed at Hayley as they stood on the third floor landing. "We're not stupid."

"And none of us are blond," Stella added. "Ready?"

They clasped hands and started down the hall.

"The problem with this," Hayley began in a voice that sounded tinny to her ears, "is that if she doesn't know what happened to her after, how will we?"

"One step at a time." Roz gave Hayley's hand a squeeze. "How are you feeling?"

"My heart's beating a mile a minute. Roz, when this is over, can we open this room again? Make it, I don't know, a playroom maybe. Something with light and color."

"A wonderful idea."

"And here we go," Stella declared. They walked in together.

"How did it look before, Hayley?" Roz asked her.

"Um. The crib was over there." She gestured with her chin. "Against the wall. The lights were on low. Gaslights, like in that movie with Ingrid Bergman. The one where Charles Boyer tries to drive her crazy. There was a rocking

chair over there, and another, straight-backed chair—the one she used—over there. Shelves here," she pointed, "with toys and books on them. And a . . ."

Her head snapped back, her eyes rolled up white. As she began to choke, her legs buckled.

She heard, through the storm surge in her ears, Roz shout to get her out. But she shook her head wildly.

"Wait, wait. God it *burns*! The baby's screaming, and the maid, the nurse. Don't let go of me."

"We're taking you out," Roz said.

"No, no. Just don't let go. She's dying—it's horrible—and she's so angry." Hayley let her head fall onto Roz's shoulder. "It's dark. It's dark where she is. Was. No light, no air, no hope. She lost. They took him again, and now she's alone. She'll always be alone. She can't see, she can't feel. Everything seems so far away. Very cold, very dark. There are voices, but she can't hear them, only echoes. It's so empty. She's going down, down, so heavy. She can only see the dark. She doesn't know where she is. She just floats away."

She sighed, left her head on Roz's shoulder. "I can't help it, even in this room, I feel sorry for her. She was cold and selfish, calculating. A whore, certainly, in the lowest sense of the word. But she's paid for it, hasn't she? More than a hundred years of being lost, of watching over other people's children and never having more than that one mad moment with her own. She's paid."

"Maybe she has. Are you all right?"

Hayley nodded. "It wasn't like before, not the way I could feel her pulling at me. I was stronger. I need life more than she does. I think she's tired. Almost as tired as we are."

"That may be, too. But you don't let your guard down." Stella looked up where once had hung an armed gaslight chandelier. "Not for a minute."

"Let's go back." Stella rose, helped Hayley to her feet. "You did what you could. We all have."

"It doesn't seem like enough. It was a brutal death. It wasn't quick, and she saw the maid run out with the baby. She reached out her arms for him, even when she was strangling."

"That's not a mother's love, whatever she thought," Roz said.

"No, it's not. It wasn't. But it was all she had." Hayley moistened her lips, wished desperately for water. "She cursed him—Reginald. Cursed them all—the Harpers. She . . . she willed herself to stay here. But she's tired. Part of her, the part that sings lullabies, is so tired and lost."

She let out a sigh, then smiled when she saw Harper pacing the landing. "We've all got so much more than she did. We're fine." She left the other women to go to him. "I guess we didn't get what we were after, but we're fine."

"What happened?"

"I saw her die, and I felt her in the dark. Awful. Dark and cold and alone. Lost." She leaned against him, let him lead her downstairs. "I don't know what happened to her, what they did with her. She was going down in the dark, in the dark and cold."

"Buried?"

"I don't know. It was more . . . floating away in the dark, drifting down where she couldn't see or hear, or find her way out." Unconsciously, she rubbed a hand over her throat, remembering the sensation of the rope biting in. "Maybe it was a soul thing—you know the opposite of the tunnel of light."

"Floating, drifting?" Harper's eyes went sharp. "How about sinking?"

"Ah . . . yeah. I guess."

"The pond," he said and looked at her. "We never thought of the pond."

"THIS IS CRAZY." IN THE HAZY LIGHT OF DAWN, HAYley stood on the bank of the pond. "It could take hours, more. He should have help. We could get other people. Search-and-rescue people."

Roz slid an arm over her shoulders. "He wants to do this. He needs to." She watched while Harper pulled on flippers. "It's time for us to step back, let them do."

The pond looked so dark and deep with the skim of fog rising over its surface. The floating lilies, the spears of cattails and iris greens that had always seemed so charming to her were ominous now, fairy-tale foreign and frightening.

But she remembered how he'd paced the landing while she'd gone up the stairs into the nursery.

"He trusted me," Hayley said quietly. "Now I have to trust him."

Mitch crouched beside Harper, handed him an underwater lamp. "Got everything you need?"

"Yeah. Been a while since I scuba'd." He took deep, steady breaths to expand his lungs. "But it's like sex, you don't forget the moves."

"I can get some students, some friends of my son's who know the moves, too." Like Hayley, Mitch studied the wide, misty surface of the water. "It's a big pond for one man to cover."

"Whatever else she was, she was mine, so it's for me to do. What Hayley said last night about maybe she'd been meant to help find her. I'm feeling the same about this."

Mitch braced a hand on his shoulder. "You keep an eye

on your watch, surface every thirty minutes. Otherwise, your mama's going to toss me in after you."

"Got it." He looked over at Hayley, shot her a grin.

"Hey." She stepped to him, crouched down. With a hand on his cheek she touched her mouth to his. "For luck."

"Take all I can get. Don't worry. I've been swimming in this pond . . ." He glanced up at his mother, and vague memories of his own tiny hands slapping at the water while she held him flashed into his mind. "Well, longer than I can remember."

"I'm not worried."

He kissed her again, tested his mouthpiece. Then, adjusting his mask, slid into the pond.

He'd swum here countless times, he thought as he dived, following the beam of the light through the water. Cooling off on hot summer afternoons, or taking an impulsive dip before work in the morning.

Or bringing a girl back after a date and talking her into a moonlight skinny dip.

He'd splashed with his brothers in this pond, he remembered, playing his light over the muddy bottom before he checked his watch, his compass. His mother had taught them each how to swim here, and he remembered the laughter, the shrieks, and the cool, quiet moments.

Had all that happened over the grave of Amelia?

Mentally, he cut the pond into wedges, like a pie, and methodically began to search each slice.

At thirty minutes, then an hour, he surfaced.

He sat on the edge, feet dangling in while Logan helped him change his tank. "I've covered nearly half. Found some beer cans, soft drink bottles." He tilted his face toward his mother. "And don't look at me, I got more respect."

She reached down, skimmed a hand over his dripping hair. "I should think."

"Somebody'd get me a bag, I'd clean up as I go."

"We'll worry about it later."

"It's not deep, maybe eighteen feet at the deepest point, but the rain's stirred up the mud some, so it's a little murky."

Hayley sat beside him, but he noted she was careful not to dip her toes in the water. "I wish I could go in with you."

"Maybe next year I'll teach you how to scuba." He patted her belly. "Stay up here and take care of Hermione."

He rolled back into the water.

It was tedious work, without any of the adventure or thrill he'd experienced when he'd strapped on tanks on vacations. The strain of peering through the water, training his gaze on the circle of light had a headache brewing.

The sound of nothing but his own breath, sucking in oxygen from the tank, was monotonous and increasingly annoying. He wished it was done, over, and he was sitting in the dry, warm kitchen drinking coffee instead of swimming around in the damn, dark water looking for the remains of a woman who, at this point, just pissed him off.

He was tired, sick and tired of having so much of his life focused on a suicidal crazy woman—one who would have, if left to her own devices, killed her own child.

Maybe Reginald wasn't so much the villain of the piece after all. Maybe he'd taken the kid to protect him. Maybe . . .

There was a burn in his belly, not sickness so much as a hot ball of fury. The sort, Harper realized, that could make a man forget he was fifteen feet or so underwater.

So he rechecked his watch, deliberately, paid more attention to his breathing, and followed the path of his light.

What the hell was the matter with him? Reginald had been a son of a bitch, no question about it. Just as Amelia had been self-centered and whacked. But what had come from that selfish union had been good and strong. Loving. What had come from it mattered.

So this mattered. Finding Amelia mattered.

She was probably buried out in the woods, he decided. But hell, why dig a hole in the ground in winter when you've got a private pond handy? It seemed right, so right he wondered they hadn't thought of it before.

Then again, maybe they hadn't thought of it before because it was lame. People used the pond, even back then. To swim, to fish. Bodies that got dumped in water often resurfaced.

Why risk it?

He moved to another area, skimmed his light.

Nearly another hour passed in the murk, in the wet. He'd have to finish for the day, he decided. Get his tanks refilled and continue tomorrow. Customers would be coming in soon, and nothing put off retail like hearing that some guy was looking for human remains.

He trailed his light through the roots of his water lilies, thought fleetingly that he might try to hybridize a red one. Something that really snapped. He studied the roots, pleased with the health and progress of what he'd begun, and decided to surface.

His light caught something below, and slightly south. He checked his watch, noted he was approaching borrowed time, but he kicked, dived, scanned.

And he saw her, what was left of her. Bones, filthy with mud, tangled with growth. Weighed down, he saw, with a stirring of pity, by bricks and stones, tied to those bones, hands, legs, waist by the rope he imagined she'd hanged herself with.

The rope she'd meant to use on her son.

Still, shouldn't she have surfaced at some point? Why hadn't the rope rotted, those weights shifted? It was basic physics, wasn't it?

But basic physics didn't take ghosts and curses into account.

He paddled a hand in the water, moving closer to her.

The blow knocked him back, sent him somersaulting and ripped the light from his hand.

He was in the dark, with the dead, and running out of air.

He fought not to panic, to let his body go loose and limp so that he would drop to the bottom, and be able to spring off to the surface.

But another wave bowled him over.

He saw her, gliding through the water, her white gown billowing, her hair floating out in tangled ropes. Her eyes were wide with lunacy, her hand reaching out, curled like claws.

He felt them close around his neck, squeeze, though he could see her still, feet away, suspended in the water over her own bones.

He struck out, but there was nothing to fight. He clawed toward the surface, but she held him down as inevitably as the bricks and stones that had carried her to the bottom.

She was killing him, as she'd planned to kill her own child. Maybe that had been the plan all along, he thought dimly. To take a Harper with her.

He thought of Hayley, waiting for him on the surface, of the child she carried. Of the daughter she'd already given him.

He wouldn't give them up.

He looked back down at the bones, tried to find a glimmer of that pity. And he looked at Amelia, eternally mad.

I remember you. He thought it with all his will. *Singing to me. I knew you'd never hurt me. Remember me. The child that came from your child.*

He groped for his diving knife, sliced his palm with the

blade. As she had once sliced hers in madness. His blood dripped and clouded in the murky water between them, and drifted down toward the filthy bones.

That's your blood in me. Connor blood as much as Harper. Amelia to James, James to Robert, Robert to Rosalind, and Rosalind to me. That's why I found you. Let me go. Let me take you home. You don't have to be alone or lost anymore.

When the pressure on his throat released, he fought the urge to kick straight for the surface. He could still see her, and wondered how it was he could see tears flow down her cheeks.

I'll come back for you. I swear it.

He pushed up, and he thought he heard her singing, the light, sweet voice of his childhood. When he looked back, he saw the beam of his light spear out from the bottom, arrow to her so she was illuminated in its shaft.

And watched her fade away like a dream.

Breaking the surface, he ripped his mouthpiece away, sucked in air that burned his scored throat. Sunlight sparkled in his eyes, dazzling them, and through the roaring in his ears there were voices calling his name.

Through the dazzle, he found Hayley standing on the verge, a hand pressed to her belly. On the wrist of that hand, ruby hearts glittered like hope.

He swam through the lilies toward her, swam away from death toward life. Logan and Mitch helped pull him out of the water where he lay on his back, drawing in air, looking into Hayley's eyes.

"I found her."

epilogue

THE SUN FILTERED THROUGH THE LEAVES OF SYCA-
mores and oaks and cast pretty patterns of light and shadows on the green of the grass. On the branches birds sang,
filling the balmy air with music.

Gravestones stood, marble white, granite gray, carved
to mark the dead. On some, flowers lay, petals fading,
petals fluttering in the light breeze. Tributes to those who'd
passed before.

Harper stood between his mother and Hayley, holding
their hands as the casket was lowered.

"I don't feel sad," Hayley declared. "Not anymore. This
feels right. More than right, it feels kind."

"She earned the right to be here. Beside her son." Roz
looked at the graves, the names. Reginald and Beatrice,
Reginald and Elizabeth.

And there, her parents. Their aunts and uncles, cousins,

all links in the long chain of Harpers. "In the spring," she said, "we'll put a marker for her. Amelia Ellen Connor."

"You already have, in a way." Mitch turned his head to kiss her hair. "Burying her son's rattle with her, his picture. Hayley's right. It's kind."

"Without her, I'm not. Without her, Harper, Austin, Mason are not. Nor are the children who come from them. She deserves her place."

"Whatever she did, she deserved better than what was done to her." Stella sighed. "I'm proud I was part of this, of giving her back her name, and I hope, giving her peace." She smiled at Logan, then over at David and all the others. "We were all part of it."

"Tossed in the pond. Discarded." Logan rubbed a hand over the small of Stella's back. "All to protect, what? Reputation."

"She's found now," David added. "You did good, Roz, pushing through the system to have her buried here."

"The Harper name still has the weight to shove the bureaucrats. Truth be told I wanted to give her this nearly as much as I wanted her out of my house, away from what and who I love." She rose up to peck Harper's cheek. "My boy. My brave boy. She owes you most of all."

"I don't think so," he disagreed.

"You went back." Hayley pressed her lips together. "Even after she tried to hurt you, you went back to help bring her out."

"I told her I would. Ashbys keep their word as well as Harpers. I'm both." He picked up a fist of earth, held it over the grave, let it sift through his fingers. "Now it's done."

"What can we say about Amelia?" Roz lifted a red rose. "She was mad—let's be honest. She died badly, and didn't live much better. But she sang to me, and to my children.

Her life gave me mine. So rest now, Great-grandmama."
She dropped the rose onto the casket.

In turn the others sent a rose into the grave, and stepped
back. "Let's give them a minute alone," Roz said, nodding
toward Harper and Hayley.

"She's gone." Hayley closed her eyes, settled her mind.
"I can feel it. I knew she was gone before you came up.
Knew you'd found her before you told us. It was like the
rope tying me to her was cut."

"Happiest day of my life. So far."

"Whatever she needed, she has." She stared down at the
casket, at the flowers that lay on it. "I was so afraid, when
you were in the pond, that you wouldn't come back to me."

"I wasn't finished with you. Not nearly." He took her
shoulders, turned her away from the grave, toward him, toward the sunlight. "We've got a life to live. It's our time now."

He took the ring out of his pocket, slipped it onto her
finger. "Fits now. It's yours now." He lowered his lips to
hers. "Let's go get married."

"I think that's a great idea."

With their hands clasped, they walked away from death,
into love, and life.

In Harper House, the wide halls and gracious rooms
were quiet, full of sun, full of memories. Full of past, open
to tomorrow.

No one sang there.

But its gardens bloomed.

Turn the page for a look at

BLue smoke

by
Nora Roberts

Available in hardcover from
G. P. Putnam's Sons

one

Baltimore, 2005

FOR BETTER OR WORSE, IT WAS DONE. REENA'S HEART was pounding, her throat bone dry, and at the base of her belly was a little tickle that could have been panic or excitement.

She'd bought herself a house.

She stood on the white marble steps, the keys in her clammy hand. Settlement was over, the papers were signed. She had a mortgage.

And a bank loan, she thought, that stretched out so long she'd be ready for retirement when it was paid off.

Did the math, didn't you? she reminded herself. You can make this work. It was time she owned property. Oh God, she was a property owner.

And hadn't she fallen in love with this house? It was so like home. What that said about her, she wasn't entirely

sure, but it had been love at first sight. Everything about it had called to her.

The location, the familiarity, even the slightly tired interior that just begged her to liven it up, her way. It even had a backyard—maybe it was narrow enough to spit from line to line, but it was an actual yard with actual grass. It even had a tree.

Which meant she'd have to mow grass and rake leaves, which meant buying a lawn mower. And a rake. But for a woman who'd lived in apartments for the last ten years, it was heady stuff.

So, here she was, moving into a three-story row, three short blocks from the house where her parents still lived.

Still in the neighborhood, she thought. And as distant as the moon.

But it was good. It was all good. Hadn't the uncles, along with her father, inspected the place top to bottom? There'd been no stopping them. Needed a little fixing up, sure. And more furniture than she could currently claim.

But that would all come.

All she had to do was put the key in the lock and walk through the door, and she'd be standing in her own house.

Instead, she turned around, sat on the steps and waited to get her breath back.

She'd taken a big bite of her savings, plus the generous lump of dough her grandparents had given her—and the rest of the grands.

Now look what I've done. Gone into debt. And didn't a house keep siphoning away money? Insurance, taxes, repairs, upkeep. She'd managed to avoid all that up till now. Those pesky details had gone from being her parents' problem to her landlords' problem.

Never hers.

Managed to avoid all that, she thought, and most every

other kind of commitment. She had the job and her family, friends she'd kept from childhood.

But she was the only unmarried Hale. The only child of Gibson and Bianca Hale yet to go forth and multiply. Not enough time, that's what she told her family if they teased or pressed the matter. Haven't found the right man.

True, all true. But how many times had she retreated from—or just sidestepped—a potential relationship in the last few years?

Dating was fine, sex was good, but don't ask me to form an attachment. Xander said she thought like a man. Maybe it was true.

And maybe she'd bought this house as a kind of compensation, the way some singles or no-children couples bought a puppy.

See! I can make a commitment when I want to. I bought a house.

A house, she admitted, she couldn't seem to make herself enter now that everything was signed and sealed.

Maybe she could just turn it over. Give it a slap of paint, fix it up here and there, then resell it. There was no law that said she had to keep it for thirty years.

Thirty years. She pressed a hand to her belly. What had she done?

She was thirty-one years old, damn it. She was a cop with a decade on the job. She could walk into a stupid house without having a crisis. Besides, some portion of her family was bound to descend before much longer, and she didn't want to be caught sitting on the stairs having a neurotic attack.

She stood up, unlocked the door, and walked deliberately inside.

Instantly, as if she'd popped a cork on a bottle labeled Stress, the tension drained out.

The hell with mortgages and loans and the terror of

picking out paint colors. This is what she'd wanted. This big, old, high-ceilinged place with its carved trim, its hardwood floors.

Of course it was too much room for one person. She didn't care. She'd use one of the bedrooms for storage, once she had enough to store. She'd make another into an office space, another into a home gym, and keep the last spare for a guest room.

Ignoring the echoes, the emptiness, she strolled into the living room. Maybe she'd take the various offers from various relatives on hand-me-down furniture. At least for now. Put some of Mama's drawings on the walls. Make this a cozy, comfortable space.

And the smaller parlor, that was going to be her library. Then she'd need a big table for the dining room. Lots of chairs for when she had family over.

The kitchen was good, she thought as she took a tour of the first floor. It was one of the points that had cemented her decision. The previous owners had outfitted it well with glossy black appliances that had a lot of years left in them. Lots of smooth, sand-colored counters and honey-toned cabinets. She might get around to having a few of the doors replaced with glass. Stained glass maybe, or some fancy ripply glass.

She'd enjoy cooking here. Bella was the only one of the lot who'd apparently escaped the love of making food. There were nice, generous windows over the sink and they opened up to a view of the skinny backyard.

The lilacs were blooming. *Her* lilacs were blooming. She could talk to Uncle Sal about putting in a little postage stamp patio, and pick Bella's brain about designing a small garden.

Of course it had been years since she'd planted anything other than a geranium in a windowsill pot. Years, she re-

called, since she and Gina had planted tomatoes and peppers and cosmos in the yard of the group house they'd shared in college.

But it seemed to her—at least with the sweetened distance of memory—that she'd enjoyed the digging and weeding.

Probably stick with flowers this time, she decided, and keep it low-maintenance. Yes, Bella would be the one to ask what would work best.

For flowers, fashion, and the right place to be seen, Bella was your girl.

She thought about heading upstairs, to tour the second floor, to mentally arrange furniture, but decided to finish off the first-level walk-through by stepping out in her backyard.

She wanted to walk on her own grass.

The yard was bordered on both sides by a chain link fence. Her neighbor to the right had some sort of spreading bushes planted along the line. Nice touch, she mused. She'd think about something like that. It wasn't just pretty, but added an illusion of privacy.

And to the left . . .

Well, well, well, she thought. She couldn't say much about the yard, but its occupant was worth the price of a ticket.

Fortunately for her, there were no bushes to obstruct the view.

The man had his back to her, and the rear view was very promising. Mid-May temperatures hadn't dissuaded him from taking off his shirt. But maybe whatever he was doing with the lumber and the power tools heated him up.

His jeans ran low on his hips, and the tool belt lower yet. But he managed to avoid the butt crack reveal, which racked up points. He wore a ball cap backward, which may

or may not deduct points from the total score, and there seemed to be a lot of wavy black hair under the cap.

She might make a pass at him right there as he was working. She caught music from the boom box beside his sawhorses and gave him additional points for keeping it at a reasonable volume. She could barely catch Sugar Ray.

Six-two, she judged. About one-eighty of good, toned muscle. She didn't want to guess his age until she saw his face. But so far, as next-door neighbors went, he looked like a nice perk.

The realtor had mentioned the carpenter next door, in case she wanted to get any bids on work. But the realtor had failed to mention the carpenter next door had an excellent ass.

His grass was mowed, and he appeared to know what he was doing with the big, sexy tool. No rings on good, strong-looking hands. No visible tattoos or piercings.

Possibilities went up.

His house was similar to hers, though he already had that postage stamp patio in some sort of stone. No flowers—too bad on that as she considered it showed flair and responsibility to pot and tend flowers. Still, the patio looked clean and boasted a muscular barbecue grill.

If the rest of him lived up to the rear view, she might wangle her way to an invite for grilled steak.

He paused, set aside what she was pretty sure was a nail gun. The noise from the compressor shut down, and she heard Sugar Ray more clearly as Carpenter Guy reached for a big bottle of water and aimed it toward his mouth.

He stepped back from his work as he did, and she made out his profile. Good nose, strong mouth—smart enough to wear safety glasses, and cool enough to make them sexy. It looked like the face was going to live up to the rest of the package.

Early thirties, she decided. And wasn't that handy?

When he turned his head and glanced her way, she lifted a hand in what she considered a friendly, hi-new-neighbor salute.

He seemed to freeze, more like she'd aimed her weapon at him rather than a casual wave. He reached up, slowly, drew off his glasses. She couldn't make out the color of his eyes, but she felt the intensity of the stare.

The grin seemed to explode on his face. He tossed the glasses on the ground, strode straight to the fence and vaulted over.

Moved well—quick and agile. Green, she noted. His eyes were a misty green—and lit up a little too manically at the moment for comfort.

"There you are," he said. "Son of a bitch. There you are."

"Yeah, here I am." She gave him a cautious smile. He smelled of sawdust and sweat—which would have been appealing if he wasn't looking at her like he was prepared to gobble her up in one bite. "Catarina Hale." She offered her hand. "I just bought the house."

"Catarina Hale." He took her hand and held it, just held it with his calloused one. "Dream Girl."

"Uh-huh." His score plummeted. "Well, it's nice to meet you. I've got to get back inside."

"All this time." He continued to stare at her. "All these years. You're better than I remembered. How about that?"

"How about that?" She tugged her hand free, backed up.

"I can't believe it. You're just here. Boom. Or maybe I'm having a hallucination."

He grabbed for her hand again, and she slapped hers on his chest. "Maybe you are. Maybe you've had a little too much sun. Better go back to your corner now, Carpenter Boy."

"No, wait. You don't get it. You were there, then you weren't. Then the other time, and then again. And you keep getting away before I can catch up. And now you're right here, talking to me. I'm talking to you."

"Not anymore." Nobody had mentioned the carpenter next door was a lunatic. Shouldn't there have been full disclosure? "Go home. Lie down. Seek help."

She turned, started back to the door.

"Wait, wait, wait." He lunged after her.

In response she spun around, caught his arm, tipped him off balance and jerked his arm behind his back. "Don't make me arrest you, for God's sake. I haven't even moved in yet."

"The cop. The cop." He laughed, twisted his head around to grin at her. "I forgot they said a cop was moving in. You're a cop. That's so cool."

"You're one second away from serious trouble."

"And you smell really good."

"That's it." She pushed him up against the back wall of her house. "Spread 'em."

"Okay, okay, hold on." He was laughing and tapping his forehead against the wall. "If I sound like a crazy person, it's just the shock. Um, oh, shit. Don't cuff me—at least until we know each other better. College Park, May 1992. A party—crap, I don't know whose house it was. Group house, off campus. Jill, Jessie—no Jan. I think Jan somebody lived in the house."

Reena hesitated, the cuffs still in her hand. "Keep going."

"I saw you. I didn't know anybody. Came with a friend, and I saw you across the room. You were wearing this little pink top—your hair was longer, just past your shoulders. I like the way you're wearing it now. Sort of exploding to the jaw."

"I'll tell my hairdresser you approve. I met you at a party in College Park?"

"No. I never got to you. The music stopped. It was a moment for me. Can I turn around?"

He didn't sound crazy—exactly. And she was intrigued. She stepped back. "Hands to yourself."

"No problem." He held them up, palms out, then lowered them to hook his thumbs on his tool belt. "I saw you, and I was . . . Pow." He punched a fist to his heart. "But by the time I got across the room—place was packed—you were gone. I looked everywhere. Upstairs, outside, everywhere."

"You saw me over ten years ago, across the room at a college party, and you remember what I was wearing?"

"It was like . . . for a minute, it was just you. Sounds weird, but there it is. Then this other time? A pal dragged me to the stupid mall on a Saturday, and I saw you up a level. Just there, and I went running around looking for the damn stairs. But by the time I got up, you'd Houdini'd again. Wow. Wow."

He grinned like a mental patient, shoved his hat farther back on his head. "Then winter of '99? I'm stuck in traffic coming from a client's place. Got The Boss on the radio. 'Growin' Up.' And I look over, and I see you in the car beside me. You're tapping out the beat on the wheel. You're just there. And I—"

"Oh my God. Weird Guy."

"Sorry."

"The weird guy who goggle-eyed me on my way to the mall."

His grin spread again, but this time seemed more amused than manic. "That would be me. Half the time I thought I made you up. But I didn't. You're right here."

"Doesn't mean you're not still Weird Guy."

"Not criminally. We could talk. You could ask me in for coffee."

"I don't have any coffee. I don't have anything yet."

"You could come to my place for coffee—except I don't have any either. See, it's right next door. You could come over for a beer, or a Coke. Or the rest of your life."

"I think I'll pass."

"Why don't I make you dinner? Take you to dinner. Take you to Aruba."

Laughter trembled up her throat but she swallowed it back down. "I'll take Aruba under advisement. As for dinner, it's one in the afternoon."

"Lunch." He laughed, pulled off the ball cap and stuffed it in his back pocket, raked long fingers through his dense black hair. "I can't believe how completely I'm screwing this up. I didn't expect to see Dream Girl next door. Let me start over, sort of. Bo. Bowen Goodnight."

She accepted the hand. She liked the strength of it; she liked the calloused roughness of the palm. "Bo."

"I'm thirty-three, single, no criminal record. Got a thumbs-up my last physical. I run my own business. Goodnight's Custom Carpentry. And I've got this real estate thing with a partner. The pal I came to that party with. I can get you references, medical reports, financial statements. Please don't disappear again."

"How do you know I'm not married with three kids?"

His face went blank. It actually paled. "You can't be. There is no God so cruel."

Enjoying him now, she angled her head. "I could be a lesbian."

"I've done nothing in my life to earn such a vicious slap by Fate. Catarina, it's been thirteen years. Give me a break."

"I'll think about it. It's Reena," she added. "Friends

generally call me Reena. I've got to go. I've got people coming over."

"Don't disappear."

"Not until my mortgage is paid off. It's been interesting meeting you, Bo."

She slipped back inside, left him standing there.

THEY BROUGHT FOOD, OF COURSE. AND WINE. AND flowers. And most of her furniture.

Since they were moving her in, Reena decided she'd better get in the spirit. She made trips back to the apartment over Sirico's for boxes, for suitcases packed with clothes. For a last goodbye.

She'd been comfortable here, she thought. Maybe too comfortable. Comfort could become rut if you didn't keep an eye out. But she'd miss being able to dash downstairs for a meal, or just to chat. She'd miss the easy routine of strolling up the block and stepping into her parents' home.

"You'd think I was moving to Montana instead of a few blocks away." She turned to her mother, saw the tears swimming. "Oh, Mama."

"It's silly. I'm so lucky to have all my children close. But I liked having you right here. I'm proud that you bought a house. It's a good, smart thing to do. But I'll miss knowing you're right here."

"I'm still right here." She lifted the last box. "Part of me worries that I've taken on more than I can handle."

"There's nothing my girl can't handle."

"Hope you're right. And remind me of that the first time I have to call the plumber."

"You call your cousin Frank. And you should talk to your cousin Matthew about the painting."

"Bases covered." Reena walked to the door, waited for

her mother to open it. "And I've got a handyman right next door."

"You don't hire somebody to work in your house if you don't know him."

"Turns out I do—or he knows me."

She told Bianca the story as they finished loading the car and started the short drive to the new house.

"He sees you once at a party when you're in college? And he's smitten."

"I don't know about smitten. He remembered me. And he's very cute."

"Hmmm."

"He took it well when I threatened to cuff him."

"So, maybe he's used to it. Maybe he's a criminal. Or he enjoys bondage."

"Mama! Maybe he's just a cute, slightly strange guy with a great butt and power tools. Mama, I'm a big girl. And I carry a gun."

"Don't remind me." Bianca waved it away. "What kind of name is Goodnight?"

"It's not Italian," Reena murmured. She pulled up, then watched the door of the house next door open. "Well, it looks like you're going to get the chance to judge for yourself."

"That's him?"

"Um-hmm."

"Good-looking," Bianca commented, then stepped out of the car.

He'd cleaned up, Reena noted. His hair was still a bit damp, and he'd put on a fresh shirt—ditched the tool belt.

"Saw you hauling stuff in. Thought maybe you could use a hand. Can I get this out of the way?" he said to Bianca. "Wow, beautiful women run in the family. I'm Bo, from next door."

"Yes, my daughter told me about you."

"She thinks I'm crazy—because I gave her pretty good reason. I'm generally less bizarre."

"So, you're harmless."

"God, I hope not."

It made her smile. "Bianca Hale, Catarina's mother."

"It's nice to meet you."

"You've lived here long?"

"No, actually, only about five months."

"Five months. I don't remember seeing you in Sirico's."

"Sirico's? Best pizza in Baltimore. I get delivery all the time. The spaghetti and meatballs is incredible."

"My parents own Sirico's," Reena said as she popped the trunk.

"Get out. Seriously?"

"Why don't you come in," Bianca said, "have a meal?"

"I will. It's just I've been working pretty much round the clock the past couple months, and— Here let me get those." He nudged Reena aside to pull out boxes while he addressed her mother. "I haven't been seeing anyone— dating—just recently. I don't like eating alone in a restaurant."

"What's wrong with you?" Bianca asked. "Young, good-looking. Why don't you date?"

"I do—I mean, did. Will. But I've had a lot of work, and I'm working on this place in my spare."

"Have you been married before?"

"Mama."

"We're having a conversation."

"It's not a conversation. It's an inquisition."

"I don't mind. No, ma'am, no marriages, no engagements. I've been waiting for Reena."

"Stop it," Reena ordered.

"We're having a conversation," he reminded her. "Do you believe in love at first sight, Mrs. Hale?"

"I'm Italian. Of course I do. And call me Bianca. Come in, meet the family."

"I'd love to."

"Slick," Reena muttered as he stepped aside for Bianca to enter.

"Desperate," he corrected.

"Just put that down there."

"I can take it where it goes."

"For now, it goes there." She pointed to the base of the steps, closed the door.

"Okay. I like your mother."

"Why shouldn't you?" She took off her sunglasses, tapped them against her palm as she studied him. "You might as well come on back—and remember, you asked for it."

She walked back toward the kitchen, avoiding a couple of her nephews who raced in the opposite direction. In the kitchen, sauce was simmering on the stove, wine was being poured, and several arguments were taking place at once.

"This is Bo," Bianca announced, and silence fell. "He lives next door. He's a carpenter and has a crush on Reena."

"Actually, I'm pretty sure she's the love of my life."

"Will you stop." But Reena laughed as she shook her head. "This is my father, Gib, my sister Fran, her husband, Jack, one of the kids running out of here was their son Anthony. This is my sister Bella—the other one streaking by was her son Dom, her other kids, Vinny, Sophia, and Louisa are around somewhere. My brother Xander, and his wife, An; their baby is Dillon."

"It's nice to meet you." Fran offered him a smile. "Can I get you a glass of wine?"

"Sure, thanks."

"Fran and Jack manage the restaurant for my parents.

Bella's husband couldn't make it by today. Xander and An are doctors, and work at the neighborhood clinic."

"It's nice to meet everyone."

She knew what he saw. The tall, handsome man at the stove giving him a careful measure. Lovely, pregnant Fran pouring wine, while redheaded Jack gave their redheaded daughter a piggyback ride. Bella leaning against the counter in her designer shoes and country club hair. Xander sipping wine and standing beside his gorgeous golden-skinned wife as she burped their six-week old infant.

Of course the questions came popping out from all directions, but he fielded them easily enough. And didn't seem surprised to see the Italian, Irish, Chinese mix in the kitchen of a nearly empty row house.

He slid into the flow so easily, she was surprised to hear him say he was an only child when asked about his family.

"My parents split when I was a kid. I grew up in PG County. My mother lives in North Carolina now. My father's out in Arizona. I guess my partner's like my brother. We've known each other forever. Maybe you remember him," he said to Reena. "He dated a girl who knew Jan, went to Maryland. I think her name was Cammie."

"No, sorry. I didn't socialize all that much in college."

"She spent most of her time studying," Bella put in, with the slightest smirk. "Then she had her heart broken by tragedy."

"Bella." Bianca's voice was sharp as a whip.

"Oh, for God's sake, it was years ago. If she's not over it, she ought to be."

"When someone dies, they stay dead no matter how many years pass."

"I'm sorry." Bo turned to Reena.

"You don't have anything to apologize for," she said with a long look at her sister. "Here, have some antipasto."

She picked up a platter. "Until I get a dining room table, we'll be eating standing up or sitting on the floor."

"I could make you one."

"One what? A table?"

"Yeah. It's one of the things I do. Actually, my favorite thing. Building furniture. Give me an idea what you want, and I'll make you a table. Ah, like a housewarming deal."

"You can't just make me a table."

"Hush." Bianca moved in. "You do good work?"

"I do exceptional work. I offered her references before. Maybe you know Mr. and Mrs. Baccho, over on Fawn Street?"

Bianca's eyes narrowed. "I know them. Dave and Mary Teresa. You're the boy who did their china cabinets."

"The oak and glass built-ins. Yeah, that's my work."

"It's good work." Her gaze slid toward her husband. "I'd like something like those. Come in here, look at the dining room."

"Mama."

"It doesn't hurt to have him look," Bianca called back, and drew Bo away.

An passed the baby to Xander. She was a tiny thing, barely five feet with a glossy wedge of coal black hair and deep black eyes. She plucked a stuffed mushroom from the platter Reena held. "He's hot," she murmured. "Serious hotness factor."

"I haven't moved in yet, and she's got me dating the boy next door."

"Hey, worst you can do is get a free table out of it." She grinned around the mushroom. "And the guy looks like he can swing a hammer to me."

"I heard that innuendo," Xander called out.

"I'm going to go separate them." Reena handed the platter to An and walked quickly to the dining room.

Her mother was gesturing, holding her hands apart, talking about necessary seating.

Bo looked over, patted a hand on his heart. "She just walks into the room and my head spins."

Reena arched her eyebrows. "You're going to want to take that down a few levels."

"It's my first day, so you need to cut me some slack. We're thinking drop leaf. That way, you'd have the smaller size, and the extension for dinner parties and family meals without the bother of the leaves."

"I don't know what I want yet." About tables, she thought, about you. About anything but the job. "I can't just say."

"I'll make you up a few designs. Get the ball rolling. It's the same setup I've got next door, so I can use my space for measurements. Lots of potential here." He smiled at her. "Unlimited potential. I'd better go."

"You should stay," Bianca objected. "Eat."

"Thanks, I'll take a rain check. You need anything," he said to Reena, "I'm right next door. I wrote down my number." He pulled a card out of his pocket. "Cell's printed on there, home number's on the back. You need anything, just call."

"All right. I'll walk you out."

He handed her his wineglass. "That's okay. I know the way. You stay with your family. I'll be in for that meal, Bianca."

"See that you are."

Bianca waited until she was sure he was out of earshot. "He has good manners. He has good eyes. You should give him a chance."

"I've got his number." Reena stuffed it in her pocket. "I'll think about it."

An all-new bouquet of novels from
#1 *New York Times* bestselling author

Nora Roberts

Read all the
books in the
~IN THE GARDEN~
trilogy:

The official
Nora Roberts
seal guarantees
that these are
new books

~Blue Dahlia~

~Black Rose~

Three women at a crossroads in their lives find in
each other the courage to embrace the future.

J989